Claire Rayner, nurse, agony aur London in 1931. She married in children were young that she began to write.

She is also a tireless campaigner on many medical and social issues, including the long term care of the elderly.

Her literary output comprises over eighty books including fiction and a broad range of medical matters.

She has three grown up children and lives in Harrow with her husband.

THE POPPY CHRONICLES

JUBILEE
FLANDERS
FLAPPER
BLITZ
FESTIVAL
SIXTIES

THE PERFORMERS SERIES

GOWER STREET
THE HAYMARKET
PADDINGTON GREEN
SOHO SQUARE
BEDFORD ROW
LONG ACRE
CHARING CROSS
CHELSEA REACH
SHAFTESBURY AVENUE
PICCADILLY
SEVEN DIALS

Claire
Rayner
The Strand

The **Performers** *Family Saga*

**HOUSE OF
STRATUS**

This edition published in 2001 by House of Stratus, an imprint of Stratus Holdings plc, 24c Old Burlington Street, London, W1X 1RL, UK.

www.houseofstratus.com

Typeset, printed and bound by House of Stratus.

A catalogue record for this book is available from the British Library.

ISBN 1-84232-531-0

FOR DR MICHAEL SMITH
a good friend and colleague

ACKNOWLEDGEMENTS

The author is grateful for the assistance given with research by the Library of the Royal Society of Medicine, London; Macarthy's Ltd, Surgical Instrument Manufacturers; The London Library; The London Borough of Camden Libraries; The London Museum; The Victoria and Albert Museum; Westminster City Library; Leichner Stage Make-Up Ltd; Raymond Mander and Jo Mitchenson, theatrical historians; Miss Geraldine Stephenson, choreographer and dance historian; Miss Judy Wade and Miss Rosalind Grose, Australian historians; The General Post Office Archives; The Public Records Office; The Archivist, British Rail; and other sources too numerous to mention.

THE LACKLANDS

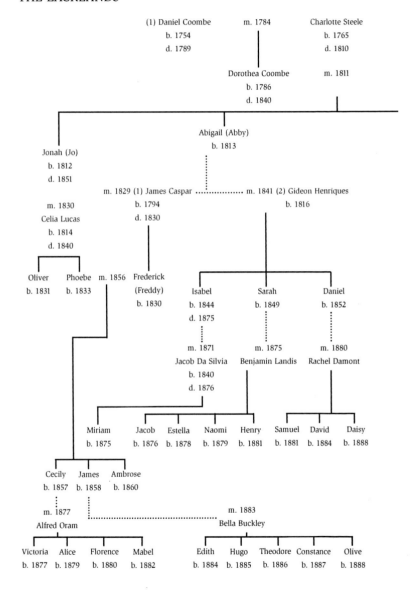

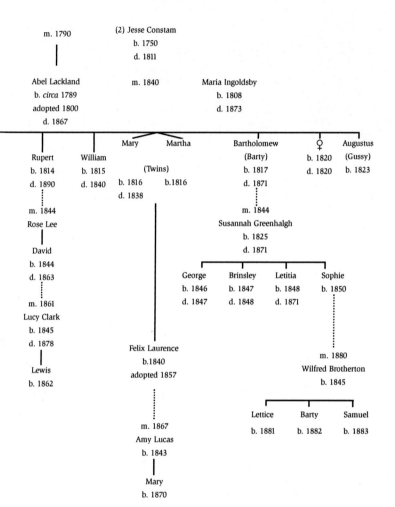

m. 1790

(2) Jesse Constam
b. 1750
d. 1811

Abel Lackland
b. *circa* 1789
adopted 1800
d. 1867

m. 1840

Maria Ingoldsby
b. 1808
d. 1873

Rupert
b. 1814
d. 1890

m. 1844
Rose Lee

David
b. 1844
d. 1863

m. 1861
Lucy Clark
b. 1845
d. 1878

Lewis
b. 1862

William
b. 1815
d. 1840

Mary

Martha

(Twins)
b. 1816   b.1816
d. 1838

Felix Laurence
b.1840
adopted 1857

m. 1867
Amy Lucas
b. 1843

Mary
b. 1870

Bartholomew
(Barty)
b. 1817
d. 1871

m. 1844
Susannah Greenhalgh
b. 1825
d. 1871

George
b. 1846
d. 1847

Brinsley
b. 1847
d. 1848

Letitia
b. 1848
d. 1871

Sophie
b. 1850

m. 1880
Wilfred Brotherton
b. 1845

Lettice
b. 1881

Barty
b. 1882

Samuel
b. 1883

♀
b. 1820
d. 1820

Augustus
(Gussy)
b. 1823

THE LUCASES

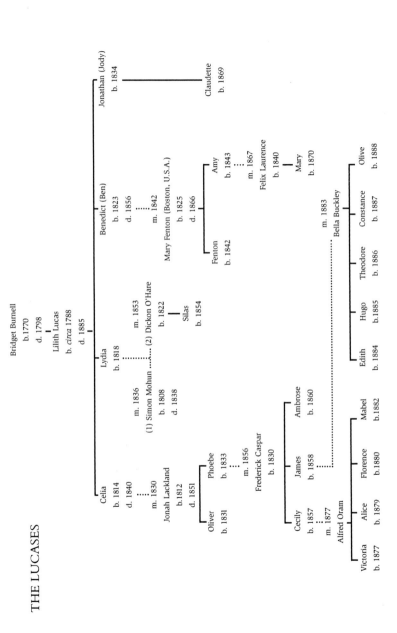

1

Alice's bottom was very cold. She had tried tucking her nightdress underneath her before sitting down on the cold linoleum, but it made no difference; the chill struck right through and she had to hug herself to stop her teeth from chattering. Victoria beside her was shivering too, but Mabel seemed totally unmoved by the cold. She was sitting with her face pushed between the banisters, staring eagerly down to the hall below.

'Look,' she whispered. 'Isn't that Cousin Amy? Yes, it is – I can see Felix – oh, doesn't she look delicious? That blue is just the colour I want for my come-out dress – and in just that style – '

'You can't wear blue for a come-out dress, silly,' Victoria said with all the lofty superiority of fourteen years old over not quite ten. 'It's got to be white. Everyone knows that. And by the time you come out the styles will all be quite, quite different. Mabel, don't lean over so far – someone'll see you and then where'll we be?'

'Back in bed,' said Alice, and shivered again. 'Don't you think we ought to go back? Someone's sure to come, or Flo will tell Mademoiselle we're not in bed, and Papa will be furious and won't let us go to the Zoo tomorrow – '

'Blow the Zoo,' said Mabel. 'I'm staying here no matter what. I think it's horrid of them all not to let us be at the Ball

1

anyway. We're cousins too, aren't we? We're just as important as soppy old Miriam – '

'No, we're not,' Victoria said, very big sister again. 'We're much younger, and we're not great heiresses in our own right and we're not orphans, and don't say "blow". It's exceedingly vulgar.'

'And you are exceedingly stupid,' Alice said and reached out and pinched Victoria's thigh which made her yelp and far below them Felix looked up and at once the three of them shrank back and were silent.

Felix grinned. The shadows were thick up there on the second floor, but he could see a glimpse of white cotton lace and he knew enough about Cecily's eager young daughters to know that nothing on earth would keep them in bed tonight. Not the night of Miriam Da Silva's very own Ball. It would be asking altogether too much of human nature, and certainly young female nature.

Amy, with her daughter Mary at her side, was already climbing the stairs towards the reception line at the drawing-room door, but he hung back and beckoned to one of the livened footmen standing impassively beautiful at the foot of the staircase and whispered to him, and the man allowed his face the semblance of a smile and nodded and went away to do his bidding. And ten minutes later the three little girls at the top of the stairs leading to the second floor were sipping hot egg nog and eating macaroons and worshipping dear kind Cousin Felix in sibilant whispers.

They weren't the only people who were cold on that May evening. As carriage after carriage decanted guests at the end of the red carpet that led from the front door of the Henriques' mansion to the kerb of the fashionable Green Street ('The Park Lane end, my dear, *of course*,' as James' snobbish wife Bella would always tell her neighbours in Balham), they shivered and pulled their wraps more closely around their bare shoulders, or huffed a little as they removed their glossy top hats, and hurried past the staring onlookers, on under the striped awning and inside. And even there, though the light was glittering in the extreme – for the Henriques' house was famous for its vast number of electric lights – it was still cold, for Abby Henriques, though a generous hostess in every other way, hated to be too warm and kept her house at a temperature that suited her. The ungenerous muttered to each other that it was all right for Mrs Henriques, so stout now that she was wider than her Majesty herself, but that lesser mortals were less well insulated. But then, as the rooms warmed up with the great press of people arriving for this most important Ball, the first of the 1892 Season, even they stopped grumbling and fluffed out their ribbons and kicked out their trains, and settled down to enjoy themselves.

And Victoria and Alice and Mabel, joined now by their other sister Florence (because she couldn't keep up her Good Little Girl pose another moment, and anyway, Mademoiselle had long since gone down to the boudoir to help Great-Grandmamma's maid, so it was safe to leave her bed), watched and whispered as their relations and their relations' friends, a glittering array of the richest and most exciting people in London, whirled and twisted and chattered and gossiped below them.

There was Great-Grandmamma herself, resplendent in gold brocade with a cream Brussels lace bodice and fichu and magnificent sleeves, smiling benevolently at all and sundry with beside her dear Great-Grandpapa, as lean as she was stout, and oh, so handsome! His crest of white hair above his startling dark eyes, his narrow, deeply lined face, his altogether delightful smile, made all his great-grandchildren adore him – although they knew that you couldn't go too far with Gideon Henriques. There was a right way to behave and a wrong way to behave, and he well knew the difference and made sure they did.

3

And there was Grandmamma, looking as beautiful as she always did, with darling Gran'pa Freddy standing beside her, and looking rather tired. But then, he always did. He worked hard, of course – all the children knew that he was one of the busiest surgeons in London, and much in demand, and worked far harder at the hospital than he really needed to, for Grandmamma Phoebe said so often and often.

And on the other side of the reception line stood Aunt Sarah, handsome as ever in purple and jet, staring at everyone through her long-handled *lorgnette*, with her husband Uncle Benjamin Landis insignificant in her shadow, and beside them Uncle Daniel and Aunt Rachel, looking, truth to tell, a little bored.

('I expect they're missing their children,' Mabel whispered. 'Poor them! Imagine having to stay in your own house when all this is going on! I'm so glad Mamma brought us to stay – '

'She had to,' Victoria said dampeningly. 'Mamma couldn't come without us, and Great-Grandmamma needed her, and Grandmamma Phoebe wouldn't look after us, would she?'

'Heavens, no!' said Alice. 'Grandmamma Phoebe never looks after anyone but herself.'

'Hush,' said Victoria, but they all knew it was true.)

And then, of course, there was The Most Important Person of All. In a drift of the very costliest white Chantilly lace, her sleek shoulders gleaming above the ruffles of her bodice, her dark hair piled on her head in the most bewitching of curls, stood Miriam, smiling brilliantly, sparkling for all the world as though she had been dusted with tinsel. Lovely, lucky, magnificent Miriam.

The cousins often talked about Cousin Miriam. The three oldest Caspar children and the four Oram girls, and Aunt Sarah's Jacob and Estella and Naomi would often sit in the old schoolroom after tea when they visited the Olds (as irreverent Jacob had once labelled them, and which had somehow stuck) and talk about Miriam. About how stupendously rich she was, for her mother and father had both died when she was a baby, and left her all they had, which was considerable, and how she was the specially adored child of Great-Grandmamma and Great-Grandpapa because they had so loved their daughter Isabel who had died giving Miriam birth, and how romantic it all was. And if some of them thought wistfully that though of course they dearly loved their own Mammas and Papas it would be rather *interesting* to be an orphan, especially such a rich and petted one, they never ever said so, even to each other. For that would be very wicked –

'Well,' Mabel would say in the end, after these discussions, 'at least she's older than us. I mean, one day, I'll be seventeen and making my come-out, and then she'll be one of the Olds, won't she? She'll be– why, *twenty-four*. Ever so old!'

But tonight, the actual night of the Ball which everyone in the family had been talking about and planning for so many months even ebullient Mabel was hard put to it not to be in awe of Miriam. She really was looking so splendid, and everyone was so obviously admiring her. There were clusters of young men standing about and asking her for a dance, just one, please, she can't have filled her programme already, *surely*? and positively pushing each other out of the way. Even Uncle Ambrose, so young and dashing and handsome with his narrow green eyes and thick moustache and daringly long dark hair was standing there beside her. Gran'pa Freddy had been heard many times to complain bitterly of his younger son's mode of dress, but above all of the way his hair curled thickly about his ears. 'Who does he think he is?' Gran'pa Freddy would mutter. 'Lord Tennyson? That bounder Padereweski?'

Tonight the curls were more exuberant than ever and the moustache most particularly effulgent, and the Oram girls, up there on the second-floor linoleum-covered stairs, could see that Miriam was as taken with him as they were. To have so young and exciting a man as a relation, they told each other in delight. Aren't we all *fortunate*?

Freddy, watching his scapegrace son flirting quite openly with his young cousin, felt far from fortunate. Why couldn't the boy *settle*, for heaven's sake? He had good example enough. James was only two years his senior, and already a well established man of affairs, with his place at the Stock Exchange and his Bella and their five little ones. Noisy, rather tiresome little ones, Freddy sometimes felt, and Bella was not precisely to his taste, being shrewish and acquisitive as well as somewhat snobbish (her own father having been a man in a small way of business, it was natural enough that she should be most jealous of her own new status, acquired by marrying James Caspar), but at least the man was *settled*. Why couldn't Ambrose be like him instead of spending his days hanging about theatres and actresses and those wretched yellow journalists he called his friends? Why couldn't he earn a living for himself instead of relying on his allowance from his father and, Freddy shrewdly suspected, whatever he could squeeze out of his mother? That Phoebe spoiled and protected her youngest son and covered up many of his peccadilloes Freddy was well aware. He really would have to speak to her again about it, he thought now, watching Ambrose lead Miriam into the ballroom for a waltz. The boy can't go on like this for ever. Boy? Dammit, at thirty-two he's a man! Something really must be done – '

'Good evening, Freddy,' Felix Laurence said in his ear and Freddy relaxed into a smile. He liked Laurence, always had, ever since the days when Aunt Martha had first brought him into the family as her adopted son, just after her return from the Crimea. 'My dear chap! Good to see you! Are you well? Family well?'

'Indeed, we all thrive. Amy is about here somewhere – and Mary, of course – '

'I must find your Mary. Charming child – perhaps she'll dance with her old cousin – if she has a space left in her programme, which I doubt.'

'Oh, she'll find room for you, I dare say. She's dancing now I think – one of Phoebe's friends from the Opéra. Can't remember his name, but he seems well enough. And Amy says he may get the child a part. These theatricals – they're a rum lot.'

'Rum indeed,' Freddy said, momentarily grim again, thinking of Ambrose and his raffish friends. 'And Aunt Martha – is she here? In this crush I can hardly see anyone.'

'She said she would be.' Felix grinned then. 'But you know Martha. No doubt some wretched street woman stopped her and needed something or other, so she went back and dealt with whatever it was and forgot Miriam's party. She takes her work very seriously, you know.'

'Too seriously. She really shouldn't be working at all, at her age – '

'I wouldn't let her hear you say that if I were in your shoes, Freddy. She'd tear you apart at the mere suggestion.'

'I dare say she would. But all the same – ' Freddy shook his head. 'I'm concerned for her. Seventy-six, dammit, no age to be working all the hours God sends.'

'Martha would take them if God didn't send them, I suspect – why, good evening, Oliver! You look to be a little put out – '

'Put out? Not at all – not at all! Good evening to you, Freddy. Quite a crush, hey?'

'Quite a crush, indeed. I haven't seen you this past month, Oliver. Are you well?'

'Well enough, well enough. Get a bit tied up with the screws, you know, from time to time. Rheumatism respects no man. Can't get out of bed some mornings, and my back – '

'Well, I'll have a word with someone at Nellie's for you – ' Freddy said hastily. He'd heard Oliver's complaints about his health too often in the past to risk showing too much interest in them now. 'Business good?'

Oliver's anxious face lifted at once. 'Indeed, indeed, very good! I'm amazed sometimes, you know, for my style of entertainment is in truth quite out of fashion! There's the Guv'nor packing them in like sardines night after night at the Gaiety, and very popular stuff at the Olympic and the Globe and the Opéra-Comique, but still they come to me. Changed my times, of course, now. Do a supper show, and get them when they come out of the Gaiety, and when Rules and Romano's are full, why, then, so am I! Got a nice little bill this week, Freddy. You must come along and bring m'sister! You too, Felix – bring your Amy and that nice little girl of yours. They'll like it. Nothing to bring the hint of a blush to any lady's cheek, I do assure you.'

'I can't imagine any show of yours ever doing any such thing,' Freddy said and grinned affectionately at his brother-in-law, and Oliver smiled too and the three men went off in search of a drink, escaping the hurly-burly of the ballroom with relief.

Abby and Phoebe were sitting side by side, watching Miriam dance with Ambrose, Abby's foot tapping gently in time to the sprightly music, and her head nodding happily above her ostrich fan. 'She looks exactly as I always knew she would,' she said and sighed. 'So like my darling Isabel. Do you remember how Isabel looked at her first Ball, Phoebe? So lovely – '

'Yes, Aunt Abby, I remember,' Phoebe said, and tried not to show her impatience. This was the third time this evening that Abby had spoken of Isabel, and sad though her untimely death had been, and painful though it must have been for her parents, Phoebe felt that enough was enough. And she wanted to speak of Ambrose and try to persuade Abby that a regular allowance made to the boy would do no harm. After all, he was her grandson –

'Ambrose is looking very well tonight, is he not, Aunt Abby?' she said artlessly as the couple swept by them on yet another turn of the big ballroom. She fanned her face gently, for the scent of the lilies of the valley and white hyacinths with which the ballroom was lavishly bedecked was becoming more and more overpowering. 'He seems to have more and more a look of my Grandpapa, although of course he is quite old in my memory.'

Abby was beguiled at once, as Phoebe knew she would be. To talk of her dead daughter Isabel pleased her well enough; to talk of her long dead father pleased her almost as much. 'Your Grandpapa, my dear? Oh, indeed he was such a figure of a man! So handsome and yet so serious! I can see him now, standing there beside my poor dead Mamma's bed and looking so sad and so noble!' The years had done much to gild the memory of Abby's young years; today when she thought of her parents – and as she moved closer to the end of her seventies it was remarkable how often she did think of those long vanished faces – she saw them lapped with softness, wrapped in a haze of loving memory that quite dislimned the reality. 'He was so devoted to her.'

'Indeed, I know,' Phoebe said, a little spitefully. 'Grandmamma Maria often told me of how it was with them.'

Abby looked at her a little sharply and Phoebe smiled sweetly back, and Abby sighed and closed her eyes for a moment. Ever prickly, this woman who was both her niece and her daughter-in-law, ever seeking for something more than she had; would she never be really comfortable with her? Abby let herself remember again, seeing the small Phoebe and Freddy making toast together over the kitchen fire at the old house in Paddington Green, and sighed again. Long ago, so very long ago, and now here she was, old and fat, and Isabel dead and – 'And eleven grandchildren and nine great-grandchildren,' she said aloud and opened her eyes.

'I beg your pardon, Aunt Abby?' Phoebe said.

'Nothing, my dear. I was but counting my chickens, now they are hatched. When will your Ambrose wed and give me more chickens for my nest? It's high time, is it not? Or is he just a happy philanderer? If he is, I cannot imagine where he gets it from. Freddy has always been steady enough, and James is as good as gold – '

Phoebe's lips tightened. For all her occasional lapses into elderly memory-polishing Aunt Abby remained as sharp as any needle. If she was in a critical mood this would not be a good time to speak of Ambrose and his financial problems. Wretched Freddy! she thought waspishly. So tight with his money, though we lack little of it, heaven knows! With the money he still gets from his father's patents, and his share of the family chemists' shops, as well as what he makes from his damned surgery, we're as warm as people can be, yet he keeps us all on such tight reins, and ties up so much for James' and Cecily's children, while my poor Ambrose – oh, wretched Freddy and wretched Aunt Abby!

'My dear aunt, I see I am booked for this dance with darling Felix. You must forgive me.' She surged to her feet in a whisper of silk and swayed across the ballroom in search of Felix, and Abby watched her go, her lips a little pursed. Phoebe was up to something, she told herself. On the touch for Ambrose again? I must speak to Freddy about that young man. High time someone did something about him. Send him out of London, perhaps to work in York. The main factory there was thriving, and could always use another member of the family among the managers. In York he would be less likely to get into lazy ways than here in glittering London –

'Oh, Grandmamma, I am having such a splendid time!' Miriam sank into a curtsy at her grandmother's feet, so prettily and with such charm that several of the chaperones sitting nearby on little gilt chairs almost cooed, and Abby looked down at her with her chubby face lit up with affection.

'Are you, my child? Then I am more than content. A girl's first Ball is very special, and we wanted you to remember it all your life, Grandpapa and I – '

'Oh, I shall, I shall,' Miriam said fervently, and got to her feet again, as graceful as ever, and the chaperones cooed again, and Miriam went whirling off into the next dance well satisfied with the impression she had made.

And she was even more pleased with herself half an hour later when once again she sank into a curtsy, a deep and particularly deferential one this time, at the feet of his corpulence the Prince of Wales, who arrived at just past midnight with Mrs Alice Keppel on his arm, and was pleased to tell Gideon that 'his little girl was as lovely and as well set up as any child he'd seen at Court these past three years', a compliment which Miriam accepted with a most charming blush and a look of trustful affection directed at her grand-father, which made everyone approve even more of the lovely Miss Da Silva, so beautiful, so modest and so *good*. That she should be admired by Royalty was not at all surprising, they told each other happily, all very gratified that they had been present at the Most Important Ball of the season to see for themselves how affable the Prince of Wales was to the Henriques family, treating them with the same easy good humour that he treated his other Jewish friends, the Rothschilds and the Cassels, the D'Avigdors and the Damonts and the Lammecks and all the others.

It was just as well that the Oram girls had at last given up their battle with drooping eyelids and gone creeping off to their cold beds just before the Prince arrived, for there is little doubt that small Mabel would have died of mortification at the thought that she still had to wait more than seven years, an eternity of time, before the Prince would tell everyone how lovely *she* was at her first Ball.

And it was also just as well that no one saw Miriam after her party, sitting on her Grandmamma's bed and arguing furiously that now she was properly grown-up she should be allowed to have her own carriage and do precisely as she pleased, for hadn't the Prince himself shown his approval of her? How could Grandmamma be so *mean* as to spoil all her lovely fun by being stuffy about making her take her maid with her everywhere? That was so old hat and *stupid*, Miriam assured her grandmother with mounting passion, and everyone would roar with laughter at her if she was treated so, and *why* could she not have her own carriage and –

Indeed, just as well.

2

While Miriam Da Silva argued with her grandmother in elegant Green Street, a mile or two away across the slate roofs and soot-encrusted chimneys of London, Claudette Lucas sat on the side of a bed in Vinegar Yard in the dirtiest and most poverty-stricken corner of Covent Garden, and argued no less heatedly with her father.

'Jody, you're being downright *stupid*. You've always been mad, but never stupid till now, and we just can't afford it. How in the name of hell are we to eat, unless I do? No one's going to come and throw sovereigns in your lap, you know, for the sake of your *beaux yeux!* Do stop being so – '

'And you stop being such a bore.' Jody closed his eyes and set his face mulishly and Claudette looked down at him and shook her head with a gesture that mixed irritation and affection and pity. 'Silly man,' she said, her voice sharp, but her movements were gentle as she leaned over and settled his woollen wrap about his shoulders and arranged the covers over his chest. 'Go to sleep, for heaven's sake. We'll settle it in the morning. No – not another word. You're as weak as a kitten – get some sleep.'

She blew out the candle and groped her way across the narrow room to the curtained alcove which was her only source of privacy, and stretched herself on her bed and lay there with her arms folded behind her head, staring up at the skylight and the thinning dawn sky beyond it. It was bitterly cold, and she had no more than a thin blanket to comfort herself, for all the covers they had she had piled on Jody's thin frame. He was cold and shivering even on warm days now, and when the weather shifted and became unseasonably chill, as it had this May in London, he suffered a lot. But she ignored the icy heaviness of her own legs and feet and lay there trying to think as, at last, Jody's breathing deepened and he slept.

Bad as things had sometimes been in the past, they had never been as bad as this. All her life she could remember they had lurched from one financial crisis to another, sometimes living on the fat of the land in the best apartment in the most select quarter of Paris, sometimes scraping along frugally in a shabby pension in a dreary suburb. But they had always had enough to eat, and clothes on their backs, and Jody had laughed and been fun and managed somehow to dredge success again out of each rock-bottom disaster. Until now.

She screwed up her face there in the gradually growing morning light, remembering. That had been some spectacular disaster, that last one. He'd gone too far that time, actually stealing money from the safe at the gambling hell he had wriggled into as a *directeur*, and the infuriated owner had set the *gendarmerie* on them, and they had got out by the skin of their teeth, baggageless, with just the clothes they wore and little more than the price of a pair of tickets on the cross-Channel steamer. She had known for some months he was ill, of course. The coughing and the complaints of pain in his shoulders, the way he became steadily thinner and weaker – she was no fool. Jody had some mortal illness, and that was probably why he had acted so foolishly. In his prime he would have been more subtle, much more likely to have swindled the man out of his possessions than to have robbed him directly. And he'd never have been caught.

In his prime. She thought of the old Jody, the father of her childhood, the lovely man who had laughed when the nurses he hired for her complained bitterly of her wilfulness and insolence, and thrown them out and sworn he would take care of her himself – until the next amusing occupation came his way, and the next handsome obliging lady, and a child became an encumbrance who needed a nurse and the whole cycle started all over again. Until she was gone thirteen and was a child no longer and could be useful as a shill in the gambling-houses he used to earn their bread. Then the fun had really begun with the two of them against the world, fighting their way through life, often fighting with each other – spectacular fights when she would hurl herself at him spitting and snarling with her fingers clawed, and he would laugh and hold her off as easily as if she was still a baby – oh, those had been good days! Sometimes he would sit and talk to her about himself; about the time when he was a boy and lived with his mother, the greatest actress England had ever known, in a beautiful house in the richest part of London, and had all he wanted for the asking. Of course she had never believed a word of all that. It made a good story, but it was patently untrue. Most of what Jody told her was a lie and she had always known it. The stories that he had offered her of her own history, of her mother, showed that, for they varied wildly depending on his mood and the amount of good claret he had poured into himself. The most likely story of the many was the one he had repeated several times – that her mother had been a dancer who had lived with him for a while, had become pregnant and managed to hide the fact from him for long enough to prevent any attempts on his part to force an abortion on her, and who had then died for her pains when the child was born.

'And what could I do?' Jody would say, staring at her owlishly over the rim of his glass. 'Couldn't leave you there with a bloody corpse, could I? No – had to take you with me, scrawny bawling brat that you were. But it worked well enough. Man with a baby under his arm – gets 'em every time. You came in good and useful that first couple of years, so I didn't mind. And then by the time you got to be a nuisance I was used to having you around, so what could I do? Anyway, you've turned out useful again now, hey Claudette? Goin' to take care of ol' Jody and make him a rich man again, hey, one of these days? Rich like I was when Mamma was alive, God rot her soul in hell – '

Good days. Good, but gone. And now what? To have fled to London seemed at the time the best thing to do, and indeed it had worked to the extent that the *gendarmerie* appeared to have given up, for no one had come near them these past six weeks. So they had nothing to fear from the law here. But what about a living? That was the most pressing problem of all, for the amount of money they had, the results of Jody's ill-starred excursion into safe-robbing, had been pitifully small. If he was going to rob a safe why the hell didn't he choose one that had something in it worth the taking? He really was losing his touch.

Had lost it. It was that fact she had made herself face up to these past weeks, and was trying to make him face. If they had stayed in Paris, they might have managed well enough. There were people there they knew who would have given her a job for old times' sake, letting her be a croupier, perhaps (there would be a novelty value in a female croupier) or deal with the restaurants that all the gambling saloons ran. She'd had good experience in that line, over the years. She understood good food and wine and knew how to present it, and could make an excellent hand of being a *restauratuese*. But here in London she was a stranger, with no contacts and little to offer anyone.

Except herself. That was what she had suggested to Jody, for it had seemed to her the best possible solution.

'For heaven's sake, Jody, why not? I saw enough of the spectacles at the *Folies Bergère* – and the *Moulin* – to know it takes little enough. A reasonable figure and an eye for clothes and a little *savoir-faire* when it comes to moving and displaying oneself – what can be so difficult? You can't tell me that every one of those actresses you used to know were great talents!

They had looks and bodies, no more. Well, I have the same. A reasonable face and a very good body. I do not flatter myself when I say it, and well you know it. There have been enough men making nuisances of themselves these past ten years – '

'No,' he had said, his face settling into the petulant childish stubbornness she knew so well. 'Not the theatre. No.'

'But why not? I can't see that – '

'No.' And he would say no more.

Well, she thought now, the time for talking is past. I shall just go and do it. I have money for food for three days, no more, and I can't pander to his nonsense any longer. He's being irrational. He's ill – '

But practical and worldly-wise though she was, she could not bear to think more about Jody's illness. The implications of it were not lost on her, but they were not to be dwelt on, for Jody was all she had in the world, and for all his faults and all his slipperiness and unreliability he was Jody, and in her fashion she loved him. So she turned on her side and curled up and with sheer effort of will banished from her mind the fact that she ached with cold and that her belly hurt with hunger, and went to sleep. Tomorrow – or rather this morning, for now it was almost full daylight – she would go to one of the theatres that studded this tawdry part of London and get herself some sort of job. No matter what Jody said.

He tried once more, as he watched her brush down her tightly waisted tailor-made gown with the gigot sleeves and pull it firmly around her hips so that every undulation of her body showed through the fine fabric. She might have been left with just the clothes she wore when they fled, but at least they had been good clothes, and that was something to be grateful for.

'Where are you going?' he said, and she tried not to notice how husky his voice sounded.

'To a theatre, Jody. No, it is no use arguing. You can give me no good reason why I should not, and we must eat. So, I shall set about remedying the situation the only way I can. Take care and keep under the covers and with luck, I'll have some *déjeuner* for you when I return – '

'Oh, God, Lilith – ' Jody said, and closed his eyes.

'What did you say?'

He remained with his eyes closed for a moment and then opened them and looked at her and she wanted to cry, suddenly, he looked so bereft. 'What is it, Papa?' she said gently. It was rarely that she called him that these days; it had been of small advantage now for many years to admit to their relationship. 'What did you say?'

'Lilith. My mother. She was so superb, Claudette. So very special. When she walked on a stage they all stopped breathing. I cannot bear to think of you – ' He shook his head. 'Lilith.'

'Your mother?' She sat on the edge of the bed and looked at him, her head on one side. 'Then it was true? She *was* an actress?'

'Yes. It was true.' He managed a smile then, almost one of his old wicked leers. 'For once I told you truly. She was – fah! such a woman! Dragged about all over Europe, and – well, never mind that. But for all else about her, she was an actress – such an actress. And to think of another Lucas woman on the stage but without her fire, without her talent – it is not right.'

'Without her – well, God damn your eyes, you wicked old sot!' Claudette said wrathfully and jumped to her feet. 'That's the damned rock-bottom of enough, that is! You lie there, you useless great hulk, and tell me I've no fire or talent? How the bloody hell do you know? Hey? Never mind your stinkin' mother – what about mine? She was a dancer, wasn't she? She had fire enough to cope with you and keep her child and – don't you dare tell me that – '

He was laughing suddenly, a breathless sound that came from his shaking shoulders in little bursts and she stopped and stared at him, and then laughed too, because it really was so absurd, to be standing here like this and arguing. So she grinned and straightened her gown and fluffed up her dark curls and picked up her tiny high-crowned bonnet and set it on her head, tying the strings perkily beneath one ear.

'Well, we shall see what we shall see,' she said. 'I shan't let down your – what was her name? Lilith, you say? Lilith Lucas? It has a certain euphony. Well, I shan't betray her memory, rest assured. But I will get the wherewithal to feed you, you ungrateful wretch. *A bientôt, mon cher!* Wish me *bonne chance!'*

And she went hurrying down the stairs from the cold attic and out into the grime of Vinegar Yard, pulling on her kid gloves as she went. She was hungry and her back and legs ached from her broken night on the hard cot that was her bed, but she knew she looked good for all that. She tilted her chin and picked her way disdainfully over the squalid gutter of the Yard and out past the public house on the corner, with its façade glittering with gilt paint and cut-glass windows, and on into Catherine Street.

There she stood for a moment looking about her. The roadway was thronged with traffic, brewers' drays and hansom cabs and four-wheelers fighting for space with delivery vans and private carriages, the drivers shouting and swearing at each other and the horses stamping and occasionally lifting their heads to rattle their harness as the reins were pulled up cruelly hard.

She had told Jody she was going to seek work in the theatre, and so she would, but which? They had found this lodging by the simple expedient of asking the cab driver they had picked up at Victoria station, after their arrival from Dover, to take them somewhere cheap and respectable, and it had been here in Covent Garden he had dropped them.

'Don't know about respectable, squire,' he'd said to Jody as he helped him out of the cab, and Claudette took his fare from her small muff, 'but Gawd knows it's cheap enough. You can get a kip 'ere for no more'n a tanner a night, and then you're payin' over the odds – offer 'em three johnnies and they'll take yer and no questions asked – ' and he'd leered at Claudette before hauling himself back up on to his perch, whistling his horse on its way.

So she had had little chance to see much of London apart from this unsalubrious neighbourhood. Catherine Street itself, into which she had ventured in search of food to buy when she was not taking care of Jody, was clearly a newly built street, with some imposing and well set up buildings flanking it, but it was abutted by many alleys and hovels which spilled their scabrous residents out into the wider roadway and made the better dressed passers-by draw aside with expressions of distaste on their faces. But Claudette had lacked pride, and wandered into many of the alleys and there had found the cheaper priced cookshops where she could buy sizeable quantities of food for a small outlay. Not good food, far indeed from the delicacies she had once enjoyed in Paris in better days, but solidly satisfying, great meat pies and lumps of bread and red herrings and slabs of Cheddar cheese. If it had not been for these shops and their offerings her meagre store of money would have dwindled away even faster than it had.

But it had not been only cookshops she had found. She had wandered out of the alleys where the gin palaces flared and the poor people lived, to wider streets where the theatres were, and seen the well-dressed and also shabbier crowds pushing their way into the Opéra-Comique and the Globe Theatre which lay between the awfulness of Holywell Street and Wych Street, and into the Olympic at the other end of Wych Street and the Lyceum in Wellington Street. And into the Gaiety here in Catherine Street itself.

It was to the Gaiety now she turned her steps, for it was the nearest, and anyway, she had liked the look of it and its audience best of all when she had passed it before. They looked so good-humoured a lot, so cheerfully set on having fun, and with none of the bored disdain showed by some of the patrons – especially the female ones – of the other theatres. The Gaiety customers looked almost French in their brightness of manner and their determination to have fun; and that made her feel at home.

So, now she went purposefully down Catherine Street, towards the Strand, and crossed Exeter Street to stand at last outside the great façade, with its half-cupola of glass over the entrance and the restaurant above, proudly labelled 'Speirs and Pond'. There were a few people standing about outside, looking as though they were part of the scenery, and they stared at her as she went in under the cupola and pushed open the big double glass doors.

Inside all was warm and quiet, and she stood for a moment breathing deeply of the smell of cigars and brandy and dust – and above all the warmth. The place was filled with heat, it seemed to her chilled bones, and she moved forwards into the centre of the red-carpeted foyer and stood with her chin up, letting it lap her round. She couldn't see the source of the warmth, but after the thin cold May morning outside it was like balm to her aching body and, after a moment, she went to the far side of the foyer to sit down on one of the broad red sofas that lined the walls. There was time, yet, before seeking out someone who could give her employment. Just a little rest first, a chance to get some warmth deep inside her, and thaw her out.

She leaned back, letting her head rest against the flock-papered wall, and stretched out her legs, and relaxed, and it felt good, and she closed her eyes to relish it. And her fatigue took over with her night of shallow troubled sleep together with her anxiety about Jody's health and her own hunger and worry for the future – and she slept.

She was dreaming. She was in the theatre in Paris, sitting in the third row dressed in diamonds and furs and applauding and on the stage was Jody holding a woman by the hand and saying earnestly in his English-accented French, 'You see my dear? You see? This is how an actress is – she is great, she is unique, she is Lilith – '

'And who might you be, young lady? This ain't a dosshouse, you know! What are you doing there?'

She opened her eyes abruptly to stare up at the heavily built man who was standing in front of her. He had thick hair parted in the middle to fall on to his forehead in modish sweeps, and a luxuriant moustache. He had one hand in his pocket and the other negligently holding a large Havana cigar which was spilling its ash down his coat, and across his broad waistcoat was a thick gold chain. He looked to be about forty years old, very well fed and very pleased with himself, and at this moment somewhat put out.

'*Pardon, m'sieu? Qu'est-ce-que vous dites?*' she said, and her voice was husky and startled.

He stared at her, and slowly grinned. He saw a round-faced girl with a pointed chin, long narrow green eyes and plentiful curly dark hair on which was perched a most charming little bonnet that showed even more clearly that her voice had its French origin.

'*J'ai dit, mademoiselle,*' he said with an accent that made her want to wince. '*Qu'est-ce-que vous faites ici?*'

'Oh, dear, I am so sorry!' she said and shook her head and got to her feet, and at once he put out a hand to help her, smiling with an arch gallantry that she found very funny – and, suddenly, very illuminating.

'*Bien sûr, vous êtes très bienvenue ici – mais, nous ne trouvons pas souvent les demoiselles françaises a la* Gaiety.' He struggled on with his excruciating French and she smiled up at him as bewitchingly as she could, and spoke in the most French of accents she could muster – which was not easy for her, since with Jody she had always learned to speak faultlessly unaccented English, so that she was at home with it as she was with her native French. Claudette had been truly bilingual ever since she had been three or four years old, but no one listening to her now would have guessed it, least of all the man standing now and beaming at her over his round belly.

'Ah, m'sieu! I am *désolée* that I should 'ave *incommodé* you in any way in sitting 'ere in such a manner – I came to seek – 'ow you say – the employment of an actress, *vous comprenez*? I 'ave – I am in England but a short time, and it is *très* – ah– ver' *nécessaire* that I obtain the position, that is – oh, *sacré bleu*, but it ees difficult, *n'est ce pas*? – *convenable* – respectable, you understand? I wish to be an actress 'ere, to make *pour papa – mon papa* 'e is in England also – I wish to obtain a – ah – job! I 'ad forgot ze word. A job, m'sieu!'

She smiled up at him trustingly and he smiled back and somewhere deep inside she wanted to cheer. There was little doubt in her mind that good fortune was smiling on her, that here in front of her was the fountainhead himself, the man she would have to beguile if she was to get the employment she wanted. After all the miseries of the past six weeks, for once Lady Luck was looking her way again. And she was going to make the best of her.

'So, m'sieu, per'aps you can tell me, to which person I should apply myself for thees purpose? I can sing a leetle – an' my mamma was a dancer, and – ' and now she was really inspired, 'and my papa, 'e 'ad an English mamma, and she was an actress – 'e tells me that she was of ze best – ' She kissed her kid-gloved fingertips with great airiness, 'and that I 'ave inherited from 'er ze – ze flair, *n'est-ce pas*? for ze work of an actress – ' Take care, she whispered to herself deep inside her head. Don't overdo it. He may speak bad French but he's no fool –

'Well, had an English grandmother, did you, my dear? An actress? And what might her name have been?'

'Lucas, m'sieu – Lilith Lucas. You know zees name, *peut-être*?'

23

'*Peut-être* I do!' the man said, and whistled softly between his teeth. 'Well, I'll be a monkey's – that was a name to conjure with a while back! Before my time, o' course, but – well, well. So you can sing and dance a little, hey? Let me look at you – just walk over there, will you?'

She walked across the foyer, allowing her hips to sway just a little bit more than they usually did, and turned, sweeping her skirt up in one hand to show a glimpse of her neat ankles, and came back towards him smiling as bewitchingly as she knew how, her head up so that she had to look at him through her lashes. For a moment she was worried, then, for he was no longer smiling but staring at her fixedly.

But she need not have worried, for after a second or two he nodded decisively and held out one hand.

'Well, there's no messing about with the Guv'nor, my dear! You've come to the right shop, indeed you have! There's *Cinder-Ellen Up Too Late* with room for a nice looking young lady in it and I'm casting soon for my new *In Town* for the Prince of Wales. You've got the position you came looking for, my dear! And a very *convenable* one, I do promise you. Welcome to the Gaiety!'

3

It had been raining with dispiriting intensity all day, and the big casualty waiting-room at Nellie's steamed disagreeably as the clothes of the people sitting on its long narrow benches gave up their water – and their smells – to the atmosphere. They had lit the big fire in the grate in the far wall, for, late May though it was, the weather was still cold, and inevitably as many patients as could had clustered near it, and they seemed to Dr Lewis Lackland to be the wettest and smelliest of the lot.

He sighed and stretched his shoulders and then bent his head again to the leg of the child stretched out on the high horsehair couch and went on with the painstaking removal of scraps of gravel from the graze that ran from knee to ankle.

'You made a fair old job of that, didn't you, young sport? Were you trying to get down to the bone?'

'Nah – fell, didn't I?' the child said, and wiped the back of his hand across his running nose. 'Fell over me boots – '

'I'm not surprised,' Lewis said, looking sideways at the tattered ordure-caked objects that bedecked the child's feet. 'You're lucky they didn't sit up and bite you. They look fierce enough.'

'You talk funny,' the child said. 'You don't talk like a toff – 'ere, mate, go easy – that's me flesh and blood you're a-diggin' in – cor stone me – felt that, I did an' all.' And he wiped his nose again and blinked and stared pugnaciously up at Lewis with suspiciously bright eyes.

'Sorry, sport. I'm trying not to hurt, but it's a problem. Those boots of yours made a right dog's breakfast out of your leg, I can tell you. Getting this stuff out isn't easy. But you're a good chap – biting on the bullet, hey? How old are you?'

' 'Leven – where d'you come from? You a proper doctor? You don't talk like one.'

Lewis sighed. This question came up so often that he had developed the habit of snapping sharply at any patient who asked it, but this child was the sort of little tough he warmed to; brave and perky and with an intelligence bigger than his scrawny underfed body could hold.

'I'm a proper doctor, friend. Very proper. I'm from Australia. We all talk funny there.'

The boy was at once entranced. 'That's the place where everyone walks upside-down, ain't it? 'Eard about it I did, when I 'ad to go to school – '

'That's right. We all walk upside-down. If you look at the top of my head, you'll see it's flat. Hold hard now, this next bit will hurt. That's got it – good lad – '

The boy took a deep breath and made a face and then, as the pain eased stared fixedly at the top of Lewis' head.

'Garn! You're bammin' me! You ain't got a flat 'ead!'

'Must have if I walk upside-down. This'll sting. Iodine. But it's necessary. You can shout if you like.'

'Not on yer bleedin' Nellie,' the boy said in a tight little voice as the iodine bit into him. 'Got me mate out there waitin' – 'ere, I reckon they told me wrong at school.'

'No, really?' Lewis said, and grinned as he began to wind the bandage round the boy's leg. 'What gives you that idea?'

'Well, you're all right, ain't yer? Just like anyone else 'ere at Nellie's, only more civil like. Last time I come 'ere there was a right snotty fella, bit me bleedin' 'ead off every word I said, and me wiv a broke wrist – see?'

He held out a sparrow-thin hand and showed Lewis the curve of a poorly set healed fracture.

'Wouldn't stay, I wouldn't, and put on his bleedin' splints, 'e was so toffy-nosed. But you're all right – ' He moved gingerly as Lewis helped him off the couch, and stood carefully on his feet.

' – and anyway, you got proper feet, ain't yer? So the school gotta be wrong. You walks like the rest of us.'

'You noticed,' Lewis said. 'Good fella. Now get on your way. Bring that leg back here the day after tomorrow and I'll change the bandage, which ought to be a fair old rag by then, looking at the rest of you. You like a bit of mud, don't you? Well, I can't say I blame you. I liked it myself at your age. On your way then, sport – and watch out for those highly regrettable boots. They'll lead you into hell yet – '

The boy limped away, collecting his friend from the fireside as he went – and as he was obviously smellier than almost anyone else in the big room Lewis was heartily glad to see him go – and Lewis stretched and came out of the surgical cubicle to make his way across the waiting-room towards the door that led to the rest of the hospital and his hard-earned supper and rest. It was now past ten o'clock at night and he had been working non-stop since eight that morning. He was hungry and extremely tired and in no condition to work any longer. Caspar would have to manage the last few patients waiting; looking round he could see that most of them had but minor complaints, and that many of them were not patients at all, but their friends and relatives who were glad to spend a comfortable hour or two in a warm dry place. They would not complain if he left.

He could see Caspar in the examination cubicle on the other side of the great waiting-hall because the curtain was only half-drawn. He was leaning against the couch with his arms folded and frowning as he listened to the young man who was standing in front of him and talking earnestly.

Lewis stopped, and after a moment turned and strolled back across the hall. Tired and hungry though he was he could not help but notice the girl on the young man's arm. Dressed in the most exquisite and even to his untutored eye costly of gowns, with a fur pelisse over it and a delectable little bonnet above it, she was quite the most beautiful creature he'd seen for a long time. Well worth looking at a little more closely.

Caspar looked up as he came into the cubicle. 'Ah, Mr Lackland – ' he said, abstractedly. Lewis stared at him, intrigued, for there was a high spot of colour in each of his cheeks that looked odd against his sandy hair and freckled skin. It was rare indeed that anyone saw the usually quiet and imperturbable Mr Caspar in anything but the most controlled of moods. Yet here he was, undoubtedly angry. Lewis was fascinated.

'Lackland?' the girl said, and her voice was high and rather childlike. 'How very interesting! That is the same name as Cousin Oliver, is it not?'

'Indeed, my dear,' Freddy said, and stood up a little more straight. 'Mr Lewis Lackland is a distant connection of yours. A surgeon from Australia. May I present him to you – Miss Miriam Da Silva, Mr Lackland, my niece. And – er – my son. Ambrose.'

'How d'do– Miss Da Silva, Mr Caspar,' Lewis said. 'Didn't mean to intrude, sir, but I thought it was about time that – '

Behind them there was a clatter as the main door swung wide and in a small flurry of rain-washed night air another girl came into the waiting-room and Lewis glanced at her and raised his eyebrows. *Two* pretty, well-dressed girls in Nellie's casualty department on one evening? This was a change with a vengeance, for most of the women who came through those doors were tired slatterns with grey faces, old before their time, or over-painted trollops with bright leering eyes and breaths reeking of cheap gin. This one, like Miss Da Silva, was however, of a very different stamp. Her clothes seemed less costly than those of the girl beside him, but they fitted exquisitely and she looked altogether very dashing and exceedingly handsome.

She stood poised for a moment in the doorway and let her gaze sweep the room and then, as she saw them standing there in the small consulting-room, immediately swept up her skirt in one hand – the other was hidden in a small muff hanging about her neck – and swept towards them. A nurse, who had come out of another cubicle, crackling with the starch in her apron and with the strings of her white lace cap flying impatiently in the breeze, tried to intercept her but with a masterly movement that gave a delicious curve to her hips the girl went past her and came directly towards them.

'Good evening, m'sieu?' she said, a slightly interrogatory note in her voice. 'You will be ze *docteur, j'espère?*'

'Er, yes,' Freddy said, still sounding somewhat distracted. 'Er – if you would like to take a seat, someone will come and see what – '

'Ah, *m'sieu le docteur*, forgive me, please, but I 'ave ze problem about time – *vous comprenez*. I cannot sit 'ere for too long, and zey tell me at ze Gaiety where *moi, je suis une* actress – I am Claudette Lucas – zey tell me zat if I tell you zis, you will understand ze problem and give me – 'ow you say – ze leetle privilege.'

Lewis stared at her, amused. It seemed to him that her accent was becoming more outrageously French with every syllable she uttered, and certainly she was working hard at getting her little bit of privilege. He looked at Caspar, and grinned. 'Well, Mr Caspar, if you don't mind, I'll – '

'Hmm? Perhaps you'd see what this young lady needs, Mr Lackland,' Freddy said. 'I have – er – matters to discuss here. I'll be with you as soon as I can and he moved forwards and somehow managed to ease both of them out into the waiting-hall, and then drew the cubicle curtain with a determined rattle, leaving Lewis staring at it with his jaw set and anger beginning to boil up in his chest.

'Ah, m'sieu, you are very kind,' the girl said, and moving carefully, withdrew her hand from her muff. 'You see ze problem? I 'ave zis dreadful swelling – it 'as quite destroyed me and is *so* painful – '

The hand indeed did look very painful. She set it trustingly in his and he looked at it, and saw the red puffiness that had lifted the skin on the back and upper parts of the fingers into a red shiny tautness.

'It is a great anxiety to me, m'sieu, for I 'ave been in re'earsal for only a few days – I 'ave ze new job, you see – and I am ver' anxious zat no stop shall be put in ze way of my being in ze performances. I am to appear next week, and zis 'and – *elle n'est pas belle*, and I am supposed to be *très belle* in zees play!'

'It's an infection,' Lewis said gruffly, and pushed her sleeve up her wrist to see how far the swelling extended. 'It needs lancing and draining.'

She looked white suddenly and pulled her hand away. 'Lancing? That sounds awful. Wouldn't that be very painful – worse than it is now?'

He looked at her and grinned. 'I thought you had rather a better grasp of English than at first appeared,' he said a little waspishly. 'You don't have to act here, you know. We're not paying customers.'

She looked a little nonplussed for a moment and then shrugged. 'I'm sorry. It – it's expected of me there. And I got into the habit. Look, doctor, can you do something about this as soon as possible? It truly is very painful, and it truly is essential it's better before next week, or I might lose my job. And I need it.'

'Come back tomorrow,' he said. 'By then it should be coming more to a head, and ready to drain. I can't open it now – it hasn't pointed enough. Look.' He touched the back of her hand, still resting in his left one, with his right forefinger. 'The pus is slowly gathering. If you bathe it in hot water tonight and wear a hot poultice while you sleep, by tomorrow it should be fit to deal with. I'll do it then. Anyway, I'll do a better job for you tomorrow – no scar. But at present I'm fit to drop. I've been working all day, and I'm not fit to pick up a knife and that's a fact.'

'Can't he – ' She lifted her chin and pointed it at the closed cubicle curtain from behind which came the buzz of voices as Caspar and Ambrose talked. There was an edge in Caspar's voice which made Lewis cock his head a little. It was none of his business, but it was interesting all the same. It was rare to see Freddy Caspar anything other than calm and polite, and to hear his voice edged with anger and heavy with control was enough to make the most bored of his junior colleagues listen. And most especially Lewis Lackland, who, though he had not expected exactly red carpet treatment simply because he had come to work at Queen Eleanor's Hospital, had rather thought he should have some recognition of his status as a great-grandson of the founder of the place. But never once had Freddy showed anything other than the coolest of interest in his antecedents. He had asked for information about his lineage, and when he had explained that his father David was the son of Rupert Lackland who had gone to Australia in 1843 and married there, and that his father had died at the age of nineteen, when he, Lewis, was just an infant (he had been killed in a tavern brawl, truth to tell, but Lewis didn't tell the remote Freddy Caspar *that*) he had simply nodded and suggested he work as a house surgeon, with special responsibility for the casualties.

'I'll assist from time to time, but I have a responsibility for all the surgical cases of the hospital of course, as well as my private practice, so you will be busy. You had experience of this sort in Sydney, I take it?'

'Oh, indeed I did,' Lewis had said, nettled. 'We have real live humans as patients in Sydney, and they get the same sort of diseases civilized people here do, take my word for it. I've dealt with the same range of work you do here – '

The heavy irony had been lost on Freddy who had simply nodded and sent him to see the Bursar to settle his remuneration, and that had been that. He was a Nellie's man. But never an invitation to meet any of the relations Lewis knew he had here in London, no hint of any friendly overtures ever came his way.

Lewis was not, of course, to know that in the past when Freddy had befriended a distant relation, newly come to London, the result had been personal pain. He had sworn then never to treat anyone at Nellie's, relation or not, any differently, and the fact that Lewis Lackland was a man whereas the Lackland who had caused Freddy's discomfiture before had been a girl, made no difference. Freddy kept his distance. And Lewis had become ever more dour in his presence.

Right now he made a small grimace, turning his mouth down expressively. 'Ask him, if you like. He's as good a surgeon as anyone else, I suppose. If you prefer him, you have him. I'm going to get myself some food. I've not eaten since the crack of dawn and I'm as hungry as hell. You asked for advice, I've given it, and you can take it or leave it as you choose. Good night to you – '

She put out her good hand and set it on his sleeve. 'Oh, dammit, I've offended you. I'm sorry. I didn't mean to.'

He looked at her, his brows a little raised. A woman who swore? That made a refreshing change from most of the namby-pamby English women he had met. 'Offended? Not on your life, lady. I'm tired, that's all. You want to get Caspar to deal with your infected hand, you go right ahead. It's no skin off my nose.'

'Ah, no – I accept your treatment, and gladly.' Claudette was liking this sharp man rather more than she would have thought. He had a big square head and a lot of untidy dark hair and hard lines that ran from his mouth to his nose, and she liked the look of him. This was no silly boy, but a man with meat on his bones. The sort she could enjoy being with, and even as the thought came into her mind, she smiled as bewitchingly as she knew how and said, 'You're hungry? I too. No food since breakfast? I too. Come, shall we sup together? They tell me that the restaurants here are good – the girls at the theatre go to Rules or Romano's and do themselves well! Shall we do the same, and I shall forget my hand till tomorrow morning and then you set your knife to me? Zat would be *très très délicieux, eh, mon brave?*'

She grinned widely and almost against his will Lewis grinned back. But he shook his head and turned away. 'No thanks, lady. I'm too tired for anything but a bowl o' something filling and my bed. Tomorrow at nine, I'll open that boil. The nurse'll put on a linseed poultice for you – I'll get her on to it now and – '

The curtain in front of the cubicle rustled and the rings rattled as it opened and Freddy Caspar came out, followed by Ambrose and Miriam. They all looked ruffled and set about the mouth and Lewis looked at them with his brows slightly raised. That Da Silva girl really is some stunner, he thought. Especially when her temper's up, and it's certainly that right now.

'Ah, Lackland!' Freddy stopped short and looked at him. 'Glad you're there. I was coming to look for you. Now, I have to get away. Can't finish this tonight, so you'll have to. Young Dawson will come at midnight and you can get away then. Now, Miriam, my dear, are you ready?'

'Now, just a minute, Mr Caspar.' Lewis was standing with his head down, his chin tucked into his collar, staring at Freddy. Great God almighty, he was thinking. Great God almighty, the brass neck of the man! 'Mr Caspar,' he said loudly and very clearly. 'I am leaving this department right now. I have been working non-stop since eight this morning, after a broken night because I had to get up to deal with a secondary haemorrhage in one of your amputation patients. I am very tired, and very *very* hungry and no more fit to deal with even the most minor of cases than – than the hall porter! So, sir, I will bid you good night. I cannot and will not see these patients, and I cannot and will not stay here until midnight. I regret any difficulty this causes you, but I have no doubt you'll agree that it would be bad medical practice to allow a man who says he is too tired to work to do so.'

Freddy stared at him, his mouth half-open, and then a tide of red rose slowly in his face. 'I'm sorry, Mr Lackland,' he said stiffly after a long pause. 'I do regret seeming to be – ah – taking you for granted. I should have asked you if you would be willing, rather than demanded your help. Now the thing is – I have a small – er – family emergency here and I would be glad if you could see your way clear to staying here at least until I can escort Miss Da Silva to her home. I'll be back here in about an hour – no more – '

For a moment Lewis wavered. The man was a gentleman, dammit. He knew when he was in the wrong and had the grace to admit it, rather than blustering as many a lesser man would have done, or pulling seniority, something he would have been fully entitled to do as chief of the surgical staff at the hospital. And he almost opened his mouth to say as much.

And then saw the smirk on Ambrose's face, as he stood just behind his father. The cocky young devil was staring at him as though he was a lackey, some tuppeny ha'penny servant there to be ordered about. God rot both their smug faces. If they couldn't treat him as a relation ought to be treated, they could both go to hell.

'I'm sorry,' he said dourly. 'I told you, I'm tired and I'm hungry.'

'And *m'sieu le docteur* 'as already promised 'e would escort me to my lodgings, m'sieu.' Claudette slipped her hand into

34

the crook of Lewis' elbow. ' 'E is in zis ze *parfait gentilhomme*. I am sure you will not weesh 'im to break 'is word – '

'Yes,' Lewis said, lifting his chin again. 'Yes, that's the other thing. I'm seeing this lady safely home. She should never have ventured here on her own in the first place. So, if you will excuse me, I'll say good night to you.'

'Well, there you are, Papa!' Ambrose pushed forwards then, with Miriam Da Silva at his side. 'You see? I told you it would be difficult for you – and really there isn't the least need for you to take Miriam home! I am quite fit to do so, am I not, my dear cousin?'

'Indeed you are, Ambrose,' Miriam said demurely, sweeping a look at him from under her long dark lashes, and for a moment Lewis felt a stab of compunction. Quite what was happening between the three of them he didn't know, but that Caspar's son was up to something or other involving this delectable child was quite obvious, and looking at the younger man's face and his elegant – indeed too elegant – clothes, Lewis knew that for all his dislike of the boy's father there was no doubt which was the better man. Perhaps he should after all agree to stay at the hospital and allow Freddy the freedom to do as he thought best, and take Miss Da Silva home.

Almost as though she divined his thoughts, Claudette's hand tightened on his arm and he hesitated, a moment that Ambrose seized in both hands.

'Good night, Papa! Sorry you couldn't accommodate us, but never mind! We shall sort well enough! Good night, Cousin Lackland! Come on, Miriam, let's away – ' And they went across the waiting-room, watched by the waiting patients and their hangers-on as though they were a side-show put on specially for their benefit, and went through the double doors and out into the street before anyone could stop them.

'Oh, dammit all to hell and back!' Freddy said explosively. 'And you too, Lackland!' And he turned and went back into the cubicle shouting 'Nurse! Next patient please!' loudly, and then dragged the curtain shut in Lewis' and Claudette's faces, leaving them standing there staring at its dull folds.

After a moment Claudette said softly, 'I think you might as well come and have some supper after all, don't you?'

And Lewis looked at her and raised his eyebrows and said, 'D'you know, I think so too. And damn all their eyes!'

4

The restaurant was buzzing with noise, ablaze with light and steaming with the most delicious smells. There were beefsteaks broiling with onions and soles frying and pies steaming with a rich clove-scented gravy. There were great bowls of hot pea soup and roast fowls and dishes of green peas and heaps of buttered potatoes and vast raisin puddings soaked in rum, and above it all the drift of good claret and cigar smoke and the bubbling of champagne. And Lewis leaned back in his chair and laughed aloud.

'I knew you would like it here,' Claudette said complacently, and held out her good hand towards him. 'Would you be so kind as to remove my glove for me? I cannot manage with my other hand so sore and stiff as it is.'

He began to peel the fine kid back from her fingers, and became aware of another smell – her scent, a warm muskiness that rose from her wrist, and he moved more slowly, enjoying the touch of her skin against his. He looked up after a moment and found her gaze fixed on his, a disconcerting narrow-eyed look that made colour lift in his face suddenly, and she laughed, a soft throaty little sound. 'This is agreeable, *n'est-ce pas?*' she said softly. 'After a long day, a leetle supper, *un peu de champagne, peut-être –* '

'Oh, come off it!' he said a little more harshly than he had meant to. 'You don't have to put on any of your fancy frenchified airs for me! I'm not one of your English wets, you know! You talk like an ordinary person, or I get up and go right now.'

She laughed again, quite unperturbed by the edge in his voice. 'Oh, but you're a hard man, sir, indeed you are! No need to take me up so sharp when all I mean to do is amuse you! Now, let's eat, hmm? A hungry man is a bad-tempered man. And has no time for – other interests.' She grinned at him wickedly, and he could not help but allow himself to grin back, for she was so transparent in her guile. 'That's better. Now, I was told to ask for the services of a particular waiter, who looks after Gaiety people as they should be and – ah, there he is! They described him well' She lifted her chin at a burly waiter in a stained coat and large white apron and wearing very luxuriant waxed moustaches.

'George,' she said imperiously, 'Rosie Boote of the Gaiety said I was to tell you that we were to have the house special, my friend and I, and that there would be no problems!'

George turned his mouth down expressively and nodded and scooped up the menu cards that had been lying on the table and went away, and she leaned back in her chair and smiled at Lewis. 'Tell me about yourself. Not an Englishman, that much is clear.'

'You're a high-handed madam, aren't you?' he said. 'Even in Sydney where we're all supposed to be as rough as the convicts they started the place with, a man expects to deal with the waiter when he takes a lady out to dine!'

'But you are not taking me to dine!' she said and raised her eyebrows. 'We are merely sharing a meal in a manner that suits us both. You wanted to put that Caspar man in his place, and I – ' she smiled, bewitchingly, 'I wanted to ensure that I was on good terms with the man who was going to be on the other side of the knife that would be cutting me tomorrow morning! A simple enough bargain, surely. And anyway – ' She leaned forwards and spoke more quietly. 'We both benefit from allowing me to deal with George. Rules likes Gaiety girls to come here – we dress up the place. So, when we are alone they will allow us to eat at half the price, as long as we insist that our rich escorts, when we have them, bring us here and spend money on us!'

'And what does that make me look like?' Lewis said. 'Obviously not a rich escort – and there's a name for men who let women provide for them in this sort of – '

Oh, pooh!' she said. 'You're talking like an – what was it? – an English wet. Just what *is* an English wet, anyway?'

'A chinless sprig of rubbish who knows no more than the spending of his Papa's money and drooping about drawing-rooms. Listen, if I am to stay here and eat, I pay for this dinner, and I pay full whack. You can use your house special business another time. Me, I don't play that sort of game.'

She shrugged. 'As you wish. You're a fool to spend money you don't need to. Or rich.'

'Rich? Ha! Do I look rich?'

She stared at him consideringly. His jacket was rather rubbed and clearly old, but it fitted him well, sitting across his heavy shoulders neatly, and his linen was white and well cared for, but equally clearly rather old. He wore no adornment apart from a plain silver chain across his waistcoat, and obviously the watch on the end of it was far from being a large and costly one.

'No,' she said. 'You don't look rich. But you're a doctor, aren't you? Why should a doctor not be rich? People who are ailing pay cheerfully for the help of a good man, do they not?'

'We don't get rich people at Nellie's,' Lewis said, thinking of the small boy with the scraped leg who had been his last patient. 'Anything but.'

'Then why stay there? Rich people get ill as well as poor ones. You should look after them.'

'I leave that to the likes of Caspar,' Lewis said, his voice hard again. 'He's got a very lucrative practice. Lives on the fat of the land, they tell me. In Tavistock Square. Got a horde of expensive children and grandchildren and a very expensive wife. Not that I gossip at Nellie's, but it's common knowledge – '

'Did I hear right?' she said. 'Didn't that young man – Caspar's son – did he not address you as cousin?'

'Aye, that's true enough,' Lewis said sourly, and then leaned back as the waiter appeared and began to put food in front of them. There was a dish of fried smelts adorned with lemon and red pepper, a pair of small fowls plump with stuffing and resting happily amid piles of baked potatoes, and a cold bottle, its sides dripping with condensation, and almost against his will, Lewis felt his spirits rise. He really was unconscionably hungry, and he set to with a will and she followed his example, displaying as eager an appetite as his. They sat there contentedly stuffing themselves amid the clatter of cutlery and the tinkle of glasses and only when there was nothing left but the bones of the chicken and a few sad-looking potatoes did Lewis lean back in his chair and sigh with repletion.

'That was good,' he said. 'I was hungrier than I knew.'

'You look better,' she said. She too was leaning back, delicately picking her teeth with a quill, and he grinned at her lazily. 'You're an odd creature, aren't you? Swear like a man, pick your teeth like a man – '

'There are other things I do that are not in the least like a man,' she said softly and smiled at him, but he shook his head a little sharply.

'None of that,' he said and after a moment she smiled again, and nodded, not at all put out. 'As you wish,' she said cheerfully. 'Tell me – you say that man Caspar is a cousin of yours? How is that, when he is so obviously an English wet, and you are not?'

'Oh, he's not so bad,' Lewis said. He was feeling better now that he was fed and some of the fatigue was leaving his bones. 'Caspar's all right, I suppose. He's a damned fine surgeon, I'll tell you that. I'm not that taken with the amount of time he spends on his fashionable patients, but there, I suppose he's entitled to make his living. Wouldn't suit me, but he's got a family, and I haven't – '

'None at all? No parents, no wives, no children of your own?'

'Not one, thank God. Miller of Dee, that's me.'

'Miller of Dee?'

He sang the song softly. 'I care for nobody, no, not I, and nobody cares for me – '

'Ah, pooh to that! Such a well set up man as you – there must be some who care for you! And anyway, if the Caspar man is your cousin – '

'He may be a relation, but that does not mean he cares,' Lewis said. 'He doesn't give a damn for me, and there is no reason why he should, I suppose. Though it would have been pleasant enough to meet some of my grandfather's family here – ' The second bottle of wine which had arrived half-way through their meal and which was now standing as empty as its predecessor was beginning to reach him, for he softened now. 'London's a long way from Sydney, and for all I've been here six months, I have no friends. Oh, there are people who work at the hospital, but they have their own lives, their own connections, and can't be bothered with an outsider like me.'

'I know,' she said. 'At the Gaiety – the girls are pleasant enough, but me, I am not English, and these English are a self-regarding lot, are they not? I have no friends here either. Just me and Papa – '

'Oh, you have a father here?'

'Yes.' She was silent then for a moment looking down at her swollen hand, which was resting on the table. 'Yes. He is ill. It is important that my hand is well before the play opens. I need the job – '

He sat and looked at her for a long moment, taking in the soft roundness of her face and the curve of her mouth and thought confusedly of how very female she was, and how long it had been since he had held a woman in his arms. At home in Sydney there had been plenty of warm affectionate girls who had been happy to share a night of warmth and comfort and laughter with him, and that side of his nature had needed strong control these past few months. But this girl was a patient and he had never been one to get involved with such. The girls at home had been first his friends, and then his lovers. Girls who had worked in the hospitals as nurses, or had been friends of the young men he had studied and worked with over his student years. He had never allowed himself to seduce a patient yet, and he was not going to start now. However long it had been –

'Your hand will be well, I assure you,' he said gruffly. 'A poultice tonight, and my attention tomorrow, and you will be comfortable and look *belle* enough for anyone. Take my word.'

'Thank you.' She smiled up at him. 'I trust you. Now tell me more of yourself! You were so very bad-tempered there before, at the hospital, and here too – but now you are charming! I am sure we could be friends – '

'We are doctor and patient. No more,' he said. 'I don't want to be insulting, but you must understand that it is not – not professional for a doctor to become a friend of a patient.'

'Yet you are sitting here with me! That is a friendly action, surely?'

He grimaced. 'I was angry, and I wanted to put Caspar in his place – foolish of me.'

'Well, I am glad it happened so. I need a friend here in London, and I am determined you shall become one! As for doctor and patient – pooh! After you have repaired my hand, then I shall not be your patient any more, for I am as healthy as a pig in a mud bath, and will need no further care from you or anyone! So we may be friends. And I like you. You are a very – you do not dissemble. I am tired of people who dissemble.'

He laughed at that. 'And you with your false accent and your – '

'It is not false!' she flared at him. 'I am half French, half English. But there are times when it is convenient to emphasize one half over the other. That is not dissembling, but common sense. I am always practical! I must use such assets as I have, and use them well. I am not one of your rich cousins who can snap fingers to get what is needed. I am a poor woman who must earn her bread, and Papa's – I told you, he is ill, and I have responsibility for him – '

'All right, all right! I believe you! No need to set my whiskers on fire,' he said. 'I dare say I'm in the wrong. There is an honesty about you, I suppose – a sort of honesty.'

'Thank you,' she said, and lifted her chin at him. 'Come, we have shared an agreeable meal, *mon brave*, we are both alone and lonely in London, and have need of each other. You agree? Friends? No more, I assure you! I am not a danger to you – I have my job and I am not a woman to use a man as a bread-basket.'

'Well, we shall see. Tell me more of yourself. How is it you are half French and half English?'

'If you will tell me of yourself, then I will. It is a bargain?'

The wine was now spreading everywhere through him. He really had not felt so comfortable for a long time, and he smiled lazily at her. 'A bargain it is.'

She set her elbows on the table and began to talk and he was first interested and then amused and finally, almost to his surprise, respecting. She had had a hard, indeed often dreadful, time during her twenty-three years, and she had clearly been, from her earliest childhood, resourceful and resilient. She spoke of her father affectionately and with never a murmur of complaint, yet the picture that Lewis got of him was of a stunningly selfish man, who had been spoiled all his life by the women around him. That he had charm was obvious, but that he exercised it only to please himself was equally obvious in every word Claudette spoke of him.

The other thing about her that came out of her description of her life was the outline of a philosophy that would, Lewis knew, shock the vast majority of the respectable matrons and God-fearing gentlemen who inhabited this rich city of London, but which appealed to him, for it was honest in its own way and showed a relish for life which he found very warming. She spoke without self-consciousness of the stealing and lying and swindling that she had been involved with as the daughter of the appalling Jody, but it was clear that she poached only from poachers. To cheat a man who gambled his money away was not dishonest, in Claudette's book; it was but making sure the fool's money went to a better use than it would in another gambler's pocket. When she and Jody needed food and clothes, where was the sin in making sure the cards were carefully stacked or the roulette wheel nicely balanced in their favour? None at all. And Lewis to his silent amazement found himself agreeing with her.

He also suspected that her attitude to physical love was one that would shock the very proper residents of rich London. This girl was no shrinking virgin, but a voluptuous experienced woman; but there was nothing calculating about her. She had had loves, clearly, but they had been true loves; men she had cared for, and whose beds she had shared for the sheer joy of it, not because she would gain any material benefit. And that made him realize something else which reddened his cheeks a little and set his pulses beating rather thickly in his ears. Her teasing of him which he had dismissed at first as the almost automatic flirting of the *demi-mondaine* had been nothing of the sort. She had made overtures because she liked him, found him attractive and might well – he found himself breathing unevenly as the realization came to him – might well share his bed with him for no other reason than that she would enjoy the experience.

When she had finished her description of their last flight from Paris, and the problems of the past few weeks here in

London he leaned back in his chair and launched willingly into an account of his own life, as much to cover up the confusion of his feelings about her, as because he really wanted to talk about himself. By nature Lewis Lackland was a taciturn man, who had learned to talk more easily than was comfortable for him simply because that was one of the necessary skills of a good doctor, but he was not used to talking easily of his own experience and feelings. Yet tonight he did; and whether it was the wine, or the girl sitting facing him across the table, with her green eyes fixed on his face, he did not know. And did not particularly care. He was just happy to talk.

He told her of his lonely boyhood as the only child of a woman who never stopped grieving for the young husband who had died in a fight in a tavern in Sydney docks, and of his grandfather, a sour silent man who had been born in England, the son of a surgeon, and who was himself a surgeon.

'He had been good once, I suppose,' Lewis said. 'But by the time I knew him all the heart had gone out of him. He had left some trouble here behind in England – he would never say what except that it had involved his father. He told me a lot about London, and about the hospital, and so I thought I'd be a surgeon too – '

He did nor tell her of the way his mind had been besieged with thoughts of London as he had moved through adolescence, how he had burned with the most passionate desire to be a surgeon too, and cure the world of its ills. How he had pushed himself and driven himself and worked at the most menial of jobs at nights and at weekends in order to pay his medical school fees at St Vincent's Hospital in Sydney, and dragged his exhausted body and aching mind through the long years of effort until he was qualified; but she, watching his face as he spoke, picked up some of it and felt herself warming even more to this heavy very adult man. There was nothing of the boy about him, and she found herself wondering if there ever had been. Even in his teens he must have been like this – solid, determined, alive with purpose.

'My mother died when I was half-way through my studies,' he said and his voice was flat and colourless. 'She had cancer and it is that disease in which I am now chiefly interested. I knew I had to come to London to obtain the experience I need. Then I shall go back to Sydney and start work there. There are few real specialists in such diseases for the people of Australia, and I intend that there shall be.'

'It is a bad disease,' Claudette said and almost involuntarily crossed herself, as she had been taught to do long ago by the stream of French Catholic nursemaids Jody had inflicted on her. 'Papa – '

He looked up sharply. 'Your father has cancer?'

'I do not know. But he is ill – he has seen no doctor,' she said. 'He won't. He is – I think he is too afraid. He pretends he's above doctors, too brave for such, but he is afraid – and so am I. Afraid for him.'

'People should not need to be afraid,' he said with a sudden passion. 'It is – it must be – a disease like others. Subject to amelioration, if no more. There cannot be an unsolvable mystery there. Pasteur solved the mystery of the infections – someone must solve the mystery of the cancers – '

'You?' she said, and smiled at him, a little crookedly, for there was something very endearing about the way his expression had lifted as he spoke.

'Perhaps. Why not? I can try, anyway.'

'So, that is why you have come to England? To find the cure for these illnesses?'

'I never speak of cure. Only of amelioration. That will be enough to start with. Yes, that is why I am here. When my grandfather died, I had at last the money to come – '

'I am sorry he died. You cared for him, I think.'

He sat and considered for a moment, staring down at his hands resting squarely on the table in front of him. 'Cared? I suppose I did.'

He had cared desperately for him, for that lined old man with the shut-in face. He had been for the young Lewis a symbol of all he ever wanted. A surgeon, a man who helped, and the fact that somewhere along the road his steps had faltered and he had lost much of his passion, and with it the vital skill that made a surgeon great, mattered not a whit. Rupert Lackland had been a beacon for Lewis, a beacon that would lead him to justify his presence in this painful world.

'And this man here – Caspar. He is a relation of your grandfather? Or was it your mother's family – '

'No – it is my grandfather who was related to him. As I understand it, Caspar's mother, who is still alive, was sister to my grandfather. But I have never met her, nor am I likely to, if Caspar has his way.'

'Why should he be so? Does he not care for family ties?'

Lewis shrugged. 'I don't know. He is just a cold fish I suppose – '

'A wet fish,' she said, and laughed and after a moment he laughed too.

'A very wet fish. But not as wet as that son of his. Did you ever see so useless an object?'

'The girl he was with did not seem to think so, did she? She was – charming – '

He looked up at her then, and allowed himself a sharp little grin. 'A good-looking woman to speak so of another? That really is praise.'

She shrugged, suddenly very Gallic. 'Not at all! I know a pretty face when I see one. She seemed a little insipid perhaps, but pretty enough – '

He laughed then. 'Not at all. The child was a vision, quite, quite delectable! You cannot deny it!'

'Why should I? Who was she?'

'Another cousin, it seems. But I do not know quite how. Caspar didn't bother to explain that. And I don't really care – '

'So that is your story. It is an interesting one indeed. You know, I think some time soon we should amuse ourselves, you and I, and make it our business to seek out these other relations of yours, so that you can discover more about your grandfather. That would be interesting, *hein?*'

He raised his brows at that. 'In the future? What future?'

She patted his hand and smiled at him. 'Oh, come, silly man! We are two of a kind, you and I! A little lonely. Looking at a world that is not as interested in us as it should be, and determined to make it so! Is that not true? Of course it is! We are meant to be friends, just as it was meant we should meet tonight. I am glad we did, and I know we shall share much in the future. Shall we not? *After* you have repaired my hand, and I have stopped being your patient!'

And he found he could not argue with her. The prospect she painted was altogether too attractive.

5

The last thing that Ambrose had wanted to do was go to Lady Rothschild's drum, for of all evening parties that bored him almost to tears, drums were the worst. Just a huge crush of the most ghastly old people who made it impossible to get near the drink and who trod on your toes and asked dismal questions about your dreariest relations, and no dancing at all to break up the ennui.

But Miriam had to go, so perforce, Ambrose had to go too, for at present Miriam was the most important person in his life.

It had started really in order to annoy his father. He had known young Miriam since her nursery days, of course, for she had always been at her Grandmamma's side when the Caspar family went to visit the Olds, and at first he had treated her much like his other childish cousins and his small nieces and nephews, for after all when he had been a grown man of twenty, and very lofty about his senior status, she had been a baby of but five years. Who would ever have thought he would take such a one seriously? Certainly not he; yet the time had come when they had sent her away to Paris for a few months of school, to polish her French and her drawing, and she had come back as poised and beautiful as any seventeen-year-old could ever hope to be, and he had looked at her again, and been amused by her, for she had looked at him and made it clear she liked what she saw.

Looking back, he realized it had always been so. She had hung about his knees during those interminable visits to the Olds, all those years ago, and listened huge-eyed to every word he said; no doubt that was when the child first developed her *tendre* for him, and to see that her feelings were as engaged as ever when she was seventeen was too much for Ambrose. She was a cousin, admittedly, but what of that? She was exceedingly pretty, excessively rich, and it would enrage his whole family and his father in particular if he were to encourage her.

So he had encouraged her, and been even more amused to see the effects; for she would turn her lovely dark head towards him and widen her eyes and part her lips and show in every way a girl could that she found him exciting. What man could fail to enjoy that? But the trouble had come when enjoyment moved over to make way for something more, and for the past weeks – ever since her Ball in fact – he had been trying not to face a somewhat disagreeable fact.

He really *cared* about Miriam. What had started as a Freddy-baiting game had become one in which he competed seriously for reward.

When other men talked to her, he got a thick dull sensation in his belly that was unfamiliar to him; and not surprisingly, for a man as attractive as Ambrose Caspar had never needed to feel jealousy before. Whatever he had wanted, be it material goods or the attention of particular persons, he had always got. He had been his mother's favourite all his life; every girl at whom he had cast a glance since he had been sixteen or so had melted before him; how could he know the pains of jealousy? But he knew them now, watching Miriam become the talk of the 1892 Season, as she went from Ball to dance, from drum to tea-party, from riding in the Park to garden receptions, always surrounded by adoring men.

It hurt Ambrose dreadfully, and made him anxious, and there was nothing he could do about it, for to change his posture as a relaxed drawling easy man-about-town was out of the question. He was a blood, a masher, one of the *crème de la crème*, and to show that his feelings were deeply engaged by one particular female would be to destroy totally his reputation among his cronies – indeed in all Society, he flattered himself – for ever.

All of which he tried to tell himself as he pushed his way through the sweating scented loudly chattering crowds at Lady Rothschild's Park Lane house in search of his grandmother's familiar bulk, for there at her side would be Miriam, and he hoped, any other young men held at arm's length, and maybe, tonight, he would be able to talk to Miriam without other damned fellows thrusting their way in –

He found Grandmamma Abby at last, overflowing one of the few available gilt chairs beside an open window, fanning herself with some vigour and trying not to show how very tired she was. It had been a long day; Miriam had been up at eight to ride in the Park, for she cut a pretty figure on a horse, and well she knew it, and had returned home at ten to prepare for a Breakfast party at the Damonts, to which Abby had felt herself obliged to accompany her, weary though she was after having chaperoned the child at the Marchioness of Collingbourne's Ball the night before. They had not got to their beds before five a.m. and to be up again at half-past ten was too much; but Abby was determined that the child should enjoy her first Season (and going by the number of young men who clamoured about her probably her only Season, for no doubt the dear thing would fall in love and marry one of the wretches, which was what the Season was all about of course, though Abby for her part would be delighted to keep her darling with her a few more years yet) whatever it cost Abby herself in lost sleep. She had managed to rest a couple of hours this afternoon, which was something, and had seen to it that darling Miriam had done so too, instead of going to the garden-party at Jerningham House to which she had been bidden, but the child looked a little pale, all the same. Abby smiled at her now, and leaned forwards to speak to her, to see if perhaps she could persuade her to come home now, instead of going on to the series of dances for which she had cards, but just as she opened her mouth to speak, she felt a hand on her shoulder and looked up.

'Good evening, Grandmamma,' Ambrose said, and bent to kiss the papery old cheek, and Abby looked up at him and smiled with genuine pleasure.

'Why, good evening, dear boy! How agreeable to see you here! I did not think to see you at such a crush as this. I thought you told me you hated drums above all things?'

'Indeed, I do, as a rule, but I thought – well, it is agreeable to see you, Grandmamma, and I knew you would be here!'

'Did you indeed?' Abby said, and looked up at him sharply. 'I do not remember you always being so devoted to your relatives, my dear!'

He smiled disarmingly. 'I grow older and wiser, Grandmamma! As a giddy boy, I dare say I did racket about a bit, but now I am at years of discretion. Anyway, I thought to see the family beauty here, and that is an added attraction.'

'Hmph,' Abby said, and hauled herself to her feet, her stays creaking a little. 'No doubt. Well, we are about to leave. It has been a long day, and now it is close to midnight, and I am determined to see that Miriam has one night's sleep at least this week. Tomorrow is another busy day, with the Ball at Marlborough House to which we have been bidden – '

'Marlborough House?' Ambrose was impressed in spite of himself. 'I did not know that you were part of that set, Miriam.'

'I am not part of any set,' Miriam said and tossed her chin a little. 'But the Prince wishes me to be at his Ball, so – '

'You must remember that your Grandpapa has long enjoyed the Prince's friendship, my dear,' Abby said a little dampingly. 'One would not wish to be – disagreeable – but the facts are that his Highness looks well to the benefits of those of his acquaintance who take care of *his*.'

'Grandpapa lent him money, then?' Ambrose said, and twisted his lip a little as he looked sideways at Miriam. This Jewish connection in his family, while in some ways a benefit, rubbed him up the wrong way sometimes; it was not agreeable when his friends made snide remarks about the special condescension the Prince showed to people like Cassel and Sassoon. And Henriques.

'No,' his grandmother said equably. 'Your grandfather is not a money-lender, Ambrose. He is a banker of considerable repute who works hard for his position in Society as do your father and your brothers, I think.'

Ambrose reddened. 'Yes – well, I meant no harm, Grandmamma. Shall I call your carriage for you?'

'Oh, Grandmamma, can we go on to Dodo Parminter's Ball? She really is a most *dear* friend, and – '

'Now, Miriam, I have told you, you need your sleep! And even if you do not, child, I do! I really cannot manage another Ball tonight. There have been four this week already and tomorrow's to come, and by far the most important – '

'I will take Miriam on to the Parminter Ball, Grandmamma,' Ambrose said easily, expertly turning one shoulder as he saw that bounder Edward Burnley moving towards Miriam through the press of bodies. 'I will assure you she will not dance more than two *valses* and then I shall bring her home to Green Street – '

'Go to a Ball without a chaperone?' Abby said, scandalized. 'What are you thinking of? As if I would allow such a thing! And as if Miriam would consider – '

'Oh, Grandmamma, don't be so stuffy! Lots of modern girls go about without chaperones! It is not so special a matter today! I shall be in excellent hands with Ambrose – why, he is my *cousin*! What possible harm could I come to? Please, dearest Grandmamma, don't be so silly!'

'Silly!' Abby's face set hard. 'Miss, you forget yourself! Indulge you I may, but that does not give you permission to behave like a hoyden or to speak so to me! I will not – '

'Oh, I am sorry, my dear one, I truly am, but I do so want to go and – '

'Grandmamma, there will be no impropriety, you know, for my sister Cecily will be there, and so, I believe, will Amy Laurence and Mary. So I will deliver Miriam safely into their hands, and there need be no anxiety about silly gossip and no disappointment for Miriam, and you will lose no sleep! Come, dear Grandmamma, is that not a practical solution worthy of your own devising?'

Abby looked at him uncertainly for a moment. It was certainly an answer; she was quite desperately tired and much in need of the comfort of Gideon's company, for Gideon, dearly as he loved his granddaughter, drew the line at going to drums and balls for her, and his wife much envied him his tranquil evenings in their comfortable drawing-room. She looked at Miriam then, and had to admit now that the child no longer looked peaky and in need of sleep, but was bright-eyed and pink-cheeked as she stood there eagerly gazing at her grandmother, her head set appealingly to one side and an expression of great hopefulness on her pretty face.

'I shall be as good as *gold*, Grandmamma, I promise, with Cecily, and who could be a better chaperone than she? I will give her your love, shall I, and tell her she is to watch me *most* carefully, and not to allow any young men to come within an inch of me except for dancing and – '

'Wretched child,' Abby said, and suddenly yawned hugely. 'You really should go to bed yourself – '

But already Ambrose was leading the way through the hubbub towards the door and waving imperiously at a powdered and liveried footman to call up Mrs Gideon Henriques' carriage, and Abby let herself be swept along. It really was easier than arguing.

'Mind that you go at once to Cecily when you arrive, my dear,' she adjured Miriam through her carriage window as Ambrose settled the rug felicitously about her knees. 'Remember, now, and do not stay out too late! Marlborough House, remember – '

'Whoosh! I thought we'd never be rid of her!' Ambrose said as the carriage at last went spanking away along Park Lane towards Green Street. 'Now, come on! We're just in time, if we hurry!'

'Just in time? For Dodo's Ball?' Miriam pulled her white fur pelisse closer round her shoulders. Close to June as it was, the weather had still not shown any tendency towards summer warmth. 'Why, it is only half-past midnight!'

'Oh, the devil with Dodo's Ball!' Ambrose said daringly, and tucked his hand into the crook of her elbow. 'We are going somewhere quite different! You will be amused by this, I think – and afterwards we shall go along to Frascati's and have lots of delicious champagne and some strawberries, for they are fresh coming into season now and I am told very good – '

He waved his stick, and a hansom cab came jingling towards them and he handed her in with great ceremony before settling beside her and closing the apron in front with a little snap.

'But Ambrose, what will Grandmamma say when she discovers from Cecily that I did not go to the Ball? She will be – '

'Pooh, to Grandmamma! We shall tell her that on the way you realized she was right, and needed to go to bed, so I took you home!'

Miriam giggled and moved slightly so that she was sitting even closer to him, not difficult in the close confines of a hansom cab. 'You are very wicked, Ambrose.'

'But very nice,' he said and looked down at her and had to work quite hard at not bending his head to kiss her, for in the flickering lights from passing street lamps, as the cab went clattering on its way down towards Hyde Park Corner before turning left towards Covent Garden as Ambrose had instructed, she looked quite unbelievably lovely.

'Where are we going?' she asked after a moment, seeming to know how close she had come to being kissed, and seeming perhaps just a little disappointed.

To the Supper Rooms, in King Street.'

To Cousin *Oliver's*?' She pulled away and stared up at him. 'My dear Ambrose, that is the most – '

'Boring? No it is not. For he has a very special act this week, I promise you! You will see!'

They arrived at the same time as a great many other people, for the narrow street was alive with cabs and carriages and a great many pushing, shouting people, but Ambrose by dint of a good deal of pushing on his own account managed to clear a way for her and in through the engraved glass doors that opened between a shuttered seed warehouse and the establishment of Odhams the publishers.

King Street had changed a lot in the forty years since Oliver had inherited the Celia Supper Rooms from his father Jonah. Then the street had been a mêlée of cheap lodging houses and dubious restaurants, but now it had come up a little in the world, and was full of publishers' offices and banks and picture galleries and other useful bastions of prosperous respectability. But the Supper Rooms had not changed.

Miriam passed between the red velvet curtains that Ambrose parted for her, on the other side of the entrance door, and stood for a moment looking about her. She had not visited the place since she was small, for she had professed herself uninterested in this sort of theatre, but now she was entranced, for the place was alive with colour and bustle and the hubbub of people enjoying themselves. White-clothed tables, each bearing their own pink-shaded electric lights were scattered about the huge room, and at the far end an expanse of rich azure-blue curtains, plentifully embroidered with gold wire, covered the small stage. There was a delicious smell of champagne and good food, and she let her fur slip from her shoulders as the warmth hit her, and smiled widely as she turned back to Ambrose.

'Oh, Ambrose, I had forgotten how charming the place is! The last time I came it was with your sister Cecily and – '

'And it was dull, dull, dull. Well, Cissie is dull, dull, dull! Come, tonight you will enjoy yourself. Hello to you, Uncle Oliver!'

'My dears, how very good to see you! Are you well? I've had a dreadful time these past two weeks. My back – and my knees you know, not a wink of sleep – oh, dear me, so busy tonight and not a table to be – yes, I kept one for you as I promised – come along – yes, as I said, my back and knees, it's as though the devil were there in bed with me with a pair of red-hot pincers, too dreadful – I must speak to your dear father again – there you are! As near as I could get you – now, order what you wish and forget the bill – '

' – And you forget we were here, right, Uncle Oliver?'

The older man blinked at him short-sightedly and then took off his glasses and rubbed them on his handkerchief. 'My boy, you're your own man, are you not? Yes, to be sure. So why should I say anything to anybody about you, hey? None o' my business. I must go and get some brandy – see if that'll ease my poor old back a little – ' and he went bustling away, stopping at almost every table as his eager customers waved to him and chattered at him and waiters went rushing by with trays loaded with glasses and the inevitable champagne bottles.

'He must be a warm man,' Ambrose said consideringly, as one of the waiters came swooping down on their table with a tray of champagne for them. 'This place – he's had it for years, and he gets such good people today that you can't get a seat for love or money – well, money, obviously. I wonder if he'd – '

'If he'd what?' Miriam said, turning her glittering eyes on him. 'Oh, I do like it here, Ambrose! I was sure it would be dreadfully dull, but the people are so funny! Do look at that woman there. Her face – it is, it really is, the *oddest* colour – '

'*Maquillage*, my child,' Ambrose said shortly, after one glance at the painted woman at the next table. 'I thought in Paris you would have seen plenty such. Heavens, but you're a protected little creature, aren't you? We'll have to take care not to let your dear Grandmamma know I have exposed you to the sight of painted ladies. She'd have a fit.'

Miriam giggled. 'It would do her good. She's so set in her ways, silly old thing! This is nice champagne. I want some more. What do you want Cousin Oliver to do?'

'Eh?'

You said you wondered if he'd and then you stopped – '

'Oh, nothing that need concern you.' Ambrose had been thinking hard about money. He always thought about money because he needed such a great deal of it, and it was getting harder and harder to persuade his mother to part with it, for his father, as well he knew, was getting ever more difficult on the subject. Since the night he had been foolish enough to try to touch the old man direct for a loan at the hospital, he'd been even more impossible, damn his eyes. But Oliver now, his own uncle, warm as toast, obviously, and as easy to handle as a day-old colt –

There was a sudden crash of cymbals and drums from the small orchestra set in front of the blue curtains, and slowly the footlights came on and lifted the colour to an even richer hue, and the audience, excited already, burst into a cry of, 'Bring her on – bring her on!'

'What is it?' Miriam cried, entranced, twisting in her seat to improve her view of the stage. 'What's happening?'

'It's his latest act. She's a wonder, I promise you. It's her last night here, for next week she goes to the Gaiety. The Guv'nor's signed her up, and she stars there in his new show *Cinder-Ellen*

Up Too Late. To have seen her here will be a real feather in your cap, I promise you. She's the best – '

'You know so much about the theatre, Ambrose!' Miriam said, shouting to make herself heard above the very lively dance music the band was now playing in a hubbub of piano, violins, drums and trumpets. 'You are almost as informed as an actor himself might be!'

'I have many friends backstage,' Ambrose said airily. 'Here she is!' And the curtains parted and there, in the centre of the stage, stood a small girl in a red dress, with a huge hat like one in a Gainsborough painting, and a mane of fair hair which fell softly to her shoulders. She held a lace handkerchief in one hand, and she looked rather shy and alone standing there.

The audience slowly subsided until all was quiet, apart from the soft thumping of the piano, and then she began to sing, in a rather timid little voice.

> 'A smart and stylish girl you see,
> The Belle of high society,
> Fond of fun as fond can be,
> When it's on the strict QT.
> Not too young, and not too old,
> Not too timid, not too bold,
> But just the very thing I'm told
> That in your arms you'd like to hold – '

And now the music lifted and there was a sudden roar of drums and the most impressive crash of the cymbals and the singer seemed to be possessed. Her legs flew up, and her red skirt disappeared in a froth of white lace petticoats, the handkerchief was waved in the air like a banner, and the huge hat bobbed like a thing with a life of its own as she roared out the chorus at the top of a very loud voice.

'Ta rara *boom* de ay, tarara*boom* de ay, tarara*boom* de ay, tarara*boom* de ay – '

It was sheer breathcatching excitement, and the audience joined in at the top of its corporate voice, shrieking its 'taras' and its 'booms' like maniacs as the little figure on the stage capered and waved and bounced and showed more of her legs than Miriam would have thought any dancer could, and still the audience roared its delight.

They wouldn't let her go. She had to sing verse after verse, each time starting with the same demure slowness and building up to the great crashing booms of the cymbals. It was one of the most exciting performances Miriam could ever remember seeing and when at last the girl disappeared behind the falling curtains, she was as breathless and as drenched in sweat as if she had been dancing and singing herself.

'There!' Ambrose said. 'Wasn't that great fun? I knew you'd like it.'

'Who is she? I would dearly like to see her perform again!'

'Lottie Collins, her name is. Enchanting – you shall see her again, if you like. I'll take you to the Gaiety. If you promise you won't tell Grandmamma.'

'As if I would!' Miriam tossed her head then. 'Anyway, why should I? I'm a grown woman now that I have had my come-out and I have my own money after all. They cannot tell me what to do all my life!'

'Can you spend your own money, though?' Ambrose asked as casually as he knew how, and poured her another glass of champagne.

She made a face at that. 'Not really. They all have to sign things – it's dreadfully boring, all of it. It is my money of course, but I cannot have the easy use of it until I am twenty-one – which is for ever! Or until I get married of course.' She giggled and drank some more wine. 'But I can usually persuade them to let me do as I wish, eventually. But it's easier if they do not know much. So take me to the Gaiety to see Lottie Collins again, and we won't say a word to the silly old Olds!'

And she smiled at him rather mistily, for she had by now taken three glasses of champagne, and the effects were showing.

'I think, dear child, we shall forget Frascati's for tonight. Another time perhaps. I shall take you home now, and we shall meet tomorrow morning in the Park, hmm? I shall ride there in the Row about nine. Don't be late. Come now, my little cousin! Home for you! Though I want a quick word with Uncle Oliver first – '

He had his quick word, and then, well satisfied, tucked the now almost sleeping Miriam in another hansom cab to take her home to Green Street. Oliver had been an easier touch than he had hoped, a much easier touch. Maybe there could be more coming from that direction, he told himself happily.

And maybe there could be more, a great deal more coming from the direction of the delicious little bundle of silk and fur who sat curled up beside him in the hansom cab. A most agreeable thought, that. This time he made no effort to control his impulse to kiss her on the way home. And she made no effort to stop him.

6

June drifted into July, and at last the weather improved, which made Lewis feel rather happier than he had been since he had come to England last November. He had not complained at all about the marked difference in climate to which he had had to accustom himself, but an English winter had been cruel to him, especially at a time of year he normally regarded as belonging to high summer. Now at last, he felt the warmth of the sun on his back as he walked in the London streets and though that meant also that his nose was assaulted with all the stenches of Covent Garden – rotting fruit and vegetables, unwashed humanity, a breath of sewage – it was worth it for the improvement in his general spirits.

But it was not only the weather that caused this change, and he was too honest a man to pretend otherwise. There were two other factors.

One was the subtle alteration in Freddy Caspar's attitude towards him, an alteration which stemmed from the night when Lewis had refused to work late for him. It seemed to Lewis that Freddy showed more respect for him than he had hitherto, and this made him feel more kindly disposed towards the older man.

They worked together a great deal now, both in the casualty department and in the operating theatres, and Lewis began to realize that he had done the man a considerable injustice. He was not, as he had first thought, a mere fashionable practitioner who was more interested in his private patients than in the poverty-stricken detritus of the Covent Garden streets who were cared for at Nellie's. In fact, he saw very few rich patients; when he was not at Nellie's, Lewis discovered, he was at a small branch hospital on the other side of the Thames, in Southwark, where 'unmentionable' diseases were treated.

He had discovered this one hot night when a man was brought into casualty in a most parlous state; raving in delirium, his face and body covered in the most repellent sores, he was clearly in the last stages of rampant syphilis. Lewis saw him first, and then tried to arrange for the man to be taken into one of the wards of Nellie's to be allowed to die there with what dignity was possible. Clearly he could not be sent back to the hovel that he called home. This was the first case of the disease which had come Lewis' way since his arrival at Nellie's – a rather surprising thing, now he came to think of it, and he discovered why it should be when he asked Freddy about arranging a bed for the patient.

'We do not take them in here,' Freddy said. 'We have another establishment – I'll have him carried there. You can come and see for yourself if you like – '

Lewis did like, and went with Freddy on the following afternoon, a particularly sultry one, to make a round of the Southwark branch known at Nellie's simply as 'the House'.

It was a big sombre building, in which long wards of twenty beds each were staffed by older than average nurses who moved from bed to bed with heavy seriousness and none of the cheerful friendliness which marked the nurses at Nellie's. Here there seemed to be a brooding atmosphere, a sense of shame among the patients who lay cocooned in their beds and made no effort to talk to their neighbours, as was usual in the hospital over the river. And as Lewis watched Freddy deal with the pitiful women there – who outnumbered the men by two to one – and saw that he showed the same respect and concern for them as he showed for patients who could not be accused, as these could, of having brought their misfortune on themselves by their own immorality, he found his respect for his cousin growing. In Sydney he had accepted as reasonable the attitude of his fellow doctors, and of his teachers, that people suffering from syphilis and other forms of pox deserved no care at all, for they were reaping the sins of their own wildness. Now he realized that this was a cruelly unjust attitude, for many of the women at the House were respectable wives and mothers who had been all unwittingly infected by their husbands; and the men could not be regarded as altogether sinful for having occasional recourse to prostitutes. After all, there were enough of them in London, and most men accepted their existence as a natural and unchangeable fact of life.

'They say there are eighty thousand of this sort in London,' Freddy said, as they moved away from the bed of a woman of some thirty-five years but who looked to be at least twice that age, so haggard and damaged was she by the effects of syphilis. 'Eighty thousand! And those are the ones who are known to be street women and to inhabit the brothels. How many there are who seem to be respectable but who engage in the same traffic on occasion no one knows. It is said that there are few servant girls who don't buy themselves an occasional bonnet this way – '

'What treatments do you use here? In Sydney mercury was popular – and iodides – and occasionally calomel – though that's of little effect, I find.'

'What else is there? I try burning with silver nitrate for some of the sores but in many cases it causes more pain, and seems to do little to redeem the disease process. It is particularly so in the children. I have lost more than three-quarters of all the babies we took in here at the House with hereditary *lues*. Three-quarters! And of those born of mothers with virulent gonorrhoea – we had more than a hundred such last year –

more than half died and many of the remainder were blinded very early. It's a sorry business – '

'Prevention – ' Lewis said and Freddy snorted.

'How? You recall what happened with the CD acts – '

'What?'

'Oh – perhaps you did not have them in Australia. We had here Acts of Parliament which provided for the arrest of women suspected of spreading infection, and their compulsory medical examination – not everywhere, you understand, but in Naval and Military garrison towns, but that was of no use for it controlled only the women and not the men, and as well you know the men carry the signs of infection sooner and much more clearly than do the women. And anyway, the radicals took such violent exception to the laws – Mrs Butler campaigned so mightily against the Acts that they were repealed these – oh, it must be six or seven years ago now. Not that it made much difference. With or without the Acts the diseases run like fire. And no one *talks* of them. Even we at Nellie's have this separate place for the patients – the Governors would not consider permitting the wards at the hospital to be contaminated by them. I become quite dejected about the problem sometimes.'

Lewis looked at him curiously. 'It seems an unusual concern for a surgeon of your stature,' he said gruffly.

'Stature? What is that? I do my work as I have always done it, as my grandfather taught me to do it – ' He stopped then, 'Your great-grandfather – '

'Yes,' Lewis said. 'What sort of man was he?'

'Oh, a most passionate surgeon!' Freddy said, and Lewis looked at him, a little startled by the word.

'Passionate?'

'Indeed yes! He made himself what he was, you know, from the most unpromising beginnings. His life was a dreadfully hard one in his youth. But he loved surgery as some men love women. Particularly obstetrical ·surgery. He became most expert in the care of women in childbirth, and I flatter myself I learned much of my present skill in that from him. It was from that work that I came to concern myself with the venereal diseases, of course. I saw so much of the destruction they cause – '

After that conversation that hot July afternoon, they did not speak again about their connection, but they were closer for all that. Lewis' new respect for the older man seemed to rub off on to his other relationships within the hospital, and for the first time since his arrival in England he began to feel more at home, sharing jocularity with the other doctors and pleasant conversation with the nurses, though he was prone to ignore the important differences between them, which caused some friction. But in time he learned to remember – most of the time – that the lady nurses, who paid for the privilege of obtaining their training in the arts of their profession, were the ones who wore blue print dresses under their snowy aprons and frilled lace caps on their heads, while the others, called simply nurses, who did the menial work of the wards and came from families of lower income (and therefore of lower class) wore housemaidish pink and no lace on their caps. It was considered low behaviour for a doctor to be as pleasant to the latter as he was to the former, an attitude which Lewis, fresh from the less rigid society of Sydney, found irksome. But he was allowed some leeway in his behaviour since he came from such outlandish parts. So, life at Nellie's became steadily more agreeable for him.

The other factor that made him feel life in London was much pleasanter than he had ever hoped it could be had nothing whatsoever to do with the hospital. It was the shapely form and delightful face of Miss Claudette Lucas, with whom his friendship had ripened to an easy camaraderie which was very precious to him. Once her hand had recovered from the lancing he had done on it – which it did in ample time for her first performance, as he had promised her it would – she told him firmly that on no account would she ever seek his medical advice again.

'For myself, that is,' she added prudently. 'Although I would not hesitate to send my friends to you.'

'That is most kind of you,' he said with mock gratitude. 'I am, as you can observe, hard put to it to find enough with which to occupy my time.'

She looked around the casualty waiting-room where they were standing, and laughed. It was most particularly crowded that afternoon, with every bench chock-a-block with ragged people, several leaning against the walls and others lounging on the steps outside waiting for space to enter.

'You know quite well what I mean!' she had said. 'I am determined to regard you as my friend, and I cannot do that and be your patient, you said! So, *qu'y a-t-il à faire*? No longer am I your patient!'

But friend she was, and one of her first actions was to present him with a ticket to see *Cinder-Ellen Up Too Late* at the theatre. He enjoyed that; the place was such a tumble of red plush and polished gilding, of bright lights and cheerful chatter, of brandy and chocolates and oranges, that none but the most curmudgeonly could have failed to find pleasure. And when the show began, he found himself laughing aloud at the capering of the comic actor of the piece, Fred Leslie, and wholly enchanted by the vigour and sheer animal excitement of the Gaiety's new star, Lottie Collins, singing the song that every errand-boy in London was whistling. He even found himself joining in with the 'tarara*boom*deay' chorus, when the ebullient Miss Collins invited – nay, implored – the entire audience to do so, and was altogether surprised at his own cheerfulness. Life was indeed different for Lewis Lackland, as he told Claudette when he went backstage to see her.

'I'm glad you enjoyed Miss Collins, to be sure,' she said a little acidly. 'Am I to take it you did not enjoy *my* performance? You have said nothing about it!'

He grinned a little. 'Well, it was hardly a *big* part, was it? I recall you crossed the stage from right to left wearing blue, then from left to right wearing green, and then were in a row of other charmers all wearing white, and finally appeared in – '

'I do not need a list of my wardrobe from you!' she said wrathfully. 'I know perfectly well what I wear in the piece! I ask only – '

'Oh, come down out of the trees, do!' he said and laughed. 'You did what you had to perfectly well. You looked delightful, you moved most wickedly, and entranced all the old men I observed sitting in the front row. I imagine that is all that the management require of you?'

She had the grace to laugh. 'Well, I cannot pretend I am Bernhardt or Lillie Langtry! And you are right – the Guv'nor wants us to look ravishing, and dresses us to that purpose.'

'Well, rest assured you were ravishing. And now, mademoiselle, I will recompense my ticket cost by taking you to supper. To a place of *my* choice!'

'*Avec plaisir, m'sieu!*' she said demurely. 'And I have the best of the bargain since the ticket came to me free of charge, from the management. And I'm *very* hungry!'

He took her to the Trocadero, to which they strolled among the crowds of the Strand and then the Haymarket, enjoying the balmy summer evening and staring at and gossiping about the passers-by and the rich shop-windows, piled high with the plunder of the whole world in an attempt to tickle the fancy of London's most fickle population, and laughing a great deal at each other's wit. Not that what either of them said was particularly scintillating but they liked each other, were at ease with each other, and after the excitement of the theatre, both were ready to be easily amused.

The Trocadero was full of elegant people, and for a moment he was uncomfortable about his appearance. He looked neat, but he knew there was an air of shabbiness about him. He was not precisely short of money – he had only himself to keep –

but he was far from lavishly paid for his services at Nellie's, and could not afford to dress as stylishly as the men he saw in the big crystal-hung and palm-bedecked rooms of the restaurant. They wore the sleekest of tail-coats and the whitest of boiled shirts and the most gleaming of diamond buttons on their shirts; but he soon lost his diffidence as Claudette moved magnificently into the very centre of the room and settled herself with great aplomb at the best table there was.

'I will eat nothing but *saumon fumé,*' she announced in regal tones. 'An' see to it, *garçon,* that it ees cut *très, très,* thin, and eez served wiz some cayenne pepper! Zat is ze only way to eat it! And champagne, *s'il vous plaît, tout de suite!*'

'You are outrageous!' he said sitting down as the waiter hastened with great deference to obey her, clearly convinced by her manner that people of Huge Importance had come to his table. 'For two pins I'd tell the world what a fraud you are – '

'Not at all a fraud!' she said cheerfully. 'I do but do as the Guv'nor said I am to do. It is part of my job. I am always to be one of his Young Ladies, he said, and to behave off the stage as I do on it – with dignity and charm and – '

'And a false French accent.'

'I've told you, it isn't false. Now, *mon ami* – I have an invitation for you.'

'An invitation?'

'My Papa. I wish to bring you to meet him. He is at home this evening – sometimes he walks out, but I am assured that this evening he will be at home. Will you come? I would have invited you before, but to tell the truth we were living in such a kennel of a place – ' She made a moue and for a moment her eyes looked bleak ' – that I could not bear to ask anyone there. But now I am working and earning a tolerable sum, we have removed to a reasonable enough small apartment in White Hart Street. It is not precisely what we would wish, but it is much preferable to Vinegar Yard! You will come after we have dined?'

'I am honoured to be asked,' he said gravely, and ordered a lamb cutlet for himself and a bottle of good wine, and settled to enjoy the rest of the evening.

When they came out into Piccadilly the crowds were as thick as ever, but the air had chilled a little as the night gave way to the small hours of the morning, and she shivered, and pulled her wrap about her shoulders.

'We shall take a cab,' he said at once, but she shook her head.

'No, it isn't so far – not if we go through Covent Garden. We can go across Charing Cross Road, and through that way.'

'I have been here much longer than you, but I don't know the streets and the ways as clearly as you seem to,' he said, as he fell into step beside her.

She laughed. 'Oh, that is Papa! As long as I can remember he has told me tales of London and when he was young. Long before I reached here I knew the map as though it were Paris! He never stopped talking about it. Anyway, I am not a person to stay a stranger anywhere for long. I make a point of finding my way about.' And she went plunging ahead into the ever narrowing streets on the other side of Charing Cross Road, towards Long Acre, and then at last to White Hart Street.

The street was darker than the wider thoroughfares through which they had first come, but it seemed respectable enough, and he took the key from her and opened the front door of number seven, and then stood back to let her lead the way.

'Papa!' she called cheerfully, as she ran up the narrow staircase that began just inside the front door. 'Here we are! Have you been waiting long for us?'

At the top of the stairs a door was half-open and light was spilling out on to the darkened landing, and she seemed suddenly to be alarmed because she called sharply, 'Papa?' and pushed the door quickly and then stood very still and silent on the threshold.

He pushed past her after a moment, and took in at a glance a small square room with a shabby green carpet and rather too much solid furniture and a small window tightly shrouded with a thick green plush curtain. Warm as the evening had been, the remains of a fire were burning in the grate, and in front of it, stretched out in an armchair, was the figure of a man. He was lying with his head thrown back and his mouth was gaping and his eyes were very wide open and staring at the ceiling. For a brief moment Lewis thought he was dead, but then a sharp jerking movement seemed to lift his chest and he rolled his eyes towards them and moved his jaw spasmodically as though he were trying to speak. His eyes showed clearly how terrified he was, and his arms and legs made convulsive little movements that made his whole body seem to writhe and twitch. He began to gasp shallow exceedingly rapid breaths that filled the small room with harsh sound.

Lewis, moving faster than he would have thought possible, was at his side and unwrapping the rug about his shoulders immediately, and he snapped over his shoulder at Claudette, 'Open the window,' and without a murmur she did so, and he registered somewhere at the back of his mind the fact that she was as sensible as she was amusing. Many women faced with such a scene involving a much loved relation would have screamed or fainted or both; but she was silent and efficient.

Already he had Jody's shirt ripped open and was investigating his chest, first tapping it expertly and then, with his head pressed against the jerking body with its pallid papery skin, listening intently. After a few moments he grunted and said, 'Help me move him.'

At once she came to his side and together they lifted the still twitching old man from the chair, she seeming to anticipate the movements Lewis wanted, and they laid him flat on the sofa against the wall, while all the time Lewis murmured as reassuringly as he could. 'Now, take it easy, slow and easy – you're all right, Mr Lucas – you're in good form. This is just a panic, you can breathe – there's no need to panic – calm down, now, slow and easy.'

He crouched beside the old man and set one hand on each shoulder and leaned forwards so that he could look into his eyes very directly.

'Mr Lucas, listen to me! There is no reason why you should not breathe normally. You're in a panic attack – no more than that. That is why your heart beats so fast and why your hands have become so cramped and tense. You must *relax*. No – you must *not* try to breathe so fast. Just slow and easy – that's it – slow and very, very easy – '

It seemed to Claudette to go on for ever, the soft murmuring voice of Lewis, the harsh chopped-off sounds of Jody's breathing, the jerking of his arms and legs, but slowly, slowly Jody relaxed until he was lying still on the sofa, his face less white and his breathing relaxed and even. He looked up at Lewis and then Claudette and said hoarsely, 'Sorry', and closed his eyes.

Lewis touched the old man's wrist lightly to check his pulse, and then moved away to the open window, and sat perched on the sill. After a moment she followed him and they both sat there staring down into the dark and now quite empty street below. The sky was very black, and their window was throwing a square of bright yellow gas light on to the cobbles beneath. Their shadows looked very clear cut down there.

'He had a panic attack. He was afraid he couldn't breathe, so – he tried to breathe too fast, and that resulted in spasm of the tubes that feed the lungs. He'll sleep now for a while, and wake none the worse for wear,' Lewis said quietly.

'That is not all, is it?'

'No,' he said after a moment, looking back over his shoulder. 'Not quite all.'

'Well?' And then, as he remained silent she said with a sudden violence in her tone but without sounding any louder, '*Mon dieu, je ne suis pas folle! Dites-moi!*' and there was no artifice in her lapse into French. It was as though she had genuinely not realized she was not speaking English.

'He has a severe blockage of the bronchus – the tube that feeds the lung – on the left side. It probably happened that he lay for a moment in such a posture that pressure was put on the right side also, and for that moment he feared he would suffocate. That started the panic which led to the situation we found.'

'If we had not come – ' she whispered.

'No – not this time,' he said softly. 'He would have lost his consciousness, the panic would have subsided and he would have breathed again.'

'Not this time?' She looked at him with blank eyes and then put her hand on his sleeve. 'Not this time?'

He took a deep breath and then set his own hand over hers. 'My dear, I am sorry, but eventually the growth will spread, for it is malignant, I believe, and he will not be able to breathe in good earnest – '

'He will suffocate, then? *Mon dieu, mon dieu, quelle mort horrible! Pauvre papa – pauvre petit papa – '* And she closed her eyes and stood there very still beside him.

He said nothing. There was nothing he could say. Listening to the old man's chest had painted in his mind's eye as clear a picture of what was going on in those tortured lungs as he would have seen had he set his knife to him and opened the whole cavity. A large uneven rock-hard mass filled the upper part of the left chest, and was growing downwards and sideways across the mediastinum, the central area, towards the other side. It was not possible for him to know how fast the growth was – he had not examined Jody before and so had no yardstick – but at the best estimate the old man could not live as long as the year that was now at its summer peak.

And he had to explain that to this girl he was coming to regard as the best friend he could ever hope to have in England.

7

In a curious way Jody's attack of panic seemed to improve his overall health, rather than the reverse. He slept well that night and woke the next day feeling, he told Claudette, 'as perky as a piglet' and determined to improve yet further. He seemed to have the idea that the attack had been some form of physical crisis, similar to the sort that happened when a person had pneumonia, and that from now on all would be well. And Claudette, knowing how wrong he was, but determined to ensure that such life as he had left to him should be agreeable, and after some discussion with Lewis, colluded in this belief.

They talked only a little about Jody, Lewis and Claudette.

'Let him do as he wishes, eat as he wishes, think what he wishes,' Lewis told her. 'He may not be able to look forward to a great quantity of life, but he can certainly enjoy what there is left to him. And until the growth enlarges more, he'll be well enough. So treat him as you always have. Too much deference to his health may alarm him. He's no fool, your father. So be just as you always have.'

And so she was. There was no point of thinking about the future, so she didn't. She worked at the theatre, and was glad to be there, and met Lewis once or twice a week for supper, and was content enough in their comfortable friendship.

As for Jody, he took to walking out each afternoon, his hat at a jaunty angle and his stick tucked under his arm, and though he looked thin and his skin had a translucence about it that Claudette hated to see, he clearly enjoyed his strolls, and that was what mattered. She tried to persuade him to come to the play to see her there, but he was stubborn on that score.

'You know I did not want you occupying yourself that way! I still dislike it, and I shan't come on any account.'

'You don't mind the fact that we're living on the proceeds,' Claudette said, stung. 'You really are absurd! The Guv'nor pays me handsomely, and I do nothing there that need distress you!'

'No, nor impress me, neither!' Jody said, and his lower lip thrust forward in a juvenile pout. 'Your grandmother was the greatest actress this country ever had – and to think of you on a stage, marching about like – like some sort of animated clothes-horse, no more, when she – faugh! I can't bear to think of it!' And now he looked so grand and full of himself that Claudette could only laugh, and say no more on the subject.

And if she had, she couldn't have denied that up to a point he was right. What she did at the Gaiety could never be called acting. That was left to the principals of the company, those who could sing and dance and cut comic capers, like Fred Leslie and Lottie Collins. All she and the other girls had to do was wear the expensive clothes the Guv'nor provided, and look haughty and gorgeous and desirable, while at the same time making sure that they remained remote from any suggestion that they ever gratified the desires they aroused.

Yet each night the stage door was besieged by hopeful admirers, top-hatted and be-caned and bearing flowers and chocolates and, often, more lavish presents. Claudette listened and learned a lot from the other girls, who made no bones about the way they circumvented the Guv'nor's strict rules of propriety. He may say that none of his Young Ladies should ever behave in any but the most proper manner, but when the luscious Ada or the mock demure Jenny found a diamond brooch or a ruby ring tucked into the bouquet an admirer had sent in, all the others knew that the trinkets had to be paid for, and were. But none of them ever said a word, for to be one of

George Edwardes' 'Big Eight', as the main line of Gaiety Girls was always known, was a privilege not to be lost lightly. Even if you had an argument with one of the others, you didn't split on her, for that would have meant her instant dismissal – and you would have to hate someone very much indeed to do that to her.

Which was why, when one of the girls took ill one night, Claudette became involved. Pearl was perhaps the most beautiful of the Gaiety Girls, with a great mane of yellow hair and very large pale blue eyes and was the most haughty and elegant of them all. She had looked pale for some days but on this particular evening she looked ghastly. She had arrived late and was hurrying into her first act costume when, with a low moaning sound, she crumpled into a faint, and at once the whole dressing-room was in an uproar. Ada rushed for smelling salts while Jenny rubbed Pearl's wrists and Kate ran to fetch her panacea for all ills, a flask of brandy. But it was Claudette who realized what the trouble was as she helped lift Pearl onto a couch.

'*Mon dieu, elle est très malade!*' she said (and even in this crisis she did not forget that here at the Gaiety she was very, very French). 'Look, she is bleeding – ' And indeed she was, the blood streaking her legs heavily and soaking the couch beneath her.

'I don't think it's 'er time o' the month – ' Jenny said, her thin cockney voice sounding puzzled. ' 'Er an' me, we always come on together – '

'Well, if it ees not zat, then she is in trouble,' Claudette said crisply. I 'ave seen zis before – *elle est enceinte, n'est-ce pas? Vous comprenez?*' Jenny looked at her blankly. 'Oh – she is – *un bébé!* She 'as a *bébé!*'

'Oh my Gawd!' Jenny breathed and stared down at Pearl, who was now beginning to come round. 'She's really bin an' gone an' done it now, she 'as! I told 'er, told 'er till I was blue not to take no chances, but she would 'ave it she could take care of 'erself. An' now look at 'er, silly bitch!'

'What'll we *do*?' Katie said. 'The Guv'nor'll go mad if he finds out – '

'She needs a doctor.' Ada was sitting beside Pearl, rubbing her hands to warm them. 'She'll bleed to death if someone doesn't do something – can we get her to a doctor without the Guv'nor finding out? How long to curtain up?'

'Oh Gawd,' Jenny said. 'It's three-quarters of an hour, no more – oh, Gawd – '

'I know a doctor,' Claudette said after a moment. She would have preferred to keep out of the matter altogether, knowing how violently the Guv'nor would respond to this situation; he might well sack all the girls in a bunch, if he thought they were covering up the sins of one of their number, for there were plenty more where they came from. And she needed her job. But Pearl was looking worse by the second and something would have to be done. 'I'll get him.'

'We got no time to fetch anyone,' Jenny said dramatically. '*Look* at 'er!'

'Then I will use ze telephone,' Claudette said calmly. 'Ze one in ze Guv'nor's office. Jenny, you get 'im out of zere some'ow, and zen leave it to me.'

The others clustered round Pearl to hide any view of her from the door, and Jenny and Claudette went out and ran up the iron stairs on the other side of the wings towards the Guv'nor's office high above the stage. 'I must be mad,' Claudette was thinking. 'I'll be thrown out with the rest of them and then what? Jody – oh, dammit, dammit, dammit – '

But she didn't stop, and when Jenny had asked the Guv'nor to come and help her sort out a problem she was having on stage with one of the props – a nice little lie to use, for there was nothing the Guv'nor enjoyed more than twiddling about on stage with such problems – she slipped into his office and hurried over to the wall-mounted contraption which was the telephone.

Even though telephones had long been part of the Paris establishments in which she had worked, they were far from familiar to her, and it was with some trepidation that she cranked the handle, as she had seen other users do, and held the earpiece gingerly. The little clacking voice that answered her made her jump, but she spoke with all the calmness she could.

'This is the Gaiety Theatre – ah, the number is – ' She peered at the telephone, looking for the label that would give the information.

'2781,' the little voice said. 'We know the number there. Which number do you require?'

'I don't know,' Claudette said blankly. 'It is a hospital – Queen Eleanor's Hospital– we need a doctor – '

'Ah,' said the little voice. '2776 – that is the number of the hospital. Please hang up and I will arrange to put you through – '

'But it's urgent,' Claudette said, looking over her shoulder at the closed door. The Guv'nor would be back at any moment, and it was little more than half an hour now to curtain up. 'Must I wait?'

'I will ascertain,' said the smug little voice and there were a series of clicks and rattles and then, at last, another voice. 'This is 2776 – ' it roared. 'Queen Eleanor's Hospital – '

It took them five minutes at least to find Lewis and fetch him to the instrument and all the time Claudette stood there trying to calm her anxiety. If the Guv'nor were to walk in and ask why she was using his telephone – it didn't bear thinking of.

He sounded remarkably like himself when he spoke, though the flat notes of his Australian voice were perhaps a little flatter than usual, and she said breathlessly, 'There's a girl here – bleeding. It's bad. Can you come?'

'Where?' he said crisply. 'Green-room?'

'Dressing-room.'

'I'll be there,' and the line went dead and gratefully she hung it up, and cranked the handle again to notify the end of the call, and hurried out. She passed the Guv'nor on the stairs coming up, and he muttered at her as he passed, 'Silly wench – can't pick up a parasol without falling over her feet – ' and she smiled demurely at him and hurried back to the dressing-room, grateful to Jenny for having drawn his wrath.

Pearl was conscious now, but very lethargic, lying with her eyes open and staring at the ceiling, but saying nothing. Her pallor was now almost grey, and Claudette felt fear rising in her. She looked as though she had no blood left in her.

He arrived breathless and with sweat sticking his hair to his forehead. He must have run all the way from Endell Street and down Bow Street and so on into Wellington Street and the back of the theatre, and as he came pushing past the girls clustered round Pearl's couch, she breathed again. It was now less than fifteen minutes to curtain up and they could hear the callboy along the corridor shouting, 'Overture and beginners – overture and beginners – ' And they were beginners.

'Get into the rest of your costume, Claudette,' Jenny hissed. 'Never mind the make up – you'll get away with it – but hurry, for Gawd's sake – '

She hurried, giving one look over her shoulder at Lewis kneeling beside Pearl, and he looked up at her for a brief moment and nodded. 'I'll do what I can,' he said curtly. 'Get these women out of here as fast as you can – '

The first act that night was hell. The stage-manager fussed and fluttered over the fact that the Big Eight was a depleted seven, but they soothed him and went sailing on stage twirling their parasols as insouciant as though none of them had a care in the world. They swayed their hips as they always did, and strolled and turned and strolled again, which was all they ever had to do, but spreading their skirts a little more widely than usual to fill the space usually occupied by Pearl.

And when at last after almost an hour the curtain fell to the sprightly tune of the first entr'acte music, they fled like a bevy of great blue birds back to the little iron stairway that led to their dressing-room.

Lewis was standing beside their washstand calmly drying his hands and there was no sign of Pearl. The couch was smooth and looked as though no one had sat on it for a week.

'Where is she? Oh, Gawd, she ain't dead, is she?' Jenny asked, and her eyes filled with tears, 'Oh, I told her that geezer'd go an' put her in the puddin' club, but much she'd ever listen – oh, Gawd – '

The door opened behind them with a loud crash, and the little stage-manager, Davis, could be seen peeping from behind the Guv'nor's broad back.

'What's going on here? How come there are only seven on stage, hey? Where's – ' He looked sharply round the room. 'Where's Pearl? And who the hell are you? No men are ever allowed in here, and all you girls know it! And we've got ten minutes to the second act and you're all still in the first act costume. Where's Pearl and what's going on here?'

Claudette took a deep breath and stepped forwards, for the others were standing wide-eyed and pale while Jenny wept helplessly.

'Ah, m'sieu, do not discommode yourself,' she said, trying to cover her desperation with a calm voice. 'Zere is no need for it, no need at all, for Mademoiselle Pearl – '

'I was sent for, sir, because the young lady was ill,' Lewis said, and came forward, putting on his coat and settling his cuffs. 'I am Mr Lewis Lackland, surgeon of Queen Eleanor's Hospital. Your young lady – Miss Frayling – has been removed there as a matter of some urgency.'

'Removed? Removed?' the Guv'nor said. 'What d'yer mean, removed?'

'She was, poor young lady, in a very severe state,' Lewis said calmly. 'She – er – ' He looked round at the other girls, and then leaned forwards and spoke in a confidential manner, but they could all hear him. 'It was her monthly flow, sir. She was taken with violent cramp and loss of blood and needs time to recover. She is somewhat anaemic, and this – ah – fault of nature has exacerbated the problem.'

At once the Guv'nor was all compunction. 'What, my poor little Pearl? Dear, oh, me, one of the loveliest creatures – well, well, we must send her round a hamper and some good stout to build her up. Poor little girl – will she be well again soon, Doctor?'

'Indeed, it is to be hoped – but she will still need a good deal of rest, you know. She has lost a considerable quantity of blood – '

'Rest? She shall have it – she shall have it! We can find someone to stand in for, I dare say – poor little Miss – imagine that – oh, it's a bad thing to be a woman, a bad thing – ' He stopped suddenly and then with a sudden change of mood his eyebrows came down and he glared at the other girls. 'Why wasn't I told? Hey? And why aren't you getting into your act two costumes?'

'There wasn't time, m'sieu,' Claudette said, and the others chorused, 'No time – happened so suddenly – no time – ' and then there was a great flurry of activity as Lewis led the Guv'nor out of the dressing-room and the girls hurried into their costumes, swearing and complaining as buttons flew and laces broke.

And after the curtain had fallen at last on one of the Gaiety's less sleek and polished performances, Claudette found Lewis waiting for her outside the green-room, ready to take her home to White Hart Street. She tucked her hand into the crook of his elbow, and they began the short walk through the brightly lit streets.

'I have to know,' he said shortly. 'That wretched girl just won't talk. You know what the real problem is, don't you? She was aborted by some ham-fisted idiot who nearly destroyed her. She'll never have a hope of a child, of course, now – and the stupid creature won't say who did it – '

Claudette was silent for a moment, looking down at their walking feet.

'I doubt she ever will,' she said at length. 'She knows which side her bread's buttered.'

'She's a fool,' Lewis said furiously. 'The man – or woman – who did this has got to be stopped – it's lethal, I tell you! They'd pushed a great length of bent wire into her cervix, pierced the fundus – it went right through her womb, for God's sake! Oh I suppose I shouldn't talk so to you, but I'm so – you never saw a girl in such a state!'

'She still won't tell you,' Claudette said. 'I'm sorry, Lewis, but there is – oh there are things about the lives girls alone have to lead that you cannot understand and never will. I know the ways things are for the girls at the Gaiety. Everyone except the Guv'nor does. But we all have our living to earn and our futures to think of – and me – ' She shrugged. 'If I had been in her situation I would have done the same. And I wouldn't tell who had helped me, if it had gone wrong, as it did for Pearl. That's common sense.'

His face was white with anger. 'Common sense? It's the maddest thing I ever heard! How can you be so stupid as to cover up like this for her?'

'You did though, didn't you? You lied to the Guv'nor. You said it was her monthly flow when you must have known full well by then that it wasn't.'

He was silent and walked a little faster. And then nodded, his face set in hard lines.

'Well, I'm not a fool, am I? I didn't want to start trouble – but that doesn't mean to say I don't want to put an end to this – the sort of butcher's work that was done on this girl. Look,

Claudette, you must help, please. Talk to the girl, will you? Persuade her to tell me. I won't make trouble, I promise. But I'll see to it that this – damned devil learns the right way to do the work, if it's got to be done. But I won't make trouble – '

She considered for a long moment and then nodded.

'That sounds reasonable enough. As long as you promise not to tell anyone that Pearl – '

'If I'd intended to do that, I'd have done it already, wouldn't I? I told you. I just want to prevent some other poor creature suffering the same damage some time in the future. You can understand that, can't you?'

'Yes,' she said. They had reached the front door now, and they stood for a moment on the step. 'Will you come for coffee or some wine?'

'No,' he said. 'I promised to go back and see the girl before the night was over. I only came back to speak to you. I think it's important, you see, to find this – '

'I know – I've said I'll talk to her, and I will. Tomorrow?'

'Tomorrow. I'll see you at Nellie's, then. She's in the women's surgical ward. Ask for me first.'

She nodded and opened the door and then, as he turned away, she stopped and said over her shoulder, 'Lewis.'

'Yes?'

'Thank you. You're a good man, and I'm grateful to you.'

Even in the dim street light she could see his face redden. 'I didn't know she was a special friend of yours,' he said.

'She isn't. But she's another female, isn't she? So – thank you. And good night.'

8

In the end she found what Lewis wanted to know from Jenny, for Pearl would not tell her. Claudette had sat beside her bed at the end of the long ward at Nellie's looking at her white face against the no less white pillow, seeming even paler because of the glow of the red blanket that covered her body, and did all she could to get the information, pleading, coaxing, browbeating. But Pearl just closed her eyes and refused to say a word.

But Jenny, who had come to see Pearl too, was obviously affected by Claudette's efforts, for as they left together, walking side by side between the two long rows of beds, she bit her lip and said softly, 'Why does it matter all that much to know 'oo 'elped 'er? I mean, 'ooever it was meant no 'arm – '

'I know that!' Claudette said sharply. 'But he did it, didn't he?'

'She,' Jenny said and then reddened.

'You *know*?' Claudette took her wrist in a hard grip that made Jenny wince. 'You know and you didn't say? You let me nag that poor wretch – '

'Well, I never fought that – 'ere, let go, will yer? Yer 'urtin' me!' and she pulled her hand away and rubbed her wrist petulantly. 'I mean, it ain't none o' my business.'

'If you ever got into trouble like that, what would you do?'

Jenny looked at her with her eyes wide and her forehead creased a little, and then looked back down the quiet ward

towards Pearl's bed. 'Me? Well, I wouldn't – oh Gawd, I don't
know! I'd go the same place as Pearl went, wouldn't I? I mean,
there ain't nowhere else as I knows of. We all goes to Mrs
Lovibond – '

'Lovibond? Is she the one who does the – does what's
needed?'

'Gawd, no!' Jenny managed to laugh at that. 'Not 'er! No,
she runs the 'ouse, see? But she's the one 'oo gets someone in,
like, to 'elp out. Lots o' girls 've bin to 'er – never 'ad no
trouble before – '

'Well, there was trouble this time,' Claudette said grimly.
'And it has to be dealt with. How do I get to this Lovibond
woman?'

'You don't 'arf sound different when you're mad,' Jenny
said, almost admiringly. 'Real serious and – '

'Well, never mind zat,' Claudette said, remembering herself.
'I weel try to sound ze same as I always do, if you will tell me
ze way I can see zis Madame Lovibond.'

Jenny took her that night, after the performance, calling a
four-wheeler cab to carry them, ' 'cos although it's only over
the road, like,' she explained earnestly. 'I mean, she wouldn't
be best pleased if the men thought we wasn't the very latest
crack, and all that. So it's got to be a good four-wheeler and
none o' yer rubbish – '

The cab took them to the other side of the Strand, to a
handsome house that lay between the Savoy and Terry's
Theatres, on the corner of Somerset Street. From the outside it
looked like so many other houses in that quarter of London;
flat-fronted, tall, high-windowed and with a most elegant fan-
shaped transom over the broad front door.

Claudette looked up at it curiously as Jenny paid the cab
driver, and saw a tall man in a very glossy black silk top hat
and a swinging evening cape lined in ice-blue satin run up the
steps and bang on the door with his silver-headed cane. It was
opened immediately and the man slipped inside so quickly that

there was no time to see the interior of the house at all, So, when they in their turn climbed the steps and rang the door bell she was more than a little curious about what she would see.

The door was opened just as promptly, and Jenny sailed in with aplomb, Claudette behind her, and nodded imperiously to the butler who stood impassively waiting.

'Good h'evening, James,' she said, and let her silk wrap slide from her shoulders. 'Miss Lucas 'ere, 'as h'accompanied me tonight.'

'Indeed, miss,' the butler said and took the wrap and also Claudette's and handed them to an equally impressive footman, as Claudette stood looking about her.

The entrance hall was a big square apartment with a black and white chequered floor about which were scattered a few small sofas upholstered in crimson velvet, and heavily gilded low tables. The walls were panelled in white and on each panel hung a large painting in an ornate gilded frame. It was the pictures which told Claudette all she needed to know. Luscious rosy nudes disported themselves amid equally naked cherubs and satyrs, with cornucopias of fruits and flowers bursting in the corners of each vast painting. The overall effect was of a great heaving expanse of pink human flesh, pulsating with life, excitement and sheer animal desire. The place smelled of roses, and Claudette smiled a little at that. They had used the same techniques in most of the Paris gambling hells with which she had been associated in the old days, soothing the senses of new arrivals in order to loosen their purse strings and encourage them to bet more than they had originally intended.

Jenny, moving with an even more exaggerated swaying movement than she did on stage, was making her way towards the broad marble staircase that faced them, and together they climbed the shallow treads and turned on the half-way landing, to complete the climb on each side of the central stairway as a double flight carried them on and up into an even larger space than the downstairs hall. This one was richly floored with obviously costly Persian rugs, and there was standing around the walls gleaming white marble statuary all as naked as the pink painted nudes downstairs, simpering blank-eyed over their tip-tilted stony breasts. The walls themselves were hung with a clearly expensive hand-painted Chinese wallpaper, showing hazy vistas of rivers and mountains and meadows populated with exotic birds and plants, and more naked ladies, this time with elaborate coiffures and slanting Mongolian eyes. The scent of roses here gave way to the fragrance of jasmine, overlaid with French brandy and Havana cigars. The total effect was of enormous opulence and colossal vulgarity, and Claudette felt her lips curve as she looked about her, for it was all very comfortable and agreeable, even cosy in its familiarity. At last, here in London, she had found her Parisian home.

The people who were standing about the great hallway seemed not to show any obvious interest in the two girls as they moved past them towards the drawing-room doors, but Claudette was well aware of the men's eyes following her as she walked, and of the sharp assessments being made by the very richly dressed women – of whom there were somewhat fewer than men – and was amused. They'd soon find out what she was made of. Claudette Lucas had not felt as sure of herself for a very long time indeed.

If she had had a mental picture of the woman who ran this establishment, it would not for a moment have meshed with the reality she was faced with when Jenny said in her thin little voice, ' 'Allo, Mrs Lovibond. Brought me friend tonight. This 'ere's Claudette Lucas an' she's French an' she's only bin at the Gaiety a few weeks. But she wanted to come to see you tonight.'

She was a very tall woman, thin as a lath and wearing only a very simple and very plain black gown. It had none of the fussy trimmings that were much in fashion this year; no flounces, no embroidery, no bows tying the shoulders; but the fabric was rich in the extreme, a heavy glowing silk, and the shoes on the long narrow feet that appeared below the hem were made of the softest and costliest of kid leather. Her hair was black too, an inky black that must have owed more to a bottle than to nature, but yet did not look as absurd as dyed hair usually did. It was plastered close to her long skull, and gleamed as though it had been polished. There was a tight knot of it firmly skewered to the back of her neck, and her face was very white so that her eyes, as black as her hair, gleamed shoe-button sharp in its expanse. She could have been any age from thirty to fifty or even more and Claudette found her a most admirable figure of a woman. Born without the benefit of natural good looks, she had created out of her essentially unprepossessing self a figure of great style and most striking originality.

Her voice was husky, and she spoke with a precision that told Claudette immediately that English was not her first language. German, perhaps? Probably.

'Miss Lucas, I am delighted to welcome you. My establishment is yours, in any way you wish to make use of it. My young friend Jenny is more than enough introduction. Indeed, any Gaiety girl is welcome here.'

'Oh?' Claudette said, and widened her eyes a little, to improve her air of innocence. 'I am sure ze Guv'nor ees mos' grateful to you for makin' 'is young ladies so comfortable. 'E is always most concerned zat we should always – 'ow you say – occupy ourselves in a manner zat is – *comme il faut* – '

Mrs Lovibond looked sideways at Jenny, her boot-black eyes flickering for a moment. 'Oh, my dear, I must tell you that Mr Edwardes is no particular friend of mine! He is only interested in his work and the activities of race horses. He has no interest in – the finer aspects of life, as I have!'

'Oh, zen we should not tell 'eem we 've visited 'ere?' Claudette said, once again all innocence.

'As to that,' Mrs Lovibond said, shrugging magnificently, 'I cannot say. It is a matter of supreme unimportance to me!' And she turned towards Jenny and smiled brilliantly at her. 'And where is your other sweet companion tonight, my dear? Miss Pearl? Lord Quantrell was asking after her not half an hour ago.'

Jenny reddened a little and Claudette said smoothly, 'Ah – Pearl. It ees because of 'er zat I wished to meet you tonight, Mrs Lovibond. Can we talk somewhere quiet, *peut-être*? *Pour un moment seulement – elle est malade, vous comprenez –* '

Again there was that flicker of the little black eyes. 'To speak to me about Pearl, my dear? Of course – of course – but I must just – in a moment perhaps – ' And she drifted away towards a tall man with a stoop who had just come up the stairs.

' 'Ere, go easy!' Jenny hissed as Claudette turned to watch the tall black figure move away. 'Don' start bein' clever wiv 'er, for Gawd's sake. She's a right smart one, that Mrs Lovibond, an' it don't do to upset 'er – '

'Why not?' Claudette smiled sweetly at Jenny as a footman bearing a tray of glasses of wine came towards them, and they both took one. 'Why ever not?'

'Because she – oh, I should never 'ave brought yer! I knew you wasn't the sort as'd understand – '

'I understand more than you think, Jenny,' Claudette said softly. 'A lot more. Now, let me tell you about this house, hmm? It's a gambling hell, *n'est-ce pas*? The men come here and bet and lose heavily, and she – ' And she jerked her head towards the tall black figure standing in earnest colloquy with a couple of men on the far side of the hallway. ' – she likes the girls to come and keep 'em 'appy. Ees that not correct? And you get ze leetle presents, *peut-être*, when ze men win – and when zey lose, why, Mrs Lovibond gives you presents instead!'

Jenny was gaping at her, wide-eyed. 'Well, an 'ere's me thinkin' butter wouldn't melt in yer bleedin' rnouth!' She giggled and drank half a glass of wine at a gulp. 'You're a right deep one, ain't yer? Never said nothin' to no one, and never misses nothin', neither – a right deep one.'

'And sometimes,' Claudette said quietly, 'Sometimes it goes a bit further than it should, *hein*? And people like Pearl get into trouble, and Mrs Lovibond helps – '

'That's about the shape of it,' Jenny said, and finished her wine and reached for another glass from a passing footman. Her eyes were beginning to look suspiciously bright as she glanced about her. 'But if yer got yer wits about yer you don't need no 'elp. I don't. I told Pearl, told 'er she could give a man a good time an' not get 'erself lumbered, but she's a bit thick, is Pearl. Reckoned she was in love, silly cow!' Jenny laughed again, rather more loudly this time, and one of the men standing nearby came drifting towards them.

'Good evening, my dear!' he said owlishly and Jenny looked at him with a sharply appraising stare and then smiled widely, showing her small white teeth and the tip of her tongue between them.

'Good evening, sir,' she said demurely and then looked at Claudette, and the message could not have been clearer if she had shouted it aloud. And Claudette was willing to accept it, and smiled vaguely at the man, who looked to be about sixty or so, from his heavy dewlaps and rather bloodshot green eyes, and moved away casually towards the middle of the drawing-room, leaving Jenny to stand closer beside her elderly admirer and look trustingly up into his eyes.

For the next half-hour, Claudette made herself merge with the wild silk hangings of the big blue drawing-room. She stood quietly against the wall and watched and listened and absorbed, and became more and more certain about what she intended to do. The question was, could she do it? It would please Jody, that much was sure, and it would please herself, too. She was no actress and well she knew it, and grateful though she was for the opportunity to earn some good money at the Gaiety, it was by no means the end of her road. Claudette Lucas could do much better for herself. And could do it here.

The rooms became busier, and then, as she watched, the crowd began to ebb and flow. One or two girls she recognized from the Gaiety came in, as well as several others, hanging on to the arms of men, most of whom were old enough to be their grandfathers, and then wandered away with them to come back later with a different escort. Some of the men stayed in the drawing-room with the girls, but most of them went away towards a pair of big doors on the far side of the great hallway. The doors were covered with the same Chinese paper as the walls, and so disappeared into the general background as soon as they closed. Claudette watched those doors most carefully and then, after a while, moved casually and very easily across the drawing-room towards them.

They had no handle on the hallway side, and she stopped and leaned against the wall, waiting, glad she had worn her blue gown tonight for it helped her to be unobtrusive in the blue ambience of the place. So much so that when a man opened the door from the other side she was able to move forwards and, giving him a bewitching smile, slip in under his arm and to the room beyond.

And here she could have laughed aloud with delight, for the scene was so wonderfully familiar. The baccarat shoes, the broad expanses of green baize with the roulette wheels whispering and clacking on their fortune-laden way, the low lights and the chairs set up close to the gaming tables. Home from home indeed.

Again she watched, her eyes missing no move of the hands of the croupiers, smooth young men in unobtrusive clothes who stood in the shadows just outside the pool of light over each table, and allowed only their hands to show, white busy hands that handled cards or brightly coloured roulette chips or the shoes with sleek dexterity. And again she smiled, and looked about the room for her hostess.

She saw her eventually, also standing out of sight near the wall, and alone, and moved towards her purposefully. She knew now exactly what she was going to do, and how she was going to do it, and there was no point in wasting any more time.

'Mrs Lovibond,' she said softly. 'You remember I said I wanted to talk to you? I wonder if you could now find the time?'

Mrs Lovibond looked at her, her eyes bright in the shadows. 'Miss Lucas? Well, now, what can we have to talk about, after so short an acquaintance?'

'A great deal,' Claudette said. 'You'd be surprised.'

'I am surprised to discover that your English is so – perfect. You seemed less at home in the tongue when we first spoke.'

'Ah, that was a while ago, now, wasn't it?' Claudette said easily. 'And the sort of – shall we say *manner* in which one approaches a stranger is not necessarily the same one would use when approaching a fellow spirit.'

'So, I'm a fellow spirit, am I?' Mrs Lovibond said. 'That is an interesting thought.'

'Oh, very much so. I have spent most of my adult life in rooms such as this – ' Claudette turned round so that she faced out into the room as Mrs Lovibond did, and together they stood leaning against the wall, surveying the scene. The soft buzz of voices, the occasional lull in sound as a table waited for the wheel to stop turning as the little ball rattled to its final resting place, the sudden bursts of laughter and chatter as a particular player made a killing came to them, and after a while Claudette looked at Mrs Lovibond and said dreamily, 'Even the methods you use are the same. I have been watching the wheel on the table nearest the door, for example. We tipped ours in just such a manner when I worked at Les Rouleaux. Near Les Champs Elysées, you know.'

Mrs Lovibond was very still, standing there beside her and looking out at her tables and her clients with their piles of chips beside them. Claudette smiled and went on, 'And the way that young man there – you see the table I mean? Towards the centre – the way he handles the cards makes me quite homesick. I was taught that style when I was very young. Of course, now I am rather more skilled than that. I would, to tell the truth, be quite ashamed to be so – gauche as he is. However, in London perhaps it is a matter of *faute de mieux*. I don't imagine that there are many establishments such as this where ambitious people may obtain their training. And employment.'

'What do you want?' Mrs Lovibond said quietly, her voice seeming no more than conversational.

'Of course there is one thing here that is very different. In Paris we did not combine the gaming tables with – other distractions. Oh, we run excellent restaurants – which I notice you appear not to do – and serve the most exquisite of wines and food. The wine I tasted in your drawing-room I must tell you does not do you justice, Mrs Lovibond. Nor, I think, do your – um – shall we say the remedies you seek for those young ladies who do not provide your other attractions as successfully as they might.'

'I am sure you are enjoying yourself a great deal, Miss Lucas, but I am becoming rapidly bored with all this. If you will tell me what it is you want, we may be able to come to some sort of arrangement. But I really cannot go on playing these childish theatrical games.'

Claudette laughed softly. 'Capital! Then we shall be businesslike, which I much prefer. Pearl was taken very ill last night, and might have died. She was bleeding, to put it frankly, like a stuck pig.'

Mrs Lovibond stared at her in the dimness. 'How is she now?' she asked sharply.

'Oh, no need to worry. She's survived. But only because I have a friend who is a doctor. A very good one. I sent for him, and he took her to hospital. But he's angry. He saw the mess that was made of her in procuring this abortion, and he's hell bent on putting an end to the efforts of whoever it was who dealt with it.'

There was a short silence and then Mrs Lovibond said in a resigned voice, 'How much? I'll tell you this. This won't be one of those long drawn out affairs with you coming back for more and more. But I'll give you one reasonable payment, to recompense you for warning me of trouble, and that'll be that. If you try to come touching me again, you'll discover the error of your ways.'

'Oh, you quite misunderstood me, Mrs Lovibond!' Claudette was enjoying herself thoroughly now. 'I don't want that sort of payment. I want a job!'

Again there was a silence and then Mrs Lovibond said, 'I think we'd better get out of here for the present. Follow me.' And she turned and moved across the big gaming-room, her thin angular back seeming as rigid as a plank, and Claudette followed her, her head up and with a jauntiness in her step that showed how confident she was feeling.

Mrs Lovibond's office was a very simple room, surprising in its asceticism. There was a desk, a couple of straight-backed chairs, a small fireplace in which a few half-burned embers lay cold and grey and a large grey iron safe, and that was all.

'You'd better sit down,' Mrs Lovibond said curtly, and settled herself in her own chair behind the desk, her back as straight as ever. 'A job you say?'

'I am very experienced. As I told you. I've run restaurants for gaming hells in Paris these past five years and more. My father was always in the same sort of activity, and he taught me a lot.' She grinned then. 'Didn't he?'

The older woman stared back at her and for a long moment Claudette wondered whether she had misjudged her, but then, almost unwillingly, the white face relaxed into almost a smile and she said harshly, 'He did.'

'We came here because – ' Claudette shrugged. 'You know how this business is. The *gendarmerie* – and Papa was ill, so I had to do as best I could. Which meant the theatre. It's suited me well enough so far, but I'm not an actress. I look well enough, and I can manage what little the man Edwardes wants of girls in his shows – but I want more! I want a job where I can use the skills I have. And I think I've been fortunate to find just the place for that. What do you say?'

Mrs Lovibond leaned back. 'And what about Miss Pearl? Is she forgotten in all this?'

'Not at all,' Claudette said briskly. 'Whoever it was you used for her must, of course, be dealt with. At once. For your own sake, if for nothing else. This time was fortunate. I got Lewis to her, and he did what was necessary. If the poor little wretch had died – '

'I know. I'm not a fool. Damn it, I warned the girl, over and over again! I told her she'd get nowhere with Quantrell! But she thought if she got herself pregnant he'd – faugh! Stupid girls make me sick! And when she told me what he'd said when she told him, and demanded I sort her out, I did the best I could. The woman I usually go to was taken to court three weeks ago, so I settled for the best I could get. But never again. Never again. I'll find someone else, a better one.'

'If you can give me the name of the one who did that to Pearl, then I think we'll have no more problems. I'll see to it that Lewis deals with the matter without involving you – '

'How can you – '

' – because of course I won't mention you! You'll be safe enough. And Lewis will be happy, and I – '

'Yes. What about you?'

'And I'll have a job. Won't I?'

'And suppose you don't? Suppose I say I can't make use of your services?'

'Then I will tell Lewis that you know who the abortion was performed by, and send him to talk to you himself. He's a large

Australian surgeon of very high principles and determination. Exceeding high. A good friend of mine.'

Mrs Lovibond was sitting with her hands clasped in front of her on the desk and she sat staring down at them, her sleek black poll bent, for a long time. And then she lifted her chin and looked at Claudette and smiled, a thin-lipped little grimace that still managed to lift her face into a more agreeable expression than it had shown all evening.

'Well, I can see that providing good food here would be no bad thing. Some of them have commented before on the lack of sustaining refreshment, but I've always found it difficult to organize and I do well enough with – other things. You think you could do a good job of it?'

'I know I can,' Claudette said vigorously and grinned too, her eyes crinkling with her delight at her own success. 'It'll be the best thing you ever did, giving me a job. I want a lot of money, of course. And a bonus on the takings. That is understood, I'm sure.'

'If you earn it, there'll be no problems. And if you can guarantee that your doctor friend – '

Claudette grimaced. 'Oh, I can handle him! Never fear that. But I'll want to know who was that woman who dealt with Pearl.'

Mrs Lovibond reached for a piece of paper and a pen and began to write, and then, after a moment moved the pen to her other hand, and wrote a little more laboriously. 'It would never do to have someone recognize my handwriting, would it? You'll find the woman there. The Ratcliffe Highway is near the river, at Wapping. An unsalubrious area. Don't go there yourself.'

'I won't,' Claudette said, and tucked the piece of paper into her *décolletage* and stood up. 'And now, will you show me the rest of your house? I've seen only the drawing-room and the entrance halls and the gaming-room so far. And I've got to learn about the place, haven't I?'

9

Abby was sitting up in bed drinking hot chocolate and eating buttered Bath Olivers and staring at the beating rain on the window-panes when Martha was announced.

'Such a time to be lying abed!' Martha said briskly as she let the maid take her wet pelisse from her, and unpinned her bonnet from her sparse grey hair. 'You should be ashamed to be so lazy! What is that you're drinking? Chocolate? Faugh! Such stuff! I shall have some coffee, please, Emily. No, nothing with it. And you shouldn't be eating either, Abby. Really, you allow yourself too much indulgence altogether. A brisk morning walk and half the food you usually take and you would be much better for it!'

Abby smiled cheerfully at her sister and reached for another biscuit. 'If I cannot indulge myself at my time of life, it is a poor state of affairs,' she said equably. 'Bless me, I shall be eighty next birthday! Why should I not enjoy myself? And I have taken chocolate and biscuits every morning for longer than I care to remember. Are you well, my dear?'

'Exceedingly,' Martha said, settling herself comfortably in the armchair beside the bed, and straightening her green merino skirts about her ankles. 'Busy, you know, extremely busy. The three hostels are full to overflowing, and far too many of them are little more than children – we have one of barely fourteen! We live in decadent times, Abby, decadent times. When I first started to run hostels for the London Ladies

– when was it – forty years ago? – the women we saved were *women*, not children. Now we think nothing odd about having mother and daughter together. It's as though all the fuss that journalist Stead made a few years ago about the ease with which children were procured for the trade encouraged it, rather than reduced it. I swear I never saw so many children brought in off the streets to us ten years ago as I do now. It's a sorry situation, and it gets sorrier.'

'Is that why you are here, my dear? For some money for your committee? Well, I dare say we can contrive to find you a little something – '

'You are always generous, my dear, and we appreciate it,' Martha said. 'That is not why I came, although,' she added prudently, 'of course we never refuse any offer of help in our work. The committee is hard put to it to find money for all that it wants to do, and we have a scheme for going out on to the streets and trying to get these children before they get involved in their wretched trade. Now there is a law to help us. So, a cheque will be most welcome – but no, it was Freddy I came to talk to you about.'

'Freddy? Why, is there something wrong?' Abby was at once alert. She loved all her children dearly, and her grandchildren and great-grandchildren too, but Freddy was most particularly special to her and always would be. The child of her girlhood, the product of her first love match with the long forgotten James Caspar, her father's apprentice all those long years ago, they had always enjoyed a closeness and an understanding that she had never found with the children she had borne to Gideon Henriques, adore them all though she did. So now she sat up anxiously and peered at her sister over the ruffles of her bedgown.

'No, there is nothing *wrong* precisely – ' Martha said. 'He is well and prospering as he always has. But he is not happy with Ambrose at the present, Abby, and it makes me anxious. He came to see me yesterday, as he always does on Thursdays and he looked so – oh, I don't know, a shade distrait, perhaps. So I quizzed him – '

'I can imagine,' Abby said, a little grimly. Martha's tendency to prod and pry at people until she had the information she wanted was a byword throughout the family.

' – and he told me that he is most displeased with Ambrose. The boy won't work, it seems, and just lazes his time away, runs up debts and sponges off his mother – '

They were silent for a moment, the two old ladies, staring at each other and then Abby said irritably, 'Phoebe? Wretched girl! She really has no sense at all, sometimes.'

'Hardly a girl, my dear,' Martha said dryly. 'She must be as near sixty as makes no never mind.'

'Next birthday – and you're right. She isn't a girl, but she behaves as stupidly as one sometimes. I've told her many times to check the boy, but will she? Not she! I know she spoils him appallingly – and Freddy is right to be concerned. He is much too idle. I shall speak to Gideon, I think, and see if work can be found for him in York. The factory can always use a member of the family to some ends or other, and you never know – he may prove to be quite useful.'

'Finding him a place and getting him to go to it are two very different matters, Abby. Unless he is cut off from money he will stay right and tight in London. I told Freddy as much, but he feels that to cut the boy's allowance would be going too far. He fears he may get stubborn and seek to obtain funds from – elsewhere. He is not as – how shall I say it – I would not wish to offend you, my dear, for the boy is your grandson, after all. But he is also my great-nephew so I shall say it. He is not quite honest. He has been known, I am told, to be unreliable in gambling matters. Bad enough he gambles – much worse that he should do it in a cheating manner. So, I think we must seek another remedy, don't you? To push him further into such ways would not answer at all.'

'But what remedy?' Abby said helplessly. 'Tell me that, Martha! If we are not to deprive him of his allowance, how are we to put any pressure on him to change his ways?'

'Why, through Phoebe, of course!' Martha said, and opened her eyes wide. 'The problem is not so much that he has his father's allowance, as that he very nearly doubles it by cadging from her. I thought it was time you had a word with her. Don't you agree?'

Abby looked at her bleakly. 'A word with Phoebe? Oh dear.'

Phoebe too was still in bed, but she was not drinking chocolate, an old-fashioned taste that she scorned. For her it was a delicate China tea with lemon, served on the finest Sèvres china, set on a handsome Venetian lacquer tray with her letters and the day's newspapers slotted in the pockets at the sides, and a comfortable fire crackling in the grate of her charming pink and white bedroom. July it might be, but a cold and dismal July with the rain pelting down heavily outside and she liked to be cosy.

Not that the morning was turning out to be at all cosy. Freddy was standing in front of the fire looking as stuffy and sour as only Freddy could, and positively glaring at her.

'So? What are we to do about him, Phoebe? For I tell you it cannot go on like this. When I saw Whittaker yesterday, he told me that he has overdrawn his account for the next three months. Three months! I do not relish being told such things about my son by my man of business, and neither should you. It's shameful, downright shameful. I've been telling you for the past ten years that we would have to do something about his idle ways, and now I'm determined. Before this year is out he must have some sort of gainful occupation – '

'Oh, really, Freddy, you're being very dull and dreary! You carry on in the most – the most middle-class fashion! Why should he not be a gentleman of leisure? It isn't as though we were paupers, is it? You could double his allowance and not feel it. You could double mine too, come to that, and be as comfortable as ever you were. I sometimes despair of your meanness, indeed I do!'

'It is not meanness to expect my sons to make their own way in the world. You'll be saying next that I should keep James and Cecily in idleness too. If James sees no shame in working as he does at the Stock Exchange and Cecily's Alfred at his shop, why shouldn't – '

'Alfred!' Phoebe said with withering disdain. 'A tradesman! A shopkeeper in Streatham! Is that the best you can wish for your own son? Ambrose is worth three of dreary Alfred.'

'You weren't so scornful of Alfred when he came courting Cecily! You were glad enough to let him marry your only daughter, seeing as clearly as I did that he was a hard-working sensible man and that his future was assured. The shop in Streatham, let me remind you, is a very large establishment indeed, employing fully a hundred and forty people, and not much smaller than Shoolbred's in Tottenham Court Road. And you're happy enough to consort with the Shoolbred wives, as I recall. As for trade – the money you wish me to allow to Ambrose so that he may be a gentleman of leisure comes from trade, and never you forget it. My father was a common apothecary, no more. The business started with just one small shop, for all it now boasts over forty. So spare me, please, any high-flown notions about being too aristocratic for trade. You can save that for your friends. I'm your husband, remember, and not to be so easily cozened!'

He was white-faced now, only small patches of colour high in his freckled cheeks breaking the pallor and she tightened her lips, and said nothing. On the rare occasions when Freddy lost his temper he was not to be argued with. It just wasn't worth it. Arguments only made him more and more mulish and more and more tiresome. And what she needed more and more of was his co-operation. Prices were rising steadily and her own expenses were climbing with them, let alone Ambrose's – '

'Now come, my dear, let us not quarrel,' she said peaceably and patted the bed beside her. 'Come and sit down and let us talk sensibly about this. There must be some way in which we can reconcile you and your boy! He isn't a bad boy, you know and – '

'Thank you, I shall remain here,' Freddy said and then added in a low voice, almost as though the words were spoken against his conscious will, 'You're not always so willing to invite me to be beside you when you're in bed.'

There was a long silence then, and Phoebe poured some more tea, fussing over the cup so that she would not have to look at him. This was an ever-recurring crumple in the fabric of their marriage, her loss of interest in his love-making. He was as vigorous as he ever had been, as aroused by the scent of her skin or the touch of her hand as he ever had been as a boy, all those years ago when they had been children and then young adults during the Crimean War, but she had become in the past few years ever more withdrawn in a physical sense. Her looks had stayed with her even though her change of life had come to her; her skin was as clear, as well coloured, though a little softer and saggier now than it had been, and her figure remained shapely. But she had lost the core of her femininity; her passion had died in a few faint splutters some five years ago, and left her remote and unreceptive to his touch. Freddy, with his knowledge of female ills, understood well enough what had happened to her but it hurt him grievously nonetheless. He knew it was no fault in him that had made her withdraw to her own bedroom and leave him in isolation in the big chamber they had once shared, but that did not alter the resentment that lurked deep in his being. Not a man to do as others in his situation did, and seek sensuous satisfaction elsewhere, he could not but help remember sometimes the pretty cousin who had caused his senses to flare and his heart to twist with hunger twenty years ago. But she was far away now, a married woman with children of her own, busy in a remote Yorkshire town about the affairs of her husband's woollen mill as well as her own work as a physician. Sophie was not to be thought of –

'You're right,' he said after a while. 'We mustn't quarrel. It will get us nowhere. But you must agree, my dear, that something must be done about Ambrose. He can't go on for ever living the life he does. Surely you want to see him settled with a wife and family of his own, like the others?'

She did not look at him. Ambrose with a wife? The very idea made her feel cold, suddenly. She was grateful when the door opened and Cecily came in, damp and glowing from the street outside and trailing her four small daughters behind her. Welcoming them and fussing over them saved Phoebe the need to answer Freddy. But it didn't stop her from thinking. Ambrose. Oh dear, Ambrose.

Ambrose was up very early, for him. It was rare that the streets of London were ennobled by his presence much before noon, and seldom at any time when they were awash with summer rain, as they were today. But he had business to prosecute and sometimes a man had to go right against the grain of his nature in order to run his life as it should be run.

Covent Garden was in a lull when he reached King Street. The morning hubbub of fruit and flower sellers had vanished to their beds leaving the streets to the sweepers and gleaners of discarded produce, and the theatre goers and strollers would not appear until well into the early evening. It was a good time to settle to a quiet conversation with Uncle Oliver, Ambrose told himself as he furled his silk umbrella and settled the astrakhan collar of his coat neatly round his neck. It was a new coat, and really a most elegant one, with its fine woollen cloth and braided seams, and it looked particularly well set off by the most gleaming silk topper that Lincoln and Bennet of Piccadilly could produce. His trousers, as well cut and fitted as the coat, were set to a nicety over his white-spatted and black-patent shod feet; altogether he looked every inch the gentleman. Normally in the hours of daylight he wore a checked lounge suit in the new style, very natty in cheviot or one of the more daring fawns, surmounted by a Homburg hat of the sort the Prince had made so fashionable. But that, he had decided this morning as he surveyed the contents of his wardrobe, would not make at all the right impression on Uncle Oliver. He was one of the old school, and would regard the newly casual elegant look as merely slovenly, or even rather raffish. And pleasing Uncle Oliver was very much the order of the day.

He found his uncle sitting at a table on the far side of his restaurant in his shirt sleeves and with his glasses pushed down his nose, poring over his account books. Ambrose made his way to him through the forest of upturned chairs on tables and said cheerfully, 'Good day to you, Uncle! You look very busy this morning.'

Oliver peered at him blankly over the top of his spectacles for a moment and then smiled a shade apprehensively.

'Well, well, Ambrose, m'boy! Good to see you – well, I trust? This weather's playing havoc with my – '

'Indeed, thriving, Uncle, and you look to be doing the same.' Ambrose took off his coat and handed it with his hat and umbrella to the waiter who had bobbed up beside them. 'Can I beg a glass of something restorative, d'you think? Not so much as a sip of breakfast has passed m'lips this morning. A brandy and soda, please, my man – '

'Tut!' Oliver said, and took off his glasses to polish them. 'You'll ruin your health taking brandy before noon. Kidneys, you know. And liver. Not to speak of – '

'Well, I continue well enough, Uncle, and when I get a twinge or two, why, then I'll take to gruel, I promise you! So, how's business?' He cocked his head at the pile of accounts spread on the table between them. 'Flourishing, I trust?'

'Come to touch me again?' Oliver said, a little acidly, hooking his glasses behind his ears again. 'You're a gifted spender, Ambrose! Can't think what m'sister – '

'Not a touch this time, Uncle,' Ambrose said, not a whit put out. 'Got an idea for business that I thought might appeal to you! Business fallen off a bit, I imagine, since the Guv'nor snaffled Lottie Collins for the Gaiety?'

'Hmph! Plenty more where she came from,' Oliver said sharply. 'Edwardes isn't the be-all and end-all of the theatre in this town, you know! The way people go on you'd think there was nothing more than him and D'Oyly Carte and that stuff at the Savoy! "Oh, 'tis a glorious thing I ween, to be a regular royal queen – a right down regular royal queen – " such stuff! Thing's been running for ever – I don't know what they all see in it, and that's the truth of it! Clever enough first time you hear it, I grant you, but after that, why, it's just a tinkle tinkle tinkle – no meat on its bones at all.'

Ambrose nodded sapiently. 'Thought you'd be feeling it a bit. Well, not to be wondered at, the way things are this season. Theatre's full of good stuff, and people're spoiled for choice. Now, listen, Uncle, you know that I enjoy a wide circle of good friends, hmm? Good lively people who know what's what and how to enjoy themselves.'

Oliver peered at him, his eyes sharp behind his glasses.

'I hear you go about with a fairly raffish lot,' he said bluntly. 'That's what I hear. All over the place. Journalists, all sorts. Doesn't please m'sister, that's for sure – still, it's your affair – '

'Journalists can be useful people, Uncle.' Ambrose was settling to his theme nicely, especially as the waiter had brought the brandy bottle and siphon rather than just a filled glass. 'Write about things they do, you know, puff things off, hmm? People read their puffs and there you are! They want to do the same things, don't they?'

'So? What's that to do with me, hey? I think I prefer an ordinary touch to this chatter. Silly – ' Oliver pulled one of his books towards him, but Ambrose set his open hand palm-down on top of it.

'Just this, Uncle. If I bring people here to see your show – and you'd better tell me what's on the bill at present – and get the place talked about by those with money to spend and written up in the sheets, what sort of bonus would that be worth? Hmm? Ought to be something in it for me, don't you think? I'd be earning m'keep that way, rather than coming on the borrow, doncha know!' And he smiled disarmingly at the older man who sat and looked at him with his lips pursed.

'Hmmph. Get the place written up, you say? But where? Don't want riff-raff here, you know! Always been a good respectable house, the Celia, and it's going to stay so! Only want the best class of customers here – '

'You don't want the suburbs up for the night, though, do you? The clerks and their dingy wives wrapped in black bombazine and their snivelling offspring! People with a bit of style, that's what you want! Not the wishy-washies who go flocking to the Savoy, or the mashers who hang around the Gaiety, but really up to the crack people. *My* people. Friends o' mine. Now, what do y'say, Uncle? I'll tell you this – I need the chance to do something useful – need the blunt, you see – '

'When didn't you need blunt, you ne'er-do-well? Hmm? Been the same these past ten years, and longer. I remember the time they sent you down from University – '

Ambrose grimaced. 'Long time ago, Uncle. Long time ago. I'm a man of sense now. Planning to get married, doncha know. Need a little grease to ease the wheels, don't I, with plans like that? So, how about it? Help the lad along, will you?'

'Married? On what?' Oliver said, and guffawed. 'Still living on your father's allowance and planning to marry? Mad, mad – '

'Not so mad when it's an heiress I've got me eye on!' Ambrose said softly. 'No, don't ask me who, because no gentleman names names, not till he's sure. But if I pull it off, you'll be the first to know. Well, almost. Now what do you say to my little business proposition, hey? Make you as busy as the Savoy or Gaiety, I could – '

'The Savoy or the Gaiety? Hmm,' said Oliver. 'Hmm.'

'The Savoy and the Gaiety?' Miriam breathed. 'Oh, Mary, that would be – well! I'd enjoy it madly. Can you really manage it? Truly?'

'Of course she can,' Amy said airily. 'Mary can do anything she says she can, can't you my love?' And she smiled fondly at her daughter who was standing patiently on a low stool while Miss Trinkett fussily pinned her new tennis dress to her figure. 'I like that Shakespeare collar, my love. Very fetching and so sporty – what colour cravat should she wear under it, Miss Trinkett? I think green, don't you, Miriam, my dear? So in keeping with a tennis-court, and very charming. The skirt a *leetle* shorter, I think, Miss Trinkett – Mary has no need to be ashamed of her ankles, and when playing tennis a well swinging skirt looks most beguiling, don't you agree? And I think one of those darling little peaked caps, rather than a sailor hat, don't you agree? Yes – you'll look quite, quite delicious, won't she, Miriam? You, I know, already have your tennis dresses ready – we were rather behind this season, what with one thing and another, Mary's piano lessons and the singing and of course Señor Alberto for her dancing and all – '

Amy rattled on, content to receive no answers, and indeed leaving no room for anyone else to say a word, even if they had wanted to. After more than a quarter of a century of English life, most of it as Felix's wife, she was the same bubbling chatterbox of an American girl she had been, though her looks had faded rather. She was more lined about the face than Phoebe, though fully ten years younger, but hers were happy lines, rather than the slightly peevish ones that were beginning to show more and more on Phoebe. Looking at Amy's face it was clear that she laughed a lot, and allowed her feelings to show in her expression, and indeed that was still one of her greatest charms. For Felix, she was still the enchanting Bostonian he had scooped up from her raggle-taggle theatrical ways, and brought to the safe haven of a good marriage and motherhood.

It had been some disappointment to him that they had managed but the one child; but since that one child was Mary, he felt he had little to complain about. Mary, as quiet and biddable as her mother was ebullient and wilful, was a source of much joy to her father, who, when he was at home rather than tending his patients in Guy's Hospital, on the staff of which he had now been for many years, or in his busy private practice, liked nothing better than to sit in his own drawing-room with her on one side, and his adored Amy on the other.

Not that there were as many such evenings as he would have liked. Amy was bound and determined, she had told him before Mary was five years old, that she would succeed where her mother had not, and be an actress. And though Felix had in the early years argued and disagreed and made every effort to block her determination to make quiet Mary into a star of the English stage, she had gone on regardless. And wise Felix, realizing as Mary moved from childhood to girlhood that she was very much more his daughter than her mother's, and quite without the push to make the sort of success for which Amy yearned, stopped arguing.

So for years now Mary's life had been a busy round of lessons in music and elocution and poetry-speaking and dancing and singing and Grecian movement and heaven knows what besides. Despite no signs at all that great success was ever to come Mary's way – indeed any success at all – Amy went sunnily on, sure of her daughter's début 'when she is ready'. Since Mary was now twenty-two, it seemed unlikely that she would ever be any more ready than she was now, but Mary herself was content enough with her activities, and her meetings with real actresses at her dancing-classes and singing-classes, to wait as long as Amy thought fit.

Mary smiled now at Miriam, sitting in the froth of a lemon-coloured grenadine blouse and a most sleekly fitting black ottoman silk skirt, who smiled back and then made a little moue.

'Though I dare say Grandmamma will fuss about it. She really does have some very silly notions, you know, Mary! She expects me to take my wretched maid everywhere, and fusses like – oh, you should just hear her when she starts! I tell her that modern girls do all sorts of things by themselves these days, that chaperones are positively ridiculous, and suppose I wanted to go out on a bicycle, or on the river or – all those things where you couldn't possibly take some boring old maid? But she just goes on and on – '

Amy looked at Mary for a moment and then said carefully, 'Well, I don't want us to be making problems with Aunt Abby, Miriam. If she isn't happy to have you go with Mary to the theatre, and to meet her friends in the green-room, well, perhaps – '

'Oh, don't you start, Cousin Amy, I beg of you!' Miriam said hotly. 'For you aren't like Grandmamma who's out of the ark and – '

'You mustn't speak so of her to me,' Amy said as reprovingly as she could. 'She's a dear sweet lady and was very kind to me when I first came to England and – '

'Oh, I know! We've all heard from everyone about how marvellous Grandmamma is,' Miriam said pettishly. 'But honestly, Cousin Amy, does that give her an excuse to stop me having fun? She's trying *ruin* my life, truly she is. She's almost *eighty* and I'm seventeen – how can she possibly know anything about what it's like to be me? How can she *possibly*?'

Amy, feeling inside much the same as she had at seventeen, despite her forty-nine years, looked troubled.

'It isn't lack of understanding, my love,' she said. 'I'm sure it isn't. But you are a considerable heiress, you know, and that means that – '

'Oh, pooh to that!' Miriam said with all the lofty airiness of someone who was born so rich that she really had no idea at all of what rich actually meant. 'It's nothing to do with it. She just wants me to sit at home and be *dull* all the time.'

'Well, she did give a splendid Ball for you and does take you about to all the best parties of the season, and lets you visit your friends alone and – '

'But she'd never let me go backstage at the Gaiety, would she?' Miriam said and looked triumphant when Amy could only look at Mary and make one of her expressive grimaces. 'You see? You think Grandmamma is too fussy too! So please, Cousin Amy, let Mary take me, and we won't say a word to Grandmamma, hmm? Promise not a word? Then I can have an adventure and no harm done. Just as I do with dear Cousin Ambrose. He takes me to all sorts of lovely places and never, never tells Grandmamma. So promise me you won't either. Please?'

10

Lewis sighed, and thrust his hands more deeply into the pockets of his Inverness. The rain was dripping down the back of his neck, guided there by the brim of his round-crowned tweed hat, and his feet were squelching inside his boots. Lousy English weather, he thought sourly, and lousy English cab drivers. The man had made a very unhelpful grimace at him when he'd demanded to be taken to Ratcliffe Highway and gone only as far as St Katherine's Dock before pulling his horse back and shouting down at him through the trap, 'This is as far as I goes, Guv'nor!'

'Why?' he'd said, peering out at the dark road. High above him, to his left, rose the almost completed twin Gothic towers of the new Tower Bridge surrounded by a tangle of cranes, and, further out, the even greater tangled rigging of the many ships that plied the river. 'Is this Hermitage Wall?'

'No, it ain't, Guv'nor, an' I ain't goin' there. You want to take yer bleedin' life in yer 'ands, yer good an' welcome. Me, I don' go no further. Ninepence the fare is, Guv, an' I'll thank yer to find it fast and let me be on my way.'

And stubbornly he had refused to budge until at last, cursing as fluently as any Australian longshoreman – which perturbed the cab driver not at all – Lewis paid his ninepence, and set out to walk the rest of the way as best he could, the man having at least had the grace to direct him.

The surroundings had become bleaker and bleaker, and less and less inviting. There were people about, undoubtedly; he could feel their presence, shadows in the darker shadows against the walls and in the dirty corners, but they weren't to be seen. They seemed to be hiding from him, watching and waiting. For what? He pushed his hands even deeper into his pockets and hunched his shoulders, knotting his muscles under the cloth of his heavy Inverness. He'd show the bastards if they tried anything, he told himself staunchly. I'm big enough for most ruffians; they won't get to me in a hurry. And wished not for the first time that his conscience hadn't pricked so hard on the matter of the damned woman who had so nearly destroyed Pearl Frayling.

The other doctors at the hospital had whistled through their teeth and made warning grimaces at him when he had asked casually what sort of neighbourhood the Ratcliffe Highway was. 'Bad,' they'd said, and, 'Rough. Keep away from there. A real thieves' kitchen, that part of Wapping. Not safe for respectable men – ' But he'd felt he'd had to go, all the same.

He'd told Claudette that when she came and gave him, wordlessly, the piece of paper with the awkward scrawl on it. 'Mrs Bessie Woodstock,' he had read. 'Corner of Hermitage Wall and Wapping High Street, just near the Ratcliffe Highway.'

'Is this the woman who did it?' he'd asked sharply and Claudette, oddly withdrawn in manner, had shrugged and said, 'So I'm told,' and hurried away on a plea of urgent private business to attend to.

'I'll let you know as soon as I can what I'm doing, Lewis,' she'd said over her shoulder as he followed her to the door of the casualty department. 'I want to – but not yet. I've got plans. Things are changing for me, you see, and – well, I'll see you as soon as I can.' And she'd gone hurrying away down the street, her skirts held high above the mud of the pavement and showing her handsome buttoned boots and a good deal of ankle above them, leaving him with a scrap of paper and only a whisper of anger left in him. Pearl was getting better after all, with remarkable speed, and had made it clear to him that she accepted with equanimity what had happened to her. That it was an occupational hazard for a girl who was making her own way in the world was obvious, she intimated, so why should he fuss about her as he was?

'Don't you care that you'll never be able to have any children?' he'd said, not wishing to be harsh, but unable to withhold the information from her. 'I had to remove your womb entirely, you know, or you would have died.'

She had shrugged, looking down at her hands clasped on her lap as she sat in the armchair beside her bed, looking as beautiful as she ever had, her face sharpened by pallor and loss of weight to an even more ethereal beauty. 'I never saw myself as a mother anyway,' she said. 'I'm not the sort. All I want is a comfortable competence to live on, and dress decent on, and I'll settle for that.'

'And the man who did this to you? Who gave you the child you – well, what about him? Did you care for him?'

She'd looked up then, her blue eyes very hard and pale in her peaked face. 'None of your business, doctor,' she'd said, her voice thin and needle-sharp. 'You hear me? I'm grateful and all that for what you did for me, and I'm glad to have me life saved, but I'm not saying who he was, nor yet who done me the favour I needed, and that's all about it. And if you care as much about me as you let on, then you'll leave me in peace to get back to the Gaiety as soon as I may, and leave my private life alone. It's none o' your concern.'

But for all that the little piece of paper had nagged at him. Maybe Pearl didn't care what happened to her, or about her sterile future, but maybe another girl would. Maybe another wouldn't have a doctor conveniently at hand to deal with the mess that was made. As long as he knew that woman was there he had to do something about her. And notifying the police wasn't enough, for all it was a felony to procure abortion. Where was his evidence? How could he offer just a scrap of paper with obviously disguised handwriting on it to a sceptical detective of the London Metropolitan Police? He'd seen enough of London bobbies in the casualty department at night when they brought in the drunks and fight victims to know that. He had to see to the matter himself if it was to be seen at all.

Which was why he now walked more and more deeply into the streets of London's most notorious dockside slum, scared sick at every sound behind him, convinced he was about to be jumped by a thief who'd gladly kill him just for his coat, let alone the contents of his pockets, but doggedly determined to do what he'd come to do.

So when someone did slide out of the shadows to put a hand on his arm he was ready, and whirled with one sharp movement and seized the soft body that met his grip in a hold so iron sharp that it hurt his own fingers.

'Jesus Gawd, mate, lay orf!' a small voice squeaked. 'Christ all bloody mighty, what yer thinkin' of? I di'n't 'urt yer, did I? Only meant to ask yer the time o' night – '

He peered into the darkness and made out a small pointed face under a draggled bonnet and a dumpy figure wearing a nondescript gown and a thick woollen shawl.

'What do you want?' he said harshly. 'Who are you?'

'Told yer – only meant to ask yer the time o' night – thought yer might like a bit o' comfort, like, on a nasty night.'

The small face leered and even in the dim light of a guttering street lamp near the corner on which they stood be could see how incongruous it was, for the face was that of a child, though the tone of voice was one of a much older and more experienced woman.

'The way yer grabbed me, I fought it was Jack the Ripper come again – '

'It could have been,' he said, and dropped his voice a little menacingly. 'They never caught him, did they? It could have been. Aren't you scared to go talking to strange men this time of night? And no one around to see you?'

She stepped back uncertainly and stared at him. ' 'Course you ain't the Ripper. And anyway, there's people around. Only got to shout, I 'ave and they'll come. I got me friends – '

They stood very still for a moment and then he nodded, believing her. He could still feel the presence of people in the shadows.

'I'm sure you have. Everyone's got someone to call a friend, I hope. Is Bessie Woodstock one of them?'

The girl put her head to one side. 'An' what if she is?'

'Could you take me to her?'

'Might do. For a consideration.' The girl giggled then, a suddenly childish sound in the darkness. 'It's the same whether yer a toff or an ordinary person, ain't it? You all get caught the same bleedin' way. Mind you, you don't find many men down 'ere looking for old Bessie. Leaves us to get on wiv it on our tods they do, usually. You put some wench up the spout then? Or got a naughty sister what the neighbours mustn't suspect?'

'Something like that,' he said after a moment. 'Something like that. There's a shilling in it for you if you take me to her.'

'Make it five and you're on,' she said promptly.

'Half a crown. A shilling now, and the rest when we get there. And if I get there safe *and* get away again, back to where I can get a cab, I might double it. You never know your luck.'

She giggled again. 'You weren't born yesterday, was you? Right fly, you are. 'Alf a crahn it is. I'll wait for yer. Will Bessie be comin' with you?'

'I – I don't know. I don't know how long I'll be either. You'll still wait?'

'Well, I got me livin' to earn,' she said, and peered at him, her eyes glinting in the darkness. Could make as much as – well, a quid I could, of an evening – '

CLAIRE RAYNER

'Try again,' he said crisply. 'Like you said, I wasn't born yesterday. If I'm a long time, I'll see you right. Maybe five bob. Take it or leave it.'

She stood uncertainly for a moment, and then nodded and turned and began to walk away, moving so that she was well shadowed by the walls of the great shuttered warehouses that lined the street, and after a moment he followed her. She could be leading him right into trouble, but that was a risk he had to take. He'd come this far, and to turn back now would be a ridiculous waste of time. And cowardly, he told himself bleakly. As if that mattered.

But there was no risk. The girl moved swiftly and surely and within four minutes they left the high warehouses behind and were standing in a better lit area, where two roads met. There was a brightly lit public house on the corner, its engraved glass windows ablaze with gas light, and the sound of noisy singing filled the air as pervasively as the stench of cheap beer and gin and heavy vomit filled the gutters outside.

'She's in that 'ouse there,' she said, and jerked her head towards a small dwelling that abutted onto the street on the opposite corner. 'Knock twice, then wait and knock twice again. She won't answer else. I'll be in the boozer when yer ready.'

He knocked as she had instructed, feeling faintly foolish, like a character in a penny dreadful, and after a long moment there was a rustling sound on the other side of the door and then rattling as bolts were pulled and the door opened, and a woman's head peered out.

He had already decided what to do; to get into the house before he spoke for otherwise the woman would refuse to speak to him, that much was obvious. So, as soon as the door opened he slid his foot forward and into the opening and then, leaning all his weight on the thin panels, pushed. She gave before him with a squeal of fear and rage and then he was inside and slamming the door behind him.

116

'Mrs Woodstock?' he said. 'Sorry to be so pushing, but I reckoned you'd be unwilling to talk on the doorstep, and it's important I discuss matters with you.'

"Oo the 'ell are you, you lousy bastard?' she said in a voice that was thickened by years of gin and rough pipe tobacco. 'I got men 'ere as'll 'ave the arse off you soon as look at you, if you don't get out of 'ere! Go on – sling yer 'ook – '

'No,' he said firmly and loudly. 'I'll risk the men. I've got to talk to you. I'm a doctor. Been treating a friend of yours. Pearl Frayling. You'll remember the lady, I'm sure – '

The narrow hallway in which they were standing was lit only by an oil lamp with a soot-encrusted chimney, dangling from a hook set in a grimy ceiling, and the walls were blackened with age and gleaming with moisture. But even in that poor light he saw her go white.

'Oh Gawd,' she whispered. 'Is she a goner? Oh Gawd – I never knew 'er, as God's my bleedin' witness. I never set a finger on 'er, poor cow – oh, Gawd – '

'Oh, of course you do,' Lewis said, and suddenly he felt deeply tired. He'd had to screw up every ounce of courage he'd had to face what he had been convinced would be a creature of sheer evil. Quite what he had expected to see during the long and unpleasant journey here, or while he had been pushing on the woman's door, he hadn't thought. But it hadn't been this wizened scrap of ageing humanity, with wisps of dirty grey hair making an aureole around a sagging shattered old face that looked like that of a wax doll that had been left out in the sun. Her eyes were bleak with years of deprivation and hunger and now were overlaid with sheer terror, as she stared at him with her mouth hanging open to display blackened stumps of teeth.

'Oh Gawd,' she said again. 'Oh Gawd.'

'Is there somewhere we can talk more comfortably?' he said more gently. 'Oh, don't look like that! The girl's all right, and

I'm not going to shop you. I just want to talk to you. No more than that. Where can we go?'

She said nothing, just standing staring at him, and after a moment he pushed past her towards a door he could see at the end of the passage. There was a thin line of light showing round it and even as the old woman moved in a too late attempt to stop him he pushed it open and looked inside.

It was a pitiful room. Not because of its shabbiness; that he was used to in his dealings with the patients he saw at Nellie's, and sometimes had to visit in their own homes. They too lived in small rooms with great mildewed patches of damp on the walls, cracked ceilings, and a few sticks of cheap broken furniture. But this one showed that attempts had been made to beautify it.

There were cut out pictures from illustrated magazines adorning the walls, peeling away because of the damp, but brave in their gay colours. There was Millais' painting of 'Bubbles' with its impossibly sweet golden-curled child in his velvet and lace suit staring in eternal wonderment at his soap bubble. There was Lillie Langtry with unbelievably red cheeks and ludicrously luscious hair staring out over the narrow mantelshelf. There were cheap lithographs of scenes of rural felicity that looked almost obscenely beautiful in this setting. The floor was covered with a scrap of carpet so worn that the shape of the floorboards beneath it could be seen, and the windows had highly glazed red and yellow cretonne curtains at them, garishly cheerful and striking almost the most pathetic note of all in the whole cheap, striving, hopeless, yearning ambience.

But he was not looking at the details of the room at all. Just at the girl sitting hunched in the battered armchair beside the empty grate, in which a crumpled red paper fan had been splayed to add another note of impossible style. She was pale and her eyes were red-rimmed, and as she looked up at him, with her face white and damp with sweat he saw her eyes were

118

swimming helplessly. She sat and stared at him, trying to focus and then said thickly, 'Bessie – 'ow much longer you goin' to be? Got the 'orrors, I 'ave – got 'em somethin' awful – Bessie?'

He turned and looked down at the woman now standing beside him in the doorway.

'Another one?' he said and his voice was flat and quite expressionless.

The old woman looked up at him, and almost as though she were aware of the way pity was struggling with anger deep inside him she said shrilly, 'Well? What would you do mate, if someone like that come bangin' at your door middle o' the afternoon? Eh? Tell 'er to piss off aht of it, would yer? Some bleedin' doctors you lot are! You'd never do nothin' fer them as reely wants yer, would yer? There's plenty o' your sort as do it fancy like for them as'll pay, but not for the likes o' Queenie 'ere. Nor fer me – ' And she blinked and her eyes glazed. ' 'Appened to me it did, 'er age or younger, I was. I misremember. An' if it 'adn't bin for an old woman down our alley, I'd a bin in it fer good 'an all. Only one way to earn a livin' I 'ad then, and you can't do that when you got a bellyful, can yer? So – ' Her voice trickled away and there was a little silence in the room broken only by the soft heavy breathing of the girl in the chair, who had fallen into the sleep of the very drunk.

'You give 'em gin, do you, to knock them out?'

'Well, we ain't got nothin' else, 'ave we? I know they 'as these anaswhatsits for them as can afford it, but we don't get nothin' like that down 'ere. Up the river like, at the 'orspital they do – but they won't do anythin' for no Queenies in the club. They 'as to make do wiv me. An' I does me best. Is she all right? That Pearl? Is she all right? Really took to 'er I did. Reel lady, she was, all dressed lovely an' all. An' paid me in advance an' all, which was nice of her. Showed trust, di'n't it? Nice that – is she all right?'

'She's all right,' he said and then put out one hand and set it on the scrawny shoulder. 'It wasn't she who told me you had – helped her. She wouldn't say. I had to find out another way.'

The old woman's eyes filled with tears suddenly. 'I di'n't think she was that sort. Ta,' she said and sniffed horribly and wiped the back of her hand across her nose.

Behind them Queenie woke with a sharp little yelp, staring around her in terror, and then her eyes cleared as she saw the old woman and she said thickly, 'Give us another pennorth o' gin, Bessie. S'wearin' orf. 'Ave yer done it yet? 'Ave yer?'

The old woman's eyes slid sideways, and she looked at Lewis. 'What shall I do, then? Eh? You come 'ere an' said you'd to discuss wiv me. So tell me. What do I do about 'er? Eh?'

11

He would not have believed it possible. He, Lewis Lackland, the man who had worked all the hours God gave him to make himself a doctor, who had regarded his profession as the most valuable possession he had, and took for granted his status as a law-abiding medical man, to be working in a back-room in Wapping performing an abortion on a girl whose only anaesthetic was the gin that made her breath reek horribly, and who rolled and moaned as he examined her. How could he let himself behave so?

But how could he not? As he picked over with a sinking heart the few bits of old metal which Bessie called with some pride 'me instruments' he was still trying to sort out a better answer.

Take the girl Queenie to Nellie's and do the operation there? Out of the question; it was illegal and, no matter how he wrapped it up in clean linen, the doctors and nurses there would soon realize what he was about.

Leave her to Bessie, wash his hands of the whole affair? Equally impossible; not after what had almost happened to Pearl.

Call the police to Bessie, get her jailed? What good would that do? Queenie would find someone else to do what she wanted done, for it was clear she was determined to be rid of her progeny. If there was one fact becoming ever more clear to him it was that the Queenies of London, like the Pearls, would go to any lengths to rid themselves of the punishment their sex heaped on them. Abandoned by men who shared the culpability of their dilemma, there was no other answer for them but to find someone like Bessie Woodstock to 'take care of them', a dreadful euphemism that filled his mind with a sick despair.

So, as he saw it, there was no other choice open to him. He had to show Bessie how to carry on her trade with less risk. She was old and poor, he told himself, looking at her, but not stupid. And handled right, she could perhaps be made less lethal than she had been hitherto.

So, he showed her how to fashion a sound from a piece of twisted wire. 'To measure how far into the womb it is safe to go,' he said. 'It's a small organ, very small. Push too far and you go right through it and that's what does the mischief. Make sure it's always blunt at the end, like this, you see? Right, now we boil the stuff – where do you do it?'

'Boil what?' Bessie said, staring at him, her face watchful and puzzled.

'The instruments, Bessie,' he said and closed his eyes for a moment. 'There are tiny creatures on them that can grow inside a body and make pus. Infection. You understand? No – well, never mind whether you understand or not. Just do as you're bid, and make sure you always do it this way. Everything you use has to be boiled for twenty minutes. And when they're cool enough to touch, you only touch the handle end, understand? Never, never touch the part that's going into the girl's body. That can kill – right, we'll do it now. Got a big pan? A fish kettle? Anything'll do – '

She brought a galvanized zinc pail, with some pride in the possession of it, and he put the few instruments in it, after having scrubbed them (to her shrill indignation, because 'I washes 'em reg'lar I do. No need for none o' that now.' 'Yes there is,' he said firmly. 'Wash them every time, before as well as after use.'), and then lit a fire in the small grate and set the pail over the flames.

It seemed to take an eternity for the water to come to a sluggish boil, and then for the twenty minutes needed for sterilizing to pass, but he used the time to teach Bessie more about her trade. He took a scrap of paper and a pencil from his pocket and drew a diagram of the female pudenda and the genitalia, explaining to her with all the patience he could how the organs lay, and what the risks of damage were, and how to deal with haemorrhage and how to place a girl so that she could get the best view of what she was doing.

And Bessie was an apt pupil. She watched his fingers as he drew and asked pertinent questions, and repeated the words he used with some relish, finding a sort of professional satisfaction in having a professional vocabulary. By the time they were ready to use the instruments and Queenie had had yet another glass of raw gin poured down her unprotesting throat, he felt almost the same sort of rapport with her that he felt with intelligent medical students when he had to teach them at Nellie's. If poverty and years of grinding struggle against the inequalities of the life into which she had been born had not claimed her, he thought, Bessie would have been a considerable person. The world is a bad place, he told himself, a bad place. Confusing thoughts for a man who had never been much given to the contemplation of society, who had spent most of his formative and working years with his head down, aiming doggedly for his goal of qualification. Now, for the first time, philosophical ideas were stirring in him; and he wasn't sure that he enjoyed the sense of confusion they created.

The operation went surprisingly well. Queenie, in a total stupor by now, allowed herself to be carried to the couch which was Bessie's operating table without a murmur, and let the old woman dispose her clothing and legs so that Lewis could get to her.

She lay there, her head back and her legs held in a froglike posture, her scrawny thighs and soft belly white and pathetic in the lamplight, and seemed to be as unaware of what was happening as she would have been had she had a chloroform or ether anaesthetic.

'Your gin works well,' Lewis grunted, as he washed Queenie's groins with the now cool boiled water and a piece of rag which he had boiled at the same time as the instruments. 'Look, Bessie, remember this. Wash, wash, wash. Over and over. You can't be too clean. Now, what you do is this – God, it would help if I had a speculum – I'll have to get you one – '

'Speculum?'

'Instrument that holds the parts open, so that you can see. I'll have to manage without – now, you need to find the cervix, the mouth of the womb – '

He took Bessie through it step by step, showing her how to use the sound to measure the depth of the uterus, and then how to use her curette, a roughened metal spoon, no more, but surprisingly effective, so that the lining of the organ was swept away. And then how to make the uterus push down and expel its contents, with careful pressure exerted through the belly wall. She was as fast a pupil for these manual skills as she had been for words and pictures, and he was relieved as he watched her mop the girl up, when he'd finished, and settled her comfortably to snore the gin out of her system.

'If you do always as I've told you, Bessie, then you should be all right. If you can persuade the girls who come to you to go ahead and have their babies, so much the better – '

'So much the better?' she said, and there was a jeer in her voice. 'So much the better for 'oo? D'you know what 'appens to kids born to the likes o' Queenie? Do yer? If they lives beyond the first week they're doin' bleedin' well, and that 'urts a bloody sight more than comin' to me when you're not yet three months gone. Them as lives – poor little bleeders never 'as a chance. If they're lucky, an' can get over Stepney way, they might get theirselves took into that there Dr Barnado's 'ome, but there's precious few can do that. The rest just – ' She shrugged. 'The girls go on the game as soon as they can, and the boys end up in clink. An' their mothers – they can never be nothin' more than alleyway brasses, not when they got kids to feed. What's so much the better about that?'

He looked at her in silence for a moment and then said quietly, 'If you have any troubles with any of them, bring them to me, at Nellie's. Say you're their neighbour or something and tell them to call me. I'll take care of them, and no questions asked. And remember what I taught you.'

Walking back through the dark streets behind the thin-faced child in the shawl, who had swallowed all of the shilling he'd given her in the form of neat gin, and was rolling drunk as a result, he felt sick and desperately tired. But not, to his own surprise, at all ashamed or guilty. Had he been asked yesterday how he would have reacted to being an abortionist, he would have recoiled with horror, and a vast fury. His task was to preserve life, not to destroy it. That had been the central tenet of his whole career.

Yet, now, faced with the realities that had been paraded before him during this past two hours, he felt only a dull anger and a sort of resignation. The world, he had discovered, was an even worse place than he had thought, and he'd never had a high opinion of it. There was nothing he could do to change it, of that he was certain. To apply the law about abortion to the Bessies and Queenies, and throw them into jail, would not touch the root cause of the evil; the poverty and spirit-grinding misery of these back streets. Nor would it alter the relationship between men and women, in which the former used the latter for their pleasure and then callously rejected them. All he could ever hope to do was alleviate. Cure was not possible.

He sat in the hansom cab he managed to pick up on the far side of St Katherine's Dock, after giving his guide the five shillings he had promised her and a couple more besides, and sat staring out into the streets as the horse clipclopped its way through the now silent and shuttered City, past banks and counting-houses, on its way to the busy populous richer streets of the West End. Alleviate. But how? Perform more abortions? And then he remembered the House and thought of the women with syphilis he saw there and felt sick again. No operation yet devised could help *that*. What alleviation could there be?

It was as the cab went up High Holborn that he suddenly leaned forwards and shouted up through the flap to the driver, changing his destination. He'd told him to take him back to Nellie's as fast as could be, wanting only to bathe the filth of the past two hours away, and then fall into bed. But now he knew he needed more.

And not until the cab wheeled through Covent Garden did he allow himself to feel any sort of surprise at the fact that the need he now felt most deeply was for Claudette. He'd told himself he wanted only to tell her of the results of his expedition, but as soon as she answered the door of the house in White Hart Street to his peremptory knock, and stood there silhouetted in the light from the hallway, he knew he had lied to himself.

'Can I come in?'

'Why – Lewis– well, yes. It's a little late, of course – ' She looked over her shoulder for a second and then stepped back a little. She was wearing a white cotton wrapper, and her hair was down, released from its pins to lie on her shoulders in a tangle of curls.

'I was just – ' she began, and then looked at his face again, and even in the shadows he could see she was puzzled. 'Are you all right? You look – '

'I'll tell you – let me come in.'

She bit her lip and then nodded and stood back and he came in and followed her up the stairs to the sitting-room, and stood in the middle of it, his head down and then after a moment looked around him, almost vaguely. 'Is your father not here?'

'No – he's gone ahead.'

'Ahead?'

She stood very still. 'Yes – we're moving – ' Now he saw as he looked about him that the few items of their own that had decorated the small room were gone. There was a new tin trunk standing in one corner, its lid open, half filled with clothes.

'Where – what's – '

'I'll tell you. Things have been happening. But you look as though you need some sort of restorative. Sit down – '

He sank heavily onto the sofa and after a while she came and sat beside him and put a brandy glass in his hand and sat there quietly watching him as he drank its contents.

He didn't usually drink so fast; a small glass of brandy and soda could last him an hour or more, for his years of hard work and poverty while he studied medicine had made him abstemious; and in consequence his tolerance for alcohol was low. And of course he was tired, and more than a little strung up by all that had happened. Whatever the cause he suddenly found that he was sitting with an empty glass in his hand and tears coursing down his cheeks, making the furrows in his face itch and angrily he drew the back of his hand across his mouth.

'I'm sorry,' he said huskily. 'Sorry – '

She set her hands on his shoulders, pulling him round to look at her, and searched his face with her gaze. 'My dear Lewis, what is it? You look – bereft. My dear, don't, please!'

She reached out then, and touched his wet cheek with her forefinger, and that soft touch and the scent that was drifting from her unbound hair seemed to swim into his senses, and he reached up and took her face in both his hands and leaned forwards and kissed her lips, gently. He wanted only comfort, the sort of kiss his mother would offer him when he was a small child who had fallen and scraped his knee; but her mouth opened under his and her tongue moved against his lips, and it was as though a long-contained river was trying to burst its banks. All the loneliness and deprivation of the past friendless months came leaping up in him to combine with the distress of the past evening, and seemed to concentrate itself in his loins. The need for sexual release was so huge that he could not have contained it no matter what she had done, but after one startled moment when she lay in his arms as though stunned, her own arms came up and round his neck and she was kissing him with almost as much fervour as he was showing towards her.

Somewhere deep in what remained of his commonsensical mind it seemed to him that she had produced one of her Gallic shrugs, to show that she accepted something not because she particularly wanted to, but because she saw no other course of action open to her, but that flash of thought was immediately overwhelmed by his ever more clamouring need, and he was scrabbling at her wrapper and his own clothes, pulling off the heavy Inverness that still lay across his shoulders and almost ripping at his trousers.

And she reached out and helped him, moving smoothly and easily and at last they were together, he pushing into her body as desperately and urgently as it was possible, thrusting at her almost violently; and then, leaping, gaspingly, the river rose in one great wave of release, followed by more waves, one after the other, and then at last he was flung on its banks, gasping, as wet with sweat as though he had in truth been immersed in some flood, and staring at the ceiling of the shabby room with wide blank eyes.

'Oh, my God,' he said after a moment. 'Oh, my God – '

She laughed softly at his side. 'God, hardly, *mon cher*. Such a delight is not precisely the product of the Divinity. More the Devil, I would think – '

'I'm sorry,' he said. 'I didn't mean – '

She put her hand over his lips. 'Never, never apologize for love, *mon cher*,' she said. 'It is an insult to do so. Unless your partner has not shared the pleasure – '

He looked at her face, so close to his, and could see the line of sweat beads along her upper lip, and closed his eyes for a moment, furious with himself. 'I'm sorry – ' he said again. 'I didn't – I was concerned only for myself. Did you – was it for you – '

She laughed again. 'My dear man, I am not a baby, you know! I am well able to ask for what I need. If I need it. And I must tell you that I am – well, very responsive to the feelings of others. Your need was enough to trigger mine – ' She smiled, a slow easy curving of her lips. 'I found as much pleasure as you, I promise you.'

There was a silence and then, as awkwardly as a boy involved in his first experience he reached for his trousers, ignominiously tangled around his knees, and set himself to rights.

'I'm sorry – ' he began again, and this time she showed a flash of anger, sitting up and pulling her wrap around her.

'Stop apologizing, man! You needed me. I was not averse, and there's an end of it. You have not ravaged an unwilling virgin, *mon brave*, so you cannot lay that satisfaction on your altar to yourself. I have had lovers before – '

'How many?' he said sharply, and was amazed at the way a shaft of sheer anger had risen in him.

She looked at him, her eyebrows raised. 'Does it matter?'

'I – no, I suppose not. I mean, it's none of my concern, I suppose – '

'Two,' she said after a moment, and reached out and touched his cheek. 'And I loved them both. At the time. One was kind and one was not, but I loved them both. For a while.'

He reddened, ashamed that she had understood him so much better than he understood himself.

'I'm glad,' he said gruffly. 'Not glad that one was unkind, of course, but – '

'Glad that I am not one of the easy ones, hmm?' She smiled at him. 'Glad I'm not a bit of muslin, a dolly-mop, a cruiser, whatever it is you call women of the night in Australia?'

'A tart,' he said, and then reddened again.

'You are really very charming, Lewis.' She was leaning back now on the sofa, her arms folded across her breasts and her knees drawn up to show her shins and bare feet. She was smiling at him, her head on one side, and with a little surge of gratitude he leaned forwards and kissed her mouth, gently this time.

'And you are more than charming,' he said huskily.

'No avowals, I do beg of you!' Her tone was light, and she scrambled off the sofa and went to refill his brandy glass, and to pour some for herself. 'It is not necessary, I assure you. We are friends, are we not?'

'Rather more, now, surely – '

She looked over her shoulder, and shook her head. 'I am French, or at least half French, my dear. I do not have the overblown notions some English women do. One can be – ' She shrugged. ' – good friends in many different ways.'

'You said you loved the other two,' he said. 'As friends? Or differently?'

She brought the glasses back to the sofa, and gave him his. 'I'm not sure. I think as friends. I was very young at the time.'

'You're hardly old now.'

'Older in living than many. Life has not been easy.' She stared broodingly into her glass and then lifted her chin at him, and grinned a perky little grimace. 'But it will be better now.' She swept her hand round in a comprehensive gesture. 'No more White Hart Street.'

'What? Oh, yes. You said you were moving – where are you going?'

She was silent for a moment, looking at him consideringly and then lifted her chin again, this time in a defiant sort of way.

'I am going to run the restaurant in an establishment that is both a gambling hell and a bordello. Very high class, very luxurious, but undoubtedly a bordello. What do you say to that, Lewis? Are we still friends?'

12

The party in the green-room at the Gaiety had been going on for some hours, and the clock was nudging its way towards two-thirty a.m. when Mary at last gave up trying to persuade Miriam to come away.

Miriam was looking enchanting, her curls as wild as plum blossom in May and her great eyes gleaming with excitement. The rosy flush in her cheeks and the tension in her movements all added up to a vision of young enthusiasm that was very fetching. Several of the men who had come to share in the obsequies of *Cinder-Ellen Up Too Late* which was giving way to the new musical comedy *Fun On The Bristol* paid a good deal of attention to her, and she was in consequence very pleased with herself indeed.

It was not that she was unused to attention; as one of the acknowledged beauties of the 1892 season she was fêted at every ball and drum she attended, dutifully trailing behind her majestic Grandmamma. But this was different. First of all Grandmamma was not there – the mere idea made her lips curve with delight – and secondly, to be accepted as a beauty at a Society Ball was nothing like so special as being regarded as one here at the Gaiety.

For there was no doubt, she thought gleefully, looking round at the glittering crowd, there were more beautiful women here than could ever have been collected under one roof before. The Big Eight, in the most costly of the Guv'nor's expensive costumes, dripping with feathers and lace and jewellery, were stunning in the perfection of their complexions, the heart-breaking loveliness of their classic profiles, the wickedly beautiful curves of their magnificent figures and the glitter of their superb eyes. The lesser lights were hardly less lovely, the 'ordinary' Gaiety girls, the twenty-five or so who made up the rest of the chorus, some pert as robins, some Dresden-doll delicate, some sweetly charming in mock rural gowns. Yet in spite of all this competition, she, Miriam Da Silva, had been the object of many admiring glances, and also of a number of somewhat outrageous compliments. Well bred as she was she knew she should have been shocked by some of the delicious things men had murmured in her ear as they had clustered round her, but she wasn't. She was just enchanted with the room, the event, the company, and above all, herself.

So, when Mary started getting restless at about midnight, when the party had been going for only an hour or so, for the curtain had come down on the last performance of *Cinder-Ellen* a little later than usual, she was far from willing to listen to her.

'Oh, dearest Cousin Mary, don't be so stuffy! You sound just like Grandmamma, wanting to go home just when the party's getting interesting. Wait a bit, do – '

So, poor Mary waited and talked quietly to her special chums, the three dancers who had had a novelty spot in the second half of *Cinder-Ellen* (and to their delight also had a place in the forthcoming *Fun On The Bristol*) and to her good friend Mrs May, who was to design the costumes for the new production, and was not at all put out at receiving no admiring glances at all.

But as the clock moved inexorably on, her fatigue overcame her, and gentle and biddable though she generally was, she was about to oblige Miriam to leave whether she wanted to or not, when to her intense relief she saw Ambrose Caspar pushing his way through the throng towards her.

'Why, hello, Cousin Ambrose!' She greeted him with rather more animation than she usually showed, and certainly more than she was feeling. 'What are you doing here?'

'I might ask the same of you, my dear!' He frowned a little, surprised to see this girl who was usually only to be seen at boring family affairs. Although they addressed each other as Cousin, out of deference to Aunt Martha, who was in effect her grandmother, they were not at all related in fact, since her father had been Martha's adopted son, and her mother from another family altogether. But it irritated Ambrose to meet someone who regarded herself as family in a setting which he regarded very much as his own. He was a regular visitor to the Gaiety green-room; not precisely one of the mashers, not being given to foppish ways or monocles, but definitely one of the *cognoscenti*, known to and welcomed by the girls and the management alike.

'I brought Miriam to meet my friends,' Mary said, looking round to see if she could see her brilliant young protégée in the crowd. 'But she's found other company – well, it is time I took her home. I feel responsible, you know – '

His face had lifted at once. 'Miriam? Damn it all, I went to the Sassoon Ball in the sure hope of seeing her there and when she wasn't I was – well, well! Here, you say?' And he too raked the mob with his eyes, looking for her.

Mary frowned. Cousin or not, he should not swear in front of her. 'We are about to leave,' she said reprovingly. 'I only brought her to talk to my friends who are dancers – and she said she was interested – '

'Oh, not yet!' He was all sunny complaisance now, taking her elbow in a warm grasp and smiling at her with eye-crinkling charm. 'Come, dear Mary, you can't tear yourself away from so charming a company so early!'

'Early! Why, it's getting close to two o'clock. And I have a singing class at eleven,' she protested. 'And I'm very tired. But I must get Miriam home, for I promised Mamma – ' She

134

reddened suddenly, remembering rather too late in the day that this visit was supposed to be a secret. 'Ah – Ambrose, I'd be most obliged if you would – if, that is you could avoid – ah – Great Aunt Abby, you know – '

He grinned at that. 'Sneaked off, did you? Well, well! Never thought you the sort, Miss Mary, that I never did! Thought you were a good little girl, and here's you encouraging naughty Miriam to flout her good Grandmamma – '

'I am,' she said at once, hot in the face. 'I mean, I'm perfectly good – oh, dear – '

He was soothing. 'Of course. Not a word, I promise. Listen, my dear, you want to leave, am I right? And energetic Miss there won't go? Yes, I thought as much – ' as Mary's face coloured. 'So I will resolve the dilemma. I will see she goes home in good time before her Grandmamma rises, and you can be sleeping sweetly in your bed! How's that, then? No – don't thank me – glad to help – ' And he smiled at her again, and almost against her will urged her through the press of people to the door, giving her just a moment to bid the St Felix sisters good-bye. But not entirely against her will, for she really was extremely weary.

So it was that Miriam and Ambrose found themselves later that night – or rather morning – sitting side by side in a hansom cab on their way to 'a delicious place which you'll adore, my dear' and laughing with conspiratorial pleasure over the way they had duped Grandmamma.

'She thought I had gone to bed early, you know, for I left the Sassoons' Ball with the headache at half-past eleven, and was no sooner in the house than out again by the area steps, and Grandmamma sipping her bedtime soup and none the wiser. I know Cousin Amy and Cousin Mary won't breathe a word, for to tell the truth, Grandmamma would be much angrier with them than with me, for encouraging me.' She slid a wicked sideways glance at him. 'Grandmamma hardly ever gets cross with me. Only with the people who lead me into naughty ways. You'd better watch out, my dear, or she'll be at your throat!'

'It's worth it to be with you,' he said with practised huskiness and slid his fingers into the palm of her hand, through the unbuttoned wrist of her glove, which made her shiver with delight and a sense of great wickedness. Delicious.

'Where are we?' She leaned forwards to look out as the cab drew up with a jingle of harness outside a house in a quiet street.

He paid off the cab and handed her out, punctilious in his care of her gown, a particularly delicate one in lime green shantung with white lace trimmings round the deep *décolletage*. 'This is a place Grandmamma must never hear about. Very sinful,' he said cheerfully. 'And great fun! We shall gamble a little – '

'Gamble?' She drew back and for the first time a hint of doubt crept into her mind. For all her headstrong giddiness and her determination to have her own spoiled way at all times, Miriam was not entirely without common sense, and one of the rules that had been dinned into her since her earliest years was that gambling was a stupid way to waste time and money. 'I'm not sure that – '

He laughed, fully understanding. 'My dear, I know exactly what Grandpapa says on the subject.' He tucked his chin into his neck and with a passable imitation of Gideon's rich old voice quavered, 'Only a fool throws his money in a hole with a dice. Only an idiot allows animals to decide the fate of his hard-earned guineas'. But, bless you, how do you think he makes his own great fortune? He's a banker, and that's just a high-flown way of gambling. Except,' he went on with a hint of bitterness, 'they're damned good at hedging their bets and making sure it's others who carry the losses. Now, do come, my dear. There's no harm in it, I promise you, and great fun.' He began to lead her up the steps and then said with a studied casualness, 'Have you any money to play with?'

'I've perhaps a few pounds in my purse,' she said unwillingly, her desire for new excitements and the pleasure of Ambrose's company pulling against her still clamouring doubts.

'And if you spent it on gewgaws, what would you have to show for it? Just a few gewgaws. Spend it here and you may end up with more than you began with! Come, don't behave like Grandmamma!'

The phrase, so common on her lips, was cunningly chosen for at once she lifted her chin and smiled brilliantly at him. 'As you say, Ambrose! You're right! We'll only have a little fun!' And if she did not notice that she had stopped calling him Cousin, he certainly did. And he grinned to himself in the darkness as they waited for an answer to his knock. Damn Mother to hell and back! He'd show her and the rest of them, see if he didn't!

It had not been an easy interview with Phoebe, and that had surprised him. He and his mother had always been on the happiest of terms, ever since the days when he had been a small boy allowed to come and perch beside her in bed every morning, much to his nurse's disgust, and share titbits off her breakfast tray. He had been said to be delicate, as the result of an attack of measles complicated by bronchitis in his sixth year which had nearly carried him off, and that had meant she would not let him go away to school as his brother James had, but made him stay at home with Cecily and learn from a governess (which fact had probably accounted for his signal failure at the University, for he was not stupid; but he had been shockingly badly educated). Thus a cosiness had grown between them during the years upon which he had come to rely.

So, he was startled to say the least when Phoebe did not greet his plan to marry an heiress with any sort of warmth.

She had sat and stared at him with blank eyes when he had said, in his usual bantering way, that he had news for her, and then had told her he had an eye on a rich bride. So cool had she been that he had not even got as far as telling her whom it was he had marked down for this signal honour.

'And why do you imagine any father of an heiress would allow you anywhere near his child?' she had said sharply. 'Really, Ambrose, if this is an idea you've taken up to mend your fortunes, it's a singularly stupid one!'

He stared at her. 'Why? Am I so unprepossessing that a rich girl wouldn't have me?'

'You know perfectly well I don't mean anything of the sort,' she had snapped. 'I mean that marrying where money is makes sense, but to marry money for its own sake leads to a great deal of misery. The girl soon finds out what you're about, for the one thing no man can pretend is a passion he doesn't feel. And then she makes quite sure you have no access to her money, and uses her father to make doubly sure. Look what happened to your friend Peter Raymouth who married the Lynton girl. As ugly as sin, miserable with it. And now look at him – a remittance man in Canada or some such wilderness and she at home again with her parents, and her money held tight in her fist!'

His brows had snapped down at that. 'I should hope I've more sense than Raymouth,' he said stiffly. 'And you do me an injustice if you think I'd choose a girl I couldn't care for. I may be free and easy in matters of cash, Mamma, but I'm not entirely without morals, I believe!'

She had closed her eyes for a moment and taken a deep breath, and then looked up at him bleakly. 'Oh, I'm sorry. I suppose I was a bit – but, really Ambrose, your father's getting more and more tiresome about you and more and more tight with money, and I'm hard put to it to pay my own bills, let alone those of yours you bring me. And now you come with some notion of buttering up an heiress – it's such a nonsense!

Who is there anyway? One of the Cray sisters? They're both nearly forty, and stupid with it. Butterworth's niece? Faugh! You really mustn't throw such foolishness at me when I'm already hard pressed.'

He had shrugged and said nothing, marvelling a little that she had not realised at once whom it was he was considering, and then, after a while, realizing that it did make sense. He had, after all, known Miriam since her babyhood. She was a cousin, one of the family, and since he had shown no interest in her before, his mother might well not think of her in the context of marriage to him.

He had stopped then, staring at her while she went on complaining about his father's complaints about him; clearly his father had not said anything to her about the time he had brought Miriam to the hospital in search of a little money and so angered him. And perhaps Freddy hadn't noticed that he was making advances to Miriam? Well, that was not so surprising after all; they saw little enough of each other, father and son, and perhaps Providence was on his side. His mind worked quickly. Perhaps the less his family knew about his plans for Miriam, the better it would be. He could suddenly see all too clearly the flutterings there would be in the various Caspar and Henriques dove-cots if it was known that he, the rakish man-about-town of the family, the only one with any style at all, had his eye on his young cousin. He almost grinned at the thought. No, the less said the better.

Gradually he had been able to soothe Phoebe, making her laugh as she usually did in his company, and entertaining her with his account of the scheme he had made with his Uncle Oliver to arrange for puffs in the newspapers about the Supper Rooms, for which Ambrose was to be paid a commission of five per cent of the house takings on the two nights succeeding the appearance of a paragraph.

'I hate to say it to you, darling Mamma, for he is your brother, I know, but really I do think that when the brains were distributed in your family, you were given Uncle Oliver's share. Any fool must see that not *all* the house takings would result from the advertisement, and that five per cent was far too much, but there – he was easily beguiled.'

'Oh, he's always been a fool about the importance of public announcements,' she said with some scorn. 'Papa was the same – ' She stopped for a moment, staring down back the corridor of long dead years to a picture of her father, Jonah, pinning a large poster to the door of the Celia Supper Rooms. And the crackle of flames and smoke while the poster curled on the door as the building caught fire. She shuddered and shook her head as if to clear it; infant though she had been at the time of his death, the manner of it always haunted her.

'But don't underestimate Oliver. He is my only brother, and so very attached to all of you. He has no child of his own, so who should benefit by his hard work? It's my guess that he agreed to your plan as much for my sake as for yours – '

In which she was most shrewd, for indeed, Oliver had accepted Ambrose's rather empty scheme as much out of concern for his sister's purse as out of any hope that the Supper Rooms would benefit. Though it would be agreeable to wipe the Guv'nor's eye, not to speak of D'Oyly Carte's –

'Well, whatever the reason he agreed, Mamma, agree he did. So I'm quids in, for a change, and you can tell Father to stop nagging you.'

'And Aunt Abby too – '

He was silent then for a moment. 'Grandmamma?' he said carefully. 'What do you mean?'

'Oh, she was here yesterday, complaining most bitterly about your lazy ways. Damn those wretched – because all her Jew relations slave away for money all the time, she thinks you should – ' and her face looked pinched and waspish suddenly.

'Oh, come, Mamma, that's hardly fair,' he said, as easily as he could. 'Grandmamma is hardly a Lombard Streeter! And you know, it's quite fashionable to be Jewish now. The Prince's friends – and he was at their Ball, was he not?'

She made a face. 'I don't care what the Prince does,' she said pettishly. 'For my part, I dislike the Jewish connection, and always have. Ever since she married into the Henriques – oh, well,' and she shrugged and fell silent, uncomfortably aware suddenly of how much she owed Gideon. He had cared for her as one of his own family from the time of her own father's death. He owed her nothing, and she owed him much. An obvious reason to dislike him, of course, but not a comfortable one.

Ambrose was watching her as she sat there in silence for a while, thanking his guardian angel for making sure he had not let slip the name of the heiress he was angling for. If his mother felt like this about Grandpapa Gideon, how would she feel about his marriage to a Da Silva? He thought of some of Miriam's other relations, on her father's side; the rather alarming Moses Da Silva of the long white beard and booming voice and the equally large Aunt Hannah with her moustache and her sharp little eyes which missed nothing – indeed, the less anyone knew of his plans the better.

And as he stood on the steps of the house in Somerset Street, waiting to take Miriam in to try her hand at roulette for the first time, he smiled down at her. It was going to be a pleasure to marry this child, it really was, and to her benefit, ultimately, for wouldn't she have him for a husband? Which would be fun for her –

He didn't think too much about the fact that until she was twenty-one she could not give her own consent to marry him; that the likelihood of her grandparents agreeing was remote in the extreme, or of his parents supporting his efforts, because he had already decided that the only answer was to seduce her, and so force marriage on to everyone will they, nill they. Why should he wait four years? It made no sense at all.

And he bent swiftly and kissed her cheek as the door opened and then grinned wickedly at her, as she blushed and shook her head in reproof. Really, it was all going to be great fun, as well as the answer to all his fiscal problems. What more could any man ask?

13

Lewis arrived at Somerset Street early, even before the house was stirring for the evening activities, bearing a laden bag in each hand and trying not to reopen with himself the discussion that had been going on in his head for the past week, ever since Claudette had set the proposition before him.

For the decision to which he had come was a sensible one; the only sensible one, in fact, which would confer considerable benefits to the girls at the house, as well as providing him with the opportunities to do more of the sort of work he was fast coming to realize mattered to him. He had always had a notion to study the ravages of cancer, to seek answers to that mysterious affliction, for hadn't his own mother succumbed to it? But over this past week the pressing need to consider the ills of women, including the effects of the venereal diseases, had become more and more clamorous. So much so, that he had found himself one afternoon visiting the House with Freddy and seeking his guidance.

'I had a bad one last night, in casualty,' he had said with studied nonchalance as they washed their hands and removed their protective gowns after their round of the women's ward. 'A street girl. Bleeding badly from a botched abortion.'

Freddy had looked at him sharply. 'Did you take her into the wards?'

Lewis shook his head. 'She refused,' he said, appalled at the ease with which the lies came tripping off his tongue.

'Wouldn't say who'd done it to her. Wouldn't do anything but let me stop the bleeding, and then ran out. I had another such a couple of weeks ago, though I admitted her. I – it's left me thinking – '

'Thinking!' Freddy said, almost violently. 'It's a matter I've thought about these past twenty years and more. It gets worse, not better, and the more the churchmen and the respectable citizens thunder on about evil and immorality, the worse it gets. I think Aunt Martha has the best solution – '

'Aunt Martha?'

Freddy looked at him over his shoulder. 'I suppose we have been remiss in not arranging for you to meet some of your connections, but – oh well, there's time yet to put the matter right. Martha is my aunt, and yours too, of course. Great-aunt. She is a most redoubtable lady.' His lips curved then and he leaned against the wash basin, drying his hands on a small towel. 'Went to the Crimea, you know, saw the whole campaign through – '

'Oh, one of Miss Nightingale's ladies?'

'Not she! Went to look after the camp followers and their children, not the Army. Miss Nightingale and she – ' He laughed. 'They didn't see eye to eye at all. No, Martha's concern has always been with bad women. Works herself to a thread for 'em. The London Ladies, you know.'

Lewis looked polite, trying not to show his boredom. He wanted to talk about the problem of abortion, dammit, not family history. There had been times when he would have welcomed this sort of conversation, but not now.

'It's a charity. Used to be called the London Ladies' Committee for the Rescue of the Profligate Poor. Once it distributed bibles in the poorer parts of Covent Garden – not much use, of course, since none of the recipients could read. Still, that's what they did. Now they run hostels for street women and children. Mostly it's a pack of old biddies who sit about drinking tea and prosing on for ever about their bunions, but they raise money, and there are of course the inheritances they have – through the family.' He looked broodingly at Lewis for a moment and then went on, 'And it's Aunt Martha who is responsible for the hostels. She lives over one of them, in Bedford Row. Spends precious little time in her own apartments though. Always running about from one hostel to another sorting out their wretched difficulties, seeing the children off into good service, and trying to keep the women off the streets. She succeeds, too, with some of them – but for the rest – well, she's practical. If they fall pregnant, and it's clear won't carry willingly to term, then she makes all the necessary arrangements.'

Lewis, whose thoughts had begun to wander looked up sharply at that. 'What sort of arrangements?'

'She has an old midwife who does the necessary for her,' Freddy said calmly. 'Dammit, man, don't look so shocked at me! What would you have her do? Throw her hands up in pious horror and toss them out into the streets she got 'em from? That wouldn't be much charity, would it? That's what so many of the others do – but not Aunt Martha. She recognizes the inevitable and bows to it, and makes sure that they get good care, illegal or not. I used to fret over it, but now – well, she's been running her hostels so for forty years, give or take a few, and there's been no hint of scandal yet. I doubt there will be, for she's not lost a woman from an abortion yet, to the best of my knowledge. And if that ain't good care, what is?'

'This midwife – she has training in what she does?'

'Indeed she does. The best.' Freddy smiled crookedly. 'Taught her myself.'

There was a silence and then Lewis said abruptly, 'Why?'

'Why what?'

'Why did you teach her? It's illegal, it destroys life, we are expressly forbidden to do it under the Hippocratic oath – '

'The Hippocratic oath!' Freddy said with a fine scorn. 'How long since you read that damned document? Hmm? Take

another look, my boy, take another look. It's nothing more than – than a trade agreement! Lays down rules to ensure physicians get the best out of their dealings with their patients and that students are taught to be as grasping as their masters. It's more concerned with protecting the mystery than with the real needs of the poor devils who are our patients. I do what is necessary for the people I care for, not for myself, but for them – for I have personal experience, and know how they suffer – '
He looked bleak then, staring down at his hands which he was still rubbing with the towel, although they were long since dry.

'You performed abortions yourself?'

Freddy looked up. 'Now, why do I talk to you? Hmm? I've never discussed such matters with any of the other people at Nellie's – '

'Perhaps because I'm family. And a stranger.'

Freddy made a small grimace. 'Aye. You could be right. Paradoxes often are.'

'You haven't answered my question,' Lewis said, after a moment. 'You've done abortions?'

'Yes. Once. A long time ago.' He looked up at Lewis then, his face was blank. 'It was a girl of breeding. Not a street girl. I had to.'

It seemed to Lewis then that a wall as solid as stone though as translucent as crystal had come down between them, for Freddy stood there, still mechanically rubbing his hands on the towel. He was staring blank-eyed at his memories, but had become totally inaccessible. To have tried to push past that wall would have been an insufferable intrusion, and Lewis did not attempt it. Enough that the man had been through the same experience he had himself. He had needed help in coming to terms with his own actions, and Freddy had given it.

They travelled back to Nellie's together in silence, but an agreeable and companionable one, for the barrier seemed to melt away as they sat side by side in the rocking clattering cab.

146

When they got back Freddy said abruptly, 'Next Sunday, Lackland. You are free, I believe. If not change your rota with young Clements. My mother will be At Home from three in the afternoon and it is time you met her. She is your grandfather's sister, and it is time. Green Street, the Park Lane end. I shall expect to see you there.'

He had gone, half eager, half frightened, trying to hide his trepidation under a bluff and insouciant manner, but deeply hopeful of making contacts that would give him the base he now knew he so badly needed. He had tried not to think of the way he had used Claudette the night he had come back in such anxiety from Wapping. He had been much in need of someone in whom he could confide, some brotherly person who would understand how things had been with him that night and who would give him understanding, and with it, some sort of absolution. Perhaps in this family, he would find such a one? The fact that Claudette had been quite unperturbed by the episode and had continued to be her usual friendly self, making no play at all upon their new intimacy, had not helped at all. She *should* have shown some reaction, damn it, he'd thought bitterly as he had walked up Oxford Street towards Park Lane that Sunday afternoon, should have been different somehow. More – more what? He had pondered, marching through the dust of the pavements past the jostling crowds, all making their way this hot afternoon to the relative coolness of Hyde Park, trying to identify what it was he wanted from Claudette; but he couldn't. All he knew was that she was still Claudette, cheerful, busy, practical, somewhat preoccupied with her new interest, but as friendly as she had ever been, while he – he was beset with confusion about his views on abortion, and of course, that new interest of Claudette's.

For after she had told him that she was to work in a brothel, albeit a high-class one, he had stood and stared at her, waiting for the wave of disapproval that he knew ought to have come – but which did not. He had said simply, 'Oh,' and stood there.

'Well, *mon brave*, you are not shocked? We are still friends?'

'I could hardly be shocked after this past half-hour or so,' he'd said dryly.

'Was it so long?' she'd murmured and then laughed. 'That is a great comfort to me, Lewis. You are a strange man in some ways, and although you seem to be less rigid than these boring English with their stuffy notions of *comme il faut* – they are like the worst of the provincial French – still you do sometimes show a sort of – oh, how shall I say it? A *judgemental* posture. You are given to making statements about what is proper and what is not and that is sometimes tiresome. So I feared – but I was wrong, and I'm happy indeed that I am.' She had kissed him then, twining her arms about his neck, and wickedly teasing his mouth with her pointed tongue, so that for a moment his senses, recently satisfied though they had been, had stirred again. 'You shall come and see my new establishment, and you will, I think, approve of it. And I want also to discuss a matter with you about it – '

And that had been when she had put her proposition before him. In the past few days, she told him, she had learned a great deal about Mrs Lovibond's operation. The real money did not lie in the gambling profits, good though they were, for Mrs Lovibond did not believe in sending her punters away skinned. They had to win as often as the house did, though in lesser amounts of course, in order to keep them coming. No, the real money came from the 'gifts' the rich and aristocratic frequenters of Somerset Street gave to Mrs Lovibond in exchange for being introduced to the girls who went there.

'It is not, you must understand, like the ordinary night divan,' Claudette had explained to Lewis. 'The girls do not live there. They are all otherwise employed, mostly as actresses at the Savoy and Terry's and the Opéra-Comique, and, when she can get them, for they are considered the best, the Gaiety. They receive considerable gifts from their admirers and Mrs Lovibond often gives them small gifts as well – clothes, mostly

– but no actual money changes hands, you must understand. So they must be regarded entirely as amateurs. It is a most *discreet* operation. There are quiet rooms there, and all that is comfortable, and – well, you see the situation. But after what happened to Pearl Mrs Lovibond is concerned, and so, of course, am I. I do not intend to be connected with a house where such things can happen. You must understand that I will not profit in any way from – from this side of Mrs Lovibond's business. I am there only to run the restaurant and help with the gaming operation. Not the girls, or their doings. But, inevitably, I am – aware of what happens there. Had it not been for you, Pearl would have died. That must not happen again. So – '

She had stopped, looking at him consideringly, her eyes watchful. 'So, we must make better arrangements, *hein*? You would agree?'

He had been silent and then sighed heavily. 'I see. I am to be the arrangements?'

'Well, *pourquoi pas, mon cher*? *Pourquoi pas*? The girls will not be *enceintes* willingly, no matter what, and someone will do it for them if you don't. Better you, surely, than someone like the woman who dealt with Pearl?'

'My God,' he'd said, almost under his breath. 'Oh, my God – ' In one night to have both performed an abortion, and to be asked to become a resident abortionist to a brothel – what had happened to him? What malevolent providence was spinning his top in such sickening, bewildering circles? Till now a simple surgeon, doing what he did because it had to be done, coping with each disease, each injury, each wound that came his way and never questioning it; how could he now be being pitchforked into the half-world Claudette inhabited?

Because I take whatever comes my way, he told himself that Sunday afternoon, as he reached Marble Arch. I cannot choose which sicknesses I will accept, any more than patients can decide which they will have. If it is these miseries which are set before me, then it is because I am meant to deal with them – and Freddy Caspar does too, dammit. Why shouldn't I? And perhaps there are ways to prevent some of the misery. Not just the unwanted pregnancies, but the infections that destroy men's bodies with huge sores and cut gleaming snail-track ulcers in women's soft faces –

And, of course, there was Claudette. That he had come to depend on her friendship he knew; now he had started to need more of her. Not just her body, but the affectionate givingness of her that regarded physical joy as just another way to comfort a friend. He knew she did not love him, not in the sense most women would use the word. But he also knew that he was within an inch of loving her. There was still time to pull away from her, and from her proposition, still time to retrace his steps. But he wasn't at all sure he wanted to.

So, by the time he reached Green Street he was in a difficult mood; hard-faced because he was coming ever closer to making the decision that was being pushed at him; confused still because of his guilt about his use of Claudette, mixed with – he could not deny it – a rising need to repeat the experience, and angry because of the sense of inadequacy which was immediately called up in him by the sight of the large sumptuous house and the exceedingly tall and haughty butler who opened the door to his knock. Added to all that was his sudden awareness of the street dust which clung to his boots and somewhat commonplace trousers compared with the clothes of the extremely elegant gleaming men he found standing about in Mrs Henriques' drawing-room.

Small wonder then, that he responded to Freddy's introduction of him to his mother, a very large and costly-looking lady in green silk, ensconced on a vast gilded and red plush upholstered sofa, with little more than a grunt. Never given much to polished speeches, today he forgot every scrap of polite conversation he had ever learned, taking an immediate and quite violent dislike to the entire company.

For they really were the most well fed, well-upholstered and sleek people he had ever been amongst. Each one wore clothes more costly than the next; each one seemed as satisfied as a cat which had fed on cream, and looked at him, he felt, with a high-bred langour and boredom which he found profoundly offensive. Which was unfortunate, for in fact no one had noticed him particularly, seeing him as just another of the many visitors who regularly arrived at Green Street on Sunday afternoons. But by now Lewis was much too tense and angry to be anything but edgy and suspicious.

So, when Mrs Henriques patted the sofa beside her and bade him sit down and tell her all about himself, he curtly refused to do other than stand awkwardly in front of her, and answer all her questions about his antecedents with the merest of monosyllables. She managed to drag from him the fact that his grandfather had been one Rupert Lackland and was now dead, and that was all. And, hot and cross already, following a disagreement with Miriam who had expressed herself forcibly on the subject of boring At Homes and who was now sulking in a corner, despite having all the liveliest of her cousins around her, Abby very quickly gave up trying to regard this uncouth young Australian as even remotely interesting.

'Relation he may be, Freddy,' she said wrathfully to her son, when Lewis had turned away to accept the tea-cup and saucer a footman was offering, 'but that doesn't give him leave to come here looking like a hobbledehoy and behaving so rude when he is spoke to. I ain't at all took with him!' Abby had a tendency to revert to the speech style of her youth when angry, and this afternoon it was quite marked. And also rather loud, for at last the old lady's hearing was losing some of its edge. Lewis, refusing the thin bread and butter he was being offered felt his face redden heavily as he caught her words and he put down his cup and saucer with a rattle on a small table and said in a low voice to Freddy, 'I'm going.'

151

'Don't be so foolish,' Freddy said sharply. 'Nor so ill-mannered! What's come over you, man? This isn't the casualty waiting-room at Nellie's, and I would have thought you had more sense than to – '

'I know no better, sir,' Lewis said. His voice was still low, for despite his rising temper he knew he was behaving badly, and did not wish to make the situation any worse than it already was. 'I'm a hobbledehoy Australian, remember? The connection with your family is slight enough, after all, and since it took so long for any of them to show any interest in what connection there was, then it can hardly matter to 'em if I go now.' He looked round scornfully at the company. 'They look to be uninterested in anything but their own affairs, anyway. So, I'll bid you good afternoon and thank you for your thought, and be on my way back where I belong. The casualty waiting-room at Nellie's – '

Freddy laughed then, a sound which startled Lewis, and taking his elbow led him away to a corner well away from Abby who was now in animated conversation with a handsome woman in pink satin, whom she addressed as 'Dearest Amy'.

'Really, Lackland, you are absurd,' Freddy said. 'To be so put out because no one paid any attention to you. Dammit, man, they don't know you! I dare say I'm as much to blame as any. You've been in London long enough – I should have told them of you, and brought you sooner. But there, I had my reasons, poor though they were – so, I'm sorry. Now, will you try again, and come back and talk to Mamma once more? She's easily won round, and would soon be much more taken with you than she is at present – and you can hardly blame her, for really – '

'I am ill-mannered, I know,' Lewis interrupted. 'But there it is. That's the way I am. I'm going all the same. Thanks for – '

'Uncle Freddy!' a voice said behind him and they both turned to see Miriam standing there and smiling up at them.

She was wearing a dress of cream lace and looking particularly fetching, especially as she was treating Freddy to the most bewitching of smiles.

'Dearest Uncle Freddy, please – will you do something for me?' she said a little breathlessly, coming close and setting her hands confidingly on the lapels of his coat. 'I am sure you will – '

She shot a bright smile at Lewis and smiled at him in a perfunctory manner, but with great charm. 'I hope you will forgive me interrupting, sir, but I must speak to my uncle, and there is so little chance in all this crush – and at the moment Grandmamma is safely occupied – ' And she looked over her shoulder at a large sofa. 'Dearest Uncle, I wish to ask you to help me with something – ' And she linked one arm in Freddy's and led him away, leaving Lewis to stand staring after them.

He recognized her, of course. The enchantingly pretty girl who had been in Nellie's casualty department that evening when he had first met Claudette – and he was puzzled for a moment about why he should have thought of Claudette just then.

Had he thought more deeply, instead of just staring at the girl's wide eyes and soft chin and sweetly rounded cheeks, he might have realized what was happening to him; the physical needs which he had managed to keep lying fallow these past seven months had been more than just satisfied by that evening in White Hart Street; they had been rekindled. Now, there was a fire in his belly that made him ripe for an emotional entanglement; he knew himself that he was as close to falling in love with Claudette as a man could be – but he had not yet so fallen. And on that Sunday afternoon, staring across a crowded scented drawing-room at a delectable child in cream lace, he slipped out of Claudette's grasp and head first into the most ludicrous infatuation that had hit him since he had passed his sixteenth birthday.

He knew it had happened, and was exasperated with himself for allowing it. But there was nothing he could do about it except hope that the mad conflagration would die down for want of fuel. For, of course, there was no chance that he would ever meet Miss Miriam Da Silva again, once he had turned and gone running down the stairs and away into the hot dustiness of Park Lane, as he had without waiting to bid anyone at all farewell.

And it was also the reason why he arrived at the door of Mrs Lovibond's house in Somerset Street a few nights later, bearing two bags laden with the equipment he might need to carry out such tasks as Claudette gave him. In a curious way, the absurdity of the effect that girl had had on him had been the final weight that had tipped the scales to make him accept Claudette's proposition. He would be the resident physician to a bawdy house, and to the devil with the law and respectability. And with pretty girls in cream lace.

14

August was a rainy month, with the gutters of London running clear rather than muddy, for by the time many of the aristocracy left for Scotland to shoot grouse from the twelfth of the month all the dust had been washed away. London was as clean as it had been for a long time (except in the slums of course, which no one who counted cared about anyway) and, far from being humid and uncomfortable, was a more agreeable place to be than remote country estates where crops rotted in the dank ground and travelling was a mud-encrusted nightmare.

So it was that the 1892 season dragged on rather longer than was usual. The Henriques decided not to leave for their usual visit to the German spas where they recouped their health and strength most autumns, partly because Abby had developed a troublesome cough and did not feel up to the tedious and protracted journey, and partly for Miriam's sake.

She had enjoyed her first Season enormously, she had told her grandparents (and why should she not? She had had no less than three proposals to add to her total and two more somewhat proper young men, both scions of very prosperous Jewish families, had approached Gideon for permission to address her) and did not want it to end yet. 'Please, please, dearest ones,' she had coaxed charmingly. 'Could we not stay in London until October at least? For lots of people are remaining in Town, and there is still so much to see and do – '

And Ambrose is not going away although his mother is to take the waters at Baden Baden, and will leave him even more free than usual; but this she forbore to offer as a reason. The less she talked to her grandparents about Ambrose, Ambrose had told her, the better.

Miriam had thought occasionally about Ambrose as a suitor. She had not been able to avoid doing so, for he had made it even more clear as the weeks went by that he regarded her with much more than cousinly affection. He had begged her to say nothing to anyone about him, however, 'because,' he had said solemnly, 'they are a narrow lot, our relations, and would regard this as positively incestuous.'

'What is that?' she had asked, and he had laughed and kissed her and told her not to worry her pretty little head, but just to do as he told her. Which was to say nothing about the happy times they spent together. And she, wise in her years, did as she was bid.

Because having Ambrose as a suitor was amusing. He was so witty, and yet so comfortable to be with. He didn't hang on every word she said, as the boring young men who adored her and proposed to her did; he teased and mocked and treated her so very comfortably that when he did laugh at her jokes, she knew she had been genuinely clever. When the boring young men laughed, it was because they were sycophantic or too stupid to know real wit from silliness. There was a headiness in the secretiveness of their relationship, too. The fact that Ambrose had said it was not to be talked about made it so much more interesting; to behave when they were with other people as though he were just good old Cousin Ambrose, and to pretend not to be aware of the naughty things he whispered in her ear, or the way he tickled the palm of her hand when he could do so without anyone noticing, that was heady pleasure indeed; and she would look with limpid eyes at bystanders while all this was going on, hugging their secret to herself with glee.

But whether she loved him or not she did not think about at all. In fact, Miriam had never been in love with anyone and did not know what it was. Protected and adored as she had always been, the need for romantic yearnings had never touched her. When in her early teens her girl friends, with whom she went to occasional dancing classes with her governess, had sighed and murmured about the callow young men who acted as their partners, she had looked at them and wondered what they were talking about. Even now she had come out and had reached the giddy heights of seventeen her heart remained untouched. It was not that she lacked any sensibility; it was simply that she had no need of romantic love. All she needed was admiration, and she had plenty of that.

Yet for all that, she thought about Ambrose as a suitor, for she was a practical girl and knew that sooner or later she would have to marry. There was nothing else a girl would do, apart from staying at home for ever with her grandparents, and that of course was unthinkable. So, a husband was a necessity and she gave careful consideration to Ambrose in this role. Would it be fun to have her own house and order her own servants about and sit at the foot of her own dinner-table while Ambrose sat at the head? Would it be delightful to go to balls with him and see all the other young ladies look at him and know they could not have him, because he belonged to her?

It was at this point that her thinking would become cloudy, for she really could not imagine how being married would be. Her closest models were, in truth, rather dull. There was Cousin Cecily with her four noisy daughters, and Cousin Bella with her tiresome five, and – Miriam would shake her head and sigh. To be married was inevitable, of course, but would it be fun? Even with Ambrose?

Ambrose himself was quite determined that it would be fun, of course. It would have to be. His income was getting ever more strained, despite his arrangement with Uncle Oliver, for Miriam was a child of expensive tastes; so expensive that she did not even know how costly a companion she was. Money to her had always run like water, and she took it for granted that Ambrose had access to as much as she did. So, she would imperiously demand more guineas with which to buy roulette chips – for which game she had developed a decided *tendre* – and never think to give him any back when her lavish allowance filled her reticule again at the beginning of the month. Which meant that Ambrose had to struggle to keep up with her. So far he had managed, by dint of a couple of lucky streaks at Somerset Street when he had won back at the tables enough to see even Miriam contented for the next couple of weeks, but time was running out. He had thought to go on as they were, sneaking away from proper balls and drums and tea parties to visit the Gaiety green-room or the gambling-houses he enjoyed with her at least until the late autumn, but it was now becoming more and more clear to him that he must move soon. She was showing no signs of becoming nearly as intoxicated with him as he had meant her to be; she enjoyed being with him, clearly, and enjoyed their occasional snatched kisses, but where was the fire he had thought to light in her? Nowhere, for she would emerge from his arms laughing equally delightedly after the most passionate of embraces as after a mere peck. Odd girl, he thought, and tried to push away the somewhat sinking feeling that came when he contemplated being married to a woman who lacked any interest in physical love. Ambrose enjoyed physical love a great deal – even while he was courting Miriam so assiduously he still found time and the need to visit one or two discreet Covent Garden establishments to slake his thirst for more than kisses from a débutante; so the thought of a chilly wife did not enthral him.

But the thought of a rich one undoubtedly did, and he began to plan more carefully.

Lewis was tired. The day had been long and effortful, for it had started with a very bad traffic accident in the Strand, in which a horse had rolled on a woman carrying a baby in her arms, and gone on to the treatment of a man who had been crushed under a falling lorry-load of potatoes in the market. There had been the usual procession of coughing old men and weak anaemic women and children with boils and sores, and now it was Friday, his day at Somerset Street, and more work ahead of him.

Not that he minded going there as much as he had thought he would, when he had started. Indeed, it was all turning out rather well. Mrs Lovibond had arranged for him at the top of the house, in one of the small snug attics, a room where he could see the girls who needed him, and do all that was needful for them. There was a small gas fire with a ring set above it, and a large fish kettle in which he could boil his instruments. There was a glass-fronted cupboard in which he arranged the store of medicaments and instruments he had brought from Nellie's for the purpose (and told himself stoutly that the hospital could afford to part with) and a shiny horsehair-stuffed sofa on high castors, ideal to use as an examination couch. There was a small desk with a light on it, at which he could write his notes on the cases he saw, and a wash basin in the corner, to which she had piped, at great expense, running water from the mains.

'Mrs Lovibond and I agreed that we don't want inquisitive housemaids emptying your slops, *mon cher*,' Claudette had said crisply on the day he had arrived with his equipment. 'They are discreet about most things here, but you never know. What are those?' She pointed to the small pile of sponges he had put on the table, as he unpacked the second of his bags.

'Ah – ' He went a little pink, which was absurd. This was Claudette, dammit, not some shrinking silly miss who pretended she had no body beneath her skirts. 'Malthusian sponges,' he said gruffly. 'They're used for – '

'Ah!' She picked one up and examined it with interest, tugging on the fine cord that was tied to it. 'I see. I have heard of these, though I have never seen one. They are used alone?'

'Alone? Oh. I see what you mean – no, it is best if they are soaked in some material which will – ah – kill the generative material. Vinegar or strong soap – '

She made a grimace. 'That doesn't sound very romantic.'

'A pregnancy that is not wanted isn't romantic either.' He stopped and then said, 'Some people use honey.'

She laughed aloud at that. 'Come, that's better! Much more – well, I can understand a girl being willing to use honey. So, tell me, how does it work?'

'Look, Claudette, this is not a matter – '

She raised her brows at that. 'Not a matter for a man to discuss with a lady, you would say? Now, come, Lewis! This is me, remember? Claudette? Think of why you are here!'

She made a wide gesture that took in not just the little attic room with its clinical furniture but the house that lay beneath them in all its luscious over-decorated richness. 'And think too, of me. Would you wish to make me *enceinte*, and to have to perform one of your services for me as a consequence?'

He had stared at her and opened his mouth to speak but she had put up one hand and covered his lips, preventing him. '*Mon cher*,' she said softly. 'It is now quite some time since our last little – encounter. How much longer are you going to wait for the next? Or have you found another answer to your needs that does not include me?'

'You know damned well I haven't,' he had said gruffly, and tried to pull away from her, but she had shaken her head.

'Then why do you stay so aloof? There is no need for such niceties with me. I told you, we are friends. Now, tell me how these sponges of yours should be used, and tonight, after the last clients have gone, we shall amuse ourselves, *hein*? On our last – meeting – we were fortunate, as I knew we would be for

I was at such a time of the month that I could not conceive. But we cannot always rely on that.'

He had stood and stared at her, at her pointed face and narrow green eyes and the curls that lay on her forehead in fashionable confusion, above all at the smile that curled round her lips; and gave in. That incredible marvellous damnable girl he had seen in Green Street had nothing to do with the case, nothing to do with the case at all. Why be so stupid as to yearn for that, when he could have this?

So he had kissed Claudette soundly and then, as clinically and dispassionately as he could, explained how the sponge was to be tucked into the body, so far as she could get it, 'to close the mouth of the womb and act as a preventive.'

She had smiled. 'I prefer it to the things some of the men here use. The girls have told me – great thick sleeves of rubber – ' She shuddered prettily. 'Not at all romantic.'

'They protect against more than pregnancy,' Lewis had said harshly. 'A man using one of those is safe from disease.'

She had looked at him then and sighed. 'It is sad, is it not? We ask little of life indeed. The satisfaction of hunger for food, the opportunity for a little pleasure from the bodies God gave us. Why is it that we should be so burdened for it?'

He had shrugged and turned away and finished unpacking his bag. 'If I knew that, I'd know more than any man can. I'll come down soon. When I have set all to rights here – '

And so a pattern of life had begun. Each Friday he would arrive at Somerset Street and, using the back stairs from the busy basement kitchens, would cut through the big new dining-rooms which had been charmingly decorated under Claudette's personal supervision in the newest of styles, all curving lilies in lilacs and purples, and on up to the third floor where Jody and Claudette had their own apartments.

This floor was as lavishly arranged as all the others, with thick red carpets and pallid wall-hangings and the inevitable marble statues flanking each of the doors. Five of the rooms were 'Private dining-rooms' which any visitor to the house could use and often did, although little food was served in them, orders for more than champagne being rare. The remaining two doors led to Jody's and Claudette's room respectively. Between the two rooms, connected to each by individual doors, was a small and charming sitting room in which Lewis would sit and have a drink with Jody each Friday evening.

The room was comfortable, and exceedingly well-furnished, since it had originally been part of Mrs Lovibond's own chambers, but she had chosen to live in a set of rooms in Cavendish Street, now that Claudette had come to relieve her of the efforts of the day-to-day running of the house. Indeed, for Mrs Lovibond Claudette's arrival had been most opportune and far from the financial burden she had suspected it would be. Not only did Claudette steadfastly refuse any of the income from the girls, she also, by her careful running of the new dining-rooms, had increased the house's revenue most markedly, and by the end of her first month had virtually taken over the organization of the whole house. Which meant that Jody lived like a fighting-cock.

'This is a very fine old Napoleon, m'boy,' he would wheeze at Lewis, pouring the amber fluid with as much reverence as if it had been the stuff of life itself. 'Just the thing to oil your wheels before you get the evening together – ' And he would laugh and nod knowingly and raise his glass in a toast. He knew perfectly well that Lewis slept in Claudette's bed every Friday evening, and did not object in the least. This life was better for her in his eyes than pretending to be an actress at the Gaiety. So he approved of Lewis, thinking him a dull stick, but a comfort to have at hand, for although his illness seemed no worse, he remembered all too vividly the alarming attack he had suffered. A doctor on the premises, even if only on Friday nights, was reassuring company.

Lewis for his part was coming to quite like the old man, reprobate though he was. He knew he should despise him, to be living as he did off the earnings of his daughter, and such earnings – and then he would remember that he too was in a sense as much a parasite as the old man was. True he took no money for the work he did for the girls (when it had been suggested his rage had been monumental, and his refusal peremptory, a decision Mrs Lovibond had accepted with a shrug and a clear display of her conviction that he was quite mad), but he dined there sumptuously every Friday, sitting in a small alcove to one side of the dining-room, for he was anxious not to be seen by any of the *habitués*. Not that he moved in such exalted aristocratic circles as these people did, but you never knew; one of them might become ill and be brought to the hospital, and it would never do for anyone at Nellie's to know what was happening with one of their surgeons on Friday evenings, or how he spent his time.

And after his dinner each Friday he would slip away and see, one by one, the girls Mrs Lovibond sent to him. So far, to his intense relief, none had required the operation he had performed on Queenie a month ago; but there was plenty to do. He taught them how to use the sponges so that they were protected; applied mercury and other medicaments to those who had been infected, and lectured them seriously on the importance of avoiding passing on the disease by not entering into congress until he gave them permission. Claudette helped here; she would take the girls on one side and tell them, in pithy straightforward language, how to give a man satisfaction without infection. 'There is more to your body than *that* portion of it,' she would say crisply. 'And don't forget it. It may not be as agreeable for you to try other ways to please lovers, but it's better than suffering the sort of sores and ulcers that you could get if you don't listen and learn.'

And listen and learn they did. Lewis had started copious notes on each of the girls he had seen, and it pleased him, as

163

he looked back on them that Friday night, tired as he was, to see how much progress he had made. Virtually all of them instructed in self-protection, seventeen cases of gonorrhoea halted if not fully cured, and three of early syphilis seeming to be under control. The elegant men of London who came to Somerset Street had much for which to be grateful to him, he thought, and closed his notebook and stretched, and looked at his watch.

Another two hours at least before Claudette would regard her presence in the rooms below as no longer necessary and would close the gaming-room and come to her room where he would be waiting. Another two hours before she would stand there beside the bed in her white wrapper and then, deliberately and with great sensuousness, drop it to reveal her small, neat but surprisingly voluptuous body to his gaze. Two hours before she would slide between the sheets and press herself against his own nakedness –

He sighed sharply and stood up. Tired though he was this evening he did not want to do as he usually did, and sit here in his attic and read until it was time to go down to the floor below. He was restless and curiously lonely. He needed the company of other people, even at a remove. Down in the rooms below he could see them, be near them, even if he did not talk to them. He never entered those rooms as a rule, always aware as he was of the need for confidentiality, the importance of preserving his anonymity, but tonight, as the inevitable rain pounded on the skylight above his head, he felt he could not remain alone another moment. He would wander down, and lean against a wall in the shadow of a potted palm and watch the expensive throng of the Best People and Most Beautiful Actresses in London, and drink a little champagne. It would relax him and make bedtime with Claudette that much more agreeable.

So it was that he saw Miriam Da Silva come up the big staircase on Ambrose's arm, laughing up at him and looking rather more flushed than a well brought-up girl should.

15

He had thought he'd got over the mad infatuation that had seized him in Green Street a few weeks ago, but as he caught sight of her his belly lurched so violently that he felt a wave of nausea. God damn it, he thought, and leaned back even further into the shade of the tall palm. God damn it all to hell and back. But he watched her; he couldn't help it.

They went to sit side by side on a sofa against the wall facing the big staircase, and he stood and tried not to stare at them, forcing his eyes to move so that he looked at the other people moving about the big room, but it was no use. Each time his gaze flickered back to the sofa, and her face.

They were drinking champagne, and she was leaning towards him, her face upturned and laughing, and after a while Ambrose slid his hand behind her and leaned to whisper in her ear, and she listened, and giggled, and went even more pink.

It was more than Lewis could bear, and he slipped out from the shadow of his palm and began to make his way towards the sofa, going round the walls, moving as casually as he could. He was very conscious of the fact that he was not wearing evening-dress like everyone else, nor yet the livery of a footman, which would of course have made him quite invisible, and could feel curious glances follow him. But he had to go, all the same.

'Good evening,' he said gruffly as he reached them, and she looked up, puzzled, staring at him with obviously unrecognizing eyes.

Ambrose lifted his brows as he too stared at him. 'I beg your pardon?' he said, and his voice had a drawl in it that Lewis found very offensive.

'It was clear enough,' he said sharply. 'I said good evening.'

Ambrose looked at Miriam. 'D'you know this fellow, my dear?'

'I – er– well, I – ' She shook her head, still staring at Lewis in some puzzlement. 'I'm not sure.'

'Then you don't,' Ambrose said. 'If you knew him or cared to, you'd be sure.' And he turned towards Miriam even more, presenting his shoulder to Lewis insultingly.

Lewis' jaw tightened. 'We have met,' he said. 'Twice in fact. Once at – '

'Oh, be off with you, man!' Ambrose said over his shoulder. 'I really don't know what this place is coming to my dear, allowing such riffraff as this in the rooms – ' And he flicked a mocking glance at Lewis' blue worsted suit, which compared most unfavourably with Ambrose's own elegant frock-coat. 'You're not wanted here. Be about your business – '

'Damn you, Caspar!' Lewis said, his temper cracking completely, and he put out one hand to take the other's shoulder and pull him round. But he had forgotten that he still held a wine glass in it and the contents splashed Ambrose full in the face as he twisted in response to Lewis' touch.

At once all was uproar. Ambrose leapt to his feet, his arm pulled back and fist clenched, clearly ready to give Lewis a facer, and Miriam yelped, shrinking back in terror against the sofa.

Claudette had been standing near the top of the staircase, talking to the Marquis of Collingbourne, a tall and very fair young man who wore a monocle screwed firmly into his right eye socket and who tended to allow his lower jaw to droop rather; neither of which facts seemed to perturb her in the least. But she was perturbed by the noise behind her, and whirled and went hurrying across the great expanse of crimson carpet, weaving in and out between the craning staring people, until she reached the centre of the fracas.

Ambrose was standing with his face suffused and was struggling against Lewis, who was holding each of his upper arms in a tight grip so that his hands flailed about uselessly, and whose own face was white with effort.

'*Messieurs, messieurs, qu'est-ce-que vous faites? Arrêtez tout de suite!* We cannot 'ave zees sort of behaviour 'ere!' Claudette had decided to go on using her more French persona for the customers of Somerset Street; it seemed to amuse them, and it could be useful when she chose to misunderstand something; and, despite the problem with which she was now faced, she did not forget her decision. '*Écoutez-moi! Parbleu, quel brouhaha!* I will not 'ave eet! – m'sieu, stop it – ' And she took Lewis' arm in a grip as tight as his own and pinched him shrewdly.

He took a deep breath and looked at her, and then at Ambrose and, slowly, let him go. Ambrose immediately brought his fists up again, and behind him Miriam yelped once more and that seemed to stop him for he unclenched his fists and then turned away and began to dust the sleeves of his frock-coat with ostentatious fastidiousness.

'I really cannot imagine, madam, what you are about to allow such persons into your rooms,' he said in a rather high voice. 'One does not expect to be molested in such a manner – '

'Now, gentlemen, gentlemen,' Claudette said soothingly. 'I am sure zere is nossing we cannot settle amiably over a leetle glass of wine. Please, both of you, come to my private office and we will see what is ze problem. I am sure – ah, *pauvre petite!*' She turned to Miriam, who was still sitting wide-eyed and anxious on the sofa. 'Zey 'ave alarmed you, 'ave zey not?

Never mind – soon all shall be comfortable again – please to come wiz me – '

She shepherded the three of them in front of her across the wide room towards her own small office, which she had taken over from Mrs Lovibond, smiling and nodding at the other guests, who by now had lost interest in what had turned out to be just a minor scuffle. There had been much more interesting and noisier ones when revellers who had lost more money than they meant to found a friend talking to a favourite girl; they were not going to be put out by such a minor incident as this.

But Claudette was, and she turned on Lewis with her eyes blazing when the three of them were at last ensconced in her small room.

'And now, please, you will tell me exactly what all that was about?' she said in a freezing tone. 'I did not expect such behaviour from *you*, Lewis! What the devil were you doing there anyway? You never come down – '

'I thought as much,' Ambrose said triumphantly. He was standing beside Miriam's chair, his hand set protectively on her shoulder, a sight which did nothing to reduce Lewis' fury. 'Some damned servant trying to muscle in – '

'I am not a servant,' Lewis said and his voice was hard and very cold. 'Had you had the common decency to stop and listen you would have been reminded that I am a connection of your father's.' He looked at Miriam, and bent his head in a sketch of a bow. 'And of yours, Miss Da Silva. You may recall that we met briefly at Queen Eleanor's Hospital, and then at your grandmother's At Home a short time ago. I was speaking to Mr Caspar, and you joined us – '

Her face cleared at once. 'Of course! I knew I had seen you somewhere before! Oh dear, I am sorry – this was all my fault, wasn't it, for not remembering? If I had Ambrose wouldn't have been so – ' She tilted her head to look at Ambrose. 'You see, Ambrose? He was only saying good evening because he knew me – perhaps you should apologize.'

'Apologize? I? Be damned if I will!' Ambrose shouted. 'Some goddamned jumped-up piece of – '

'We will 'ave no such language 'ere, m'sieu,' Claudette said frostily. 'If you 'ave no shame to speak so before me, consider ze feelings of this young lady – ' She looked again at Miriam and then turned to Lewis.

'Am I to understand you know zis lady, Lewis? She is not– ah – she is not one of ze usual guests we enjoy?'

He looked at her and nodded. 'Precisely. She is not an actress, not yet – may I present Miss Da Silva? Of Green Street? She lives there with her grandparents. Miss Da Silva, Miss Lucas – '

Miriam bowed her head, but she looked a little puzzled. 'How d'you do. Is this your house, Miss Lucas? I mean – ' She giggled. 'Perhaps I shouldn't ask. I know gambling is really rather – ' She looked up at Ambrose. 'I'm being rather indiscreet, I think, Ambrose, aren't I?'

'Just a little, my dear,' Ambrose said. He was staring at Lewis. 'Who did you say you are?' he asked abruptly.

'More to the point, sir, is to ask who *you* are,' Claudette said. 'I am a little surprised to find – shall we say – a young *lady* here. Did you bring her?'

Miriam looked at her, her brows slightly furrowed. 'But there are lots of ladies here!' she said. 'I saw them downstairs – and in the gaming room. Oh dear, I really shouldn't mention that, should I? Ambrose told me – '

'I'm glad you were at least discreet enough for that, sir!' Claudette said, her voice low but unmistakably angry. 'I am amazed, however, that you should bring so – so young and inexperienced a lady here. It is not a suitable place at all for – '

'For a well-bred girl,' Lewis said. 'I really think, Miss Da Silva, that you should return home, you know. And you should not come here again. It truly isn't suitable.'

'And who are you to decide what is or is not suitable for Miss Da Silva?' Ambrose said furiously. His face was white now with barely controllable fury and a certain amount of anxiety. He knew as well as anyone that he should not have brought a girl like Miriam to this house – and he also knew that one of the private rooms on the third floor was booked in his name and several bottles of champagne were cooling there waiting for them. Ambrose's plans for this evening had been very different to the way it was turning out.

'My name, sir, is Lackland,' Lewis said crisply. 'Lewis Lackland. We have met before.'

'Lackland.' Ambrose stared at him, his face blank. 'Did you say – '

'We are distant cousins, as you seem to have forgotten. I work with your father at Queen Eleanor's Hospital. Perhaps you remember now.' The time had undoubtedly come, he felt, to put all his cards on the table. 'I would be loath, Mr Caspar, to – shall we say *discuss* the events of this evening with your father, but I really will feel some compulsion to do so unless Miss Da Silva leaves at once. And does not return. *Ever.*'

Claudette nodded in firm agreement. 'Mr Lackland is quite right, Mr Caspar,' she said. 'I am glad of course to welcome gentlemen at any time. But this is not a place for ladies, as I'm sure you know perfectly well – '

Ambrose stood there with his teeth tightly clenched, staring first at Lewis and then at Claudette while Miriam looked up at him, her face creased even more. 'I wish someone would explain to me what all this fuss is about,' she said pettishly. 'I know you have gambling here, and that's rather fast, but the place is full of ladies! Why shouldn't I be here too? I like playing roulette! It's a very amusing game, and I think Grandpapa is quite wrong about gambling, isn't he, Ambrose? Why, I won twenty-five sovereigns last time we were here and – '

'Well, my dear, you must accept that win as your last. I cannot possibly agree to allow so young a lady as yourself to visit this house!' Claudette said sharply. 'It is not suitable for a débutante. And that is the end of the matter. I am sure we can rely on Mr Caspar not to bring you again. *N'est-ce-pas, m'sieu?*'

She went to the door and held it open. 'Perhaps you will allow me to see you on your way – ' She looked out of the door and beckoned. 'Edward, Mr Caspar and Miss Da Silva are leaving. Please find their wraps, will you? Good night, Mr Caspar, Miss Da Silva, I am sorry we cannot continue what might have been a pleasant association, but I am sure you understand that it just cannot be – ' and she opened the door wider, so that Ambrose and Miriam could see the footman waiting to escort them to the front door.

After a moment Ambrose put his hand under Miriam's elbow and raised her to her feet, and led her towards the door.

He stopped for a moment as he passed Lewis. 'You bounder!' he said in a low tight voice. 'You rotten cad! I'll give you what's coming to you for this, you see if I don't – how dare you – '

'If you've any sense at all you'll keep very quiet indeed about it,' Lewis said, as Claudette took Miriam's hand to lead her on her way. 'I'm not sure it isn't my duty to tell your father exactly what it is you're doing with this girl. You know as well as I do that to bring her to this sort of place is – '

'And what are you doing here, then, if you're so high and mighty? If you can blab, so can I. A fine thing if my father hears one of his surgeons comes to a place like this!'

Lewis laughed at that. 'You really are a fool, aren't you? As if he'd give a damn! There's nothing wrong with the house as far as I'm concerned, or for any man come to that. But I don't bring innocent girls here. So blab if you like – but if you've any respect for that child's reputation you'll keep quiet. Now get out! My temper's short and fraying fast. If I have to look at your stupid face any longer, I'll push it in. Good *night*, Mr Caspar,' and he thrust him aside and went out, walking swiftly to the back staircase and the privacy of his attic. He was shaking like a leaf now, and could trust himself no longer not to let his feelings show.

She came to him when the rooms closed at last, already undressed and with her hair loose on her shoulders. He was lying on his consultation couch, his hands linked behind his head, staring up at the skylight which was still dripping with rainwater.

'Well, my dear, that was quite a little episode there! Who are those people? I gather the girl's respectable, but – '

'Don't you remember her? She was at Nellie's the night you went there with your hand – '

She frowned and then her brow cleared. 'Yes – of course, I'd forgotten – well, well. But why should that stupid young man bring her here? And book a room, too?'

Lewis sat up and stared at her. 'What was that?'

'He'd booked a room. Champagne on ice, and instructions not to disturb them till tomorrow. It's annoying, because now of course the room's wasted. And I turned the Earl of Mark away – '

'Christ!' Lewis said loudly and she put her hand on his shoulder and peered into his face.

'What's the matter?'

'What's the bloody man up to? That girl isn't one of – what's he *doing*?'

'Well,' Claudette said judiciously. 'It sounds as though he had intended a little seduction, wouldn't you say? Interesting – '

'Interesting? Is that all you can say?' Lewis said wrathfully and pushed her aside and swung his legs over so that he was standing beside the couch staring down at her. 'That bastard trying to – *interesting*?'

'But what is it to you? I mean, I know they're your cousins, but they've not shown all that much concern for you, have they? Why should you care what they do? As long as they don't do it here, there's no problem.'

172

'You make me sick, Claudette!' he said and his voice was thick with anger. 'D'you know that? Did you see the child? She's little more than a schoolgirl. And a damned rich one, into the bargain. You should just see the grandparents' house. She's obviously in line for a fortune – and that piece of – my God, have you no morals at all?'

She lifted her brows at him coolly. 'When they make sense, *mon brave!* But I don't see that I've any moral involvement with a pair of people who mean nothing to me. As for you – ' She shrugged. 'They're your cousins, I suppose, even if they have treated you like street dirt. You can take an interest if you like. Though I'd have a closer look at my own morals before I meddled if I were you.'

'What do you mean?' He had been marching about the room, but now he stopped and stared at her. 'I'm only interested in protecting a girl who's obviously at great risk of being – '

'Oh, Lewis, for heaven's sake! You're talking to me, you know, not one of your half-wit patients! You've obviously got a *tendre* for the girl. Haven't you? And I must agree she's very pretty – if rather silly. And an heiress you say? Well, I dare say you could do worse – '

'Shut up,' he said quietly. 'Do you hear me? Shut *up.*'

She stood up and pulled her wrapper more closely around her and shook her hair back from her shoulders.

'With pleasure. It really is no concern of mine. I promise you they'll never come here again, all right? I'll see to it that, if Caspar ever shows his face here, he'll be shown the door. Will that satisfy you? And now do come to bed! I'm exhausted, really exhausted.'

'I'm going back to the hospital,' he said curtly, and went over to the chair on which he had left his overcoat and hat, and she watched him with her head on one side.

'Oh, my dear, then I was right,' she said softly. 'You do admire that child. But how difficult for you! Do you intend to pursue her?'

He stood there with his hat in his hand, feeling the anger drain out of him at the sound of genuine concern in her voice. 'I don't know,' he said after a moment. 'How can I? As you say, the girl's as rich as Croesus, and me – it's not to be thought of.'

'I don't see why not,' she said. 'I think of a great many unthinkable things.' She hugged herself for a moment and her eyes seemed to glaze as she thought thoughts of her own. 'Very unthinkable. And you know, sometimes they happen. If you want them enough – '

He looked at her, his forehead creased. 'You don't mind?'

'Eh? Mind what?'

'Dammit! That I – that I care for another girl? When every week I come here and – '

She came and stood close beside him, and set her hands on his shoulders. 'My dear boy,' she said softly. 'We are *friends*, real friends. We do not own each other. I do not hold you in any sort of thrall, or you me. If we were married or even betrothed, it might be different. But we are not. Just friends. Very *close* friends.' She lifted her mouth to his and gave him that familiar tongue-flickering kiss that always aroused him so. 'Now dear one, come to bed. I'm beyond exhaustion, almost, and if I don't lie down soon I shall fall down. Leave it now – there's no harm can come to your little cousin tonight. Not after the fuss that went on. Anyway, I checked with Edward. The cab was told to take them to Green Street, and she should be safe enough under her own grandparents' roof! Leave it till the morning when you feel better. Now come to bed.'

So he did. But not to make love. He lay there beside her, cradled in her arms, her breath warm on his chest, and watched the darkness shading into dawn against her bedroom window, and thought hard. He had a great deal to think about, after all.

16

Not that his thinking got him very far. Really there were only three salient points. One, that he was besotted with a girl with huge eyes and an enchantingly pretty face, and secondly that she was exceedingly rich. Even if his own gorge hadn't risen at the idea of pursuing an heiress there was no chance that her family would ever consider him as a possible husband for so special a person. They'd be mad if they did, he told himself. They must, surely, be constantly on the watch for fortune-hunters.

Which brought him to the third point: Mr Ambrose Caspar. Was he fortune-hunting? Lewis knew nothing of the man's activities, apart from the facts that he was Freddy Caspar's son and had been squiring Miss Da Silva for some time, since May at least, if not earlier. Freddy was obviously a rich man in his own right, so his son could hardly be a pauper, as Lewis regarded himself. He seemed not to have any employment, so was probably a gentleman of leisure, unlike Lewis who had to earn every penny he had. And Miss Da Silva clearly liked and trusted him, and was on happy close terms with his parents – certainly his father. All of which added up to a highly suitable match which surely the girl's grandparents would approve.

Yet Caspar brought the child to a house of assignation, and had booked a room. Which suggested surely that his plans were far from honourable. Why not just marry the girl and be done with it? He could hardly be planning just to enjoy a romp with her and then go on his way whistling. There were actresses for that sort of game; surely a man didn't need to go fishing in his own family's pond for such adventures?

There was, of course, another possibility; that Miss Da Silva was far from being the innocent well-bred child she seemed; that she was a girl with a taste for sensuality which she was prepared to gratify in less than respectable surroundings. But that he dismissed from his mind almost as soon as it entered it; besotted he may be, but he was not entirely devoid of sense. Miss Da Silva, for all her charms and beauty, was no great intellect. She was quite unable to dissimulate, of that he was certain. She was a much indulged girl who gave little thought to consequences, doing only what she wanted to do when she wanted to do it, and it had clearly never occurred to her that her escort was anything more than an amusing companion.

So, what was he to do about the situation? Lewis was still thinking after he had left Claudette asleep at Somerset Street and was walking back to the hospital through the early morning bustle of the Strand. Go and knock Caspar down, after telling him that he knew he was trying to seduce Miss Da Silva? Highly satisfying though that would be, would it do any good? The man would pick himself up, and then go on in the same way.

Tell the girl's family? That would make sense, perhaps. Freddy could be told bluntly that his son was –

Lewis shook his head at himself, and walked faster. Dammit, that would be impossible. He liked the man and enjoyed working with him. How could he possibly go on at Nellie's if he interfered in his private family affairs? That would never work.

Go to Green Street and tell her grandmother then, and warn her that the child was at risk? He thought of the large old lady in green overflowing her sofa and tightened his lips. She'd hardly listen to him, after the poor impression he'd made on her at their last meeting, and anyway, would she believe him?

Who was he, after all? A distant connection, a poor man, just another surgeon at her son's hospital. Perhaps after the rich girl for himself. She'd send him off with a flea in his ear. 'And I wouldn't blame her,' he whispered, as he took off his coat in his small room on the top floor of the hospital's main building and put on his working-coat, and then made his way to his brief breakfast in the stuffy surgeons' dining-room behind the operating theatres. 'I wouldn't blame her.'

There was really only one thing he could do, he told himself as he chewed leathery cold toast and drank stewed tea; breakfast at Nellie's was a far from enjoyable repast. Only one thing. Talk to Miss Da Silva herself. She might be a silly giggly girl, but surely she wasn't beyond plain speaking. It had been obvious that she had been quite mystified last night by the fuss; she had no idea that Somerset Street was anything more than a gambling-house. Well, she would have to lose some of that innocent bloom, and be told –

The morning's work was a great help. While he was lancing boils and setting broken wrists and dealing with suppurating ears he could not think about anything other than the work he was doing, and he went doggedly through the rows of patients who shuffled their way along the benches as their turn arrived, waiting with the resigned patience of the very poor who never expected their own time to be anything but expendable.

By two o'clock the press of patients had eased up, and only half a dozen or so remained to be dealt with. Lewis stretched his tired back and nodded at young Mr Nicholls, the newest of Nellie's house surgeons, who had just arrived to work the afternoon in casualty having spent his morning dealing with patients on the wards.

'Nicholls, can you manage here?' he asked him. 'I don't like to leave you, but I have some private business to attend to, before I see my ward patients. I'd like to be away till – oh, about six. I'll finish the evening for you, if you can hold the fort till then.'

Nicholls' eye brightened. 'Glad to. I've been given a pair of tickets for the Gaiety and I thought I'd have to waste them. Great – there's a rather charming nurse on the children's ward – '

'The Gaiety – ' Lewis looked blank for a moment. 'Oh, damn and blast.'

'What's the matter?'

'I'm supposed to be going to the green-room party there tonight after the performance. I'd forgotten.'

Nicholls' face fell. 'Oh, well, I suppose it doesn't really matter – '

'No, you go. I can come on later. Peter Charterhouse is on call after midnight, isn't he? Well, that'll have to do. I'll go then. If I don't, she'll never forgive me.' He grinned a little crookedly at Nicholls. 'Women!'

'Is that the pretty actress you go around with?' Nicholls winked knowingly. 'A lovely little French salad, that one – we've all noticed her.'

'I'm sure you have,' Lewis said dryly, and went to snatch some much needed lunch before setting off for Green Street. That was another reason for not speaking to Freddy about his son's behaviour. The walls in this place had ears; there was nothing that happened among Nellie's doctors and nurses that did not become common knowledge and a rich spicy stew of gossip in a matter of hours. And though Lewis would not at all object to young Caspar being talked about, he'd object most strenuously to having Miss Da Silva's name part of the currency of the surgeons' dining-room. They were a ribald lot in there –

So he shored up his resolve to face the girl and warn her. That it would be a disagreeable task was undoubted; but he never for a moment thought that he would not succeed in his mission. Which was, for a usually sensible man, rather surprising.

So he was at first dumbfounded and then angry when she laughed at him. He had taken a hansom cab to Green Street, almost enjoying the ride through the busy clean-washed streets for at last the rain had stopped and there was an autumnal nip in the air as clouds scudded busily across London's pale blue skies. The park was still green, but here and there a tinge of yellow on the edges of leaves warned of the end of the summer, and he pulled his coat more closely about his shoulders as he stood on the doorstep of the big house waiting for an answer to his knock.

The butler let him in without a murmur, which comforted him; he had wondered whether in fact he would be denied access to Miss Da Silva and made to come back another day, so it was with a light step that he climbed the broad and very thickly carpeted stairs to the double drawing-room. But he stopped short in the doorway, a little startled at the sight of the cluster of girls who were sitting about in elegant droopiness on the plush sofas, their skirts a froth of lace and silk about their ankles.

They had been babbling cheerfully, but came to a stop as he stood there, all staring at him, and he thought for a moment of the rows of people with whom he had spent his morning. There had been girls of this age, eighteen or so, among them, but they had not looked like this. These girls could have belonged to a different species, with their thick glossy hair and sleek figures and shining soft skins. This morning's girls had been scrawny and grey with fatigue and the ever-present hunger that they accepted was as natural as the sky above their heads. These girls in the sumptuous drawing-room didn't live on bread that had been polluted with chalk, and rotten potatoes and stewed tea and beer, with an occasional herring to add a relish, as the girls of Covent Garden did; and the awareness of the chasm that yawned between his morning and his afternoon sharpened his mood into a sort of anger, so that

179

when he spoke his voice was rougher than he had meant it to be.

'I came to see Miss Da Silva. On a private matter,' he said loudly, and the girls looked at him blankly, and then at each other. 'A private matter,' he repeated.

Miriam had been sitting on a large sofa with a girl on each side of her and now she stood up, her face rather pink.

'Mr Lackland,' she said a little stiffly. 'Good afternoon.'

'Good afternoon,' he said crisply. 'I am sorry if I disturb you, Miss Da Silva. I had not thought that you might be giving a party – '

She looked around at the other girls and then at him, her brows slightly raised. 'A party? Hardly, Mr Lackland. Just the normal morning calls, you know.'

'Morning calls? It is almost three o'clock!'

'So? Morning calls are always paid in the afternoon!' she said a little pettishly.

One of the girls behind her clapped her hands. 'Oh, Miriam, my dearest, he is an *Australian!* I am sure of it! My papa has an acquaintance who speaks in just such a manner and he is Australian! Are you Australian, Mr Lackland? Of course there people probably pay their morning calls in the middle of the night, for they are far further behind than we are! And we have got as far as three o'clock!' And they all giggled, a shrill little babble of sound that made him think of the way the sparrows shrieked in the plane tree outside the house in Somerset Street.

'No doubt, madam, no doubt. But I never pay calls at any time, so I'm not the person to ask.' Deliberately he allowed his vowels to flatten back into the accent that he had been beginning to lose here in London, and the girls giggled again and then Miriam said sharply, 'You wished to speak to me?'

'Yes – if you could spare some of your valuable time. I have to get back to the hospital soon – ' It seemed important to him suddenly to make it clear to this collection of empty-headed dolls, each wearing a dress that had cost the price of a month's food or more for the beshawled ragged creatures he had spent his morning with, that he was not as they, but one of the world's workers. But it was a pointless exercise, for they were already chattering to each other and giggling again, as Miriam came forward in a susurration of silk.

'We can go to the morning-room for a few moments,' she said and marched out of the door, not turning her head to see if he was following.

The morning-room, a large and almost equally sumptuous apartment on the floor below which looked out on to a charming garden, was bright and warm and he felt his face dampen as sweat broke out on it, but he couldn't be sure whether it was due entirely to the warmth, or to the proximity of the girl now standing with her back to the marble fireplace, and staring at him. She was wearing a lilac-coloured gown of heavy silk, its skirt pleated and trimmed into a sculptured perfection that showed off her extremely narrow waist to great advantage, and with huge sleeves on the snug and equally heavily pleated bodice, which gave her hands an ethereal look. But there was nothing ethereal about her face, which was set in a very mulish expression.

'What are you doing here?' she said, with an attempt to be both remote and angry, but sounding only childlishly cross. 'You've no right to come meddling here at all, the way you did last night!'

His pulse was thumping in his ears. God damn it, why did she have to have this wretched effect on him? He hadn't suffered this sort of madness since he'd been a schoolboy. Mad, mad, mad –

'I've every right,' he said gruffly. 'The right of any man who sees something wrong going on and wants to put an end to it.'

'Really, you're the most ridiculous creature I've ever had to do with!' she exploded at him. 'I've seen you but twice in my life, and you think that gives you permission to come and tell me I mustn't go to a gambling-house and – '

'Oh, gambling!' he said, almost wearily. 'Gambling isn't important! You've obviously got far more money than you know what to do with, and if you want to waste it throwing it around on stupid games, that's your affair. I don't care a pin if you gamble every penny you own down the drain. It might do you good if you did – then you'd find out what life is really like!'

She shook her head at him, totally bewildered. 'I think you're mad! I know you're supposed to be some sort of relation – but you're quite, quite mad.' She turned towards the bell pull beside the fireplace. 'I'm going to have you removed at once before you do something dangerous – '

He was across the room in two great strides, pulling her back. 'You can ring in a minute,' he said. 'When I've said what I've come to say.' She felt extraordinarily soft under his hands. He'd taken her by the waist, and he registered somewhere deep in his mind that she was not as tightly corseted as most women were. Her shapeliness was her own. Oh, God, this was mad –

'Look, I don't want to alarm you.' He spoke more gently now, for she was staring at him with real terror in her eyes, and he let her go. 'I dare say I do seem to be behaving oddly. But this is an odd situation.'

Deliberately he turned away and went and sat down on one of the chairs near the window well away from her. 'Look, here I am. I can't hurt you here, can I? You can run to the door and out of it without any hindrance. But please don't. Let me talk to you. It really is necessary that I should.'

She moved to the door at once and then, as she reached it, stopped and turned round, her curiosity pushing down her alarm. 'Well?'

'I came to tell you – ' he stopped and swallowed and started again. 'That house in Somerset Street isn't just a gambling-house. It's also a – it's a divan.'

She stared at him, uncomprehending.

'A house of assignation. A brothel, damn it! The women you saw there weren't like you! They're – actresses and such-like who make a good deal of money out of the men who go there to gamble. Is that clear enough for you?'

She had gone very red, and now the colour was receding to leave her looking pinched. 'I don't believe you. Ambrose would never – '

'Oh, yes he would. He did,' he said brutally. 'The man's dangerous, you stupid child! Thoroughly dangerous! He'd booked a room last night.'

'A room?'

'Yes!' He almost shouted at her. 'A private room! For you and him, obviously. I don't know what sort of – what arrangement exists between you two, and it's none of my affair, but you ought to know that whatever your plans are, his seem to be different. He's a very dangerous person for you and if you've any sense at all, you'll keep well away from him.'

That was when she laughed. She had listened with her mouth half-open, and then, as he finished, stood there staring at him, and then shook her head, and said flatly, 'You're mad,' and laughed. And turned and pulled the door open and went running away up the stairs.

17

Had he been able to get a message to Claudette in time to tell her that he would not be there, he would have cut the party altogether. The last thing he wanted tonight was the noise and jollity of a lot of bouncing self-important theatricals. But he felt it would be wrong to let her down, for she had made a particular point of asking him to be there; it was her first visit back to the Gaiety since she had left, and she needed, she had said, some support.

'I will feel strange,' she had said. 'No, don't look so unbelieving. Even I can have my moments of uncertainty. Especially now I have – now I'm here. So don't forget. I'll be counting on you.'

That had been last week, and he felt that his promise must hold, despite the intervening events that were now so much exercising his mind.

Which indeed they were. He had gone back to Nellie's in a cold rage; how dare she laugh at him? How dare she be so stupid? And what was he to do now? For he couldn't just wash his hands of the affair, however stupidly she behaved. She was at risk of damage, and needed protection. If she hadn't the wit to look after herself, someone else would have to do it for her. And as far as he could tell, he was the only one available. Anyway, there was this crazy infatuation –

The afternoon had been a tangle of work, for when he reached his ward he found that a woman who had had an ovarian cyst removed the previous afternoon had slipped a tie, and was bleeding fiercely into her abdomen. She had been returned to the operating theatre when he arrived, and a thankful Mr Nicholls had immediately relinquished his place at the patient's side to Lewis, who had precious little time in which to scrub his hands and apply the carbolic spray before reopening the incision and searching for the bleeding point. He found it, his hands almost wrist deep in free blood, and managed to secure it with a firm horsehair suture, cursing under his breath meanwhile as the anaesthetist fretted and fussed with his bottles and masks over the woman's pinched and pale face.

She was carried back to the ward in a parlous state, and he spent the rest of the afternoon supervising the fluid replacement she needed, with his own hands trickling the sugar water through the rubber tube into her rectum, not fully trusting the vital task to the nurses. She almost died twice as the afternoon ticked away, but somehow held on to the thread of life and by eleven o'clock seemed to be in rather better condition. She was fit now to be left to the care of Mr Charterhouse, who was the night duty surgeon, and Lewis was free to stop work.

But it was too late to get a message to Claudette, which meant that, like it or not, he had to bath and change his clothes, putting on his modest evening frock-coat, which, though it fitted him well, enjoyed no satin trimmings or elegant braiding as did that of most men of fashion, and make his way to the Gaiety stage door.

He almost turned and went back the way he had come when he got there. The small lobby by the stage-keeper's little box was athrong with men, their evening capes swinging on their shoulders to give glimpses of ice-blue and crimson satin, and their glossy curly brimmed toppers set to one side of their heavily brilliantined heads with great rakishness. There was much flourishing of Malacca canes and twinkling of monocles, which were all the rage this year, even those with perfect sight feeling out of things unless they too had a gold-rimmed glass disc to dangle on their gleaming shirt fronts on a silk ribbon, and the place was clacking with the most inane chatter Lewis could ever remember hearing.

But a promise was a promise, and anyway he felt obscurely guilty about Claudette. She claimed to be no more than his friend, but she had spoken of the fact that they were neither married nor betrothed. Could it be that she wished they were? She was a lively and independent young woman, and well able to take care of herself, and her ailing father, but she was still a woman; marriage and home and the hope of children of her own must surely figure in her plans for her own future, as it did for every other female. And he had used her for his own needs shamelessly.

He stood in the narrow corridor that led from the stage door to the green-room, letting the other men on their way there push past him, smelling the violet-scented brilliantine on their heads mixed with the rich effluvium of greasepaint and stale fish-glue from the scenery and coal gas from the hissing lights that lined the way, and thought about marriage to Claudette.

He thought of her body, soft and yielding, yet oh so knowing, so well able to tweak the tiredest of emotions into new life, and the comfort there was to be found in her laughter, for she regarded love as an amusing pastime rather than a solemn rite, and laughed a lot when other women might have sighed or wept or moaned. He thought of Claudette in his arms every morning, and not just once a week. Of Claudette ministering to all his needs and not just – the vision shattered. He could not see Claudette ever being other than she was; cheerful and amusing enough, but always more concerned with her own needs than anyone else's. Could she be the sort of wife a busy surgeon needed?

Could Miriam Da Silva, with her soft undulating waist and her huge eyes and her extraordinary effect on him be such a wife? Miriam with her money and her spoiled childishness, and her flat refusal to listen to him?

'Damn,' he said aloud, and went stumping down the corridor towards the noise coming from the green-room. He needed a drink.

The place was jammed with people and it took him some time to push his way through the chattering crowd to the table at the far side where he knew wine was available, for he had visited this green-room with Claudette before, when she was still at the Gaiety. He found himself a glass of claret-cup and drank it thirstily and had it refilled at once by the sweating, hectically busy man behind the table before turning to survey the crowd and find Claudette. He would see she was comfortable, stay a half-hour or so and then be on his way back to his bed. He needed sleep, and needed it badly.

His brows clamped down hard as he saw her at last. She was standing in the middle of a group of men, looking very fetching in a gown of deep crimson ottoman silk, and with an aigrette twinkling with crystals set in her hair which had been curled on her forehead into the most exuberant of fringes. She was making much play with her ostrich fan and even above the hubbub Lewis could hear her being very French indeed, with trills of the most silvery laughter pealing from her lightly rouged lips.

Needed him? Like the devil she did! he thought wrathfully and pushed his way towards her. He need not have come here at all! His face was set in very hard lines by the time he reached her.

'*Ah, mon cher Lewis!*' she cried as soon as she saw him. 'At last! M'sieu – ' She turned to the big man at her side. ' 'Ere 'e is! I promise you 'e would come, did I not? *Enfin*, 'e is 'ere! *Mon cher*, M'sieu Edwardes ees most anxious 'e should speak wiz you!'

'Ah, Dr Lackland!' the big man said.

'Mr,' Lewis said. 'I'm a surgeon, not a physician. Claudette – '

'Well, whatever you are, you're a genius at it,' the big man boomed. 'And I'm very grateful to you for what you did for our little Pearl.' He turned his head to look at the crowd. 'She's here somewhere, and looks as pretty as paint, never think she'd had a damned thing wrong with her – ah! There she is – Pearl, my dear – '

Lewis remembered the man now; the Guv'nor, and he shot a glance at Claudette who smiled limpidly yet warningly back at him.

Pearl came pushing through the crowd and stopped for a moment as she caught sight of Lewis, and then, moving a little less quickly, came to stand beside the Guv'nor.

'Hello,' she said in a small voice. 'Hello, Dr Lackland.'

'Mr,' Lewis said again, looking closely at her. She had left his ward two weeks ago, and had looked thin and peaky, but now she was magnificent. Her skin was as warmly coloured as it had ever been and her hair was a mass of golden curls piled on her small head in artful confusion. Her shoulders rose richly creamy from her extremely low décolletage and she looked altogether a picture of perfect womanhood. Sterile, destroyed womanhood, Lewis thought and his tired eyes seemed to prickle as he stared at her.

'You're looking well, Miss Frayling,' he said gruffly after a moment and at once she smiled sweetly at him, but there was a hint of appeal in her eyes. 'I am well. I've never been better. I just want to forget all about being ill and all, as though it never happened. I feel wonderful,' and she slipped her arm into the Guv'nor's. 'Everyone's been ever so sweet to me – it's as though nothing at all happened – '

He nodded. 'Good. That's the way it should be,' he said and after a moment she smiled brilliantly at him and then leaned forwards and kissed his cheek. 'Ta,' she said. 'Ta ever so much – ' and with another smile directed at the rest of the group she went drifting off again as a man in the most sleek of evening suits and the most gleaming of monocles came towards her with a glass of champagne in each hand.

'Wanted to thank you m'self,' the Guv'nor was saying heartily. 'You were good to my little lass – I insist they're all the best of girls, you know, so they all have to have the best of care. Rule o' mine. And I know my little Pearl couldn't have had better care than she had from you. Very grateful indeed, we are – and to Miss Claudette here, for finding you.'

He smiled down at Claudette and patted her shoulder.

'Sorry that the dear girl chose to leave us, of course! I'd have thought working here was the best life a beautiful girl could have, even if she had come into a bit o' money. But there, she would go and live a lazy life, hey, my dear?'

Claudette glanced up at him and then at Lewis. 'Indeed, m'sieu, I felt I 'ad to go and make room for someone else 'ere when my in'eritance came to me – but I am busy enough. I leev wiz my friend – *elle est très très charmante!* – in 'er 'ouse in Somerset Street and we are very comfortable togezer – ' She watched him carefully, but he just nodded and smiled and nodded again. Clearly the reputation of her house had not reached him, and Lewis felt rather than saw Claudette take a breath of relief. 'Also, eet is very pleasant to be able to invite my old friends 'ere at ze Gaiety to come to veesit wiz me – '

'Very nice too, my dear, very nice,' the Guv'nor beamed at her. He was beginning to look abstracted, and then brightened as someone beckoned him over the heads of the crowd. 'Damme, if that isn't me old friend D'Oyly Carte! And Gilbert with him! Well, well! Not often they cross over the Strand, hey? See you again, Lackland, old man, and thank you. Always grateful – ' And he was away, leaving Lewis standing beside Claudette, who turned to speak again to the men amongst whom she was standing. But he pulled her aside and said in an angry low voice, 'What was all that about?'

She smiled up at him, her eyes positively glittering with self–satisfaction.

'Obvious, I would have thought! I want only the best for my house, and the best is here, at the Gaiety! Girls, that is – I wanted to be sure to get the Guv'nor on my side. If he ever hears anything about Somerset Street now he'll just pooh-pooh it. I told him I'd come into a legacy and was living with a companion there – now when he hears where his girls go after the performances, there'll be no problems – bless you for coming. I knew he'd be pleased to see you – and Pearl does look much better. Doesn't she?'

'Does she?' he said. 'What about the parts you can't see?'

'Don't be tiresome, Lewis.' She tapped his hand with her fan, looking as gaily casual as she had throughout, but her low voice was sharp. 'She's grateful for the help you've given her and she's ready to go back to her own life. Who are you to judge it? What's the matter with you these days? You're full of judgements and complaints all of a sudden! Do hush – and,' she raised her voice a little, and turned back towards the group of men patiently waiting for her. ' – I want to introduce you to le Marquis de Collingbourne, Lewis, *mon cher!*'

She put her hand out to draw towards her the tall figure of a fair-haired man with the inevitable monocle screwed into his eye socket. 'Lewis is a great old friend, David! 'E 'as always been so kind to me, ever since we first met, so many years ago – abroad – ' She looked at Lewis challengingly. 'We are like brozzer an' sister, are we not, *mon cher*?'

'Oh, very fraternal,' Lewis said after a moment, and grinned ferociously, baring his teeth in the most obviously insincere manner, but Collingbourne seemed not to notice.

'Ah, good to meet yah, doncherknow. Yerss – good to meet yah! Good party, what? Pretty ladies – none so pretty as our mademoiselle here o' course, but pretty ladies, pretty ladies!'

'Very pretty!' Lewis said. 'Best there are. What would you give for the lot of them? Available as a job lot, I shouldn't wonder. Cash down – '

'What? Oh – yerss – very funny – very witty – ha ha!' Collingbourne said and blinked at him and Claudette, her chin up, laughed too, that same silvery trill but with an edge to it now.

'Lewis 'as always been ze great wit, David – 'e is most outrageous when ze fit is on 'im!' And she tapped Lewis' hand with her fan, a pretty, roguish gesture, while with her other she managed to pinch his thigh sharply through his thin trousers.

He reached out for another glass of wine as a waiter with a tray came on his perspiring way past them, and drank it at a gulp, and then reached for another. His thirst in this stuffy over-scented room was mounting, as was his recklessness.

'Oh, I'm often taken with fits,' he said. 'Fits of judgement, doncherknow?' He looked directly at Lord Collingbourne, grinning again. 'Like judgements about the sort of people who can spend more in one evening on one of these clothes-horses than men in the streets outside get to feed their families for a year. Doncherknow!'

Collingbourne stared at him, looking oddly blank as the light glinted on his monocle and then he let it drop to his chest. 'Not sure of your drift, old man,' he said stiffly.

'Aren't you? Well, why should you be?' Lewis finished the glass of wine and looked round for more. 'You haven't spent the day at Nellie's, up to your elbows in – ' He caught Claudette's eye and began to feel some shame at what he was doing. It was hardly fair to take out his anger about Miriam's laughter on her, dammit. Nor his fatigue. Nor his guilt about his work at Somerset Street which had come surging back at the sight of Pearl, who had in a sense been the start of it all. ' – Well. It doesn't matter. Care for another drink?'

'Yerss – ' Collingbourne said after a moment. 'Thirsty work, this – ' and Claudette smiled at him and beckoned the waiter back, and began to chatter about the new play *Fun On The Bristol* and how well it was doing, and Lewis watched her and listened to her and thought confusedly about how lovely she looked in her new gown, and how lovely she looked without it; which made him laugh suddenly and after a moment Claudette and Collingbourne laughed too, picking up his change of mood and glad to do it.

Across the room Ambrose was watching them. He'd seen him come in, and had at once moved to stand more in front of Miriam, so that she would not see him too. She had been behaving oddly all evening, already; the last thing he wanted to do was give her any further cause for alarm.

He'd tried all he could to make a joke of the previous evening's escapade. 'That madman!' he'd said to her, when he came to collect her, to take her to the opera. 'I must tell you – ah, dear Grandmamma!' as the old lady came slowly into the drawing-room. 'I hope you are well tonight? So sorry you cannot come to the opera tonight – they're doing *Lohengrin* you know, last night of the season – '

'Your grandfather is away in York, and I dislike the opera without him. And I am a little tired, my dear,' she had said, kissing him, and indeed even to his generally unobservant eye she seemed a little less than her usual self. Her face seemed a little drawn and she was somewhat breathless. 'I am sure you will enjoy it, however. Don't bring her home too late, now. She's had a great many late nights recently, and she's looking less blooming than she was – ' and she pinched Miriam's cheek.

Miriam was indeed looking rather pale tonight, and listless too, and he looked at her apprehensively as he led his grandmother back to the door where her maid waited to escort her to her room. ' – For I'm going to spoil myself and have an early night! – ' she told them. 'That damned man last night!' he thought viciously. 'If it hadn't been for him, I'd have been able tonight to stand in front of Grandmamma and tell her flat that we are to be wed, and there's nothing she could do but give her consent. *Bloody* man.'

'I will tell Mamma I saw you, Grandmamma,' he said. 'As soon as she returns from Baden Baden.'

His grandmother looked at him with her sharp knowing gaze as she leaned on her maid's arm and began the laborious climb to her bedroom on the next floor. 'I'm sure you will, my boy. She likes to be told she has a dutiful son, I'm sure,' and he looked a little put out and then managed a smile.

He wasn't smiling when he went back to Miriam's side. 'What is it, my dear?' he said with all the gentleness he could muster. 'You seem out of sorts tonight.'

'Out of sorts!' she said, in a little flash of temper. 'I have every right to be – '

She wanted to tell him about the horrid experience of the afternoon, the way that unpleasant man had frightened her so, but somehow she couldn't. Because unpleasant though the experience had been, the man himself had not been quite as nasty as she had thought, a fact she had realized as the afternoon drifted away and she lay on her couch in her boudoir, pretending to have a headache so that she would be left alone.

He had been quite interesting to look at, she had told herself, with his heavy unruly hair, and carved face. A face with just a few lines on it, she now realized, was much more interesting than a smooth one, even one embellished with luxuriant whiskers like Ambrose's. It had a – she had tried to put a word to it and could only come up with manliness. It had a manliness to it that was somehow comforting.

But how could she have found herself comforted by a man who sat there and told her that Ambrose was a bad person, trying to seduce her? It was nonsense, absolute rubbish. It had to be; Ambrose was her cousin, for heaven's sake! He had known her all her life, and clearly cared about her, for hadn't he been her constant delightful companion throughout the whole of the now almost ended Season? Of course he had! He would never harm her in the way that interesting – no, not interesting, horrid – man had said. Would he?

She looked at Ambrose again now, trying to see behind the familiar smooth face and the smiling crinkled eyes to the mind beyond, and couldn't. And after all, he did kiss her a great deal, and whisper naughty things rather often, but surely all that was a game? It had been for her – a silly amusing game. And if she'd thought about it at all she would have thought it was the same for him. And yet – perhaps it was true? Could it be –

He relied on instinct. He had nothing else. That last night's episode had alarmed her was clear, and he had somehow to defuse the situation. He could have tried coaxing – which would have been disastrous, for that would have convinced her he was trying to ill use her in some way. Instead, he became suddenly very masterful indeed.

'Miriam, you are being rather silly, I suspect. A stupid man said nonsensical things to you last night and you've allowed it to spoil your day today. Well, I won't have it. You're a silly little donkey and you should be beaten as donkeys are! Now come along. We go to the opera, and after that to a party. And you will smile and laugh and be your usual lovely self. Now do as you're bid!'

It had worked and she had capitulated and listened to *Lohengrin* and chattered about the other people around them as gaily as he could have wished. But the memory of the afternoon's events remained in her mind; and she still did not tell him of the visit. Which worried her rather. It made it seem to herself as though she didn't really trust Ambrose –

Now, at the party, she was trying to revive her flagging spirits with a little more champagne than she usually took. Somehow it was not as gay and sparkling here as it had been the last time she had come, with Cousin Mary. The glitter seemed to have gone out of the lights and the men seemed less exciting, though there were still admiring glances at her. But it wasn't the same; so she drank some more of the wine, trying to transfer its sparkle to her view of the proceedings.

Ambrose, beside her, was thinking hard. He'd had a very bad day, worried sick that that wretched man would do as he had threatened and tell his father. There was no doubt at all in Ambrose's mind that once his father heard, that would be an end to it. His allowance would be cut at once and he would be thrown on to his own earning ability. And his mother would be as likely to turn against him too, as not, remembering her reaction to his talk of a rich wife. Altogether an appalling prospect and one to be dealt with at once.

What were the remedies? To lie in wait for the unspeakable Lackland and beat him to a pulp would be agreeable, but would solve nothing; but what else was there? He could think of no way to silence the man, and it seemed his days of freedom were numbered, for his parents were due to return from Baden Baden shortly, and that would be that.

As the day wore on and he sat in his club in St James's drinking rather more brandy than he usually did in daylight hours he became more and more convinced that Lackland would behave like the cad he was and blurt it all out. What *was* to be done?

The answer was so obvious that he was amazed it had not come to him sooner. He had to do only as he had planned to do all along. That there would be trouble with Freddy as well as with his grandparents when they were faced with the *fait accompli* of what he was planning, he knew. But he wasn't worried about that. Once he had Miriam firmly in his grasp they could fuss till they were blue; he'd win in the end. So, he had to get Miriam firmly in his grasp, didn't he?

The problem was that he had been banned from the house in Somerset Street, and there was nowhere else he could think of persuading her to go which would serve as well. His own parents' house was shut up while they were away, since he had

chosen, fool that he was, to move into his club, and silly
though Miriam was she wasn't fool enough or wild enough to
agree to go to a hotel with him. The Somerset Street house
which she believed to be just a gambling establishment was
the only one he could use. But how?

And then he saw that not only was Lewis standing there on
the other side of the green-room, so was Claudette. He had not
seen her clearly before, in all the hubbub, but now, as the
crowd thinned a little, he could. That meant that if he and
Miriam left now and went to Somerset Street, they would be
admitted. Someone else must be in charge tonight. And maybe
he could get again the room he had lost last night? Why not?
The Season was almost over and people were leaving Town in
droves. There'd be room – '

'My dear,' he leaned closer to Miriam, who looked up at him
with slightly unfocused eyes. 'I think it's time we moved on –
and I want to show you that that stupid man last night was just
that. Stupid. Let's go and play a little roulette, shall we?'

18

Claudette, Lewis told himself, was getting more and more outrageous. She was flirting with Collingbourne in a way that was making that smooth-faced young man almost purr. Lewis had moved away from them, so irritated was he by her frenchified trills of laughter and so disgusted by Collingbourne's gullibility. Couldn't he see what a performance it all was? 'She'll be saying ooh-la-la next,' he told himself sourly and drank another glass of claret-cup. It was a good claret-cup with rather more brandy in it than was usual and he was feeling better for it.

He leaned against a table littered with glasses and drooping flowers and smilax trails and watched her over the rim of his glass as the crowd thinned out a little and people went off to Romano's and Rules and the Trocadero to eat lobster patties and drink even more champagne. Dammit, where was her *sense*? How could she possibly waste her time on such a flat, boring, dreary idiot as that? He scowled at Collingbourne who was now laughing with his head thrown back and his mouth wide open to reveal large, rather yellow teeth, and wanted, quite urgently, to push those teeth down his stupid throat.

Claudette caught his eye and smiled at him, but he stared back at her straightfaced, and after a moment she said something to Collingbourne who glanced up at Lewis and then nodded and turned and went pushing his way towards the door of the green-room, while Claudette made her way to Lewis' side.

'My dear boy, you look as sour as a basket of lemons! Why are you standing here sulking instead of coming to talk to – '

'I've better things to do with my time than chatter rubbish with an idiot,' he said loudly. 'That man is a useless hulk of – '

'Stop that at once,' Claudette said quietly but sharply. 'You may not like him – that's your right, I suppose. But there's no need to be insulting in public. He's gone to get my wrap, and his own, and to collect Polly Brown. She's a dear girl, and you'll enjoy her company. I thought we could all go on to supper at Somerset Street and – '

'With him? No thank you!' Lewis said and finished his drink. 'Nor do I need you to procure some female for me. I'm not one of your customers, Claudette, and I won't be treated as one!'

She was very still for a moment. 'No,' she said then, in a level voice. 'You are not. You are my friend. As David is, and as Polly is. My *friends*. I thought we could spend an agreeable hour or two together, that's all.'

'Friends?' he said, and he knew he was being unjust, and it made his voice harsher than ever. 'Friends? How can you make a friend of a half-wit like that?'

Suddenly she laughed, and came closer to him. '*Mon brave*, you're jealous! Oh, dear, dear, Lewis, I do adore you! You're actually jealous! Head over heels in love with another girl, yet jealous of me! I do find that delicious – '

'I am not!' he began wrathfully and she leaned forwards and set her fan to his lips.

'Of course you are! But why should you be? Have I not the right to make friends with whomsoever I choose? Just as you have? I don't try to control your feelings, Lewis. You really mustn't try to control mine, must you?'

'I'm not trying to control your feelings,' he said, still angry, but with a lower tone to his voice. 'I know perfectly well that

I – of course you're free to do as you choose. I just can't see what that man has that makes it possible for you to spend so much time with him.'

She pursed her lips judiciously. 'Close on a hundred thousand a year in rents,' she said coolly. 'And a good family. Just to start with.'

'So?' He looked at her and lifted his brows. 'Does that make him interesting? A friend worth knowing?'

'Perhaps not. But it would make him an excellent husband.'

'*Husband*? For you?' He laughed then. 'You're off your rocker. Do you think he'd marry you?'

She leaned against the table beside him and stood with her head bent, watching her fan as she tapped it rhythmically against her skirt. 'Why not? He's got to marry someone. And I'm more fun than most of the women he knows. And very knowledgeable about what a man needs in a wife. I'd make an excellent marchioness. I *intend* to be an excellent marchioness! You will see – '

'Oh, Claudette, stop being so – ' He shook his head, suddenly very tired. 'As if he or his *good* family would even consider you! An actress – or once an actress and now – '

'Why not?' she flared at him. 'Why ever not? Connie Gilchrist is going to marry the Earl of Orkney and be a countess! And Rosie Boote and the Marquis of Headfort are inseparable. She'll get him to the altar yet. What two can do, three can. And I shall – '

'Running a brothel?' he said softly. 'A Gaiety girl is one thing, but a madam?'

'I am running a restaurant and gambling-house!' she said furiously. 'Never you dare say otherwise! If some people choose to make use of my premises in other ways that's their affair! I have private dining-rooms for those who wish to eat and drink in peace and – '

'Oh, do stop trying to pull the wool over your own eyes, Claudette! You know as well as I do what you're doing! If you weren't concerned about the girls you provide *dining-rooms* for, what the blazes am I doing there? I'm not a cook or a waiter! I'm a doctor with a couple of most delicious specialities. Venereal disease and abortion – '

She stared at him, her face white with anger. 'How dare you, Lewis? How *dare* you? To blame me for – what you do, you do for your own reasons. If I choose to try to help the girls who come to my house and who are stupid enough to get themselves into trouble, is that something with which to castigate me? I am not – I take no money from anyone apart from the payment for food and drink that is consumed there, and a reasonable percentage of what crosses the tables. If you ever *dare* to suggest that I am making a profit from – '

He shook his head, more tired than ever now. 'I know – I know. No one pays you any money for the girls. There are some presents given, perhaps – '

'To Mrs Lovibond, not me,' she said at once.

'To whoever – it's not the money that matters. It's the – the – oh, dammit, woman, you know bloody well what I mean!'

'I know that you're a mean-minded jealous prig!' she said, and her voice was ice cold. 'One who can't face the results of his own actions, and seeks others to blame for them. Whatever you're doing at Somerset Street you do because you agreed to. No one twisted your arm. I thought you cared about people – *all* people, not just polite ones, respectable ones, mealy-mouthed *good* ones. Everyone. Including girls who have bodies they enjoy and who have the generosity to share them and are too silly to protect themselves. I thought you were a real man – the sort of man who understood women and the way we're punished for the accident of our sex. But you're the same as the rest of them – you want to use us and then make judgements about how wicked we are for letting you do it. You want to be comfortable and enjoy yourselves among people who won't despise you for what you are, and then despise the very people who make it possible for you to do just that – you want to be free yourself, but own us. You make me *sick* – '

She snapped her fan shut and stood there staring at him, white-faced, and then, as Collingbourne came through the door on the far side, turned on her heel and walked away with her head up, and he watched her go. He watched her shake her head as Collingbourne looked across at him, and put her hand on his arm and then link her other hand into the elbow of the pretty red-headed girl who had come in with Collingbourne. He watched as Collingbourne held the door open and the three of them went, leaving him to the wreck of a party in a room rapidly being denuded of guests, as weary waiters began to clear up the mess.

She was right, of course. He had been unjust, unkind, everything she said he was. She hadn't merited the way he'd treated her, and if she never spoke to him again, he richly deserved it. He rubbed his forehead with a tired hand and suddenly yawned hugely. His head was aching thoroughly now, and his mouth felt dry and sour. I need some water and some sal volatile and some sleep, he told himself muzzily. I've drunk far more than I should and I've behaved badly and this afternoon was hell and what am I to do about that wretched girl and I want to get today over and done with. I'm going to bed.

But he couldn't. Claudette's words hung over him like a pall, a weight of anger and pain and loss. She was his friend, the only real friend he had in this benighted town, and he needed her. He couldn't go to sleep knowing he had left her feeling so about him. He'd have to go after her, explain, apologize –

It's nearly two in the morning, he told himself, blinking blearily at his pocket watch. I've worked my tail off today and I'm tired, tired, tired. I've got to apologize – oh, God damn everything. I hate her. I hate Miriam. I love them both. I'm tired.

He had to go, and he knew it. He wrapped himself in his overcoat and pushed his hat to the back of his head and his hands deep in his pockets and set out to walk there. He was still muzzy with claret-cup, and, now he came to think of it, hunger. He'd hardly eaten a thing since his dismal breakfast, half a lifetime ago. No wonder the drink had gone to his head so nastily, made him so bad-tempered and difficult –

There you go again, he told himself as he walked along the Strand, now settling to its night-time silence with just a few other late home-goers scuttling along its shadowy pavements. Looking for excuses for your own bad behaviour. You get nothing out of a bottle that isn't already in you. If you're nasty and sour when you're drunk then you're a nasty sour person all the time. End of equation. Oh, God, I'm tired. I must find her, apologize, make friends again, get to bed. Tomorrow – I've got operations in the morning. A woman with a procidentia, and a man with a huge umbilical hernia. They're lying awake worrying about what I shall be doing to them in a few hours' time and I'm walking the streets of London sozzled with wine and not fit to talk to anyone –

By the time he reached Somerset Street he was a little less muzzy. The pint of water he had downed before leaving the Gaiety combined with the exercise of the walk had started to burn off the alcohol in him. His head still ached – it ached rather more in fact – and his mouth still tasted dry and foul, but he was at least clear-headed and his vision was no longer impaired by the hazy glitter through which he had scowled at Collingbourne and Claudette. But, he realized, as he shrugged out of his coat for the butler who let him in, other physical effects from his drinking were taking over. He needed a lavatory and needed it badly, before he could talk to Claudette. Painful though his conscience was, his bladder was causing him more distress at the moment.

The rooms were full and bustling and he could see a steady stream of men moving towards the doors of the upstairs hall that led to the lavatories. Damned place would be mobbed, obviously; he wasn't the only one who'd taken more alcohol than his kidneys could easily deal with. And anyway, that damned fop Collingbourne might be there and he wanted to see Claudette first, before facing him; he felt obscurely that he couldn't trust himself to be civil to the man until he'd put matters right between himself and Claudette – and knew that if he were uncivil first, he would have little chance of putting matters right afterwards. So, he must find another lavatory.

Upstairs, to the third floor where the rows of discreet doors gave on to the long, red carpeted corridor with its soft lights and statues and air of opulence. At the far end was a private bathroom complete with bidet and lavatory. Claudette – or was it Mrs Lovibond? – had thought of every aspect of the guests' comfort. He'd go there and then back to the restaurant below and find Claudette and be charming to her and polite to the egregious Collingbourne and then to bed and sleep. There was work to be done in the morning – just a few hours away.

He left the lavatory feeling much better. The pint of water taken from the elegant dolphin taps over the shell-shaped basin (for the Somerset Street house boasted all the most modern of conveniences, including that rare pleasure, water from the mains on every floor) and drunk out of his cupped hands had cleared his mouth a little and even seemed to dull the edge of his headache somewhat. He dried his face and hands, feeling rather more himself, and with a hint of humour coming back into him. Really, this whole episode was absurd – almost funny –

The corridor outside was still quiet, still opulent, and he began to walk along it to the far end where the staircase started. And then stopped.

It wasn't so much that the sound was an unfamiliar one, or even particularly distressing to his doctor's ears. Retching and vomiting were part of his daily experience, after all. It was the small sounds that punctuated the more obvious ones that seemed to reach down inside him and tweak his concern. Whoever it was who was being so ill behind one of these doors was suffering a great deal as a result. The little moans were pitiful, and were becoming more pitiful by the moment.

He stood hesitantly, trying to think. It was a rule of the house that when a customer had booked a private dining-room and the food or drink had been served and the cloth drawn, no one, but no one, entered again until the bell was rung. The whole point of these private rooms was their unassailability. Everyone knew that.

Yet – and yet. He stood there and listened and the diagnostic bit of his mind flicked over the possibilities. Over-indulgence in alcohol. That was the most likely cause. In which case no harm done if he left the wretch to get on with it. He or she would bring his heart up and be thoroughly miserable and might think twice next time before over-indulging again.

But the sounds coming from that room were more than that. There was real distress, and he worried. Acute gastric irritation? That could prostrate a weak subject in no time, and some of the people who came here were thoroughly weakened by the lavishness of their lives. A sudden apoplexy of the heart? He had seen many men die that way, collapsing with violent pain and being dreadfully sick and dying –

He couldn't decide what it was. Standing with a thick wall and a solid door between himself and whoever was suffering so would hardly enable him to make a diagnosis. But of one thing he was sure – a diagnosis had to be made. Whoever was making that sound was very ill indeed. As a doctor he couldn't ignore it. And wouldn't ignore it, however rigid the rules about privacy in these rooms. If Claudette or Mrs Lovibond didn't like it, then that was too bad.

He moved along the row of doors, listening intently at each one. It was from behind the third door that the sounds were coming and he knocked on the panels softly. There was no need to alarm any of the occupants of the other rooms –

The sound of moaning and retching went on, and he knocked again, a little louder, and this time the moaning seemed to get louder and even more piteous, and he waited no longer but turned the knob gently and pushed the door open.

The room was almost dark. On the far side a small table lamp was alight, with a red cloth hanging over it so that it threw only the faintest of glimmers. A table set with dishes was pushed to one side; it had obviously been used, because he could see the faint gleam of the silver covers on the sideboard, and the half-filled bottle on the table amid a tangle of dishes and crumpled napkins. Beyond it was a wide sofa and huddled on the sofa was a small shape. He could hardly see, so dim was the room and he moved forwards, peering at the sofa. The moaning had stopped for a moment and there was no movement from the figure that lay there in the shadows.

'Can I help you?' he said softly, and then again, but there was no reply, and he stood for a moment, uncertainly, and then closed the door behind him and moved closer to the sofa.

'You're ill,' he said. 'And I am a doctor. Can I help you?'

The shape on the sofa moved slightly and there was another soft sound, almost the ghost of a moan, and he moved closer. And then the door behind him opened and someone came in and closed it swiftly again.

'It's all right,' a voice said quietly and with a breathy urgency about it. 'I've got you some – ' The voice stopped and then said sharply, 'Who's there?'

'Put the light on, for heaven's sake!' Lewis said sharply, already knowing who had come in but not wanting to believe it, and he moved across the room towards the shaded light and twitched the red cloth from it, and then turned to stare at the newcomer.

Ambrose was standing there with a glass in his hand, and a face as white as the tablecloth on the table beside him. Lewis stared at him and then turned his head to look down at the sofa.

Miriam was lying there, her face chalk grey and gleaming with sweat and her eyelids half-closed so that a rim of white showed beneath the uprolled eyeballs beneath. She was breathing in tiny, very shallow breaths and was obviously very ill indeed.

19

The next half-hour went by in a blur of activity. He ignored Ambrose, turning at once to Miriam, checking her pulse, and immediately arranging her so that her head was set low and her feet were at a higher level. He rang the bell and as soon as the waiter came bustling in said tersely, 'Throw this man out – at once. Fetch Miss Lucas. And I want some things from the room upstairs. Move man. This is urgent!'

The waiter gave one open-mouthed stare at Miriam, and then nodded, bobbing his head like a doll on a string and went hobbling away as fast as he could and within moments the room was full of people.

Ambrose was still white and said not a word, glaring at Lewis with a wide-eyed fury that was unnerving in its intensity. Even when the footman, the tall and somewhat lantern-jawed Edward with shoulders that were twice the width of Ambrose's own, set his hand on his shoulder, he said nothing. But he stopped at the door and looked back and said in a tight voice, 'I shall call upon you Lackland. This is not the end of the matter.'

'You're bloody right it isn't,' Lewis grunted at him over his shoulder. He had taken off his coat and was in his shirtsleeves and waistcoat, and had pulled Miriam's gown down so that he could set his ear to her chest and listen to her erratic heart-beat. 'By God, it isn't. Get out of here – go on, Edward. Throw him into the gutter where he belongs and if you break his neck on the way, it'll be all to the good.'

'Treat him sensibly, Edward,' Claudette's voice cut across, cool and calm. 'Lewis? What's happening?'

'She's had a violent reaction to some food or other, I think – she's already had too much wine, obviously, but it wasn't that – you – ' He threw a glance over his shoulder at the still hovering waiter. 'What did they eat?'

'A chicken, sir,' the old man wavered. 'At least, they'd ordered it, like, but they 'adn't et none, yet. They 'ad a few oysters, like, to start with – '

'Oysters? That's what did it. Were they good?'

'Our oysters are perfect,' Claudette said at once. 'I check every barrel myself as they arrive. They're the first of the season, and came here straight from the sea below Colchester. There's no harm in them – '

'You – ' Lewis said then, as Edward, who had been waiting large and impassive and very threatening as Ambrose picked up his coat and hat, began to urge him with gentle shoves towards the door. 'How many did she eat?'

'Only one,' Ambrose said after a moment. 'She – ' He reddened. 'She's a Jew, so she's never had them before. They're forbidden to her religion. I thought she'd enjoy one – '

Lewis threw him the most withering look he could. 'Not enough to plan to seduce her, I suppose? You've got to make her break all her rules of behaviour? Man, you're the biggest, most lousy – '

'Not now,' Claudette said crisply. 'What will happen to her?'

Lewis looked down at Miriam. 'She's vomited all the damaging material, obviously. But the reaction is still the same – but I think she'll do. She needs some water put back into her. And sugar. And some salt, I think – '

'Salt?'

'She's lost a lot. It makes people very ill,' he said shortly. 'Like sunstroke in Australia. They sweat it out, damn near die for want of it. Get me those rubber tubes from the cupboard in my room Claudette, and a funnel – and send for some boiled water. And make sure that Caspar is out of here – he pollutes the air – '

When Claudette returned with his equipment and the boiled water arrived from the kitchen he mixed his potion, using sugar and salt from the dining-table, and then, with Claudette's help, gently turned Miriam to her side. He hesitated for a moment before uncovering her, remembering suddenly with embarrassment the fact that this girl had aroused feelings in him of the sort that did not normally exist between doctor and patient, and then pushed the memory aside.

Claudette, under his guidance, took off Miriam's gown and chemise, and then, carefully, her frilled and beribboned drawers.

Her small pink buttocks looked pathetic in the lamplight, like those of a child waiting to be spanked and he bit his lip and reminded himself savagely that this was a human organism in desperate need of care. Not Miriam, not a pretty child he loved, just a human organism. And he carefully and expertly pushed the rubber tube home so that the liquid in his jug could be poured into her intestines through the funnel.

It was a repeat of this afternoon. He had stood there in a ward in Nellie's performing the same task for a woman who had lost a great deal of liquid in the form of blood, and now he was doing it for a girl who had lost almost as much in a very different way, but the actions were the same and the need to be slow and deliberate in all he did was the same and he stood there, holding the tube gently kinked so that the liquid ran in oh-so-slowly, and could be absorbed, and not immediately thrown out again by the protesting gut, and tried to remember where he was, who the patient was and, indeed, who he was. It was as though he had been doing the same things for an eternity, and would go on doing them for even longer.

But at last, as the dawn sky outside pushed against the windows and thinned the lamplight to a puny dullness he withdrew the tube and stood staring down at her. She was asleep now, her greyness having given way to a more ordinary pallor, and her eyes were properly closed. She looked far from well, but equally far from desperately ill.

'I'll dress her again,' Claudette said in her practical voice, and he almost jumped. He'd forgotten she was here, and he looked at her, almost bewildered.

'Yes – and I must get her home,' he said after a moment.

'Home?' Claudette said, expertly sliding Miriam's drawers over her hips, and then settling her chemise over them. 'This child needs to go to bed to sleep this off, and you need to do the same, my friend. You're fit to drop.'

'No,' he said stupidly. 'No, I must – I have cases to operate on this morning. And she must go home – at once – '

'As for the cases,' Claudette said calmly, pulling Miriam's elaborate gown over her head, and settling it tidily about her ankles. 'If you were to operate on anyone in your state it would be sheer murder. You're not fit to shave your own face, *mon ami*. Look at your hands.'

He did, holding them out in front of him, obedient as a child, and stared at them. The fingers shook with a fine tremor and the harder he tried to hold them still the more they shook.

'You see?' she said. 'I shall telephone the hospital. Tell 'em you're ill and they must find another surgeon. No – ' as he opened his mouth to protest. 'Don't be so arrogant. You're not the only surgeon in London, nor even at your precious Nellie's. A man is entitled to be ill sometimes! Today it's your turn. I shall put this child to bed and then settle you, and then telephone. Then I shall go to bed myself. After I have breakfasted with Papa and seen him happy for the day – '

He shook his head stubbornly again.

'The hospital, yes – ' he said, and was surprised at how hoarse he sounded, and coughed, but the rough sound was born of his fatigue and could not be banished. 'You're right – I can't operate. Young Nicholls'll have to manage. Or postpone till tomorrow. But she – ' He looked at Miriam. 'She's got to go home.'

'Of course! – I don't want her here, be sure of that! But later – '

'Don't be stupid!' he flared at her, suddenly infuriated by what seemed to him to be her wilful misunderstanding of the situation. 'She's a respectable girl! What d'you think'll happen if she goes home during the day in these clothes, looking like that? After being out all night? She'll lose every atom of reputation she's got – '

'And that would be no more than she deserves!' Claudette snapped back at him. 'She's behaved like a – like a hoyden! What decent girl would allow herself to be brought to such a house as this? She can't even pretend she didn't know! She was told, wasn't she? Of course she was! Yet still the stupid creature comes here and makes trouble for all of us! Even you can't go on having a care for such a one as this!' Her righteous indignation would have been funny if it hadn't been so intense.

'Be careful, Claudette,' Lewis said, and his voice was almost menacing, he was so angry. 'She is a good girl – foolish, I don't deny. Easily led by a very wicked, cruel – ' He shook his head to clear it. 'Easily led, but not bad. And she's got to be protected from that bastard, you hear me? I'm going to get her home now, before any of her family realize she isn't there. It's not that much later than the finish of some of those balls they all rush around to, so she can get away with it. Either that, or I get a message to her family and have them come and fetch her. They'll keep what happened quiet, obviously, and none need know. They'll see to it she's properly protected in future – in fact – ' and he produced a sudden jaw-cracking yawn ' – in fact that's probably the best idea. If I turn up with her on the doorstep and I'm seen she'll be no better off than if she goes

home in the middle of the day looking like a ragbag. I'll get a
message to her grandmother – '

'Are you completely mad?' Claudette had covered Miriam
with a rug, and now stood, arms akimbo, staring at him over
her sleeping form. 'Tell her *grandmother*? Have her family
collect her here? And what will that do to me, hmm? What
about my house and our reputation, hey? Do you imagine the
grandparents of such a one as this wouldn't blame us for
letting the stupid creature come here in the first place? They
never lay blame where it belongs, that sort. Always look for
others – working others like me – to carry their guilt for 'em.
Well, I shan't have it. I'm willing to look after the stupid little
thing for the day if you want me to. If not – to hell with you!
Take her and do what you like with her. But bring anyone here,
and so help me – I'll – I'll – '

'What will you do, Claudette?' he said softly, staring at her.
'What will you do?'

She was silent, standing in the rapidly strengthening
morning light and glaring at him. And then she lifted her chin
at him.

'I'll do what I have to do to protect myself and my living.
And Papa's,' she said flatly. 'Even if that means – talking about
you. And what you were doing here in the first place.'

He nodded, slowly and heavily. 'I see, Claudette. I see.
That's the sort of friend you are, is it? One who'd really protect
someone she was supposed to care about? One who'd – '

She shook her head and put both hands out to him
appealingly. 'Dear, dear Lewis, please let us not fight. I really
can't bear it – and anyway it's so unnecessary!'

'Unnecessary? When you're being so heartless and – '

'Not heartless! Practical! What do you suppose will happen
if the girl's family come here and collect her? *Hein*? Will they
smile sweetly and say, "Oh thank you" and go on their way
with never a backward look? Or will they take one glance and
call all their lawyers and police and magistrate friends and

have us all clapped into jail? Hmm? Do think, man! I know you're dead-tired, but think, *je vous en prie!*'

He was silent, standing with his eyes screwed up to sharpen his now hazy vision, trying to get some sense into his mind. His fatigue was bone-deep and he could hardly think. But after a long moment he nodded.

'Yes. Yes, I see. You're not entirely heartless.'

She smiled a little thinly and looked down at Miriam on her sofa, who took a deep breath and turned over like a child half-waking from a dream. 'Not entirely.'

'I'd better get a cab,' he said, but he didn't move.

'You'll need a four-wheeler. And that won't be easy at five in the morning. I'll send Edward to the livery stables. He, *pauvre diable*, has had no sleep tonight either, of course. I'll have to pay him double for this night's work – '

She went away, turning off the light on the table as she went, and he stood there for another moment after the door closed behind her and then went to the window and opened it and leaned out, taking deep breaths of the damp morning air. It had rained some time in the past couple of hours and the pavements below were reflecting the shapes of the trees that lined the street and the pale sky above his head. It was all very quiet and very clean.

The air helped, and he felt his head steady and some of his strength returned to his muscles and he drew his head in again, and stood there staring out at the sky, not wanting to look at Miriam. But after a while he turned and came to crouch beside the sofa, to look down at her sleeping face.

She was lying with her hand curled into a fist and pushed into her cheek, so that she had the crumpled look of a baby. Her face was rosier now, and indeed she looked far less the worse for wear than he would have expected. So young, he thought, and touched the crumpled cheek with one finger. So young. So vigorous.

Her eyes opened, slowly, and she stared at him in the half-light of the morning, her eyes puzzled and unfocused.

'Ambrose?' she said sleepily. 'What's the – ' She closed her eyes as though she were about to fall asleep again and then snapped them open and lay very still, staring at Lewis. 'Oh, no,' she whispered after a moment. 'Oh, no!'

'Listen, my dear,' he said gently, and set his hand on her forehead. It was agreeably warm, not overheated nor yet with that dreadful cold clamminess that it had had when he had first examined her. 'You've been ill. You're better now, but you were ill. How do you feel now?'

She tried to sit up, but he put his hands on her shoulders and gently held her still. 'No, don't move. Just tell me. How do you feel?'

She frowned, like a child again, trying to find the right answer. 'I've got a pain. Here,' she said, and put her hand on her belly.

'I'm sure you have. You were – you were sick,' he said. 'The muscles have been strained. That'll feel better soon. But otherwise?'

'Otherwise – ' She shook her head, bewildered. 'Where's Ambrose?'

His jaw hardened as he clenched his teeth. The words that rose to his lips to describe Ambrose Caspar couldn't be said to this child. Not possibly. 'Gone away,' he said at length. 'Gone away.'

'Gone away? And left me alone?' Now she struggled again to sit up, and was so determined that he couldn't stop her. Shaky though she was, her young strength was too much for his own fatigue. 'Left me here? And – ' She looked around the room, at the mess on the dining-table and then at the sofa on which she lay and at once her face changed as a tide of colour rose in it. 'Oh, no,' she whispered again. 'Oh, no.'

'No,' he said firmly and loudly after a moment. 'No. You did nothing you need be alarmed about.'

She stared at him for a long moment, and then said, 'Are you sure? Nothing that – I had champagne, you see. Grandpapa always says ladies shouldn't take champagne for it makes them stupid, but I was – I was cross and miserable and I took a lot and – ' Her face clouded. 'Oh, what happened to me, Mr Lackland? Why are you here? And where is Ambrose and can I go home?'

'I'm here to look after you and I've sent Ambrose packing because he's a – he meant you no good, and I shall take you home as soon as may be. I've sent for a cab.'

'Ambrose,' she said after a second, and her eyes narrowed as she stared at her memories. 'He talked about – ' She laughed, uncertainly. 'He said we were to be married. It was too absurd – '

'Married?'

'Yes. He said after last night being here and in this room they would have to let us. And I was so – I was stupid, wasn't I? The champagne, and all – I only laughed at him. I remember that. It was all so silly, I laughed at him. But he said that we would, and last night it seemed such a funny idea that – ' Again she frowned. 'Then he said we would have supper and some more champagne and talk about being married. So we had supper – '

'And you ate an oyster which made you very sick.' Lewis stared down at her and felt the corners of his lips quirk as he thought about it all properly for the first time. 'You almost have to pity the wretch. He feeds you oysters from some mad notion about the way they make women lubricious, no doubt, and all they did was to make you very sick – '

'Oysters?' She looked at him closely. 'Did you say *oysters*? I ate – '

'That's right,' Lewis said. 'Only one, I gather, and then – '

She set her hand to her mouth and stared at him over it with wide horror-stricken eyes. 'Oh, no, not oysters – they're trafe.'

'Trafe?' he said, puzzled.

'Forbidden food. Not kosher. Oh, God did punish me, didn't he, for being so wicked?'

He smiled at that, and pushed her gently so that she had to lie down again. 'I don't know about punish you, my dear. He used 'em to protect you from something rather more worrying than eating food that is forbidden, I rather think – ' He laughed then, a sound of real amusement. 'It is funny, really it is – '

The door opened and Claudette stood there, a rug over her arm and looking at them with her face quite expressionless. He looked over his shoulder at her and then scrambled to his feet, dusting his knees a little awkwardly with both hands.

'The cab's waiting downstairs,' she said. 'He's a good man – won't talk more than he needs. I've oiled his palm so you needn't fret over that. Now get this wretched child off my premises and never let me see her here again.'

Miriam looked at her and then at Lewis, and after a moment her face puckered as though she were about to cry. 'Please Mr Lackland,' she said in a small voice, 'will you take me home? I do so want my Grandmamma.'

20

The journey through the rain-washed streets was almost idyllic. He sat there beside her, with one arm supporting her back and her head resting heavily on his shoulder and stared out at the pavements where a few working men hurried about their affairs, and at the sparse traffic that was beginning to appear as London stirred and woke and set about its daily business. She was warm and confiding and somehow reassuring there beside him; and in his own fatigue he slipped into an occasional doze and it was as though they were curled up together in the same bed the way married couples did, an idea which he let his weary imagination play with and much enjoyed.

But then they arrived and the cab drew to a stop outside the house in Green Street and he sat and looked down at her, still asleep, and tried to think what came next.

'This is it, Guv'nor,' the cabbie said hoarsely, opening the door for him. 'D'yer want the doorbell rung?' and he leered a little at Miriam, who had now woken and lifted her head to blink at the man in puzzlement.

'No – don't do that, for God's sake,' Lewis said swiftly. 'Miriam, my dear, have you a key?'

'She frowned. 'A key? What for?'

'The front door, of course! We have to get you into the house and to your bed before anyone realizes that you've not been home till now. Your front door key, child – give it to me – '

She shook her head at him. 'I don't have one. I've never needed one. I just ring the bell and my maid comes, if the other staff have gone to bed. Just ring the bell, Mr Lackland! Francine will come – '

'And so, I imagine, will half the household,' Lewis said dryly. 'No, that won't do. Is there no other way in?'

She giggled. 'We could go down the area and in through the kitchens – there's a door down there, I believe. Ambrose has come in that way sometimes – '

'Will that be open at this time of the morning?'

She yawned suddenly. 'I expect so. Maids get up early, don't they? I really don't know.'

'No, I don't suppose you do – ' Lewis said dryly, and then he sighed. 'I'll go and try. And for your own sake, pray that it is unlocked. Or you'll be – oh well – I'd better go – ' And he untwined his arm from behind her back and made to get out of the cab. But at once she was scrambling after him.

'I won't stay here on my own,' she said, 'I'll come with you – '

He stopped and looked down at her. 'You really are remarkably resilient, aren't you? A bare couple of hours ago you were as sick as – well, very sick. And now – ' He shook his head. 'I wish I had half your strength.'

'I do feel shaky,' she said, and took his arm so that he had to lead her out of the cab, and then stood beside him on the pavement, clinging to him. 'I do, truly. And I'm afraid that – will they be very angry with me?' And she looked up at the frontage of the big house with its blank-eyed curtained windows that gave it an air of faint menace.

'I don't know,' he said. 'How can I? Only you can know how much your family expect of you. You tell me – *will* they be angry, if they discover what has happened?'

'I think – ' She bit her lip and looked up again at the windows on the third floor, behind which she knew her grandmother lay sleeping. 'I think this time they may be. I've been very foolish, I think.'

'Very,' he said, and now it was his turn to yawn. 'Well, standing here will get us nowhere. Come on – no, don't wait,' he said to the still hovering cabbie. 'I'll find a hansom for myself when I leave – '

They stood side by side for another moment or two after the cab had gone clattering away and then Lewis took a deep breath and moved towards the area steps behind the ornate iron railings that flanked the steps leading to the front door. 'Pray for us,' he whispered, under his breath more to himself than to her, but her hand tightened on his arm.

They walked down the narrow, steep stone steps until they were standing in front of the green-painted door, and Lewis had reached forwards to try the handle when he felt rather than saw her sway beside him. And caught her just as she began to crumple. She was white-faced again and her eyes had rolled back in a faint, and though she recovered her consciousness swiftly she remained white and obviously confused. Clearly the energy she had displayed as she had got out of the cab had been a small and temporary spurt and the effects of the night had not completely worn off.

He lifted her a little awkwardly so that she was resting across his left shoulder and felt his back creak under the strain. She might be a slender and small-boned creature but she was well fed for all that, and carrying her hundred and twenty pounds with his own weary muscles was not easy.

He reached for the door knob and breathed again when it gave to his hand and the door opened. Someone somewhere was watching over them, that much was clear.

He was halfway across the dim stone-floored kitchen before he realized that the room was not empty. A small and very grimy kitchen-maid was on her knees in front of the big range, blackleading brushes in her hands and staring at him wide-eyed over her shoulder.

'Oh, damn,' he said and then shook his head at the girl and tried to smile. 'My dear, there's nothing to worry about. Miss Da Silva was – ah – she became a little overcome with the heat of the ball, and I brought her home. I did not wish to wake the entire household, so I – er– I thought I would bring her in this way.'

'Eh?' the girl said stupidly, and he gritted his teeth and said it all over again.

'Oh,' said the girl and scrambled to her feet and came to stand behind Lewis and stare up into Miriam's face. 'Is that there Miss Da Silva, then?'

'Well, of course it is!' he said, trying to brace his legs more firmly, for her weight really was pulling cruelly on his back. 'Surely you know your own employer! Or rather her granddaughter.'

' 'Oo, me?' the girl said and laughed and went back to the range, and flopped onto her knees in front of it to start working at the expanse of blackened metal with her brushes. 'Bleedin' likely that is, ain't it? I never claps eyes on them upstairs, do I? I'm just the bleedin' tweeny, that's me. I never sees nothin' but this bleedin' range and them bleedin' pots what I scrubs and that bleedin' cook, may 'er soul rot in 'ell and er feet drop off.'

Lewis was now leaning against the vast scrubbed wooden table in the centre of the kitchen. Miriam felt less heavy that way, because he could rest part of her weight on the table-top. 'Well, this is Miss Da Silva, take my word for it. And she will, I think, be grateful if you say nothing of having seen her this morning like this – '

The girl sniffed revoltingly and he thought automatically – adenoids. 'Would I be likely to say anythin'? Would anyone bleedin' well listen to anythin' I 'ad to say anyway? It's none o' my business. I got me range to think about. I don't care what you quality people does. S'long as I gets me work done, I gets me vittles, an' that's all as matters to me – '

He looked at her and saw for the first time how scrawny her back was in its calico dress and how thin her red hands were under their layer of grime, and he said abruptly, 'How old are you?'

'Eh?' She looked at him, her eyes sharp and knowing. 'What's that to you? Seventeen, if yer must know. I bin earnin' me own keep these past five years, so don't go thinkin' otherwise. A respectable girl I am, an' – '

'I'm sure you are,' he said and smiled. 'I'm sure you are. And thank you for your help. As I said, Miss Da Silva will be grateful when I explain to her,' and he moved towards the door, trying not to think about the depth of the chasm that yawned between the life of the girl he was carrying on his shoulder and that scrap of a creature who was her exact contemporary but who was kneeling in front of the kitchen range. It was a wicked, wicked world in which one girl need worry only about her reputation, and another about whether or not she'd get enough food to fill her belly.

The stairs outside the kitchen door were shadowed and he had to make his way up them slowly and painfully, terrified of slipping and dropping Miriam, who was now trying to move from his shoulder, lifting her head to look about her, and making his task much more difficult in consequence.

'Do keep still, you silly girl!' he hissed at her as he reached the door at the top of the stairs and pushed on it. It gave way easily before him and he was through it and out into the wide hallway beyond almost before he realized it.

The green baize door swung back behind him and he stood for a moment, taking deep breaths and waiting for a new surge of energy to come to carry him the rest of the way. He was almost dropping with fatigue and effort, and his vision was hazing a little, and his eyes were smarting as sweat trickled into them from his forehead. 'Where's your bedroom?' he managed after a moment and she said in a muffled voice, 'Put me down.'

'And have you fall down and need picking up again? I can manage as I am a little longer – where's your room, dammit?'

'Put me down!' she said again, more loudly, and began to wriggle, and somewhere above his head a voice said calmly. 'I think she means you to put her down, you know. Perhaps it would be as well if you did.'

Miriam slid from his slackened grip and stood beside him, still holding on to his arm and staring up and over his shoulder and after a moment he turned and looked up too.

There was plenty of light now, as the morning sun came pouring in through the big glass transom over the front door, and through the great stained-glass windows that flanked it, and the staircase was brightly illuminated with bands of crimson and green and electric blue as well as more commonplace sunshine. And standing at the turn of the staircase in a pool of vermilion and holding on to the banisters with one hand was the square figure of Mrs Henriques.

'Oh dear,' Miriam said, and shrank closer to Lewis. 'Oh dear, Grandmamma.'

'Indeed, Grandmamma,' the old woman said and began to make her slow and painful way down the stairs, obviously finding her progress difficult. 'And you, young lady, are to go to your bed at once. I will talk to you later.'

'Oh, but Grandmamma – ' Miriam said, but the old woman shook her head and went on with her slow and careful paces, coming down each step as awkwardly and slowly as a baby who has just learned how to deal with such complex structures.

'No, Miriam. This time you will do as you are bid, at once. Go to bed. I shall talk to you tonight. Francine is waiting in your dressing-room, I imagine. You have kept the poor girl up all night, so be quick about it, and get to bed. Then she will be able to. You, sir – ' She had now reached the hall and was standing in front of the pair of them but staring up at Lewis. 'You sir, will come to my morning-room. Sleep well, Miriam.'

And she flicked her gaze at the white-faced girl standing there beside Lewis, and for a moment her resolve seemed to lessen as anxiety moved into her expression. But then, as Miriam opened her mouth to expostulate again, Mrs Henriques said sharply, 'No, miss. Be told!' And Miriam went, stopping only at the turn of the stairs to say breathlessly to Lewis, 'Mr Lackland, I do thank you – you have been most good and kind. Please – ' And her eyes seemed to question him and warn him and plead with him, all at the same time, and he nodded as encouragingly as he could. 'Don't worry, my dear,' he said, as heartily as was possible. 'I will explain all to your grandmamma,' and she managed a thin smile and at last disappeared.

'This way, Mr Lackland,' the old woman said, and he followed her, still in a haze of exhaustion, to the room where he had first tried to warn Miriam, and he stood in the doorway a moment, remembering, and felt a sudden stab of acute irritation. If only the stupid child had listened then, they could all have been sleeping peacefully in their beds now.

'Another time, when you want to bring a gal home at some disgusting hour, it would be better to tell the cabbie to take you only as far as the corner. To arrive with great clatter of hooves and harness outside people's bedroom windows at six in the morning is hardly likely to make such an arrival inconspicuous.'

'Oh,' he said stupidly and then, 'May I sit down?'

'Indeed. If you are to avoid falling down you'd better. Man, you look completely ruined! What has been going on, that my granddaughter should be the colour of shop milk, and you twice as bad? Hey? And be warned – I haven't reached my eightieth year without developing a deal of knowledge of the world and the way it wags. If you tell me a pack of lies I shall know it, and deal with you accordingly.'

He leaned back on the sofa he had chosen to fall into and closed his eyes for a moment. 'I'm sure you will, ma'am,' he said. 'I'm as sure as I sit here that you will.'

He forced his eyes open then and sat more upright. If he got too comfortable there was no question but that he would fall asleep and completely antagonize this alarming old woman now sitting very upright herself and staring at him. And even though she was wearing only a lace pelisse and had her sparse grey hair tied up in an old-fashioned cap, she looked formidable.

'Well, Mr Lackland? What explanation have you for this – behaviour? What were you doing with Miss Da Silva?'

Saving her virtue, he thought madly. Shall I tell her that? Saving her virtue and saving her life? How that would make the old bitch sit up! How would she feel then with her haughty face and her cold fishy stare?

He smiled as emolliently as he could under the circumstances. 'I was at a – a ball, ma'am,' he said. 'And Miss Da Silva ate some food that disagreed with her, and was sadly put about. Very sick, to tell the truth.'

Suddenly he remembered one of his grandfather's more exotic phrases, 'Quite cast up her accounts, I do assure you.'

She stared at him, her face unmoving. 'At what ball? And what did she eat?'

He seized on the second of her questions with gratitude. Anything that would prise him out of the trap he had so unwittingly led himself into; what did he know of which balls the child had been invited to attend?

'Oysters, ma'am,' he said, without stopping to think. 'She ate oysters. Very ill she was indeed.'

'*Oysters*?' She sat up even more straightly if that were possible. 'Oysters? That's a lie. That can't be possible.'

Too late he remembered Ambrose's explanation that oysters were forbidden to Jews, and Miriam's own distress when she realized she had swallowed one. But it was too late to turn back. He set his lips mulishly. 'It is and it was. She ate an oyster. And damn near died of it. If I hadn't been there – '

'Who gave it to her? She could never have known what it was, for she had been most carefully reared – who did such a thing?'

He sat and stared at her owlishly. The lined old face swam in his vision, and the sharp little eyes almost buried in the pouches of age stared back at him. There was a bluish tinge to her lips which his trained eye noticed and he thought – she's got some heart disease – but that thought was banished at once by others. Should he tell her the truth, and risk her wrath descending on Miriam's head? And what harm would it do if Miriam did suffer some grandmotherly anger as a result? Wasn't the girl spoiled and wilful? Didn't she need protection from the likes of Caspar? Wouldn't it be better to tell this wise old face just what happened, and leave it to her to deal with?

He closed his eyes, letting his weariness wash over him and the decision was made somewhere deep in his mind quite without his conscious thought. The last time they had met, he and this old woman, they had not liked each other at all. He had thought her insufferably proud and she had thought him – what was it? A hobbledehoy, she had said. All the same, she was Miriam's grandmother –

'And my aunt,' he said absurdly, opening his eyes. 'My great-aunt.'

'What's that?'

'It doesn't matter. Listen. I'll tell you. And try not to be too hard on Miss Da Silva. She did as she did from silliness and from – well, wilfulness. She is very indulged by you all, you know, and this does not usually make a young girl into a sensible young woman. The person for whom you should reserve your anger – well, listen.'

And he told her, from the beginning. Told her of young Ambrose Caspar's behaviour, of Miriam's reaction, of every detail of the previous night's exploits. He told her too what

Miriam had told him, how Ambrose had spoken of marriage, and in what terms.

It was not until he had finished and saw her stricken face as she stared back at him that he remembered that he was speaking not only of her much loved granddaughter, but also of her grandson, the child of her own favourite son. And he felt sick with distress for her as he saw the look deep in those old tired eyes, a look that he had put there.

21

She could be remarkably masterful when she chose, his great-aunt. When he had finished speaking she sat for a long moment and then nodded, her face quite expressionless. 'Be so good as to pull the bell, Mr Lackland – what did you say your given name was? Lewis. I shall call you so, for you are, after all, my brother Rupert's grandson. Lewis, pull the bell.'

Bemused, he did as he was told. In speaking as he had, throwing not only Miriam but in a sense himself upon her good sense, he had shot his bolt. Now he could do nothing but concentrate on keeping his eyelids prised apart and his body in an upright posture.

'Light a fire in the green bedroom,' Aunt Abby instructed the startled housemaid who answered the call – for the butler was much too lofty an individual to be stirring yet. ' – And warm his bed. Mr Lackland, my nephew, is to stay the day, and he needs some sleep. A cup of hot milk to sustain you, I think, Lewis, and we shall speak later. No, I will not be argued with. I have made up my mind.'

She got to her feet, with some difficulty, and Lewis noticed that her lips went a little more blue with the effort, but he was too stunned with his own state of body and mind now to be able to do more than simply notice the fact and register it somewhere deep in his mind.

'See to it, girl, at once!'

'The hospital – ' Lewis said.

'They are expecting you?'

He nodded, dumbly.

'I shall see a message is sent. I shall tell them you are ill – and you really seem to be close to it – and then all will be well. I am known there.' And she nodded a little solemnly, so that he wanted to laugh.

'I'm sure you are,' he murmured, and wanted to tell her that a message about this so-called illness of his had already been sent to Nellie's, and that her further message would only add verisimilitude.

'Verisimilitude,' he said absurdly. 'It will lend verisimilitude to an otherwise bald and unconvincing narrative – '

'Ah,' Aunt Abby said equably. 'Mr Gilbert and his *Mikado*. A most diverting fellow. Sleep you well, Lewis. We shall talk later.'

He did sleep well, eventually. He found the green bedroom to be a large and very lavish apartment with a bed of heavily decorated brass, a set of rich mahogany wardrobes and wash-stand and dressing-table and a lavish display of emerald silk curtains, bed-hangings and sofa cushions. He also found an adjoining bathroom in which a huge marble tub had been filled and sponges and pumice-stone and expensive French soap set about in abundance, and vast Turkish towels arranged before the bright fire that burned in the bedroom grate. He bathed and drank the hot milk with gratitude and then slid into the bed with its thick linen sheets and lace-trimmed pillows, to lie and stare at the greenish shadows thrown by the curtained windows which were shutting out the October light, and listened to his own heart thumping erratically in his chest as it tried to cope with the punishment his night's work, following the previous day's efforts, had inflicted on it. Hearts, he thought drowsily. Hers is none too sound –

And he slept. All through the long afternoon as the shadows wheeled on the ceiling and finally thickened into night, as the coals in the grate burned with a glowing orange flame and then settled to a dull crimson glow, as the activity of the house went on peaceably round him, and his tired bones and muscles found their new strength, he slept.

He woke suddenly as the door of his room closed softly, to lie, puzzled and disorientated, staring at the unfamiliar ceiling, trying to remember where he was; and then did, and sat up sharply.

The fire had been mended and was burning afresh now, with a cheerful crackle and leaping flames that made horrendous patterns on the ceiling with the shadows of the great wardrobes, and there was hot water on his wash-stand in a pair of covered and gently steaming copper jugs. There was a new razor set thoughtfully beside the jugs and a tray of hot tea on the table beside the bed. Indeed, nothing had been neglected to give him comfort, as he discovered when, tea swallowed and face shaved, he went to dress. Someone had, while he slept, laundered his shirt and pressed his frock-coat. He looked as spruce and neat, once he was clothed, as any gentleman could hope to be.

He made his way downstairs a little uncertainly, still feeling somewhat lethargic after his day's deep sleep, but aware of new energy in his bones, and stopped in the hall when he reached that richly carpeted expanse.

The butler appeared as from nowhere. 'Madam is waiting in her morning-room, sir,' he said and led the way there, though by now Lewis felt he could have found the door without any difficulty at all. This house was becoming quite familiar to him.

She was sitting beside the fire in a high-backed armchair, her feet on a footstool, and wrapped in an all-enveloping robe of dull crimson silk. Over her grey head was thrown a square of what even the uninformed Lewis could recognize as very costly old cream lace. Altogether she looked comfortable and relaxed and very very rich.

He stood there looking at her for a moment, trying to see some sort of message in her profile, and then she turned her head and looked at him and said equably, 'Lewis! Come and sit down. I thought we would have a little quiet dinner here, just you and I. Miriam is to eat her own supper in her room, though I gave her leave to come down later to say her thanks and her good nights. And her farewells.'

'Farewells?' he said sharply and moved forwards to stand beside her on the thick rug.

'Yes,' she said with great tranquillity, looking up at him with a small smile. 'I am sure you will agree that it would be better if she were to leave London for a while. The Season is well over, of course, and it's high time she left the Town. It is very jaded at this time of year. And my grandson – ' Her voice trailed away.

'Yes,' he said, and bobbed his head in a sort of bow. 'Yes, of course. It's very wise indeed.'

And you have no right to feel so bereft about it. Of course it's the best thing that could be done. You would have advised it yourself if you'd been asked. But that did not help make him feel any better.

'Sit down, my boy.' She indicated the chair facing her, and he sank into it, surprised at how glad he was to do so. He felt a little shaky, as though he had been in bed for some time with an illness, and had only just risen.

As though she had identified the feeling she said, 'I told them at Nellie's that you were far from well, and were to stay with me, your aunt, for some days until I thought you fit to return. They did not argue with me,' and she smiled then and he thought suddenly – she must have been a pretty girl. She has a lovely face. Friendly –

'Thank you,' he said. 'But I doubt I will need so long. Tomorrow, I will be back at work, of course. Tonight, I am grateful for your hospitality, but I really must – '

'Oh, pooh,' she said. 'Pull the bell. I am hungry for my dinner, if you are not. You must be, in fact, if you think about it. You have not eaten for a long time, I imagine.'

He hadn't and he was ravenous. He hadn't realized how ravenous until she mentioned it and when the footman brought in a wheeled table and set it on the hearthrug between them he needed little encouragement to settle to the viands. There was a rich game soup of most majestic body and flavour, and a large beefsteak pie which would have done service for three times as many people and crisp salads and quantities of vegetables, and chablis so cold that drops of moisture trickled down the sides of the glasses in which it was served. A delectable meal, and he leaned back at last in his chair and sighed softly and found he had hooked one finger in to the waist of his trousers to relieve the pressure on his full stomach.

She laughed aloud at that. 'A pleasant variation on the food at Nellie's, hmm?' she said. 'I remember many *dreadful* luncheons there, when my son was younger, you know, before my father died and left him to be chief of the place in his stead. Dreadful, with boiled suet puddings and the most lamentable mishmashes they would call soup, and which I regarded as veritable dishwater – '

'It hasn't changed,' he said feelingly. 'I sometimes wonder whether it is the Bursar's way to save the hospital funds. If the food is poor enough none will eat it except the patients who, poor wretches, are glad to fill their bellies with anything they can get. But the doctors and nurses dislike it above all things, and that must save the exchequer.'

'You could be right,' she said, and then, as the footman took away the table and left only a decanter of port beside Lewis and a dish of fruit beside her, said a little abruptly, 'Lewis, I must apologize to you.'

'Apologize? To me? Whatever for?' He smiled at her a little crookedly. 'I owe you great thanks for as comfortable a night's – day's sleep as I have ever had, and a most delectable dinner. There is no other debt between us.'

'Indeed there is. A double debt. First I must apologize to you for being so – unfriendly when we first met. I did not see you as clearly as I should. It was a dreadful afternoon for you, was it not? All those people, so well fed and – and glossy! I can imagine how it must have seemed to you. I should have been more aware of how difficult it might be for you, but I was not feeling as well as I might that day and – '

'You often do not feel well, I imagine,' he said, and leaned forwards. 'I know it is none of my concern, but I am a doctor and – have you told your son, Mr Caspar, of the breathlessness and lethargy you sometimes have? And the pain in your chest and arm?'

She sat and stared at him for a long moment and then her face relaxed into a small grimace of a smile. 'Dear me, you are a knowing young man, aren't you? Well, keep your knowingness to yourself, young fellow! Freddy has noticed nothing, for I have made sure he doesn't. And he sees me every day, you know, so any change in me would be missed. It is insidious, this sort of thing, is it not?'

'It is treatable,' Lewis said vigorously. 'A little digitalis may be needed or perhaps – '

She shook her head. 'No, my dear. I am eighty years old, all but a few weeks. I shan't live for ever, and certainly have no desire to live as an invalid. I shall go on as long as I can as I am, and then, when the time comes to draw a line beneath my total, why, a line I shall draw! No hanging on of odds and ends for me – I like to keep all square – so let us now forget my health which is all I could ask of it at my time of life, and complete that which I started. I apologize for my misunderstanding of you, and welcome you most warmly to your own family. And I thank you most deeply for your care of your young cousin – '

There was a long pause and then he said awkwardly, 'She is a very special girl, Mrs Henriques.'

'You are to call me Aunt Abby. Yes she is. Pretty, and charming and very rich. Her parents died young, you know. My daughter Isabel – ' The old eyes shaded for a moment. 'She was a lovely girl, my Isabel. Lovely. She inherited money from my husband's mother, in her own right, and of course her husband Jacob was rich too. The child is a substantial heiress, Lewis.'

'Do you think I did not realize that?' he said, almost harshly, and then controlled his voice. 'I knew as soon as I saw this house that she was what is regarded in the marriage market as a most special prize.'

'You need not sound so sardonic. I dislike the way people think and talk these mercenary days as much as you do. But facts are facts. And I have been blinding myself to an important and dangerous one for some time. Ambrose is a villain. I thank you for making sure I know.'

'I wouldn't say a villain exactly – ' Lewis said uncomfortably.

'I would. A stupid villain which is almost worse. If the boy had courted my Miriam properly and made her love him, doesn't he know he could have had her for the asking, all above board? We have, as you so rightly pointed out, indulged her all her life. Would we have refused her her heart's desire, if it had happened to be Ambrose? Stupid, stupid – it must come from the other side of the family. Freddy would never be so – but Phoebe – ' She shook her head. 'Poor Phoebe was spoiled too, of course. Jonah, her father, you know, was so set about after Celia died that he – well you know how these things are – '

She sank into the momentary reverie of the very old and he looked at her and was silent. These names meant nothing to him, but he would not say so to her. However harsh she had seemed the day he first met her, now he was beginning to feel the warmth of a remarkable personality. A wise and caring woman. He liked her. I wish I'd known her when she was young. She must have been –

'So, you see I am grateful.' She had roused herself now and was smiling at him in the firelight. 'I know Miriam is.'

'Miriam?'

233

'Oh, we have talked today. She is younger and more resilient than either you or I, Lewis. She woke at five this afternoon as chipper as could be. We talked and she – well, she does know how foolish she has been, and how fortunate in having you to care for her these past few days. She will tell you herself – '

'There is no need,' he said. But I hope she does. To see her again will be – 'No need at all.'

'I think there is,' she said and smiled again. 'Now, my dear boy, let us talk of you. I know so little of you. Tell me more about poor dear Rupert and what happened to him. I must tell you too, what he was like when he was a boy. A charmer, you know, a charmer.'

She laughed aloud then. 'Not so charming later on, I must confess. He quarrelled bitterly with my father – who was, I can't deny, an easy man to quarrel with, and that was why he went to Australia. And why you are a citizen of the Antipodes.'

He talked, easily and happily. The stiffness of that first meeting was long since melted away, and he chattered as happily as a child, and not only about his Australian life but also of his life in England now. Glossing with some delicacy over some of the aspects of Claudette's operation in Somerset Street, and also saying as little as possible about what he actually did for the girls there – though he suspected that this shrewd old lady knew quite well without being told – he talked of her too, and now Abby, who had been listening comfortably, stiffened and sat up more straightly.

'You say her grandmother was an English actress?' she said sharply. 'What is her own family name again?'

'Lucas,' Lewis said, a little surprised by her vehemence. 'It seems odd for a French woman to have so English a surname, but it was only her mother who was French, you see. Her father Jody – and I must tell you that he is a charming old ruffian, but a ruffian all the same – is as English as – as you are.' He grinned at that. 'He objected to Claudette being a Gaiety girl, you know, because his mother Lilith was so marvellous an actress that he could not bear that poor Claudette, who is not so talented a performer, should tarnish her memory! I know it is good for a man to love his mother, but all the same, there should be limits, I feel!'

'Lilith Lucas,' Abby said softly. 'Lilith Lucas. Won't she ever leave us alone?'

'I beg your pardon?' Lewis leaned forwards to stare at her in the soft lamplight. Her voice had changed so much, and she seemed to have become remote. 'I did not quite – '

'I'm sorry.' She roused herself and leaned back in her chair and he saw with some alarm that her lips had become even more blue.

'What is it? Do you feel – '

'No. I am well enough.' And already she was looking better as her first reaction to the realization of who Claudette was faded. 'Well enough. So, it was at this girl Claudette's house that my Miriam was so nearly brought low?'

'Indeed it was not Claudette's fault,' Lewis said, loyally. 'She was as anxious as I that she should not be – connected in any way with the house. I do assure you – '

'It doesn't matter,' Abby said, and she sounded weary now. 'It is of no consequence. Miriam knows now that she must keep away from that place, and also that she cannot trust her cousin Ambrose – ' She nodded then. 'He will be dealt with in my own good time. My son Freddy will return from Baden Baden soon and then – well, I think Ambrose will be going to York. It is a good place for an impetuous and stupid young man to learn to better himself.' She looked grim for a moment.

'I don't like being involved in this family upset,' Lewis said abruptly. 'It's no concern of mine, really, and – '

'You are family,' she said and, moving carefully, got to her feet. 'You have every right to involve yourself. And as I say, I'm grateful that you are and so is Miriam. I will send her down now to say her thanks and her apologies, and her farewells, as I said, because we leave for Harrogate the day after tomorrow.

Gideon will meet us there from York.' She smiled at him. 'I spoke to him on the telephone, you know. Is it not remarkable? When I was a gal, why, the very journey there took some days! And now we cannot only ride there on a train in a few hours, we can actually talk down a wire! I find the world a sorely changed place, indeed I do! I don't think I'll miss it too much when it's time to be on my way. Except for Gideon – '

Her face clouded and then she tapped his hand, for he had moved as soon as she had raised her bulk from her chair to stand protectively beside her. 'But never mind that! I'm going to bed. And Miriam will come to speak to you before you return to your own bed, for extra sleep will do you no harm. Don't let her talk too long, will you? She needs some rest as well. Oh, it is a comfort to know I can leave her safely with you after that wretched boy Ambrose!'

She hobbled to the door and stood there for a moment before leaving the room. 'Where did you say this Claudette lived?'

'Er – in Somerset Street,' he said guardedly. 'But – '

'Oh, I mean no harm in asking,' she said. 'It's just that – I knew her grandmother, you see. It might be – I might wish to talk to her one day. Perhaps. Good night, Lewis. I shall see you in the morning, no doubt.'

And she went, leaving him to stand on the hearthrug waiting for Miriam, and only able to think of the way in which his great-aunt had said that it was such a comfort to her that she could leave her vulnerable granddaughter so safely with him. The last thing he wanted to be for Miriam was safe. And it was the only thing he could ever be.

22

'You told her everything,' Miriam said. 'Didn't you? Absolutely everything.' She was standing in the doorway, her curly hair on her shoulders and holding her arms crossed over her white lace wrapper, hugging herself. The firelight set soft shadows on her cheeks and deepened her eyes and he found it painful to look at her, she was so stunningly lovely. But he couldn't take his eyes away, either.

'Yes. I couldn't help it. And I'm not sorry, because it really was the best thing to do. She's good, your grandmother. She's remarkably good, and you're lucky to have her. To tell her more lies would have been – ' He shook his head. 'It would have been wrong and anyway it wouldn't serve. She's very clever as well as good, and she'd have known they were falsehoods.'

'You're right,' she said, and came across the room to the hearthrug and sat down on the floor, and curled her feet in their fur-trimmed slippers under her. 'Sit down, do, Lewis. You look all stiff and miserable standing there. Do you mind me calling you Lewis? To address you as Mister sounds so – it isn't family, is it? And we're cousins. And will you call me Miriam?'

'Miriam,' he said, and sat down, leaning back in his chair. If only he could be less tense. His knees felt shaky and he was sure she could see the tremor. 'You aren't too angry then that I told your grandmother about all that happened?'

She smiled. 'I would have no right to be angry, would I? It is you who should be angry with me, for being so stupid. You came here and warned me, and I – well, I'm sorry. Ambrose is – ' She made a face. 'He is *dreadful*. I shall never speak to him again. No matter what. He ruined my first Season – '

'I don't think that's entirely true, Miriam,' Lewis said. 'As far as I can tell, you had a great deal of pleasure.' I sound like a dreary old man. She's only a girl – why should she concern herself about the sort of lives less fortunate people than she have to lead?

'Well, yes, I suppose so.' She pouted. 'But he was so attentive and so – I paid no attention at all to the other men, and that was stupid, wasn't it? Why I might have had much better beaux if I hadn't been so beguiled by him.'

He felt his forehead crease into a frown. 'Is that all that concerns you, Miriam? That you might have had better beaux? And what's better, anyway? Richer? For all Caspar's faults clearly you enjoyed his company. Isn't that worth something?'

She was silent, staring up at him, for she was now sitting with her arms twined round her legs and her chin resting on her hunched knees. 'Oh dear,' she said after a moment. 'I really am rather silly, aren't I?'

'I don't know. You've behaved in a very foolish fashion, and you talk rather foolishly, but I doubt you're naturally stupid. Your relations seem to be people who are rich in intelligence and in my experience this is something that family members share. It is not usual to find clever men among a family of dolts, or idiots among one made up of industrious, sensible people.'

'And of course you are a relation are you not? And you're clever, so really that ought to mean that I am.'

He reddened. 'It's quite clear that you have no lack of native wit, Miss Da Silva,' he said stiffly. 'How you use it, of course, is another matter.'

'Now you're angry! Oh, I'm sorry. I was pert, and I shouldn't have been. You're the last person I want to make angry, for I'm very grateful to you – ' She moved then, coming across the hearthrug to kneel at his feet and look up into his face. He had to work quite hard at sitting still, with his hands resting on the arms of the chair. To lean across and kiss her would have been very easy, for her face was upturned to his and her mouth was half-open and she was looking at him with an expression of great admiration in her eyes.

'There is no need for gratitude,' he said. 'If you've learned something useful out of this escapade, then I'm content enough.' Boring old creature you are! You sound like some dreary old schoolmaster, lecturing a baby. She's a woman, young and lovely and very exciting and you ought to be doing something better than talking at her so.

'Well, I am grateful, all the same. And I'll try not to be so frivolous in future.' She sat back on her heels and looked at him consideringly. 'Grandmamma says I have to go to Harrogate with her, to take the waters and be good. I wish I could stay in London. Then I could see you sometimes, couldn't I?'

'I have a great deal of work to do,' he said. 'I'm at the hospital all day and – '

'Visiting that house at night?' she finished sweetly. 'Men really are lucky, aren't they? They can go wherever they like and no one thinks ill of them, but girls – we have to be watched over all the time, and watch over ourselves or there's such fusses. It isn't fair, is it?'

'No, I suppose it isn't. But that's the way life is. Look, Miriam, I want you to understand – I'm there because I'm a doctor. You see? Not as – not for any other reason. I'm a doctor and I look after people's health and – '

'Why? Can't the visitors there look after their own health? Go to their doctors? Why should you have to be there to look after them?'

'Because – because – oh, dammit, that I can't, and won't, explain. You'll just have to take my word for it.' He was hating himself now, and hating Claudette too, for it was she who had made him do – and that was another cause for self-loathing because of course she had made him do nothing of the sort. He was his own man; what he did he did because he chose to.

He stood up abruptly and moved away towards the door. 'I must say good night, Miss Da Silva – '

'Please, Miriam!' she said. 'I thought we were to be good friends, Lewis? It's so delightful to have so interesting a new cousin and now you're angry and – '

'No, I'm not. But you – how can I be your friend? Just look at the differences between us! You live here – ' He swept his hand round in a comprehensive gesture. ' – and you're very very rich. I'm a working man who hasn't a penny he hasn't earned by his own labour. The gulf between us is much too big for us to be anything but what we are. Distant cousins. I'm glad I was able to help you, and I hope you are happy and successful in the future and – and good night, Miss Da Silva – '

'You're a dreadful snob, aren't you?' she said after a moment.

His hand was already on the door but he turned back at that. 'I, a snob? That's the most stupid thing you've said yet! How can you possibly accuse me of such a – I'm not Caspar, you know, dazzled by money and – '

'Oh yes you are. I never consider money, you know that? Oh, I know what you're thinking. I don't have to. That's why I can be so insouciant about it. But at least I don't value people in terms of what they have! I didn't think Ambrose did, but obviously he does – and it's that that's made me most sick about what happened. I didn't think you were that sort either – heaven knows I know enough toadies and tuft-hunters, but you – I thought you had more sense. And now you say you can't be my friend because I'm too rich.' She was on her feet now and her face was pink with the energy she was putting into her speech. 'What's the crime in it? Why should I be punished because I had parents who left me a lot of money? It's nothing to do with me, is it? Can't we be friends because of the sort of people we are? You were kind to me, and I like you. Isn't that good enough?'

He was silent, staring at her, a little startled by the way she seemed to have changed. He had thought of her so far as a silly child who happened to have a face and a body that enchanted him, but little more. Now, for the first time he could see a glimmering of the sort of woman she was likely to become in time.

In time. 'You're very young, Miriam,' he said then, and tried to smile. 'It's that as much as the difference in our situations that concerns me. I suppose you're right up to a point. I do worry about the fact that you're rich and I'm not. It's not because I value money itself so highly, though. It's because the world does. People have a label for poor men who dangle after heiresses. You said yourself you knew – what was it? Toadies and tuft-hunters. I don't want to be regarded as one of them. But it isn't just that, as I said. You're so *young.*'

'And you of course are so *old.*'

'Thirty.'

'Oh, that is a vast age, is it not? Quite cobweb-hung, you are! I'm surprised you can walk about without a stick.'

'It's all very well to pretend it doesn't matter. It does. I'm thirteen years older than you. I've – you've still got to find out who you are and what you are, but I'm already a grown man. How can you expect us to share a friendship when real friendship, surely, is based on similarities? I saw you here with all your girl friends that afternoon I came – a roomful of children. You looked comfortable with them, and happy with them and I felt – '

'Old?'

'Yes.'

'Then you are stupid. Yes you are. I am speaking only of an agreeable friendship, between cousins. Why to listen to you you would think I had declared myself as seeking to marry you! And I did not, did I?'

She was looking at him with a challenging sort of stare and he looked back at her, nonplussed. What had happened to this girl? She had seemed so malleable, so foolish and now here she was fencing words with him and making him feel that he was the foolish one. And she knew it; she was half smiling now, still holding his gaze, still seeming to be all wide-eyed innocence, yet knowing perfectly well what she was doing.

He took a deep breath. 'Miriam, I am going to bed now, and early in the morning, very early, I shall be returning to the hospital. I will try to visit your grandmother after your return from Harrogate, whenever that may be and I hope that when I do I might have the pleasure of seeing you. But that is all. I really cannot see that we can in any way support a friendship between us, since we both live such very different lives. And are so separated by age. Good night, and I hope you feel better than you did last night.'

He slept badly that night and not entirely because he had slept so long during the day. Whenever he closed his eyes, he saw her standing there on the hearthrug in her white lace wrapper, staring at him with those great dark eyes as he closed the door between them.

Abby slept poorly too. It was not only because of what had almost happened to her beloved Miriam, not even the fact that her grandson Ambrose had been displayed in so poor a light. That would be sorted out, she was sure, once Freddy came home. Abby had for many years had total faith in Freddy's ability always to put matters right. He would soon make sure his own son saw the error of his ways, and would, whether Phoebe liked it or not, see the boy set on the right path.

No, it was the way she felt at the news that Lilith Lucas' granddaughter was involved in what had happened that robbed her of sleep. Her involvement may be of the most tenuous, but that didn't matter. Involved she was. Abby, remembering the long-ago events that had so affected her family; the way her mother, long dead Dorothea, had taken her with her when she had gone to see Lilith Lucas, to beg for her beloved son Jonah; the accident that had robbed Dorothea of her awareness and had left her to rot the rest of her life in a coma; the misery Jonah had suffered at the hands of Lilith's daughter – the memories spun in her head making her dizzy and miserable, for all through them the name repeated and repeated itself. Lilith. Lilith. The trouble-maker. And now her granddaughter was here in London ready to start it all again.

Somewhere deep inside herself she knew she was being less than just. However hateful Lilith had been, however much she had caused Abel and all his family to suffer, she was long since dead, like Abel himself. This granddaughter, this Claudette, could bear no malice towards the Lacklands now. Could she? There had been no deliberate act of wickedness against young Miriam simply because she was Abel's great-granddaughter. It was fortuitous, it had to be. Yet for all that Abby lay heavily in her bed and stared at the ceiling in the darkness of the night and felt all the old fears and all the old hostilities stirring in her. More than sixty years ago, it all was, yet still it reverberated down the years to break her sleep.

Quite when it was that she decided what she must do she was not sure. But by the time her maid arrived with her hot chocolate and buttered biscuits she knew what she had to do. She would have to spend the morning arranging the Harrogate visit, of course, but this afternoon – this afternoon she would sort it all out.

Lewis had gone long before she left her room, sending a polite message of thanks for her hospitality and a promise of a visit as soon as she returned from Harrogate, and Miriam was in a most sensible mood, helpful and biddable, all of which helped speed the morning on its way. By the time their luncheon was served in the morning-room their boxes – all seventeen of them, for they were to stay for several days – were packed and corded and ready to be carried down.

'Miriam, I have a private call to pay,' Abby said, as she finished her bowl of soup, and refused the plate of bread and butter the footman was proffering. 'I wish you to remain at home this afternoon to greet any callers we may have. There will be few, I imagine, for London is very thin of company at present. But I wish you remain at home. Is that understood?'

'Yes, Grandmamma,' Miriam said. 'I have nowhere else I wish to go, anyway.' She looked dispirited and tired, Abby thought, looking at her with surreptitious anxiety. It's not surprising, of course. Foolish child – Harrogate will do her good. And me, too, I'm more tired than I've been for a long time –

Her carriage was at the door at three o'clock sharp and she settled herself in it with some trepidation. This wasn't going to be an easy meeting, and she really would have preferred to spend the afternoon snoozing on her comfortable chaise-longue in her boudoir. But necessary is necessary, she told herself sturdily, and gave her coachman his instructions.

Claudette was in the dining-room when Mrs Henriques was announced. She had chosen today to make a total rearrange-ment of the tables and the service system, for in the few months since she had started the restaurant, she had learned much about the ebb and flow of diners and the sort of food they most liked. Now, she was enveloped in a vast white apron and her hair was tied up in a large kerchief, for she had no intention of letting the waiters slack at the work she had instructed them to do, for want of supervision. They would do it and do it well, with her own eye firmly on them.

'Who?' she said a little irritably, looking up from the pile of napkins she was counting. 'Mrs Henriques? Who is she? I don't think I know her. Do I? Though the name is perhaps – '

'Don't know, miss,' Edward said. 'Old lady she is, very big and old. Says it's important she sees you right away.'

'Probably some charity-queen,' Claudette said, and finished counting the napkins and made a note of the total. 'I suppose Mrs Lovibond – '

'She's out, miss,' Edward said. 'Won't be back till late.'

'No, I don't suppose she will,' Claudette muttered. In the months since she had arrived Mrs Lovibond had taken to living a life of leisure, coming to the house only to check the books and collect some money from time to time which suited Claudette's independent nature well enough, though at the same time it irritated her; the woman should not get all that money from her, Claudette's, labour, damn it all! Even if the house was leased in her name, and she had furnished and equipped it, it was now Claudette's, efforts which brought the fine income pouring in, paid the rent and the staff and generally filled the coffers. She'd have to buy her out, soon. Either that, or of course, bring young David to the boil –

'You'd better bring her in here, Edward,' she said. 'I have no time to see her anywhere else. And if she's still here in fifteen minutes time, come and tell me I am required to be somewhere else to get rid of her – '

The old lady, when she arrived, startled Claudette a little. She had expected some elderly twittery bundle who would prose on about poor children or distressed clergymen's wives or some such charity and then go on her way with a donation in her pocket, but this was someone very different. She was large, indeed, more wide than she was tall, almost, but there was an air of command about her, a quality of pride that made it clear that she was a Personage.

'Miss Lucas?' she said, and her voice was stronger than her age would have led Claudette to expect.

'Yes. Mrs Henriques, I believe? I am not sure zat I 'ave 'ad ze pleasure – ' The French accent appeared automatically. 'You must forgive my *déshabillé*, but as you see, zere are some duties to which I 'ave to attend – ' She waved vaguely in the direction of the waiters who were busily rearranging tables and carrying stacks of cutlery and china from one side of the dining-room to the other. 'I cannot be a lady of leisure, sad to say!'

'I am Miriam Da Silva's grandmother,' the old lady said, and Claudette stood very still and then nodded, putting on a bright smile.

'Oh, dear! Zat poor little girl the other night who was taken so ill? I am so sorry zat should 'ave 'appened, though I am sure we cannot be blamed 'ere for it. I understand from Dr Lackland, who took care of her, zat there was no fault in the food she ate – just a constitutional distaste for oysters which made her ill. I trust she is well again now?'

'Thank you, yes. I am not here to complain about the food she ate under your roof, Miss Lucas.'

Claudette relaxed and her eyes which had been bright and hard softened in their gaze. 'Well, I am glad to hear that!' she said heartily. 'To tell you ze truth, Mrs Henriques, I am sometimes a little suspicious when people – well, let it be! As long as she is well.'

'I do however wish to complain about the fact that she was here at all. Tell me, Miss Lucas, this establishment is a bordello, is it not? Masquerading as – ' She looked about her with an expression of cold dislike on her face. ' – as a restaurant? And gambling-house?'

Claudette's face became very still. 'No, ma'am, it is not. It *is* a restaurant, and yes, a gambling establishment. There is no reason, I believe, why a lady should not choose to entertain her guests with games of chance in her own home?'

'As to that, I cannot say. I am not as acquainted with the law in these matters as I might be. But I do know that places used for such immoral purposes as I believe this house to be used are likely to come under official scrutiny. And I have come here to tell you that – '

'Claudette, where have you put my new tobacco?' The voice behind them made Abby turn. A thin man, very thin and somewhat bent was standing in the doorway peering in at them. He was wearing carpet slippers and a red smoking jacket and his face was set in an expression very like that of a cross baby. 'I want it, and I won't be stopped from having it. Now where have you put it, wretched girl?'

'Oh, Papa, you know you should not smoke!' Claudette said sharply, and she moved forwards to hurry the old man away. 'Lewis has told you and told you – and I am sick and tired of telling you. I threw it away, and that's all about it. It only makes you cough when you use it and – '

'I will smoke if I choose to!' He moved away from her, towards Abby, and now she could see him more clearly and she thought – he's ill. Very ill. His face had a waxiness about it that was clearly unhealthy, and his eyes a glittering anxiety that showed he knew as well as anyone that he had a mortal disease.

Claudette put a hand out to stop him and he turned on her and with the pettishness of the weak stamped his foot, and Abby heard her own voice say suddenly 'Jody – '

The old man whirled and stared at her. 'Eh? What did you say? Who are you? Do I know you?'

'I haven't seen you since you were a baby,' she said. 'So long ago, you won't remember. Your toy boat went out of reach on the Long Water in the Park, and you shrieked and shrieked – '

Claudette was staring at her now with her brows tightly clamped together. 'You say you knew my father when he was a child? How can that be? I mean, are you – '

'I knew his mother too,' Abby said, never taking her eyes from the sick man's face. 'I knew her too. Lilith – '

'Lilith – ,' Jody said, and he frowned and his face became more childlike than ever. 'Lilith – '

'And I want to tell both of you that I won't have either of you interfering with me and mine the way she used to! Do you hear me? I won't have it. That is what I came here to tell you – ' Abby felt all the fears of her sleepless night come welling up in her again. She knew she sounded shrill and over-excited but she couldn't stop herself.

'What on earth are you talking about?' Claudette said. 'You knew my – and how did she ever – really, this is a nonsense. I mean no harm to you or yours, whoever they may be – '

'You harmed my granddaughter,' Abby said. 'Allowing her to come here and – '

'The devil I did!' Claudette said, her face pinched with fury. 'I did nothing of the kind. I don't check on every person who walks through my doors. If she's so ill-cared for and ill-protected by *you* and *yours* that is no fault of mine, is it? Deal with the man who brought her here, and leave me alone! Do you understand that? I won't be bullied in this fashion by someone who – '

'You knew Lilith,' Jody said, and his voice was almost dreamy. 'Tell her, please, was she not the most beautiful creature you ever saw? Tell my daughter, ma'am, for she doesn't always believe me, I think. And I want her to know. Wasn't she beautiful?'

Abby was tight-lipped now. Somewhere deep inside herself she knew that Claudette was right, that it was no one's fault but her own in her handling of Miriam that it had all happened but that didn't help her anger, and she turned to look at Jody, words of dismissal on her lips. But at the sight of the pallid face and eager eyes she couldn't. It seemed to matter so much to him, and after all, what did it matter to her? I'm eighty, she thought. After all these years why can't I forget it? Why persist in hating someone for so long? Why did I come here? I shouldn't have come at all –

'Yes,' she said. 'She was beautiful. Before – until her accident she was the most beautiful creature you ever saw.'

'Oh, the accident! I never think of that. I just remember her as she was at her greatest. The best actress London ever had – the very best – ' And he smiled, a wide smile of great sweetness and to her own amazement, Abby found herself smiling back.

'I think it would be better if you were to be on your way, Mrs Henriques,' Claudette said and her voice was frosty. 'My father is tired and should rest – '

'I'm going,' Abby said. 'I just wanted you to know that – ' She sighed, suddenly aware of her own tiredness again. 'I was foolish perhaps. Old feuds should be forgotten. But be warned, Miss Lucas, that this house of yours is one upon which I shall be keeping a close watch. If I hear of any – any other contretemps, I shall see to it that something is done to deal with you. I am well able to, you know. Well able to – '

23

Ambrose sat in the window of the smoking-room at his club staring out into the street and trying to devise some sort of answer to his dilemma. He had just three days left before his parents returned from their holiday, and heard from his grandmother of his behaviour. Three more days until his allowance would be withdrawn completely, and he would be thrown on his own devices, to make his own living.

He had no illusions at all about that; Freddy would seize on the affair to sever finally his financial connection, and as for Phoebe – he grimaced. He remembered all too well how she had reacted when he had first talked of marrying an heiress. She too was likely to be alienated by this wretched business, and so withdraw her support. It really was the most diabolical mess.

He drank some more brandy and brooded. That bloody man, that stinking, lousy, jumped-up sawbones daring to interfere in his private life; who the hell did he think he was, anyway? He deserved to be given his come-uppance, one way or another, by God he did. I'd like to beat his head to a pulp, he told himself. I'd like to take that stupid face and mash it into a jelly.

He drifted into an agreeable fantasy in which he confronted Lewis Lackland and told him exactly what he thought of him, while Lackland cowered against a wall and bleated his terror. He watched himself square up to the snivelling creature and rain blows on his head while Lackland gave at the knees and slid down the wall, a helpless cowering mess. It was very agreeable, and made him feel a lot better, so he ordered extra brandy and thought about it some more.

Where could he find him to do his punishing? Outside the hospital? That wouldn't work, because some interfering passer-by would be sure to join in, or call the police or something. He'd be too near his own cronies there too. At Somerset Street, then, where he seemed to be an *habitué*? He liked that idea. It was a quiet street where people minded their own business, and a good place to deal with the man – and there would be a poetic justice in fitting the punishment so neatly to the place where the bastard had first earned it with his meddling. If it hadn't been for him, Ambrose thought with muzzy fury, Miriam and I would have been married by now, or damned near it. The relations would all be running round in a fuss and talking about how much extra money I'd need to be her husband with, instead of doing what they're going to do which is strip me of every penny a man requires. His eyes smarted with the pain of the injustice of it all. Bloody Lackland – he deserved all he was going to get, and get it he would. Ambrose Caspar would see to that.

For by now the fantasy had changed gear, had become no longer an agreeable day-dream but a real plan. Lackland was to be beaten for his meddling, and made to feel the error of his ways. It wouldn't help Ambrose's present situation, of course. He could cut Lackland into cat's meat and feed him to the gutter moggies, and he, Ambrose, would still be left without the hope of marrying his pretty cousin and with the prospect of his parents' financial wrath to face. But by God, he'd feel better, knowing Lackland had paid the price.

He drank more brandy, and settled deeper into the armchair. He needed to think about such things as weapons. Fists? Or something more punishing? The man looked fairly beefy and might be stupid enough to try to fight back.

As the afternoon wore on Ambrose felt better and better.

Claudette sat beside the sofa in their sitting-room and listened to Jody's breathing. It was rough and noisy, yet shallow, as air seemed to have to fight its way into that fragile chest. Each time it rose and fell she found herself holding her own breath, waiting for the next bubbling intake. Please let it be easy, she prayed to someone somewhere, though she would have been hard put to it to say whom. Please let it be comfortable for him –

She heard a door open and close softly along the corridor outside, and then footsteps and the hiss of a whisper as someone went towards the stairs and she thought – that's Lord Cowan on his way, with Pearl. I wonder if she's got a performance tonight? If she has she'd better put a move on, or she'll be late and if the Guv'nor finds out, and that it was because she was here – her lips tightened. Suppose that woman carried out her threat? By the time she'd left this afternoon she had seemed softer, somehow, less angry, but all the same she'd said that she'd make trouble for the house, and she looked the sort who could. And would.

Claudette sighed and settled herself more deeply in her chair. Thank God Mrs Lovibond had agreed to come and work tonight. One way and another Claudette needed the break – and needed too to be with Jody, who as a result of Mrs Henriques' visit had become more agitated than she could ever remember seeing him. He had also become more childlike, petulantly refusing to eat any supper and then demanding some special *quenelles* which the chef went to great trouble to make, only to find that Jody had changed his mind and refused to eat them. It can't be long now, a corner of her mind whispered, it can't be long now. He's slipping through my fingers, going backwards to his death –

No. No. *No.* That thought had to be banished and she said the word aloud. 'No.' And Jody stirred and opened his eyes.

'What?'

'Nothing, Papa, my love. Nothing at all,' she said soothingly and pulled the rug over his chest and he caught the edge of it and began to pick at it with his thumb and forefinger, restlessly and erratically.

'Is she still here? Lilith's friend? I want to talk to her. About Mamma. Tell her to come and talk to me – Lilith – I want Lilith – '

She set her hand over his twitching one, wanting to stop that restless picking. She'd heard of that sort of behaviour, of the way it presaged death as surely as a rattling throat did, and she couldn't bear to see it. 'She's gone now, Papa. Gone away. Go back to sleep, sweet one, and tomorrow we will see if you can see her again. Tomorrow. Sleep now, Papa – sleep now – ' She crooned the words, over and over again, like a lullaby, and his eyes, wide and puzzled in their stare, hooded and then closed and he slept, his breathing resuming that shallow noisiness that was so distressing to hear.

She sat there listening, feeling the activity of the house around her, but not stirring. It was early yet but some diners had arrived for the restaurant. She could hear the carriages and hansoms in the street below delivering their passengers. They would eat and then go to the theatre and then come back and play the tables and use the private rooms and eat again, feeding their partners midnight suppers – an eternal round of playing and eating and drinking and playing again. And eating again – it's sickening, she thought suddenly. Stupid, pointless, wasteful; what sort of life is this?

It's the only one I've ever known, the only life he could ever give me. She looked at the waxy face on the sofa pillow and tried to see the young rip-roaring man he'd been; the witty outrageous delightful companion who had carried her lurching from disaster to disaster all her life. And all she could see was a tired, dying old wreck who could hardly get air into his tortured lungs –

What good has it all done you? she thought, letting the words form in her mind. Where has it brought you? Dying miserably in a hired room over a restaurant where greedy aristocrats fill their faces and pad their already bulging bellies before going on to throw coloured chips at a spinning wheel or a decorated card and get ludicrously excited over it. It's a mindless crazy *waste*. I'm sick of it. I've had enough. I want peace and comfort and my own home and children –

She leaned back in her chair, smiling a little in the shadows. A home and children! She, Claudette Lucas, to have such ideas? What had happened to her? To spend the rest of her life worrying about the arrangement of flowers for her drawing-room, the behaviour of her cook, the spots on her children's chests? Absurd!

Not absurd. It's what I want. Comfort and security and no greater anxiety than a child's spots. I'm sick of doubt and excitement. I want dullness and peace.

Lewis. His face came drifting in front of her mind's eye and she tried to blink it away. Not Lewis. A pleasant lover, undoubtedly, but an uncomfortable man with his sharp eyes and his moral doubts and his edgy questioning of all he did. Life with him would be exciting, not dull and comfortable. It would be effortful and wearing, not cushioned and lazy. I want easiness now, lots of easiness. It's been long enough, the work and the struggling. Long enough. When Papa is dead I'll have to think again. When he is dead –

But please, not yet. Give him a little longer if you can.

'Yes, Grandmamma,' said Miriam. 'As soon as he gets here, I'll waken you. I promise.' She kissed the papery old cheek and smiled. 'You do miss him, don't you?'

Abby was sitting in the big armchair in the bedroom of their suite, her feet on a footstool and a large shawl over her shoulders. Her face looked drawn, not its usual plump self at all, but she smiled now.

'Yes, I miss him,' she said. 'Does that seem foolish to you? After so many years?'

'No, of course not,' Miriam said, but her tone lacked conviction.

'It's more than fifty years, you know, since we were wed. A long time – '

'Yes, Grandmamma.' Miriam was standing by the window now, looking down at the gardens tumbling down the hillside into the valley. The hotel was one of the most elegant in the town, built at the very highest point of the ridge that overlooked the spa buildings, and the view was really rather charming. But Miriam was not seeing it, any more than she was really listening to Grandmamma prosing on about how long she had been married.

All she could see was Lewis' face, with its deep lines and that thick unruly hair crowning it, and all she could hear was his voice, deep and serious, with that fascinating flattening of the vowels. He was the most remarkable and exciting man she had ever known, and how she could ever have regarded him with fear and dislike she could not now imagine. All through the journey here, with Grandmamma fussing over the luggage and having the guard on the train and the porters on the platforms of every station they went through running hither and yon about her errands, all through the long dull afternoon as the train went rattling through the golden autumn landscape, she had thought about him.

And from time to time she had taken from her reticule the square of white cambric that was now her most treasured possession, and held it to her nose, pretending it was just a handkerchief she was using, but in fact taking deep breaths of the smell that clung to it. He had given it to her from his own pocket during the journey from Somerset Street to Green Street, to dry her tears of weariness, and she had not returned it. She never would. It had a faint odour of carbolic, of bay-rum hair-dressing, of sheer masculinity, and it made her chest lurch as it reached her nose, made her skin creep on her back and made her breathe rather more deeply than she had been.

Is this being in love? she asked the deepening twilight outside as the lights of the hotels and the houses on the hillside below her began to twinkle. Is this what the other girls used to go on about and be so boring about? Has it happened to me? And now what if it has? What will happen next? Lewis, darling Lewis, I want you. I can't bear to be so far away from you. Please, Lewis, love me. I want you. I want you –

'I do need him, you see, my dear,' Grandmamma was saying. 'The more now than I ever did. It's been so lonely these past days while he has been in York. I know he had to be there, of course. No one understands the business better than Gideon, and no one could have coped with these wretched Unions better than he, for he understands the men and their anxieties, but all the same – ' She sighed heavily. 'I will be glad when he arrives. Did you do as I asked and check that the message had been delivered?'

'Yes, Grandmamma,' Miriam said. 'Of course I did. Now, you said you were going to sleep – though why you won't go to bed, I can't imagine – '

'Oh, I shall do well enough here,' Abby said. 'And I want to be up when Gideon arrives – if he can get here this evening, that is. I should have asked the man downstairs to tell me the times of the trains from York, so that I could send a man from here to meet him at the station – '

It was a tolerable lie, she told herself. Miriam would not understand that it was easier to breathe and be comfortable sitting up like this, than lying down. It had been a long time since she could remember feeling quite so ill; the journey had been wearing in the extreme and there had been a moment, somewhere between Gainsborough and Doncaster, when she had been afraid she would actually lose her senses and make a complete fool of herself. More than a moment, in point of fact; for the attack, whatever it was, had lasted fifteen minutes or more. Her chest had felt as though it was seized in a most cruel vice, and her head had spun with dizziness. But fortunately Miriam had not noticed, sitting there staring dreamily out of the window, her handkerchief held to her lips, quite unaware of her grandmother's discomfort. And that is how it should be, Abby had told herself when at last the pain had worn off and her head had recovered its usual equilibrium and that hateful ringing sound in her ears had faded to silence. That is the way it ought to be. I don't want her feeling bad about the fact that I had to make the journey on her behalf and that it is tiring me. She has suffered enough for her foolishness. I don't have to burden her with guilt.

'Dear child, go down to the restaurant and order yourself a little dinner. I will not come down, if you will forgive me, but I dare say you will find it amusing enough without me. You can look at the other people here and tell me all about them.'

'I'm not hungry, Grandmamma,' Miriam said, turning from the window. I only want to think about my Lewis. I don't want to *eat*. 'Shall I order something for you?'

'No, my dear, nothing for me. Perhaps later, when Gideon gets here – ' And she moved awkwardly in her chair. Oh dear, the pain was coming back.

Lewis tied the last suture with a practised twist of his wrist, and snipped the ends and the man said anxiously, 'You're sure that's the last, then?'

'Sure as I am that I've made as neat a mend as you'll get anywhere,' Lewis said. 'And another time, friend, don't start conversations with drunken fools carrying broken bottles. You could have lost your hand altogether.'

The man peered down at his forearm nervously and then looked away, unable to contemplate the jagged, carefully sewn wound that covered the wrist and ran down into the palm of his hand.

'Not my fault, mister,' he said, aggrieved. 'I jus' walks along mindin' me own business 'n this geezer comes up to me wavin' this bleedin' bottle, don't 'e? Did what any man would, I did – puts me 'ands up to defend meself – '

'Well, so you say,' Lewis said, and began to set a bandage over the wound. 'But this isn't the first time we've had you here, is it? You seem to have a great propensity for having geezers come up to you in the street with murderous intentions. I can't suppose you're always the innocent in these affrays.'

'Well, I am,' the man said pugnaciously. 'So what you goin' to do about it?'

'What we always do, I suppose,' Lewis said equably, fastening the bandage with a final turn. 'Sew you up. Come back next week and I'll remove the stitches. And try, just till then, to keep out of trouble, will you? We're busy enough already – '

It had been the usual panic in the casualty department and he'd been glad of it, but now he had to stop work. Mr Nicholls had arrived a couple of hours ago, and with both of them working, the waiting-room had been cleared rapidly. Now, at close on midnight, he had to wash his hands and bid Mr Nicholls good night, and go to bed. There was nothing else he could do.

Which, though he was tired, was a painful prospect. Lying in bed trying to sleep and not think about Miriam Da Silva was becoming, it seemed, part of his life. In the three days since he had returned her to her grandmother's home, and had himself come back to Nellie's, he had simply existed; he could hardly call it living. Each day he filled with relentless activity, taking on other men's work gladly, spending longer hours than he needed, in the operating theatre and wards, and each night he had fallen into bed, aching for sleep, and unable to find it. She haunted him, and he hated himself for his weakness in letting her have such an effect on him,

Worse still, he found his body betrayed him. When he did sleep, his dreams were so erotic, so very explicit in their imagery that he would wake with his heart thumping and in actual pain with the urgency of his need. He found himself thinking often of the comfort that Claudette could provide and that filled him with even more self-disgust, for how could he love one girl, and desire another? It was appalling. Yet it was so.

When the message came from Claudette, as he made his way out of casualty, brought to him by a panting servant-girl he recognized as one who worked at the Somerset Street house, he was tempted for a moment just to screw up the piece of paper she pushed into his hand, and ignore it. Wasn't life complicated enough without getting involved again with Claudette? But he didn't; she could hardly be blamed for his emotional turmoil, after all.

He was very glad indeed that he had reacted so, when he read it. 'Tell your mistress I shall be there, at once,' he told the girl shortly. 'I'll collect some things I might need and I'll follow you – '

24

'There's nothing I can do, my dear,' Lewis said softly. 'I'm sorry. But you knew this was coming, didn't you?'

'That doesn't make any difference,' she said, her voice flat. 'Will it be bad for him?'

He shook his head. 'I don't think so. He's almost in a coma now. I can rouse him, but only with the use of very painful stimuli. And there's no need to inflict that on him. I know you were afraid he would have a bad death, but– '

She shivered, looking over her shoulder at the bedroom door behind which Jody was lying in bed, propped up on half a dozen pillows. 'I was afraid he would suffocate,' she said. 'I – it's all too imaginable.'

'I know. But it seems it won't be so. He's breathing still, without too much effort, but he's obtaining less and less air from each inspiration. I believe he'll sink more and more deeply into unawareness, and the end won't be too painful for him.'

'He's dead already,' she said, and sat down on the sofa, her hands clasped in her lap and her head bent as she stared down at her interlaced fingers. 'Dead already.'

'Not quite. I think it may be some time yet. It's a hard time for you – '

She shook her head and looked up at him. 'Not if you can assure me he's not suffering. It's that I can't abide. I can't bear to see a cat in pain, let alone – and I know he was frightened of that too. If he's unconscious, though, it's all right, isn't it? He's already dead to himself. So he might as well be dead to me – '

He stared at her, his face still but feeling the coldness rise in him. Was she as heartless as she seemed? He had thought she cared for that old man in there, for all his faults and for all the distress he had brought her over her young years, but looking at her calm tearless face now and hearing her words, so cool, so collected, he wondered. But she did care, of course she did. Didn't she say she wanted no suffering for him? That she could be practical and accepting about the fact of death did not rob her of her humanity and it was wrong in him to think otherwise.

He smiled then, trying to be as comforting as he could. 'This is a hard time for you, my dear. I do sympathize – '

'There is no need,' she said. 'I can cope.'

'I'm sure you can, though I could arrange for him to be taken into Nellie's if you would wish that – '

She shook her head. 'No, thank you. It will complicate matters when it comes to arranging the funeral,' she said calmly. 'It will be simpler from here.'

'Really, Claudette!' He could not help but protest. 'The poor man isn't dead yet! I know he's in a very bad state, but all the same – '

'All the same it is not *comme il faut* to speak of the interment so soon? Pooh to that! I must think ahead. If I just sit here and beat my breast, I'll – ' She stood up. 'Try not to be so English, Lewis. I had hoped for better from you. Tell me, how is your little beauty?'

'Well enough,' he said shortly after a moment and took his stethoscope from his pocket and put it in his hat. 'I have not seen her since I returned her to her home.'

'And told her grandmother all about my house, while you were there? Hmm? That was a most comradely action, my friend, *most* comradely.'

He looked up quickly. 'I had to, in the end. I couldn't prevaricate – why? What has happened?'

'She came here. Threatened to make trouble. I knew that would happen if I let you – oh, well what's the good of talking about it? I'm getting out anyway. As soon as – ' And she jerked her head towards the bedroom door.

'Why wait so long?' Lewis said bitterly, and put his coat on. 'I'm going. If I'm needed again, send a message. I've done all I can tonight to ensure his comfort. I'll come tomorrow in any case – '

'Aren't you interested that I'm going?'

He looked up at her, his face expressionless. 'Going where?'

'To live in Wiltshire.'

'What's in Wiltshire?'

'David Collingbourne's seat. Simister House, it's called. Very large. Quite a château.'

He stood very still, not looking at her. 'Collingbourne's house,' and his voice was as expressionless as his face.

'That's right!' Her chin was up. 'Have you any objection?'

'Objection? Why should I object? Your life is your own affair. I'm just – '

'Just a friend,' she said softly. 'I had hoped you would wish me happy. Friends usually say that to brides-to-be, I believe.'

'Bride-to-be? Oh! I thought that – ' He stopped and she laughed aloud.

'Yes, I dare say you did. Well, you are wrong. I am to be a Marchioness. I told you I would, and so I shall.'

'But he's so – oh, damn. I'm sorry, I have no right to – '

'But you're not wrong in your assessment, my dear! He *is* so. So dull, so unintelligent, so boring. And do you know something? That's part of his charm. Just like his fortune and his title. I've had enough of clever men and sophisticated men and moral men, like you. I want to be comfortable and have children and live in peace and – well, I will with him. I'll be in charge and everything will happen as I want it to. He adores me, and he'll do anything to please me – including putting his ghastly old mother out of Simister House and into the Dower House. I've made up my mind to it that I shall have nothing to do with her because she's the most unpleasant creature alive, and that's how it shall be. Everything done *my* way.'

He shook his head, wonderingly. 'Well, if that's what you want – '

'It is. And when I get bored then I shall take a lover. Two lovers. As many as I want. It will be a very agreeable life and I shall enjoy it very much.'

He was at the door now, his hand on the knob. 'You sound very vehement,' he said softly. 'Who are you trying to convince?'

'No one. Just telling you, that's all.'

'Well, I do wish you happy, Claudette. It sounds as though you'll do your best to be as happy as you can. I'll be back to see Jody – '

'That is up to you,' she said, and turned her back on him, and after a moment he went, closing the door behind him with a little snap. This was the girl he had regarded as a warm and loving friend? The girl he had found himself thinking of as a source of comfort even while he ached for love of Miriam? How could he have been so misled in his judgements? How could he? And he went down the stairs towards the front door with his face set as hard as granite in its expression.

Ambrose had taken all day to work himself up to his exploit. The fantasy that had seemed so delicious when he had first thought of it had lost some of its savour by the following day but had recovered that same evening, only to wilt after yet another night's sleep. But now it was the eve of his parents' return to London, he felt he had to do something. Tomorrow was going to be absolute hell, when the storm would break around his ears. Tonight at least let him punish the author of all his misfortunes.

He was not drunk, though he had taken a lot of brandy during the day, and he stood in the shadows of the house opposite Claudette's in Somerset Street, watching the front door and keeping his hands thrust deep into his pockets, for there was a more than wintry nip in the air now, promising a hard winter ahead. Suppose he doesn't come here tonight? What do I do then? Suppose he's already inside and doesn't plan to leave till morning? I could send a message up, I suppose, telling him he's wanted at the hospital. Then he'll come down and I'll get him – I'll have to do it that way. I've been here an hour or more already, and that's an hour too long.

He began to move forwards, planning the wording of his message in his head, and had reached the bottom step of the flight that led up to the front door when a shaft of yellow light sprang across his feet and he drew back. The front door had opened and, almost as though his prayer had been answered, Lackland was standing there, pulling gloves on his hands, and then closing the door behind him and beginning to descend the steps.

A great exultant rush of satisfaction lifted in Ambrose; this was meant to be; this was actually designed for him. If this didn't prove beyond any shadow of doubt that it was necessary for him to punish this hateful man, nothing would. If he weren't meant to be beaten, he wouldn't be here.

So Ambrose told himself as he stepped forwards to stand in Lewis' way.

'Lackland,' he said and his voice was rough and he had to cough to clear it, which somewhat spoiled the effect. 'Lackland,' he tried again, more clearly now.

'Well, what is it?' Lewis couldn't yet see who it was who was accosting him, for his eyes were still bedazzled by the bright lights of the hall he had left behind him, and he peered into the shadows, trying to see the face under the hat brim. The hoarse voice was vaguely familiar, but no more than vaguely. 'Who are you? Get out of my way, man. I've better things to do than stand about here, wasting my time – ' And he tried to push past the figure that stood in his way.

'Not so fast, you,' Ambrose growled. 'I've got a score to settle with you. And I'm bloody well going to settle it here and now.' And he thrust his hand forwards and grabbed Lewis by the front of his coat and began to drag him down the steps.

It was here that the fantasy went wrong, dreadfully, painfully wrong. Lackland was supposed to whimper, or at least to show some sign of terror. He was supposed to try to escape the grasp of the better man, but to be impotent in that iron grip. He was supposed to be pinned against the railings – which would have to do service for the wall which had figured in Ambrose's original day-dreams – and be beaten to a pulp, a jelly or any other amorphous substance Ambrose felt like making of him.

But it didn't work that way. Lewis, already as tense as a high-wire in a circus, as strung up as any man could be by his ill-slept nights and hard days, and above all filled with pain and distress at the way Claudette had been in the conversation he had just had with her, responded to the insult of an unwanted hand on his coat with an enormous upsurge of rage. How dare this creature, whoever he was, lay a finger on him? How *dare* he?

He thrust forward with his own hands and without any difficulty at all got them both firmly clasped around the other man's neck and began to shake him the way he would shake a rag doll, snapping the head from side to side while at the same time pressing hard on the man's windpipe.

His adversary tried to resist, at first, scrabbling furiously at his coat, but after a moment he shifted his attentions to his own desperate need for air and began to scratch at the hands that were so cruelly fastened round his neck. He began to splutter, too, as his eyes bulged and saliva began to dribble down his chin.

Lewis, in a white-hot rage, shook on, and it was only when the man's body began to sag that he actually realized just how violent he was being, and he let go, and grabbed the shoulders as the figure slid lumpishly to the ground at his feet.

Behind him the door opened, for the noise they had been making was not inconsiderable, and again a shaft of yellow light sprang out across the steps, and Lewis bent down and pulled at the shoulder of the crumpled figure on the lowest step.

The face was red and wet with sweat as well as spit, and the eyes were bulging still and a large bruise was rapidly appearing on the throat beneath the lax jaw, but all the same the man was recognizable.

'Caspar!' Lewis said disgustedly. 'I might have known! Caspar, you stupid idiot. I might have killed you! What the hell did you think you were doing?'

And Ambrose could only grunt and close his eyes as dizziness overcame him and he slid into a dead faint.

'Next time,' Claudette said acidly, 'choose somewhere else to settle your private scores. We have no need of this sort of behaviour!'

She had come down to the hallway, called there by Edward the footman, and was standing watching as two of the other menservants bore the prostrate figure of Ambrose away up the stairs.

'Private score!' Lewis said furiously. 'The man attacked me! I thought he was just a common thief until someone opened the door and I was able to see his face! It wasn't I who chose to – '

'Please, gentlemen, gentlemen!' Claudette was saying soothingly as some of the guests peered over the stairway in great interest to see what the hubbub was about. 'Zere is nossing to worry about, I do assure you! *S'il vous plait, messieurs, retournez à vos jeux!* Ze poor gentleman, 'e jus' took a trifle more wine zan was good for 'eem – we will soon settle 'im – per'aps, doctor, you will see to 'im? I will 'ave to see Mrs Lovibond and explain to 'er what all ze trouble is – ' She stared at him, her eyes bright with fury. 'And then get out of here, you hear me?' she said in a low voice. 'You've caused me enough trouble with that damned Henriques woman without picking on another of her wretched family! This is her grandson, isn't it? Yes – I knew it. Now she really will make problems. And Mrs Lovibond will – oh, you make me sick!' And she turned on her heel and went sweeping away up the stairs, leaving Lewis flaming with rage in the hallway beneath, unable to say another word, for the watching audience were all far too interested in what was going on.

He was very tempted to turn and go, leaving her to cope with Caspar as best she might. She didn't want him here? That was fine – absolutely fine as far as he was concerned; he wanted no more to do with her or her establishment. But then he stopped even as he turned back towards the front door.

He had wrought some considerable damage on young Caspar. He knew that, for his fury at being accosted had been so great, and the dammed-back irritation and frustrations of the past few days too much to handle. He had been much harder on the man than he had needed, truth to tell, and there was the possibility that he had done him some real harm. He would need to be dealt with by some man of medicine, and it would be best if it were himself.

And of course, he *was* Miriam's cousin. True enough that she no longer had any feelings of friendship for him; true enough that his family would be venting their fury on him; all the same, he didn't want to be the one who caused any lasting damage to the young man. For all his peccadilloes, he was their relation, and they would surely feel animosity towards anyone who damaged him badly. And although he had made up his mind firmly that there was never any hope of there existing between himself and Miriam more than the most cool of cousinly relationships, he wanted to do nothing that would risk making it any cooler than it had to be.

So, he turned and went up the stairs, following the footmen who were carrying Caspar's not inconsiderable weight up to the small room on the top floor where his medical equipment was. He might as well go up, if only to collect all that, anyway, he told himself. Because after tonight he would never set foot in this hateful house again. He'd had enough. If they needed help with the dying man on the third floor he'd send Nicholls to them. He would not come himself. Never again.

25

In fact the damage wasn't all that bad. Ambrose lay on the narrow couch, groaning in a husky voice, though he was fully conscious and well aware of who was looking after him; but it suited him to pretend he did not know. Sore as his throat was, and aching though his shoulders were, it was his pride that was most damaged, and to have this hateful man who had been the source of all his troubles bathing the broken skin on his throat with swabs soaked in mild disinfectant and expertly checking on the state of his larynx was almost more than he could bear. So, he kept his eyes closed and groaned but said not a word.

'You'll do,' Lewis said brusquely after a while, and covered him with a blanket. 'You'll be hoarse for a few days, but no more. You're a fool, Caspar, you know that? Behaving like a common footpad – what did you expect me to do? Stand there and let you do what you wanted? And it's stupid to lie there with your eyes shut like that. I know damned well you're conscious, so performing like some schoolroom miss won't get you anywhere.'

Ambrose kept his eyes even more tightly closed, and lay still as a log. Get the hell out of here, you bastard, he shrieked inside his head, get out before I – before I let you half strangle me again? another corner of his mind whispered jeeringly and again he groaned, this time with frustration.

'Oh, damn you,' Lewis said disgustedly. 'I don't know why I bother with you! For two pins I'd have you taken out of here and over to Nellie's and call the police to you so that you can be charged with your attack, except that that would cause embarrassment to your father, and I care for his peace of mind, if you don't. Stay here and God rot you. You can go when you feel like it. And keep out of my way in future – '

And he slammed out of the room and went clattering down the stairs to the floor below, pulling on his coat as he went. Damned idiot, stupid young fool – and not all that young at that, damn it!

There wasn't all that much difference in their ages, as he well knew, yet that spoiled lazy good-for-nothing seemed to be a mere boy in comparison with himself. I'm old, next to him. Old.

And next to Miriam. The thought came unbidden to his mind and added to his edge of anger. I ought to go back to Australia, he found himself thinking, as he reached the third floor and began to walk along the richly carpeted corridor to the staircase at the far end. Life here in London is just one great big mess –

The sound that stopped him wasn't at all like the sound that had once before stopped him in this corridor. Then he heard retching, the obvious signs of illness, but this was different. This was a sobbing, a tearing weeping that seemed to be coming from the depths of someone's soul and he stood and listened, his head up and cocked to one side.

Whoever it was was very unhappy indeed. She was crying desperately – and there could be no doubt that the voice was female, for it had that high unmistakable pitch – and with a desolation that made the hairs lift on the back of his neck.

It's none of your business. Bad enough you got yourself involved with this damned place in the beginning; don't involve yourself any further than you need. Get out now, and send someone to collect your things tomorrow, and draw a line and end it. The girl cried again, the sound muffled behind a door but no less poignant, and he found himself suddenly thinking of Queenie, there in Bessie Woodstock's hovel in Wapping. He saw her face, white and narrow in the guttering light, the anxious figure of Bessie hovering behind her, the shabby room and its pitiful attempts at gentility with its torn pictures on the damp and peeling walls. Why he thought of that night all those months ago he did not know, nor why the memory should affect him as it did, but suddenly he found himself with his hand on the door which led to the sound that was now settling to a low moaning, broken occasionally by a convulsive sob.

The room was brightly lit, and there was no sign of any food on elegant tables, this time. Just the sofa, with its tumble of coverings, and in the middle of it a small figure, hunched into such a bundle that it was hard to distinguish it from the shawls and blankets that were piled round it.

He closed the door behind him with a small click, and at once the figure on the sofa moved and sat up, resting on one elbow. A girl was looking at him, her face streaked with rouge and tears and her nose running and she lifted one hand to wipe the back of it across her upper lip. She was wearing a low-cut dress of vivid blue and yellow net lavishly trimmed with feathers and spangles.

' 'Oo's that?' she said huskily. ' 'Oo are you?'

'I heard you crying,' he said. 'What's the matter?'

She looked at him for a moment and then shook her head piteously. 'It hurts,' she said. 'It hurts *awful*,' and she cried again, lifting her chin and closing her eyelids and making no attempt to control the tears that squeezed under them and down her cheeks.

He came across the room and sat on the sofa beside her, and put one arm across her shoulders, and she made no attempt to shrink away from him as he had half expected. And his brows snapped into a frown as he felt the bones of those fragile arms, and the delicacy of her shoulders.

'How old are you?' he said and at once the crying stopped and she opened her eyes and stared at him, apprehension on every line of her face. Not that there were many. Looking at her more closely he could see, under the smudged paint and the runnels left in it by her tears, the smoothness of youth – indeed childhood.

'Seventeen,' she said, and sniffed thickly. 'Seventeen, I am – '

'Twelve,' he said heavily. 'If you are twelve it's a lot – '

'No!' Her voice lifted to a thin whine. 'No, I ain't. I bin seventeen fer ages – '

'I'm a doctor,' he said. 'I know about such things. Twelve – '

'Firteen – ' she whispered after a moment. 'Oh, Gawd, she'll kill me fer tellin' you that. Don't tell 'er I told you – '

'Don't tell who?'

'Me mum. And *her.*' She flicked her eyes at the door and put one bird-thin hand on his arm. 'You won't tell her, will you? The lady 'ere – '

'The lady here – ' he said and his throat tightened. 'What about the lady here?'

'She fixed it with me mum, didn't she? They got an understanding – ' The child sniffed again, and once more used the back of her hand to dry her upper lip. 'It's all right, you know. I mean, I don't mind – and like me mum says, I could do worse'n this. It's a good house, this is – nice. Not like you usually has to put up with, Mum says. And good vittles. But this time it *hurt* – '

'This time?' Lewis said, and took the child by the shoulders and pulled her round so that he could look into her face. '*This* time? Tell me what happened. And – '

She shrank back from him, her face crumpling with fear at the roughness in his voice. 'Oh, Gawd,' she whispered. 'Me mum'll kill me if I – '

'I'm sorry if I frightened you,' he said more gently. 'It's just that – listen, my dear. I'm a doctor. I told you that. I look after people. Now tell me. What happened?'

She bit her lip and then she said, 'Well, it was the alum really – '

He frowned. 'You'll have to explain more than that,' he said carefully. 'What about alum? I don't understand – '

'Funny sort o' doctor you are, if you don't know about alum,' she said, pert suddenly. 'Everyone knows about alum!' and she wriggled away from him and that made her face crumple once more into lines of pain, and she was crying bitterly.

'You'd better let me look at you,' he said after a moment. 'Tell me where it hurts. Maybe I can make it better – '

She shook her head and again tried to pull away, but this obviously increased her pain, and she scrabbled at the gaudy blue skirts that were tangled around her thin knees, trying quite obviously to reach her own crotch. 'It hurts,' she whimpered. 'Make it stop hurting – '

He examined her, quickly and delicately, and his face was a mask of fury when he pulled her skirts down again, and laid her back against the cushions.

'I need some ointment,' he said gently. 'I won't be a moment. I'll bring it – ' And he went quietly out of the room and up to his little room on the floor above, trying to batten down the sick rage that was clamouring inside him. That such a thing could have been done to so young a child – it seemed inconceivable. And that Claudette could have done it –

He pushed open the door of the little room, almost forgetting that Caspar was there and stopped on the threshold. Caspar was sitting up now with his legs dangling over the edge of the couch and leaning forwards towards Claudette who was standing in front of him, helping him to put on his coat.

She looked up as Lewis opened the door and said collectedly, 'I thought you'd left.'

'I was on my way,' he said, his voice clipped and very controlled. 'I was delayed.'

'Well, you need not be any longer.' She put one arm across Ambrose's back to help him slide down from the couch. 'Now, my friend, there is a cab waiting downstairs to take you on your way. And if ever you set foot in this house again, there will be more trouble than you could ever imagine. You hear me? Edward will take you down. Sit here and wait and he will come to you. Now, Lewis, shall we call a cab for you also?'

'No,' Lewis said, and crossed the room to his medicine cupboard, totally ignoring Caspar who was sitting now with his hands dangling between his knees and his head slumped forwards on his chest. 'No. I have work to do here. And you're going to watch me do it. Come on.'

He took a pot of emollient cream and a bundle of lint from the cupboard, and after a moment's thought a bottle of chloral hydrate as well, and moving purposefully snapped shut the cupboard and relocked it and then crossed the room towards Claudette. He took her elbow in a firm grip and without a backward look at Caspar, led her to the door.

She resisted for a moment, and then, after one look at his face, gave in. Whatever it was that had made him so angry, she had never seen in that expressive face a look of such controlled passion, not ever; and she was too practical a woman to argue when she could not be sure she would win.

'I will send Edward as soon as I can,' she told Caspar over her shoulder and then they were gone, leaving him alone, and hurrying down the stairs. Edward was hovering at the foot of them and Claudette nodded as she saw him. 'He's ready,' she said crisply. 'Get him on his way. Don't let him talk to anyone as he goes, if he's fit to, which I doubt.' She looked up at Lewis then. 'You made a considerable job of him, *mon ami.*'

'Did I?' he said. 'Someone else has made a considerable job of the next person you'll see. Come along – '

The child was lying as he had left her, still weeping, still with her knees drawn up to her scrawny little chest, and he knelt beside her and said softly, 'My dear, I've brought you something to make you better. Just lie still and let me help you – '

She tensed as he set his hand on her belly over her dress, and opened her eyes, and then relaxed and straightened her legs at his gentle urging and let him rearrange her clothes.

Claudette was standing just behind him as he finally revealed the child's bare body and he was aware of her there, but he didn't look, concentrating on applying a layer of thick soothing ointment to the excoriated and torn tissue that was so swollen and obviously painful.

'She tells me it was alum,' he said. 'Alum! I've seen what that can do to ordinary skin. How could anyone apply a violent caustic like that to a child of this age and on such delicate membrane? Hey? What have you to say to it, Claudette? How can such an action be defended?'

She was silent, and he still did not look at her, arranging a layer of lint over the area and then tucking the child's dress about her knees and covering her with a blanket.

'I have some medicine for you, little one,' he said then and reached into his pocket for the small leather case which he always carried, and which contained a minim measure. He poured a small dose of chloral into it, carefully, and then, setting one hand behind the child's head, lifted it so that she could drink, and obediently she opened her mouth and then swallowed, grimacing a little at the taste.

They stood there staring down at her, both quite silent, and after a very short time she slept, worn out by her tears and her pain, rather than affected by the sedative, and then Lewis said harshly. 'What have you to say, Claudette? How could you have done it?'

'How could I have – ' She stopped and stared at him. 'What have I done?'

275

He swung away from the side of the sofa and went over to the fireplace, and stood with his back to its empty grate, his hands thrust deeply into his trouser pockets. 'Oh, for God's sake, Claudette, this is me. Remember? Not some idiot you can bamboozle with a sweet smile and a fancy accent. *Me*. Lewis. So, let's stop playing games, hey? Why was that child treated so? How could it ever have been done?'

'I can tell you *why* it was done,' she said after a moment. Her head was up and her face was white now with control. There was as much anger in her as there was in him, but he was staring across the room at the sleeping child, and did not see how Claudette looked.

'I will tell you,' she said again. 'It is because men are in constant hunger, always wanting to please their own bodies. They use women for their hunger and they use them in any way they choose, thinking that money is enough to recompense them. Some of them, the very rich ones, prefer virgins. Shall I tell you why? Because they don't want to catch the diseases that they and their kind spread around among women. Virgins don't carry the pox, do they? They get it fast enough, God knows, but they don't carry it, not the first time. So, there's a trade in virgins. It's kept up by you and your kind – no, don't look at me like that.' For he had turned now and was staring at her with his eyes wide with fury. 'You and every other man – you're all the same! Didn't you yourself come to use me, straight from dealing with the mess another man had wrought on another female? You were so sick with *distress* and *pain* and *compassion* and all those other high-minded emotions that you came to me and used me in the self-same way others had used the girl who had made you so upset. You're as much a hypocrite as the rest of them, and you always will be, every man jack of you! Men want virgins, so virgins are supplied. And that means young – like this poor little object – because men see to it that poor girls don't stay virgins for very long.'

She looked over her shoulder at the child sleeping on the sofa, her mouth partly open and snoring slightly.

'Like this poor creature. As for the alum – ' She turned back then to stare at Lewis. ' – I'll tell you about alum. They use it, after they've first been entered, to tighten up the torn tissues. It's a caustic, isn't it? It shrivels the membrane and makes the opening so tight that some stupid man can come and try again and think he's got himself a nice clean little virgin – and pay the rate that's demanded for virgins. And all the time she's probably got diseased already. How's that for poetic justice, hey? It's something they can do two or three times, if they're lucky, and don't get a stricture that damned near destroys their bladders.'

She moved then, a little convulsive action that took her to the door, and stood with her back to it, staring at him, her face shadowed.

'So, that's why alum,' she said after a moment, her voice heavy and dull. 'That's why a child like this. It makes me sick – '

'It makes you sick?' he said, and he felt his mouth twist as he looked at her. 'It makes you sick, yet you do it – '

There was silence between them that almost crackled in its tension and then she said softly, 'You really believe that, don't you? You really think that I got this girl to come here and be used so? You actually think I provided the alum that did that to her?'

'Who else?' he said and now he sounded weary, almost as though he were losing interest. 'Who the hell else? Don't you run this house? Aren't you responsible for all that happens here?'

She closed her eyes for a moment and then opened them and stared at him. 'I run the restaurant,' she said. 'I run the gaming-rooms. I do not run this side of it. I know I asked you to come here to look after the girls in the house, but that was not because I – there was nothing in it for me. Ever. Can't you

277

see that? Or can't you believe that anyone other than you can ever have good motives? Do you believe you have the monopoly of compassion? That none but you high-minded doctors can care for others? It isn't so, Mr High and Mighty oh-so-good Lackland. It isn't so. Mrs Lovibond deals with all this. I hate it – I told her I did, and that I would have no part of it and she agreed it would be so. I make no moral judgements – people can use sex and love any way they choose. It's their affair. I won't involve myself, and won't make any personal profit out of it. What I do with love I do for myself. I do what I do for the sake of my feelings, and nothing else. But you – you don't understand that, do you? I gave you comfort when you needed it. I was the loving friend you told me you wanted, and what do I get in recompense? An accusation that would – faugh! If anyone makes me sick, it is you!'

There was a long silence then, broken only by the even sound of the child's snoring.

'I'm sorry,' he said then. 'I – I'm sorry. I didn't think that – '

'No,' she said. 'You didn't think, did you? Well, it doesn't matter any more. It's over. Everything is over. I'm leaving here as soon as – as soon as I may. I never want to see you again – you hear me? Take this child away from here, get her into your hospital – I shall tell Mrs Lovibond to tell her people where she is – and then never come back. I never want to see you again.' And she pulled on the doorknob and went, her skirts whispering in a rush of blue silk.

He stood there for a long time after she had gone, his eyes closed, trying to sort out the confusion in his mind, but he couldn't. She had been so right, and yet so, so wrong. She had understood him, and yet so cruelly misinterpreted him. She had been his friend and now she was gone.

He opened his eyes at last and looked across the room at the little girl sleeping on the tumbled couch. 'I don't even know your name,' he said aloud to her open mouth and blankly-lidded eyes. 'I don't even know your name – '

26

The night-sister was sitting in the middle of the ward, the light above her head shaded with a red cloth and casting a pool of light on the table in front of her. He stood at the entrance of the ward for a moment, the child feather-light in his arms, and looked at Sister, and at the serried rows of beds, each with its bright red blanket, and at the occasional glimpse of highly polished brass that winked out of the shadows, and felt curiously at peace. That this room in which thirty women lay suffering from illness, some of them with diseases that would kill them in the next few days or weeks, should seem so comforting, so good a place to be, is strange, he thought confusedly. Yet I'd rather be here than anywhere else in the world. At Nellie's in London, doing my job –

'Mr Lackland?' Sister had seen him and come soft-footedly down the ward, her white apron gleaming over the blue serge of her dress. Her face was concerned and friendly under her lace-trimmed cap, but the chin under which the cap ribbons were tied in a neat bow was resolute and had a certain hardness about it. 'What can I do for you?'

'Good evening, Sister Woodbine,' he whispered. I don't even know her name, he thought then. The ward sisters at Nellie's always bore the name of their wards, rather than their own; Sister Marigold, Sister Violet, Sister Elm, Sister Spruce – she's like this child, so familiar, yet such a stranger.

'Sorry to be a nuisance, Sister,' he murmured, very aware of the sleeping women around him. 'But I have a patient for you. I have to admit her tonight, for there is no other way to arrange it – '

She pursed her lips disapprovingly. 'Well, you know the rules, sir,' she said, looking down at the child in his arms. 'It's Marigold ward's intake tonight for women, and Larch for men – Mr Caspar is very strict about it, usually. Except for emergencies – is she an emergency?'

He looked down at the child's sleeping face. She was so deeply sedated by the chloral he had given her that she had not stirred from the moment he had gathered her up in his arms in Somerset Street, all through the cab ride or while being carried up the stairs of the quiet hospital to the ward. And still she slept on.

'I think she is,' he said softly. 'And she should be on this ward. She has – severe lacerations of the vulva, Sister. She has been treated in the area with alum, which made the membrane exceedingly scarred and brittle and now they have – there has been further trauma, you understand. I had to bring her here. She may need some surgery, I fear. She is thirteen years old.'

Sister sighed and then nodded crisply. 'I understand, sir. Poor creature – how is it that no one can put an end to such things? In a Christian city like this, it's little short of – ' Muttering busily she led the way to a bed on the far side of the ward, and pulled back the covers so that he could set down his burden.

'Nurse?' A figure in a blue cotton gown and white apron came gliding out of the shadows, as silent on her feet as Sister herself had been. 'Nurse, settle this patient, will you? She need only be undressed and gowned. We can bath her properly in the morning. She seems sedated at present – '

'Chloral hydrate – ' Lewis said. 'I'll write her up for more should she need it. Her pain will be considerable yet, I think. She has already suffered a good deal.'

'Yes – ' Sister said grimly. 'I dare say she has. Very well, Mr Lackland. I shall book her in under the care of Mr Caspar, then, shall I? Then you can be sure to look after her yourself, since he isn't here.'

'But he'll be back tomorrow, will he not? His holiday's over, isn't it?'

Sister was back at her table, busily writing out a folder for the case notes of her new patient. 'Indeed, his holiday is over, sir, but he won't be back – what is the patient's name?'

'Er – I'm afraid I don't know. You'll have to wait till she wakes and ask her. She has a mother who may just possibly come and see her. I have my doubts though, since she was the author of the child's injury, inasmuch as she agreed that she should be – that she should be used as she was.'

'Yes,' Sister said matter-of-factly. 'We all know of these cases.'

'What do you mean, Mr Caspar won't be back?'

'He has been called away,' Sister said, as she closed the folder and added it to a pile on the table. 'Some family trouble, I believe. We received a message late in the evening. Now, sir, will you write up the prescriptions for your patient? And when will you see her again and decide upon surgery?'

He took the prescription chart and began to write. 'Tomorrow – after the morning casualty session is done, and before I do the rounds on the men's wards. Did the messages say when Mr Caspar might be back?'

'No, sir. Just that there was this family matter.'

It can't be his son, can it? Lewis thought as he went to look down at the child in the bed now hidden behind discreet screens. The nurse had already put her into a thick calico hospital gown and washed her face and combed her hair back from her brow. Without her bedraggled finery and streaked paint she looked what she was; a tired sick child, and a frail one at that. No of course it can't be his son. The fracas with Ambrose Caspar had taken place late at night; the message from Frederick Caspar had come to Nellie's in the evening Sister had said.

And yet the possibility nagged at his mind as he said good night to Sister ('Good *morning*, sir,' she answered reprovingly) and went away to his own room at the top of the building. He was not himself culpable in any way for what had happened to Ambrose, of that he was sure, but all the same, he shrank from the idea of talking to Freddy about his dealings with his son. It was all so seedy and nasty – and anyway, to talk about Ambrose would mean talking about Miriam – and that he could not bear to do.

Outside the ward the hallways and stairs lay in silent tidiness in the half-light that was always provided for them during the night and he went over to the handsome wrought-iron balustrade that had been presented to the hospital by the Guild of Leather Workers only two years before, and looked down onto the wide stone-floored hall below. The statue of the founder, his great-grandfather Abel Lackland, stood foreshortened and squat beneath him and he thought with sudden irreverence – I could spit on his head from here. And then wanted to laugh at his own childishness.

He folded his arms on the balustrade rail and leaned over a little further. There on the far wall, beyond the statue, was the Benefactors' Wall, on which were brass plaques bearing the names of rich city men and assorted aristocrats who had donated money to the hospital over the years, or who had left it legacies. I wonder how many of you used little girls as that child in Woodbine ward was used? he asked the Wall. Did you think it right and proper to take a virgin child and subject her to your temporary needs, just so that you wouldn't risk becoming a patient in our care yourselves? Is it children like that who keep all of you rich men out of the House across the river? For there are no rich patients there; only poor men and women who know too little about protecting themselves by using children, who get their sex when and where they can and their diseases with it –

He stood up, and began to walk towards the stairway, on his way to bed, and then, almost without thinking, wheeled and went down the main flight to the hall beneath, his heels clacking lightly on the stone stairs. Bed was what he needed, but bed was what he couldn't face.

The casualty department was blessedly empty, the wooden benches standing tidy and quiet in the big waiting-hall. There was a pleasant clean smell in the air, of carbolic soap and ether, and he breathed it in, gratefully. So familiar, so reassuring. There was a fire burning in the big grate and in front of it, on a square-backed chair, Nicholls was sprawled with his feet up on the brass-edged fender. Beside him a nurse was crouching, her face a little red as she leaned towards the glowing embers, holding a long toasting-fork in her hand.

A new smell drifted to Lewis' nose, the faint and agreeable scent of hot toast and he was suddenly aware of how hungry he was. Had he taken any supper that evening? He couldn't remember. They'd sent for him to see old Jody after his evening's work in casualty, hadn't they? Maybe he hadn't had supper now he came to think of it.

Nicholls scrambled to his feet in a little panic, and then relaxed when he saw it was Lewis.

'Oh, Lackland, it's you! Glory be! I thought it was Frankenstein's Bride – '

'Who?' Lewis said, startled.

The nurse giggled. 'Night-sister. That's what we call her. But she's Sister Woodbine tonight because Sister Night's got the bronchitis, and she won't be down unless she's sent for. I keep telling Jimmy that – ' She dimpled then, casting a sideways glance at Nicholls. 'I mean, Mr Nicholls. But he won't believe me. But it's all right, really it is. You wouldn't catch me risking making supper for you if there was any chance that old bat would show her face. Do you want some toasted cheese, Mr

Nicholls? And can I do something for you, Mr Lackland? I've got the keys to the larder on Larch, and I could soon get you some bits and pieces – '

Lewis sat down on the fender, stretching his cold hands to the embers in the grate. 'And here's me thinking all you young ladies are just that, ladies. Yet you're suggesting you steal food for me.'

'Pooh to that, Mr Lackland,' the nurse said pertly. She was a round-faced girl with a voluptuous little body, her apron straining over her well-filled bodice and her hips springing impudently from beneath her tightly clasped black belt. There were a few wisps of reddish hair escaping from the frilled edge of her white cap, and her face was rosy from the heat of the fire. It was easy to see why Mr Nicholls found her company so enjoyable. 'Pooh, I say. We all work very hard indeed, and get little enough in return. I see no harm in helping yourself to a little of this and that, if it doesn't deprive anyone else. Sister Larch is so absent-minded that when she sees her larder is low she just tut-tuts and orders more. So no one's hurt, because she makes sure her patients get plenty.'

'Except the hospital's funds, perhaps,' Lewis said.

'You're in a black mood, Lackland, fussing about such things,' Nicholls said, his mouth full of the hot buttered toast his nurse had bestowed on him before setting about making another slice. 'You're not usually so pernickety – didn't we share a bottle of medicinal brandy from the casualty cupboard ourselves not two days ago?'

'That was different,' Lewis said. 'We'd just had to deal with a man who was damn near sliced in half by a great dray-mare stamping on him. We needed a restorative after that. You were the colour of putty and swaying like a field of corn! You needed it. So did I, come to that. So that was quite different – '

'It's always different,' the nurse said, turning the toast on her fork, and wincing a little as the heat caught her fingers. 'It's easy to be good when you aren't short of anything. But when

I get hungry, I don't worry about good and bad. Just about being hungry.' She giggled then. 'I'm usually hungry, aren't I, Jimmy – Mr Nicholls?'

'I'll have some toast, and thank you,' Lewis said abruptly. I'm talking about morality again, he thought. It's stupid. Life has to be lived the best way you can. If you spend too much time agonizing over what's right and what's wrong, you never get anything done. You stay hungry, too. Perfect morality has to be the greatest luxury of the rich. I'm sick of worrying about it –

The toast was good, and he ate it as fast as the little nurse, whose red hair was escaping the confines of her cap in ever wilder tendrils, could make it. As Nicholls and the nurse sat side by side and drank hot tea and giggled and chattered, Lewis watched them, feeling like an indulgent and rather elderly uncle, though in truth he was no more than a handful of years older than either of them.

The tall clock in the corner struck two, and he stretched and yawned. 'You're lucky tonight, Nicholls. Whenever I'm due for night standby, the place is full of broken heads and vomiting drunks. What's the secret?'

'Make sure you've something better to do than work,' Nicholls said, and daringly set his arm about the nurse's waist, making her giggle and slap his hand, though without any real conviction.

'Well, I'll leave you to it,' Lewis said and stood up. 'Who am I to intrude my company where it isn't wanted? Thanks for the tea and toast, nurse. You mayn't have any patients tonight to do anything for, yet you did a lot for me – '

The big double doors at the far side of the waiting-room whispered and swished and then swung open and Nicholls gave a small groan. 'Now see what you've done, Lackland! If you hadn't said we were quiet, we'd have stayed that way. Now what's coming in?'

The nurse hurriedly cleared away the impedimenta of her supper-making as the casualty-porter came across the polished floor with a self-important bounce that made the brass buttons on his tunic glitter in the gaslight.

'Ah, Mr Nicholls, sir, it's you as is on call, I believe?'

'You know perfectly well that I am, Bravery!' Nicholls said. 'You know everything that goes on here – '

'Right sir. Then there's a young lady outside as you ought to see. She says as 'ow she's got to see Mr Lackland, but I said to 'er, I did, as 'ow it was you as was on duty and I wasn't to call Mr Lackland from his bed for nothing, not on no account.' He winked at Lewis and tapped the side of his nose in a music-hall gesture. 'So will you see 'er, Mr Nicholls, sir? Don't know what the trouble is, but she seems in a rare old taking – '

'Probably one of your special ones, Lackland!' Nicholls said with heavy jocularity. 'One of those Gaiety girls you know so well, or – '

'No need for that, Nicholls,' Lewis said sharply, and turned to the porter. 'What sort of girl is she, Bravery? Actress?'

Bravery shook his head with great conviction. 'Oh, no, sir. She's a real lady. Mind you, she looks a bit draggled like, all of a heap, you might say. But a lady, all the same – '

'Perhaps I ought to see her, then – ' He stood irresolute.

'If you hadn't happened to be here, you wouldn't have known anything about her, and I'd have to see her anyway, wouldn't I?' Nicholls pointed out reasonably. 'So why not go to bed and pretend you didn't know? You look as though you need your sleep. And you've got an early start tomorrow in the theatres, which I haven't.'

'But if she's my patient, perhaps I ought to – '

'It's up to you,' Nicholls said. 'But I'm damned if I would. You can't always do everything you ought to, after all. But it's your affair – '

Morality again, Lewis thought and closed his eyes, feeling the weariness in him and the clamorous need for rest. 'You're right,' he said. 'I'll go. You see her – '

Which was why it happened that when he came on duty the next morning to start his casualty session before going to the operating theatres, he found that one of the cubicles was closed, and there was a note waiting for him from Mr Nicholls.

'Dear Lackland,' he had written. 'Once you'd gone to bed last night I didn't like to call you down again, especially as I'd been the one who said you ought to let me see this patient anyway. And she said I wasn't to disturb you either, and would wait to see you this morning, so long as I could find her somewhere to wait for you. She wouldn't say what the trouble was, only that it is personal, but she's clearly a lady, and most anxious to talk to you. So I thought as we were quiet, I'd let her use the far cubicle to sleep in, and told Night-sister she was your case. She wouldn't give her name. I hope I did the right thing. Yrs. J C R Nicholls.'

Lewis frowned and walked across the waiting-room, past the old woman on her knees scrubbing the floor in readiness for the rush of patients that would come as soon as the doors were opened to the dressing-clinic at eight o'clock, and pulled open the curtain of the far cubicle.

She was lying on the narrow examination couch, her pelisse pulled up about her ears, and fast asleep. Miriam, looking like a tired and rather grubby child.

27

She woke as he came into the cubicle and pulled the curtains closed behind him, sitting up suddenly, her eyes wide with alarm.

'It's all right, my dear,' he said, and came and perched on the edge of the couch, his hands pushed into the pockets of his coat, so that she would not see how they were shaking. To react so at the mere sight of a girl! It was lunacy. 'There's no need to look so frightened! What on earth are you doing here?'

She took a deep breath, and sat up, putting her hands up to her rumpled hair with the classic gesture of a startled woman. 'I – I had to come to you,' she said huskily. 'I just had to – oh, Lewis!' and she shook her head at him and closed her eyes. 'I didn't know what else to do. I just had to come to you – '

'You'd better explain,' he said after a moment, trying to sound practical, cool, relaxed. Anything rather than let her know how hard he had to exert control to prevent himself throwing his arms around her. She looked so vulnerable and so very weary.

'I – it's yesterday,' she said, and opened her eyes. 'It was dreadful, and I just couldn't bear it, and so I just ran. I sat at the station for – oh, hours, it seemed, until I could get a train and then it got to London so late, and I couldn't get a cab to bring me here from King's Cross – ' She began to shake and then made fists of both of her hands and held them in front of her chest like a child trying to keep itself warm on a cold morning.

'You'd better have something to restore you,' he said matter-of-factly, and pushed her back gently against the pillow before going to find some sal volatile and ask the nurse, now hovering curiously outside the cubicle, to bring some coffee for Miss Da Silva.

Miriam drank the coffee gratefully, sitting up on the couch with her feet dangling over the edge and he sat beside her watching her.

'Now,' he said when she had finished, and seemed in better control of herself. 'You'd better tell me – '

There was a rush of sound from outside and he lifted his chin and listened and then cursed softly under his breath. 'Oh, damn it all! It's half-past eight – the dressing patients are waiting. I'll have to see to them – and then I'm supposed to be in the theatres at half-past nine. Look, wait here, will you? I'll get through as fast as I can, and then come back to you. The nurse will show you where you can wash and make yourself comfortable and I promise I won't be long – '

She looked up at him, her eyes wide and trusting and he couldn't help it. He leaned forwards and kissed her cheek, and she reddened and put up her hand and touched the place and smiled, a slow and happy smile and he smiled back. For a moment they sat there in a private bubble of joy, aware of only each other, and then the curtain rings rattled and the nurse put her head into the cubicle and said breathlessly, 'Mr Lackland, sir – ' and the bubble shattered into shards of light and then melted away.

'There's a lot of people waiting, sir. Shall I start to take their dressings down? I could get them cleaned up a bit ready for you to see them. Only Sister'll be here soon and if we haven't started, you know how she'll be – '

'Yes – yes, I'm coming,' he said, and patted Miriam's hand. 'I won't be too long, my dear. Nurse will look after you –

Nurse, see Miss Da Silva to the bathroom will you? And then see if someone can find her some breakfast – no, don't argue, Miriam. You obviously need it. And nurse, book her in as – as a case of oh – severe headache. That'll do. And looking at you it's not far wrong.'

'It does ache a bit,' Miriam admitted, touching her hair again. 'It was dreadful last night – when I – ' She looked at the nurse and then back at Lewis. 'Please don't be too long – '

'I won't,' he promised and put out one hand as though to touch her and then pulled it back and just smiled and went away, leaving her to follow the nurse to the bathroom on the far side of the waiting-hall where she could wash and tidy herself and be comfortable again.

The nurse led her to a small office-like room that had just one comfortable chair in it and gave her a bowl of porridge and at first she wrinkled her nose at the dreary stuff, and then, overcome by sudden hunger, tried it, and found it hot and sweet and milky and very comforting, and wolfed the lot.

She sat back in the chair, then, listening to the sounds of the casualty department coming to her from the other side of the closed door. Children whimpered and occasionally one wailed its pain loudly, a sound that made her shiver a little, but there were other more agreeable noises; the rattle of a nurse's heels as she hurried across the wide floor, the chattering voices of the patients, the clatter of glass and metal as trolleys were wheeled past. There were smells too, drifting to her, lye and carbolic and anaesthetic and, oddly, far from being unpleasant they soothed her and made her shoulders loosen and she drifted into a half-sleep. She had slept little and poorly on the hard examination couch, and fatigue was deep in her. Now, fed and warm and relaxed, sleep crept up to her again.

And brought with it the memory. She lay there, her head thrown back, trying not to see it all again, trying to push it all down inside her, to keep it enclosed until Lewis could come and take it away from her, and make her feel right again, but she could not. She tried to rouse herself, to be awake and listening to the sounds from outside, but she couldn't do that either. It was as though the memory was a juggernaut, pushing slowly but inevitably on her, making her live it all again.

The light had dwindled more and more until the room was almost blotted out. She could see, still, the lights below the hotel, gleaming on the hillside, and in the room itself, the faint whiteness that was her grandmother's face against its pillows. But that was all, and suddenly she was restless, unable any longer to cope with the feelings inside her without some sort of action. Her body seemed to be pressing on her awareness; she could feel her legs, her arms, the curve of her breasts, the way her thighs fitted into her hips, her whole body seeming to clamour for her attention. And the stillness, broken only by the soft sound of Grandmamma's breathing, became more than she could bear and she moved sharply from the window and went across to the lamp on the table and struck a match from the box beside it and lit it, fiddling with the burners a little awkwardly so that the chimney smudged with black. The room lifted into light abruptly and her grandmother stirred and opened her eyes widely.

'Gigi?' she said, her voice a little thick. 'Gigi, is that you, my love?'

'No, Grandmamma.' Miriam knelt beside her and looked up into her face. 'He's not here yet. I dare say he won't be long – Grandmamma, I must talk to you – '

The old woman moved awkwardly, raising her left hand with a huge effort and then grimacing. 'I – what do you say, my love? I do wish this did not ache so abominably – '

'Oh, I dare say you've been lying on it,' Miriam said impatiently. It was imperative that she talk to her grandmother now, absolutely imperative, and to have her fussing over an aching arm was almost intolerable to her. 'Grandmamma – it's important. Listen. It's Lewis – '

'Lewis?' Again Abby grimaced and tried to move her arm, using her right hand to pull on it, but the pain seemed to increase and she closed her eyes.

'Grandmamma!' Miriam put out her own hand and took her grandmother by the shoulder and shook it slightly, and the shadow of a frown rose on the older woman's face, and she opened her eyes heavily.

'Miriam, my love, I think – I need to talk to a doctor, I think. I am not feeling well. Will you call them in York? On the telephone? They will know to whom we should send, and I think it would help. I do feel so very tired – '

'Call them in York, Grandmamma? But it's gone eight o'clock! The counting-house and the offices will long since be closed, won't they? Would it not be better to wait for Grandpapa? He must surely be here soon, and he will find you a doctor – '

She's fussing, she thought furiously. She's being just like she was all day getting here, fussing over her sillinesses. She must listen, she must. 'Grandpapa will find someone for you to talk to, Grandmamma, I'm sure, when he gets here. Shall I get you a drink – some water?'

'No, thank you, my love,' Abby said after a moment, and then smiled. 'There, it's gone off now. It hurt rather when I woke, you know, but it is nothing. You are right, I am fussing – '

Miriam reddened. 'Oh, Grandmamma, I did not say – '

'No, love, you didn't. But I can read you like a book, you know. And I know you were thinking so, and you were right. I am more comfortable now. It is just that I want to see your Grandpapa – he must come soon – '

'Yes – soon,' Miriam said. 'Grandmamma, while we wait for him, I must talk to you. About Lewis.'

'Yes – Lewis, you said.' Abby took a slightly deeper breath, almost experimentally, and then made a small face again.

Obviously it would be better to keep her breathing shallow. 'He is an excellent person. Sensible and careful – '

'Grandmamma, I want you to – I want him.' She had not meant to say it so baldly, to be so childish about it, but how else could she do it? Grandmamma was not listening properly as it was, and to try to be delicate would make her even less attentive. 'I want him.'

'Want – how do you mean?' The old eyes snapped open again and stared at her, wide in their surprise. 'What are you talking about?'

'He said we were just cousins – that we could not be more than cousins, but that is nonsense, Grandmamma, and so you must tell him.' The words came out in a rush, and again she leaned forwards and took her grandmother by the shoulder. 'Do you hear me, Grandmamma? I love him dearly, I truly, truly do. I never knew what it was everyone meant when they talked of love. I thought it was all a sham, but it isn't, is it? For I love Lewis, and I want him so much, and he said we were to be only cousins for I am rich and he is – oh, such a snob! But that need not be a difficulty, Grandmamma, need it? Can you not arrange for him to have money? He is family, after all, and if you arrange for him to be given the right money then we can be – not just be cousins. I want him so very much, Grandmamma. Please help me – he won't consider me without some help, I know – '

'Dear one, I can't – please, not now – ' Abby said, and closed her eyes again. 'I – when your Grandpapa arrives, we will talk of it, but not now. I cannot – '

'But you know how he will be, Grandmamma!' Miriam almost wailed it. 'He fusses so about money – he always does. He'll never understand unless you make him do so. If you tell him he must do it, then he will – you know that. Everyone knows that. But if I ask him – Grandmamma, please, don't go to sleep now. Listen to me!' and she gripped those plump shoulders and this time really shook her.

293

CLAIRE RAYNER

It was dreadful, absolutely dreadful. Miriam, sitting on the comfortable chair in the little office in the casualty department at Nellie's, her head thrown back and her hands lax on her lap, would have seemed to an onlooker to be relaxed in sleep, but inside she was as cold and tight as though a sharp frost had seized her in its grip. The scene unwound itself before her eyes, over and over again, the way her grandmother's face, that familiar, beloved, irritating, all-of-my-life-I've-known-it face crumpled into a hideous rictus, the mouth opening and frothing, the eyes rolling back; the way the shoulders under her hands tightened and hardened and then flopped like those of a dead doll; the way the old woman's back had seemed to arch and then crumple as though it had been exploded; the way the sound that came out of that unrecognizable gash of a mouth echoed in the still room and then, even more horribly, fell to total silence, until she was kneeling there in front of the slumped figure of her much beloved grandmother, knowing her to be dead, and yet refusing to believe it, as she shook those unresponsive shoulders again and again, shouting her fear and her despair and her huge overwhelming guilt; for hadn't she herself shaken her grandmother's life out of her, with her very own hands?

And then the door behind her opening, and she stumbling to her feet and turning to see who it was, crying, 'Grandmamma, she's dead, she's dead! Grandmamma – ' And seeing him standing there, Gideon, her grandfather, his face white and hard, his hat in his hand and his shoulders as rigid as the dead Abby's were collapsed.

He had stood very still for a second, and then come across to stand in front of the chair with Abby's plump shape in it, and had looked down at the bluish face in the lamplight and then, horribly and terrifyingly, had lifted his chin and looked up at the ceiling and opened his mouth; and a great wailing sound had filled her ears, a sound of such desolation and pain that she could not bear it, and she shrank away and put her

294

bands over her ears, saying over and over again, 'No, no, no – ' as though the sound of her own voice in her ears would blot out all else.

And when she had looked again, he was standing before his Abby, his coat thrown on the floor beside him but his hat on his head and he was praying, loud words she had heard before, but never really thought about – 'Yitgadol veyitkadash shemay rabba be alma deebera chirootay' – the Kaddish, the Hebrew prayer for the dead.

'No,' she said again, whispering it this time. 'Please, no – not Grandmamma – not Grandmamma – '

The prayer went on, the sonorous words rising and falling in the quiet room, and she watched him, half-fascinated, half-horrified, until at last the prayer ended and he was just standing there, looking down.

'Grandpapa,' she said, softly. 'Grandpapa – '

'I should have said a barucha – a blessing. To say Kaddish without a minyan is a sin,' he said almost dreamily. 'There should be ten men to say Kaddish – '

'Grandpapa.' Her voice was stronger now. 'Please, what must we do? There must be something we must do.'

He looked at her, turning his head slowly and jerkily. 'Miriam? I said Kaddish for your mother, so little a time ago. But it was easier then. My Abby was beside me. Who is beside me now?'

'Grandpapa, we must do something, tell someone – '

He shook his head.

'There is nothing I wish to do. I will stay here with my Abby. That is all.' And he turned his head again so that once more he was staring down at Abby, crumpled in her chair and somehow looking smaller than she had been. Her bulk, that comfortable stoutness that had been so much a part of her and that had made her lap so delightful for a child to clamber on seemed to have fallen in on itself. There was just a shadow of it there in the armchair, and a tall man looking faintly absurd in his shirtsleeves and hat standing in front of it.

The memory slid about inside Miriam's head, became blurred at the edges, and, sitting there in Nellie's with her eyes tight-closed in her white face, she was glad of that. She saw herself in snatches, running down the stairs to the hotel lobby, talking to someone – whom? She couldn't remember that – explaining, talking, telling, pointing – and then running upstairs again, and standing outside her grandmother's room unable to set her hand to the knob and open it, visualizing all too clearly her grandfather inside. And then people, people, people, coming from everywhere and nowhere; hotel people, and doctors and, absurdly, a heavy-set man in a thick gaberdine coat and tall hat and luxurious beard. A rabbi? she had thought ridiculously, a rabbi, in Harrogate? But he had come and then gone into Grandmamma's room and then someone was giving her brandy for her to swallow so that her throat caught and she coughed dreadfully and was afraid she was going to be sick, as she had been that horrible night in Somerset Street.

And that of course had been the worst thing to think, because it had brought Lewis back to the forefront of her mind. Lewis, careful and caring, strong and safe. Lewis who could make bad things go right. Lewis –

The night had drifted away in bustle and noise, worried faces looming up in front of her and then disappearing and voices coming and going, talking all the time. 'Mr and Mrs Caspar are coming, Miss Da Silva – ' and then, 'We have notified Mr and Mrs Oram,' and 'Mr Daniel Henriques has telephoned and says to tell you that he will arrive tomorrow morning early, Miss Da Silva,' and 'Mrs Landis has called to say she is coming with Mr and Mrs Oram, Miss Da Silva – ' 'Miss Da Silva, Miss Da Silva, Miss Da Silva,' until she wanted to scream and run away and leave it all behind her, the sight of

Grandpapa staring down at Abby, and the memory of her own hands, shaking Grandmamma's shoulders –

And at last she had cracked. As the light had come creeping into the broad lobby of the big hotel and cleaners arrived with mops and buckets to stare at her with beady-eyed curiosity, and she could no longer stay there, curled in the corner of a sofa as she had sat all night, the moment had come when she knew what she must do. She had run to her room, and taken her wrap and her reticule and nothing more, leaving her clothes scattered about for the maid to tidy up when she came in, and had just gone, running through the streets of the town as though some horror were chasing after her. She could not bear another moment of it, and there was only one person who could help her, and she was going to him. *Now.*

And now I am here, she thought, opening her eyes to stare up at the half-green, half-cream painted walls of the casualty office. Now I am here. Please make him understand. *Please.* I need him so.

And as though he had heard her thought, the door opened and he was standing there looking at her, and almost smiling.

28

She told him all of it. In plain simple language, concealing nothing. Not even the fact that she had shaken her grandmother to death, begging her to buy Lewis for her.

'Because that is how I was thinking,' she said bleakly, not looking at him. 'That was how it was with me. I was stupid and greedy and hatefully selfish. I know now – oh God, I know now how wicked I was – '

He was silent, leaning against the wall with his hands in his pockets, looking at her unblinkingly. And then he straightened and sighed a little and shook his head.

'Let's get one thing clear first,' he said. 'Clear the air and your muddled mind. You did not cause your grandmother's death. She had quite severe heart disease. I knew as soon as I saw her – that blue look about her mouth – and it was just a matter of time. And she was quite old, you know, and heavy. To be honest, she was fortunate to have lived as long as she did. That she died after a long and tiring journey and during a conversation with you – that was almost a coincidence. It could have happened to her at any time, at home in her own bed after a night of peaceful sleep. You mustn't, now or ever, lay the blame for this at your own door. To carry such a load of guilt would be absurd – it would destroy you – do you understand me?'

'I knew you would want to help me feel better,' she said, and managed a small smile. 'I think that was one of the reasons I had to come – '

He shook his head, almost violently. 'Damn it, I'm not trying to make you feel better. Don't talk like a child. I am not your nurse to kiss your injury and then castigate the ground you fell on for hurting you. If I thought you'd injured your grandmother I'd tell you so, even if the telling gave you pain. But you didn't, and you shouldn't see yourself as so – so omnipotent. Your grandmother died of her disease and her age, and they were God given, if you like. They certainly weren't created by *you*. You haven't that much power, and never think it.'

'Oh!' she said and blinked. 'Oh!'

'You understand?' he said, his voice gentler now. 'Do you really understand? You mustn't fall into the error of taking this to yourself. Grieve, of course. Regret her loss, naturally. But don't luxuriate in guilt – '

'Luxuriate!' she said, stung into a flush of anger. 'How can you use such a word when I'm so unhappy? As though I'd get any satisfaction out of – '

'Oh, but you could. People do. There's a sort of grim satisfaction in putting yourself firmly in the wrong. It makes you – important. But it's an importance you don't need, Miriam. Never forget that.'

There was a silence then, as she sat looking down at her hands clasped on her lap, trying to fit his words into her view of herself and her world. Most things were simple for Miriam; she wanted, she needed, she got. That was all. To be made to look at her deeper feelings and reactions and analyse them was foreign to her, and it confused her.

'I'm very stupid, Lewis, aren't I?' She looked up at him then with no trace of artifice in her face or voice. She sounded only surprised, perhaps a little puzzled. 'So ignorant and stupid – '

'Ignorant, yes, stupid, no,' he said. 'You're very young and you've been kept young by the adoration you've always been wrapped in. It's understandable. You're an easy person to adore – ' And his voice was unsteady for a moment, and he closed his mouth firmly and took a sharp little breath in through his nose.

'I love you, Lewis,' she said then, still sitting there with her hands clasped on her lap, and looking up at him with her face open and her gaze very direct. 'I know it's selfish and wicked to think of myself and my own feelings when Grandmamma is dead, but I can't help it. I love you, and I had to tell you, and – ' She shook her head then and looked away. 'Last night I thought if I could just get rid of this silly fuss over money and all that – I thought it would be easy. You'd love me too, and then we'd be happy. Now – ' Her voice dwindled away. 'Now I don't know. I don't understand any more – '

He was still leaning against the wall, his hands in his pockets, seeming to be the same. But his voice showed how tightly controlled he was. 'Love is a very easy word, Miriam. I'm not sure you really know what it means – '

'I know!' She flashed at him. 'Oh, I didn't before. I admit that. I thought it was all silliness and – put-on stuff. But it isn't. I love you, and I know what that means. I feel – I'm only half a person. It's as though I've always had a gap all down one side of me and I didn't know it. Now there's you and I know what's missing from me. You're the other half of me. Without you, I'm – I feel like a person with no arms, or no legs – isn't that love? If it isn't, and it's something else, well, that doesn't matter. You can call it what you like, but it's what I feel. I want you – '

'Miriam, stop it! You really must stop it – ' He almost cried it, but she shook her head.

'No, I shan't stop it. I can't. How do you stop needing the other half of yourself? It's the way it is – '

Again he shook his head. 'You're barely eighteen, Miriam. A child – '

'Oh, for heaven's sake, Lewis, *you* stop! The things you fuss over – age and money and – '

'The fact that you don't understand that such things are important shows just how young and spoiled you are. It's romantic bosh to think you can ride rough-shod over – over the conventions of normal life. I'm both much older and much poorer than you and if I take advantage of the way you say you feel, I'd be looked at by everyone as – it doesn't bear thinking of. And before you say I care too much about others' opinions of me – ' for she had opened her mouth to interrupt him ' – it's my own opinion of myself I'm concerned about. If I was sure that I was right for you, that I could give you what you need, then I'd not hesitate. As it is – '

'As it is, you don't care for me.' She said it in a small flat voice, her eyes fixed on his face. 'I've found my other half but you haven't. Is that what you're saying?'

He stood there very straight and still and then, to his own surprise as much as hers, he laughed.

'My dear, I don't know, I truly don't know. I – I'm fascinated by you. I'll tell you that. I want to touch you, and hold you and kiss you and – but that's just *physical*. It's the rest of it I'm not sure about. The friendship, the sharing part. We've lived such different lives, we're such different people – how can I know how we'd be together?'

'You're frightened of me,' she said softly. 'You do love me, but you're frightened of me.'

He shook his head. 'Not frightened. Uncertainty doesn't mean fear. And in a way, yes, of course I love you. I want to. It's taking every bit of self-control I've got to stand here and not touch you. No – don't move. Don't you dare leave that chair. I'm trying to be sensible and honest and – '

'But why do we need sense and – *why*? If I love you and you want me, isn't that good enough?'

He shook his head. 'No. Because it wouldn't last. It would be like – ' Again he shook his head.

'Like the other girls you've loved?'

He managed a smile then. 'Perhaps you're not quite as naïve as I thought – well, yes. There have been others. I'm a man of thirty, remember, Miriam. I've had a – busy life. There'd be something odd if I hadn't been involved with other women before this – '

'Involved, yes. But have you loved them?'

'I've thought so.'

'Oh.'

'You see what I mean? I felt as powerful an urge to touch them and kiss them as I feel for you – and when I did, it was, oh, marvellous. For a while. And then it stopped being marvellous.'

'And you don't want that to happen with me?'

'No.'

She smiled, a wide smile that seemd to be of unadulterated happiness and he looked at her, puzzled. 'Then that's all right.'

'All right? What do you mean? I don't understand you, Miriam – '

'You do love me. If you didn't – if it was just *physical* then you wouldn't hesitate would you? I don't mean you'd marry me – that'd upset your opinion of yourself and all that – but you'd certainly be touching and kissing me, wouldn't you? You wouldn't be standing there with your hands tied in your pockets with ropes! So you do love me. You'll find out eventually – '

'Miriam, for God's sake!' He almost wailed it. 'you're not supposed to be so – oh, God, you confuse me, horribly. You're a baby one minute and the next you're – '

'Almost grown-up,' she said softly. 'Do I have to apologize for being young, Lewis? Is it so dreadful to be eighteen?'

'No,' he said and then smiled and took his hands from his pockets. 'No. It doesn't last, after all – ' And he put his hands out to her and she rose from her chair in one smooth easy movement and came to stand in front of him, putting her hands in his, looking up into his face and smiling.

'Don't think about it, my darling,' she said softly. 'Just let it be. I love you, and you do love me, even if you're trying not to – '

'I'm not trying anything,' he said. 'I'm confused. Bewildered.'

'That doesn't matter. It doesn't last – '

The door opened and he turned his head to see who it was, his face a little red, and pushed her gently away from him, and the nurse who put her head round the door smiled knowingly and then said demurely, 'Mr Lackland, they're waiting for you in the operating theatres, sir, and they said will you be long because they want to start the anaesthetic and the patient's getting very agitated – '

'Oh, hell,' he said distractedly, and then nodded. 'I'll be up in ten minutes, tell them. No more – '

'I'll wait here for you,' she said, when the door closed.

'No – no, you can't do that.'

'Then I'll wait somewhere else. And when you've finished work we can talk again.' He shook his head. 'No. You've got to go back to Harrogate, now – '

She shrank back from him, her face crumpling as though she was about to weep. The woman she had been for the few minutes while they were talking seemed to disappear as he looked at her, to be replaced by the child she had always been, and, staring at that soft face and wide eyes, he felt the doubts he had been trying to express, and which she had almost vanquished with her newfound wisdom, come flooding back.

'But you must, my dear,' he said gently. 'Your grandfather will be needing you. And there will be things that have to be done – a funeral, family matters – '

'I can't,' she said, and now tears appeared in her eyes. 'I can't – it's all too horrible. I won't – they don't need me – I'll stay here in London with you, and then when – when it's all over Grandpapa will come back and you can go and see him and tell him – '

He shook his head, and moved away from her, to stand by the door. 'No, Miriam. I won't. Because he'll be in need of comfort and support, not – not someone nagging him. It would be nagging of the most cruel kind to go to him about your feelings of love when he had just been deprived of his own. Can't you see that?'

She was crying in good earnest now. 'No – he's old! It can't be so – '

'It can't be as important as your feelings, is that it? Oh, Miriam, Miriam, can't you see that all this is impossible? How could I say I loved you, as you want to be loved, when I see so many flaws in you? I seem to spend as much time telling you how to behave as – no, it just won't *work*. Not yet, anyway – '

She rubbed her face with the back of her hand, and sniffed and then took a deep breath.

'And if I go back to Harrogate and – and everything, then you'll love me?'

'Oh, don't be so childish! I'm not making bargains with you! I'm just telling you what I believe you ought to do. After that it's up to you. I'm not in charge of you, Miriam. You own your own life. You have to do with it what's right for you. As I must – '

There was another silence and then she nodded. 'All right, I'll go back to Harrogate. They're all there – and they'll all be so angry with me – but I'll go back, because you said I must. And then, after we come back and it's all over, maybe – '

'No maybes,' he said. 'No promises. I don't know what will happen. I need time to think. And you need time to grow. Come along. I'll get them to call a cab for you.'

He stood at the hospital door, looking out into Endell Street and watched her climb into the hansom. The driver leaned forwards and touched the horse's flank with his whip as soon as she had closed the apron over her knees, and the animal was off with a rattle of harness. She had time to look back just for a moment, her small white face appearing round the edge of the hood and he lifted his hand briefly and then let it fall. He was watching his heart trotting away through the drays and vans and pushing crowds of Covent Garden, knowing he'd sent her away, knowing he needed her as much as she had said she needed him, and yet knowing he had to let her go.

ENVOI

Alice was feeling very hot. Her new gown was rather tight and scratchy round the neck and they had frizzed her hair up in tight curls that made her head ache, rather. But none of that mattered because she was being treated very much as a Young Lady by everyone today. Not quite as Young Ladyish as Victoria, who was being thoroughly insufferable, to be honest, ordering Florence and Mabel about like a duchess, but still, pretty satisfactorily for a person of only just fourteen.

'Look, Alice,' Mabel whispered, and pinched her arm. 'Down there – isn't that the cousin from Australia?'

'Where?' Alice craned her neck, trying to see beyond the waving feathers on Mamma's and Aunt Bella's hats, to the main part of the synagogue far below. But it was impossible to see anyone recognizable down there. From up here everyone looked the same, all the men in their white prayer-shawls, trimmed with blue stripes and funny little fringes, and their shiny top hats. 'I can't see anyone – '

'Ssh,' Victoria said reprovingly. 'Mind your manners, Mabel, and Flo, stop fidgeting.'

'Pooh to you,' said Mabel and leaned across and pinched her older sister, which made her squeak, and Mamma looked round and tightened her lips at them and they all subsided. Even Mabel.

The service seemed to have been going on for hours, and they still hadn't got to Samuel's bit. Alice could see him all right. He was standing on the raised section in the middle of the synagogue, the bit they called the Bimah, with his father, Uncle Daniel, standing beside him, and as she looked at him, she wanted to giggle. He looked as though he'd been polished, he was so round and shiny and important-looking. Is that what happened to men when their sons were having their Barmitzvah? Did someone come along and polish them with brushes and dusters?

She turned her head to look along the rows of seats up here in the ladies' gallery. They were all here, in their best hats and gowns and looking very pleased with themselves, a bit polished as well, come to think of it. She wanted to giggle as she thought that, looking at the bobbing cherries on Aunt Bella's hat and the smoothness of Grandmamma's fur pelisse and Aunt Sarah's green skirts. But then she saw Cousin Miriam, and didn't want to laugh any more. She looked as she always did these days, quiet and rather dull.

'She's gone right off, you know,' Mabel had said confidently, when they'd seen her arrive at the synagogue that morning. 'That happens to people who don't get married in their first season, you know. They Go Off. All dull and dreary, and then they're old maids for ever. That's what happened to Miriam because she's had two seasons now. She's Gone Off.' She giggled. 'I won't. I'll get married the minute I've had my come-out, and then I'll be beautiful and perfect for ever.'

Poor Cousin Miriam, Alice thought, and wanted to go and sit beside her and tuck her hand into the crook of her elbow. They'd all been sad when Great-Grandmamma had died last year, of course they had, but it had been Miriam who'd been worst. Ever since then she'd been quiet and stayed home with Great-Grandpapa, and looked – well, Mabel had said Gone Off and it really was like that. As though there had been a light inside her once, one of those lovely electric lights that they had in the street outside her bedroom window, but someone had come and turned it off. Poor Cousin Miriam.

Samuel started his bit, and they all leaned forwards in a whisper of silk and a rustle of feathers and Aunt Rachel Damont started to cry, the tears running down her face for everyone to see, and then Aunt Sarah began, and of course that made Alice's eyes feel hot and prickly. Until she saw Mabel looking at her, grinning all over her silly face, and that stopped her.

And at last it was over, and all the women went trooping down the stairs to be greeted by the men and be kissed on both cheeks, and people were shaking Samuel's hand, and Daniel's hand and Aunt Rachel's hand and congratulating everyone else, and it was all very noisy and bewildering, but great fun, because they kissed her, Alice, as well and offered her congratulations though for the life of her she didn't know why. But it didn't matter because it made her feel every inch one of the grown-ups. Lovely.

They came out on to the steps into the thin November sunshine to stand there waiting for Mamma and Papa to come, so that they could walk home – for no one rode in a carriage on the Sabbath – and Mabel pinched her again.

'Look, see, Alice? Over there. It's that cousin, the one who Grandpapa brings to visit sometimes. Don't you remember? He's a surgeon, like Grandpapa. I like him – he's got such a messy sort of face, hasn't he?'

'Messy?' said Alice, trying to see through the crowds to where her sister was pointing.

'Mmm. All sort of chopped up and all over the place. Nice – there, do you see?'

Alice saw him, talking to Cousin Miriam, who was standing beside Great-Grandpapa with her hand tucked protectively into his elbow.

'Oh, yes, I see. He *is* quite nice – ' And then she looked again and said, 'You know, Mabel, I think you're wrong about Cousin Miriam. She doesn't look Gone Off at all. Not now.'

Claire Rayner

Gower Street
(Book One of *The Performers*)

The early 1800's. Jesse Constam, a highly respected spice merchant, lives in fashionable Gower Street. Saved from poverty himself, he rescues two children from the gutter.

Jesse's intervention changes their lives forever. The fate of Abel Lackland and Lilith Lucas and their families become inextricably entwined as they are destined for the vastly different worlds of medicine and the theatre.

The Haymarket
(Book Two of *The Performers*)

Abel Lackland, rescued from the gutter as a child, has achieved great success as a surgeon. His eldest son, Jonah refuses to follow in his father's footsteps. He secretly nurtures a desire to act on the stage.

Lilith Lucas, saved from destitution at the same time as Abel, has achieved equal success and adoration as an actress. One night, Jonah steals away to watch Lilith, unaware of her thirst for revenge. He meets her after the show and is enchanted by her, as his father was many years before. Lilith sees in Jonah an opportunity to settle old scores...

CLAIRE RAYNER

PADDINGTON GREEN

(BOOK THREE OF *THE PERFORMERS*)

Abel Lackland's children are grown up in the early years of Queen Victoria's reign and are making their way in the world. Two of his sons have followed their father into medicine. Jonah, now married to Lilith's daughter, has followed his dreams of a career on the stage. But the reality is harsh as he struggles to provide for his wife and children.

Then suddenly into their lives comes something that casts a shadow over all their personal crises and drives a wedge between them.

SOHO SQUARE

(BOOK FOUR OF *THE PERFORMERS*)

Lydia Mohun is the daughter of the famous actress, Lilith Lucas. She comes to live in Soho Square, prepared to achieve the same success on the same stage as her legendary mother had.

Phoebe Lackland is the seventeen-year-old daughter of Jonah Lackland. When she is introduced to Lydia an exciting and glittering world is opened up to her. Freddy, her cousin feels very protective towards her and feels that Lydia poses a threat to his beloved Phoebe.

Jonah is now widowed and middle-aged and anticipates an inevitable tragedy for them all.

CLAIRE RAYNER

CHARING CROSS
(BOOK SEVEN OF *THE PERFORMERS*)

Sophie Lackland is the granddaughter of the great surgeon, Abel Lackland. She is twenty-one, alone in the world and virtually penniless.

A letter tells her of the death of her step-grandmother and of a strange bequest. This legacy could make it possible to fulfil her ambition of becoming a doctor.
Sophie sets off for London to a new life and to meet her Lackland relatives. She also meets the charming and passionate Gilbert Stacey...

SEVEN DIALS
(BOOK TWELVE OF *THE PERFORMERS*)

It is 1946 and London is still reeling from the destruction and suffering of the Second World War.

The formidable Letty Lackland helps to raise funds for Queen Eleanor's Hospital, destroyed in the Blitz. Dr Charlie Lucas helps Brin Lackland come to terms with a devastating wartime facial injury. Brin's sister, Kate is forging her way to success on stage and screen.

Here, at the end of the vast and panoramic 'Performers' series we see the two formidable families united at last after more than a century.

OTHER TITLES BY CLAIRE RAYNER AVAILABLE DIRECT
FROM HOUSE OF STRATUS

Quantity	£	$(US)	$(CAN)	€
THE POPPY CHRONICLES				
JUBILEE	6.99	11.50	15.99	11.50
FLANDERS	6.99	11.50	15.99	11.50
FLAPPER	6.99	11.50	15.99	11.50
BLITZ	6.99	11.50	15.99	11.50
FESTIVAL	6.99	11.50	15.99	11.50
SIXTIES	6.99	11.50	15.99	11.50
THE PERFORMERS SERIES				
GOWER STREET	6.99	11.50	15.99	11.50
THE HAYMARKET	6.99	11.50	15.99	11.50
PADDINGTON GREEN	6.99	11.50	15.99	11.50
SOHO SQUARE	6.99	11.50	15.99	11.50
BEDFORD ROW	6.99	11.50	15.99	11.50
LONG ACRE	6.99	11.50	15.99	11.50
CHARING CROSS	6.99	11.50	15.99	11.50
CHELSEA REACH	6.99	11.50	15.99	11.50
SHAFTESBURY AVENUE	6.99	11.50	15.99	11.50
PICCADILLY	6.99	11.50	15.99	11.50
SEVEN DIALS	6.99	11.50	15.99	11.50

ALL HOUSE OF STRATUS BOOKS ARE AVAILABLE FROM GOOD BOOKSHOPS
OR DIRECT FROM THE PUBLISHER:

Internet: www.houseofstratus.com including author interviews, reviews, features.

Email: sales@houseofstratus.com please quote author, title and credit card details.

Hotline: UK ONLY: 0800 169 1780, please quote author, title and credit card details.
INTERNATIONAL: +44 (0) 20 7494 6400, please quote author, title and credit card details.

Send to: House of Stratus Sales Department
24c Old Burlington Street
London
W1X 1RL
UK

Please allow for postage costs charged per order plus an amount per book as set out in the tables below:

	£(Sterling)	$(US)	$(CAN)	€(Euros)
Cost per order				
UK	2.00	3.00	4.50	3.30
Europe	3.00	4.50	6.75	5.00
North America	3.00	4.50	6.75	5.00
Rest of World	3.00	4.50	6.75	5.00
Additional cost per book				
UK	0.50	0.75	1.15	0.85
Europe	1.00	1.50	2.30	1.70
North America	2.00	3.00	4.60	3.40
Rest of World	2.50	3.75	5.75	4.25

PLEASE SEND CHEQUE, POSTAL ORDER (STERLING ONLY), EUROCHEQUE, OR INTERNATIONAL MONEY ORDER (PLEASE CIRCLE METHOD OF PAYMENT YOU WISH TO USE)
MAKE PAYABLE TO: STRATUS HOLDINGS plc

Cost of book(s): —————————— Example: 3 x books at £6.99 each: £20.97

Cost of order: —————————— Example: £2.00 (Delivery to UK address)

Additional cost per book: —————— Example: 3 x £0.50: £1.50

Order total including postage: ———— Example: £24.47

Please tick currency you wish to use and add total amount of order:

☐ £ (Sterling)   ☐ $ (US)   ☐ $ (CAN)   ☐ € (EUROS)

VISA, MASTERCARD, SWITCH, AMEX, SOLO, JCB:

☐ ☐ ☐ ☐ ☐ ☐ ☐ ☐ ☐ ☐ ☐ ☐ ☐ ☐ ☐ ☐ ☐ ☐

Issue number (Switch only):

☐ ☐ ☐

Start Date: **Expiry Date:**

☐ ☐ / ☐ ☐   ☐ ☐ / ☐ ☐

Signature: _____

NAME: _____

ADDRESS: _____

_____

POSTCODE: _____

Please allow 28 days for delivery.

Prices subject to change without notice.
Please tick box if you do not wish to receive any additional information. ☐

House of Stratus publishes many other titles in this genre; please check our website (**www.houseofstratus.com**) for more details.